THE
LAST
ENCORE

ALSO BY REBECCA HEATH

The Summer Party
The Dinner Party
The Wedding Party

THE LAST ENCORE

REBECCA HEATH

An Aries Book

First published in the UK in 2026 by Head of Zeus,
part of Bloomsbury Publishing Plc

975312468

A catalogue record for this book is available from the British Library.

ISBN (PB): 9781035914319
ISBN (eBook): 9781035914302

Cover design: Simon Michele | Head of Zeus
Typeset by Siliconchips Services Ltd UK

Printed and bound in Great Britain by Clays Ltd, Elcograf S.p.A.

MIX
Paper | Supporting
responsible forestry
FSC® C018072

Bloomsbury Publishing Plc
50 Bedford Square, London, WC1B 3DP, UK
Bloomsbury Publishing Ireland Limited,
29 Earlsfort Terrace, Dublin 2, D02 AY28, Ireland

HEAD OF ZEUS LTD
5–8 Hardwick Street
London, EC1R 4RG

To find out more about our authors and books
visit www.headofzeus.com
For product safety related questions contact productsafety@bloomsbury.com

For Caroline and Rowan

*You've known so many versions of me
and loved them all. Thank you.*

Sound check – Hours before the show

I exhale hard, making the softest whistle between my teeth. It's done now. Everything is in place, waiting for the star of the show. Ironic, since there will be no adoring crowd tonight.

I'm not sure what I expected to feel. Regret, maybe? That some instinctive desire to preserve human life would kick in?

It doesn't.

Instead, a slow smile spreads across my face.

I should get the hell away from the scene of the crime. Logic would have me far from here when what is about to happen, well... happens. But I linger.

Knowing suddenly isn't quite enough. I need to see it happen. More than that, I want a moment where our eyes meet and there's understanding. For what is justice if no one knows it has taken place?

The shadows provide some shelter, but I'm not exactly hidden away. There's risk in staying here. But still I linger.

My ragged breath is loud in my ears, a backdrop for the staccato hammer of my heart, and I fear I won't hear your approach. There is so much that could go wrong. *So much*. Like the fact that you should have got my note and been here by now.

Sudden, bowel-loosening terror slices through me. Have I made a mistake? Are you not coming?

But then you step onto the stage, and I can breathe again.

You sashay to the microphone, accepting the spotlight as your rightful place. You lean close, take a breath, and then notice the cord isn't plugged in to the amp at your feet. Bending over, you pick it up and frown as though you've never seen that end of a mic before. Maybe you haven't. Maybe you're not as sure you belong up there as you would like to believe. Maybe your palms are sweating and you're worried the note was meant for someone else.

I don't move. Don't breathe. Don't blink. Goosebumps rise on my skin. It's time.

The silver end of the cable's socket catches on the sunshine overhead and glints as you reach down to make the connection. In my head, I practise what I'm going to say.

Something terrible has happened.

A STORYBOOK LOVE:
THE CEDRICS BAND FAN BLOG

13 December 2003

I am typing this through actual tears.

What you've heard is true.

The headlines, for once, are correct, and it seems Jonny – *our beautiful Jonny* – is dead. I know you guys have been waiting for me to post since the news first began trickling through two hours ago, but I've been praying that there has been a terrible mistake.

There hasn't.

Our Jonny is dead in Paris. His body fallen in a foreign land.

I've only just left the stadium, where some of us diehard fans were already gathered outside ready for the show.

I. Heard. The. Explosion.

Guys, I *heard* it. I felt the blast through my body. I can confirm it's true.

Singer and songwriter Jonny Rake is dead at twenty-two.

There are rumours the explosion was caused by an electrical fault, and there is no news of other casualties. However, I wouldn't be surprised if there's something they're not telling us, because there was more than one emergency vehicle at the scene.

I know you guys want all the details, but it is seriously hard for me to even type. I can't stop shaking. When I close my eyes, I hear the sound again. At the time it was barely a rumble, but now I know the truth of what happened... well, now I can feel it in my heart.

We were questioned by the authorities, and I think some of us were shown crying in the background of news reports. Some reporter asked me for comment, but I wanted to keep my words for you guys, the true fans, the ones I know understand what I'm feeling right now.

I've lost more than an idol; I feel as though I've lost a friend.

Our beloved band is broken, literal hours before what should have been their greatest triumph, another stepping stone in an already meteoric rise to the top.

Guys, I can't even begin to process this. Only a few hours ago I was outside the stadium trying to guess the set list for their show. It was supposed to be the best day of my life. Now, I can't imagine arguing whether they should open with 'Be Yours Tonight' or 'Light the Soul'.

Jonny was but a young man, about to hit the best times of his life. I just know he would have gone on to become a legend. I can only imagine the pain the band is feeling right now. Especially Adam, as his beloved brother.

This is a dark day, not just for fans of The Cedrics Band, but for the music industry as a whole. These guys were something special and Jonny the best of them all. We've lost a light today.

Rest in peace, Jonny Rake.

'as long as the spark still flickers,
the flame will burn again.'
LIGHT THE SOUL – The Cedrics Band

Yours,
Ricky
The Cedrics Band Number One Fan

18 Years Later

ACT I

A STORYBOOK LOVE:
THE CEDRICS BAND FAN BLOG

November 2021

I know it's been a while, friends and devoted fans, but you had to know I couldn't ignore the circulating rumours. The Cedrics Band are apparently getting back together for a one-off private show and filming of a documentary, giving unprecedented access to the band.

This will be the first performance for them since Jonny Rake's tragic death nearly eighteen years ago.

As you'd expect, I have the inside word. The show will take place on a remote island off the coast of South Australia and is not to be missed for serious fans. And, well, I'm not missing it.

Surprise!

Yes, I can reveal, just between you and me, that your friend Ricky is invited. Only the most passionate fans are invited, and we all have to sign strict confidentiality agreements. But I promise I will share what I can with you in our little corner of the internet. Even after all this time, I think of you guys as my friends – in fact, practically family. When we lost Jonny, it formed a bond between us that can never be broken.

You can trust me to share everything I can.

However, if you want the juiciest details, including live video updates (depending on the island's internet), you can get it all for just a small fee. Just click on the link below and follow the instructions, and you can live this with me (without seeing my face, of course – because guys like me and Batman need our privacy).

So, settle in and sign up, and in a few weeks I'll be live to your screens with the spiciest of inside looks into The Cedrics Band's reunion show.

'I never thought such a thing could happen,
to a boy like me.'
BE YOURS TONIGHT – The Cedrics Band

Yours,
Ricky
The Cedrics Band Number One Fan

Florence – Friday – Two days before the show

'We have quite literally gotten the band back together,' I tell my sister, Elsie.

She doesn't comment on my movie reference, but I know she gets it. We've always been able to read each other's minds, and growing up only two years apart gives us an unending supply of in-jokes.

I'm staring out over the bay, hardly daring to blink, lest I lose the smudge of white that will be the boat with our first guests.

'Well, most of the band,' I amend.

Not Jonny.

A thought impossible to ignore, considering it's been splashed across the headlines. However, every story has mentioned our Three Chains Lodge and Distillery as the location for this highly anticipated, exclusive event.

My neat, practical nails dig into my palms as I try to stay focused. I've never been the type to believe in destiny. In fact, when my husband, Bruce, said, 'What about that record executive guy I went to school with?' when I threw out 'a concert' while brainstorming how to launch our rebuilt venue after the fire, I'd laughed. But it turns out life is very much 'who you know'.

The Cedrics Band is coming to perform their reunion show on our little Sparrow Hawk Island. And I made it happen.

A nervous chuckle escapes me as I scan the light-filled space and spot an empty vase on the dark wooden mantle accenting the huge stone fireplace.

'That was close,' I tell Elsie.

I hurry out through the kitchen, my steps loud on the stone floor, to one of the smaller fridges I've reserved for the weekend's bought flowers. Our fire-ravaged garden is still struggling, and I didn't want to pillage it. I select a single, buttery banksia and some foliage. Back inside, I place the flower and step back to admire how it ties in perfectly with the hints of pale yellow through the room, offsetting the white, wood, glass and stone.

The view out of the huge windows shows the boat getting closer. I look to the cobblestone path towards the villas perched along the escarpment edge, but there's no sign of movement. Bruce disappeared that way about twenty minutes ago for one last check on the private suites we have ready for our visitors, six that will be occupied and a spare.

What could be taking so long?

He should be back by now. When I walked through each suite earlier, the drinks were cold, the towels fluffed and the air-conditioning humming.

When my gaze returns to the water, the boat approaching the island is close enough that I can see individual figures on board. Great, I nearly missed them arriving. All because I got distracted by the missing Bruce.

There's a gust of warm air from the door opening, and then his familiar, heavy tread sounds behind me. 'Where have you been?' I snap.

He takes his time finding his words, a habit I used to think meant he was deep. Now it makes my teeth grind together.

'Had something to do,' he says eventually.

That tells me exactly nothing. But I don't probe because I fear I can guess the answer. 'They're almost here,' I say instead.

He turns his blockish head to look at the water. The boat is now toy size, bobbing on the waves. 'Yep,' he grunts. The stubble on his jaw glints golden in the morning sunlight.

My shoulders tense. 'You said you would shave.'

He rubs a hand over his chin, then shrugs.

I breathe in, then out, trying to keep control. Tears prick my eyes. Everything we've worked for comes down to these next few days. The band, the media, the documentary. All of it the kind of publicity that a fledgling business can only fantasise about – and my husband can't be bothered shaving.

The restaurant and tasting room I'm standing in wobbles at the edges as rage blurs my vision. 'You said you'd shave,' I repeat through gritted teeth.

I shouldn't push him. God knows I'm more aware of that than anyone – can never forget what happened last time – but he's not the only one with a temper, and I can't help myself.

Bruce's huge, calloused hand grips my shoulder, which is bare but for the thin strap of my white summer dress. Unwanted heat skitters through me, despite my revulsion at the dirt under his nails. The strength that attracted me to him makes my body respond even now like it did that first time.

And – not that I need reminding – if not for him, none of this could happen. Any thoughts I have of extricating myself, from his grasp or from this marriage, disappear as fast as they form. We're in this together.

'Breathe,' he growls, his grip tightening enough to hurt.

The message that he'll shave or not as he sees fit is clear, if unspoken.

I obey his command. Inhale, exhale. Sense returns, and I step away. 'We need to meet our guests.'

Then, I head for the path down to the dock. I don't wait for my husband to follow.

Lara – Friday

Nausea climbs my throat in a wave like those beneath the boat we're on. It's bucking like some possessed animal. I ignore the threat of my breakfast reappearing, instead shielding my eyes and focusing on the spot high above us pointed at by the gruff, bearded boatman who collected us from the mainland.

'Oh, my goodness! The building is gorgeous. Don't you think, Edward? The white of it so different to the dark grey of the cliffs and the green around it.' Next to it the smaller buildings almost disappear into nature, but I can make out private balconies jutting out over the edge of where the rock falls away. 'Those must have an incredible view.'

Edward, frowning at his phone, doesn't look up.

'Oh, Edward, ever the workaholic.' I force a chuckle past the rising need to spew.

The boatman might not look interested in our conversation, but you never know who's going to sell a story to the tabloids.

Unexpected seasickness can't dampen the thrill of being here. And my three pregnancies were good training for something at least, letting me maintain an upbeat smile. Hopefully, my makeup has held for any waiting media. There was none at Port Este, the tiny coastal town where we were taken from the airport, so I'm guessing they're already across. I lift my hand to smooth back some flyaways.

'No one cares how you look,' Edward says.

I drop my hand and keep my tone light. 'You're such a kidder.'

He doesn't correct me, even though both of us know he wasn't joking. I'm not sure when Edward stopped looking at me like he couldn't believe his luck, but he will not ruin this for me. This is my chance and it's been a long time coming. I'll never forget that not one member of the band came to the wedding.

Edward said he didn't care, but I'd already gone and hinted about special guests to half my family. Besides, I saw the hurt he was trying to hide. There had been so much pain after Jonny died. A wedding – *our wedding* – would have been the perfect way to bring everyone together. I'd even allowed myself a little hope that they'd perform.

All day I'd clung to them making a surprise appearance, ignoring the snipes from my family. It had been fancier than any wedding any of us had seen, but no, they'd had to point out what was missing.

I shrug off the memory of their smug faces. I'm here now. Admittedly, it's not a sell-out stadium tour, but the documentary rights have already been sold to streaming services all over the world.

All. Over. The world.

And, the itinerary we were sent noted I might need to make myself available tomorrow afternoon for an interview. *Me*. For my perspective as the keyboardist's wife. I allow myself a little glow inside. So much for not making anything of myself, hey Mum?

I realise my nausea's gone. Good timing, because the dock is clearly visible at the foot of a long, wide path that curls out of sight upwards through rugged bushland.

I toss my hair back. A move I know from mirror practice shows off the line of my neck.

'You look like a peacock,' Edward mutters.

I will not let his negativity affect me.

'Here we are,' the boatman says once he's tied up the vessel and hauled our suitcases onto the jetty.

It's the most he's said since we got on the boat, and I think he's only talking now because neither Edward nor I have moved. Edward because he's staring at his phone, and me because I am trying to make sense of what I'm seeing. Or, more accurately, what I'm *not* seeing.

The place is deserted. There's literally no one in sight.

A wide, sweeping beach curves around the small bay, surrounded by the silvery grey of gum trees, splashes of yellow wattle and other low green scrub that makes up decidedly inhospitable bushland. Apart from two small tin buildings – barely big enough to be storage sheds – the now out-of-sight resort at the top of the cliff is the only sign of human habitation on this wild island.

Unease ripples through me that once the boat leaves we'll be abandoned here, but I brush it aside. The brochure described where we're staying as the epitome of luxury, and I know the island is much bigger than what I can see and includes farmland as well as a swathe of national park on the far side – it's just a matter of working out where we need to go.

Edward is already up on the jetty when I make myself move. It's not that I don't appreciate that Edward isn't the main attraction for this event – keyboardists turned accountants don't make for headlines – but surely our arrival is worth a picture, given the tabloids' need for constant new content.

Then there's the issue of how we get our luggage up to the top of the cliff.

I step from boat to dock as Edward grumbles, 'There's really no phone signal at all in this godforsaken place.'

It takes me a moment to steady myself, and the boatman is already untying the vessel.

'But where do we go?'

He points towards the path. There's a couple of small vehicles, like golf carts, that were hidden by the tin buildings. They're parked next to what looks like a sign with a map of the island.

Edward perks up like a little boy seeing a toy race car. 'This might be fun.'

Yes, when I read 'luxury' I pictured driving myself through unknown wilderness.

My smile drops once Edward and I are alone, but he's too busy examining the welcome instructions attached to the cart's steering wheel to notice. With the luggage stowed on the back, I pause on the passenger side and swallow past a lump in my throat. My black dress sticks to my skin from the heat but, eyes closed, I exhale the negative thoughts threatening to derail my journey and inhale the new opportunity to grow and have a deeper life experience.

'If you're done?' Edward says.

I open my eyes.

He's gesturing to the seat. 'Today would be nice.'

It turns out Edward is as bad at driving golf carts as he is good with numbers and the piano. We lurch along what appears to be a smooth – if not for his driving – path up through the trees. I cling on as Edward mumbles that it's more difficult than it looks. As the house comes into view – the place is even more impressive up close – the path levels and he picks up speed. Taking a bend around a stunning jacaranda tree, he veers off the path.

'What are you—?'

He shoots me a glare and overcorrects. We're on the lawn now. It slopes down towards a picturesque pond with a cute wooden bridge arching across it. We're not stopping. We're not changing direction.

I will not end up in that pond.

'Edward!'

His foot stomps on the brakes and we jolt to a stop about a foot from the water. Edward's hands grip the wheel. 'I was handling it.'

I get out, stalk back across the lawn and stand with my arms folded as Edward finds reverse and manages to park. A thin woman in a white dress, her poking-out collarbones showing veins beneath pale skin, floats down the stairs to meet us. She brushes back wispy, white-blonde hair and shows neat teeth. If friendly is what she's aiming for, she's falling well short.

'My name is Florence Harper, and I'll be your host during your stay on our beautiful Sparrow Hawk Island. If you have any questions, or need anything – anything at all – please don't hesitate to ask.' She reaches the last step, and I realise she's tall, taller than Edward, and must be at least six foot. 'Edward, I recognise you from old pictures,' she says. 'You've hardly aged a day.'

I think she's stretching it there. His strawberry hair's thinning on top, and he could do with getting out from behind his computer once in a while to join me in a workout. Not only that but, in his white polo shirt and brown checked shorts, he's more 'dad on vacation' than keyboard player for a worldwide phenomenon.

But his cheeks redden. 'That's me.'

She turns to me. 'So, you must be Lauren?'

My lips press together. 'Lara.'

'Of course, many apologies. It is a hectic time here at Three Chains Lodge, as you can imagine. So sorry I couldn't meet you off the boat, but I am pleased to see you found your way. As far as staff, there's only myself and Bruce until the concert, to prevent any leaks around the documentary, and by this evening there'll be nine guests.'

I try to do some mental maths of who else might be coming, although numbers have never been my strong point, but lose track after the two other members of the band and the manager.

'Does that include the media?' I ask.

Edward stiffens beside me, but I ignore him. Just because fame is beneath him doesn't mean I can't ask.

'A select group will be brought across with the fans on show day. The documentary director, Marco, and his wife arrived just before you and are settling in. I didn't expect you to get here so soon.'

'We don't mind,' I say generously, although my heart's still racing from my near-pond experience.

'I'll be happy to show you to your suite, where you'll find maps of the estate and more information, but first I'll have to take your phones.' Florence says the latter politely but firmly, indicating a basket at her feet. 'They'll be returned when you leave the island.'

'I'm sorry, what?'

I feel my neck get hot at Edward's tone, but Florence appears unfazed. 'It was in the information as it's crucial there are no leaks to the press,' she says. 'There's only a single tower serving the island, so reception is intermittent at best anyway.' She waves inland.

'That's why I told you to bring your laptop,' I chime in. Unlike Edward, I read every word we were sent.

Edward is still glaring.

'They have Wi-Fi,' I say quickly. I look to Florence. 'Right?' She nods.

'There you go,' I say to Edward.

'But no social media. We'll monitor anything that's transmitted through the firewalls we have set up,' Florence explains. 'The exclusive part of this event needs to remain exclusive.'

'That's what makes it special,' I agree. I pull out my camera I bought for the occasion. It's not my only purchase for the next few days, but she doesn't need to know that. 'I'll be using this. We want to be able to share our experience with the kids.'

She hesitates, but I don't wait for her agreement.

And it's not for the kids, really. My three mini-Edwards have little interest in the event.

This is all for me.

Adam – Friday

Slouched on a metal chair outside a tiny, corrugated shed optimistically signed 'Welcome Lounge', I'm in the pitiful excuse for shade. Still a drop of sweat runs down the side of my neck from where I tied my hair back under my cap, adding to the dampness of my vintage Nirvana T-shirt, which is beginning to stick to my skin. The girl at the counter inside said that the boat to take me to Sparrow's Fart Island, or whatever the hell it's called, will be back soon.

Apparently, there's no other way across, but she'd be happy to get me a drink while I'm waiting. Happy unless it's whiskey, however. Discovered that the hard way. And I shouldn't have dared ask, if her horrified expression was anything to go by.

I caught myself before I went with the *Don't you know who I am?* line.

Mostly because either she does and doesn't give a shit, or worse, she's way too young to have heard of me. My jaw tightens. There was a time she'd have been lining up to drop her panties with the rest of them.

My knee bounces and I squint through my dark aviators to scan the horizon. I should have kept the car that drove me here waiting. Damn the officious guy who bustled me out. What use is a luxury ride if I'm stranded here?

What if someone else turns up and I'm here like a chump, sweaty and – I sniff the salty air, catching the hint of body odour – starting to reek? That's not how this was supposed to go down.

Man, this whole thing was a mistake.

Before I can think too hard, I have my phone in my hand. A couple of taps and it's ringing. He answers as I start talking.

'I'm out.'

'Now, Adam,' he says gently. 'Don't be hasty.'

I jump to my feet and pace out towards the dock. 'Don't use the baby tone with me.' A few more steps and I glare at the expanse of boat-less water. 'I don't know why I agreed to this in the first place.'

'Because you don't have a choice.' There's steel there now. 'And I'm not going to stand for you pulling prima-donna fits every five minutes. You wanted a job. Well, my boy, this is quite literally the only one that's going.'

My hand involuntarily tightens on my phone. The words to tell him to shove it – the reunion, and his offer to represent me as a solo artist, and the documentary – where the sun don't shine, fill my mouth.

But even I'm not that stupid. At least, not anymore.

I grit my teeth. My eyes close and my breath shudders like I've finished a three-hour session on stage, not sat on my arse in business class and then a limo.

When I open my eyes again, I see my guitar case where the driver dumped it out of the way with my battered suitcase and backpack. The black and gold 'Rake' special that I like to think they designed as much for me as in memory of Jonny.

I exhale hard, stand a little straighter. While a no-show is pure rock, I'd rather everyone see I've still got it. This is my way back into the spotlight that always should have been mine – I'm putting the comparisons and the ghosts to rest once and for all.

And there's the lack of other options.

'Yeah, well. The boat better get here soon,' I mutter.

'It will.' He's back to charming now. He knows submission when he hears it. 'In fact, if you look out to your right, you can probably see it.'

When silence tells me he's ended the call, I lift my head and see the boat. A sleek white mid-sized craft, with shelter and space for a few passengers, is rapidly approaching. A glance back towards the road shows a stretch-car winding down towards the small car park, explaining how he knew.

Of course, his transport from the airport is bigger than the one that brought me.

But when the door opens, it isn't my old band manager, Ian 'Bugsy' Malone. Instead, a tall guy, who's always looked more like a surfer than a musician with his blond streaks and effortless muscles, steps out.

My gut squeezes at the sight of Dylan O'Conner.

Even as The Cedrics Band's former drummer flashes me a grin, I can feel my mouth twist into a grimace. I haven't seen my brother's best friend since Jonny's memorial, which is the last night the rest of the band were in the same room, if you don't count distantly at a couple of awards shows. We'd come together at this tiny pub back home, the place we'd first played, to share a few beers and memories of the departed.

To turn Jonny into a saint, more like it.

I'd wanted to talk to Dylan about a gig. Of course, not too soon after burying Jonny, but the band was on a precipice, and I didn't want to lose all the momentum we'd gained.

So much for that idea.

When my jaw tenses, there's the faint click that's the lasting reminder of the answer he gave me with his fist. But now he's only a few feet away, and he's striding towards me like nothing happened.

Shuffling backwards, I look for Bugsy behind him. Hoping for someone to step in. Man, I told Bugsy I couldn't do this. He promised the contact with the others would be minimal, said it would be professional only.

'Adam, my bro,' Dylan says.

He's close enough now that I can smell him. Fresh, clean, oceany. With his white fitted T-shirt and casual navy shorts, he could be from a cologne ad. He's probably been in one, for all I know. Sometime in the last decade I've developed the ability to skim over anyone who looks like him on any form of media.

Better that way.

I endure as he gives me a loose hug. I've got to get through the next few days, and I've promised Bugsy I'll play nice. Besides, Dylan was my brother's best friend since they were two. I've probably shared a bathtub with this guy.

Despite everything, that kind of history is hard to shake.

'Hey,' I say, stepping back.

Dylan looks back to the posh car and the girl next to it. Young, lithe and freshly gorgeous in shorts so tiny they're borderline indecent and a halter top displaying a whole lot of golden flesh. Typical that, despite his age, Dylan can still pick up.

I turn away to where the boatman is tying up the craft.

'Maximum three passengers at a time to cross,' he says. About as rough-looking as you'd expect, the guy's guttural voice carries command.

This is good. Maybe with Bugsy here too I'll be free of Dylan and his little piece for the trip over to the island. Bugsy's out of the car now. Wearing a suit and his trademark braces – bright purple today – holding his pants up, he strides around the long vehicle to open the last closed door with a flourish.

And my knees go numb.

I know I'm staring – probably jaw hanging open, the works – but I'm powerless to do a thing about it. The woman who eases her limbs from the luxury leather seat with a languorous smile at Bugsy hasn't changed a bit in all these years. This I already knew; hell, I've wanked over enough pictures of her that I can recall every detail just by closing my eyes. But in the flesh...

Oh, in the flesh it's a whole other thing.

Ivy St Fleur – name acquired sometime after she wiped her past and before she shot to fame as a cross-genre jazz singer – is the kind of woman to inspire anything but innocent thoughts. And her every move feels like it's designed to attract the eye, while at the same time lacking obvious artifice. Naturally full lips, curves for days, dark silken hair, smoky eyes and a sinuous grace that quickens the blood.

The sex kitten and the Madonna in one.

My brother's ex.

Able to move suddenly, as realisation hits, I look again at the girl at Dylan's side, searching her features for any sign of familiarity. She approaches, closing the distance such that even my old-man eyesight lets recognition slam through me.

'That would make you...' My mouth isn't working properly, and I can't quite get the words out. This just gets worse and worse.

The girl, close enough now to hear my mumblings, raises her eyebrows, a hint of smirk on her mouth. 'Monet St Fleur. Nice to meet you, Uncle Adam.'

Monet – Friday

To say that Adam Rake is not what I expected is an understatement. Time has not been kind. Sure, the jeans are expensive, and there's a hint of the old pin-up boy in the brown hair falling over his eyes from beneath his cap. But his skin is sallow, and there's a rank smell. The few pictures I've managed to find on the internet from the last few years must have been liberally air-brushed.

My uncle – the reason I'm here – is still staring at me like a stunned mullet when gold-wrapped fingers encircle my wrist. The proprietary action of the man standing far closer than necessary starts a crawl of revulsion across my flesh. Instinctively, I shudder, disguising the reaction as an airy, girlish laugh.

'Would you like some assistance in boarding the boat?' Bugsy asks me.

Apparently, I'm some delicate flower. An idiot might think he's being kind, but I know he's simply protecting the merchandise. That being me, and my voice, and the show that he probably still can't believe he's getting a cut of.

'Maman might need a hand,' I say as I dislodge myself from his grip with the expertise gained since my figure developed about age eleven, and certain men stopped looking at me as my mother's annoying sidekick.

Adam hasn't said a word since I greeted him.

Not sure if it's a shock thing or what. I leave him to get himself in order, but a sudden thought makes me snag my foot on the gravel, and I nearly stack it. God, I hope he wasn't checking me out before…

'*Ma belle fille*,' Maman says, taking my hand when I reach her side. 'You nearly fell. I told you nothing good would come of this. There is still time to change your mind.' She lets me go and addresses Bugsy. 'You take us to the airport, now. *Oui*?'

I give it a beat just to enjoy his panic.

'No, Maman,' I say. 'I have a show to perform. You, however, can leave if you feel the trip is too much.'

I wait. She might not want this to happen but she's not going to leave.

Her sigh in response is long and pained. 'I will get through.' The huge black straw hat and oversized dark sunglasses she wears might hide most of her face, but I know she won't miss a thing, so I'm careful not to roll my eyes. At least, not until I turn away.

Part of me would prefer she stayed home where she has carers close to hand, in case her illness takes a turn, but the doctors assured me she was fit to travel. Besides, Dylan is here to look after her.

I flash him a grin and his eyes twinkle in response. He'll have caught the exchange and Maman's dramatics. I lower my voice so only he can hear. 'You'll make the crossing with us?'

I didn't miss the boatman's announcement about passenger limits, and although I have plans for Adam Rake, I can't leave Maman, and I'm not sure either of them is ready to be in such close proximity.

'Of course, my filly,' Dylan replies, his French accent deliberately cartoonish.

'I heard that,' Maman says. But there's amusement in her tone. Dylan always makes her laugh, something that's become more and more valuable over the last couple of years.

Straightening, I turn back to Bugsy. 'We'll be crossing first. I'm sure you and Mr Rake have plenty to catch up on while you wait.'

The spider-web of red veins in the apples of the manager's cheeks darken. 'My dear, I thought that you and—'

'Don't,' I snap.

Bugsy frowns. 'Don't what?'

'Think. It doesn't suit you and it's certainly not what I'm paying you for. In fact, that is a good question. What am I paying you for?' I give him every bit of haughtiness I can muster. My reputation as someone hard to work with, cultivated over the last six months, allows me freedoms the old me would never have imagined. And I can't pretend it isn't kind of fun, particularly when dealing with men like Bugsy.

His mouth opens and closes but nothing manages to come out.

I turn my back on him, avoiding Dylan's eye so I don't get the giggles.

Maman takes my arm as we cross to the boat.

'Got the bags for you, Miss,' Dylan teases. 'Hope that's acceptable.' He's grabbed our luggage from the car and easily caught up thanks to Maman's leisurely pace.

'More work and less chat,' I joke back.

I think I can feel Bugsy's ill-concealed glare and Adam's bemusement as we pass them.

'You shouldn't be quite so mean,' Maman whispers. 'You'll get a reputation.'

Again, I have to fight not to roll my eyes. She's not a fan of what she refers to as this 'new side of me', but she's more interested in quashing it than questioning.

'Bugsy Malone is a pig,' I say quietly.

That, she doesn't have an argument for. She can't really, since she discouraged me from hiring him as my manager, using that as one of her reasons. That fight lasted days and needed a visit from Dylan before she'd speak to me again.

I'm guessing he said something about letting me make my own mistakes and having decent lawyers give me get-out clauses for when I come to my senses.

He was less thrilled when I told him about the reunion I wanted to use to launch my first song. But he's never been able to deny me for long. Some might say he spoils me; I just kind of think he's doing his best to make up for the father I never had.

Dylan helps both Maman and me into the boat while the boatman is otherwise occupied with the same ropes I'm sure he was untying before. Maybe he's just not a fan of old pop stars and their offspring.

Unlike the obviously irritated Bugsy, Adam seems relieved by the travel arrangements. He's skulked back to a small seat in the shade of the only building, basically as far from us as he can get without leaving.

A twinge in my chest hopes it's not me he's so keen to avoid, but as the rumble of the boat's engine springs to life, I don't waste time dwelling on the prospect.

The guy will like me, everyone does.

He just doesn't know it yet.

Florence – Friday

Having heard that the young Monet St Fleur can be a bit of a prima donna, I expect an argument when I ask for her phone outside the guest suites. 'It'll be well cared for, and we do have Wi-Fi in the suites you can connect your laptop to, if you have one. Activity will be monitored, however.'

Earlier I met her, Ivy and Dylan, the drummer, at the dock and escorted them past the main resort building – along the only garden path wide enough for the carts beneath the canopy of some of the gum trees we managed to save from the fire – to where the route splits off to each of the seven new cabins.

'Of course,' Monet says, immediately handing hers over. 'We all want the same thing this weekend. For this event to be a huge success.'

Her smile is so warm, her voice like dark, golden honey, that I find myself smiling back. Really smiling for the first time in hours.

'Yeah, sure, no worries,' Dylan says. 'Catch.'

His phone loops through the air and I catch it at the last second.

'You'll give the poor woman a heart attack,' Monet berates him. 'Sorry,' she adds to me.

He hangs his head. 'I'm sorry, too,' he agrees. 'I'll make up for it by taking the girls' bags if you can direct me to their suite?'

Unlike Edward, who's barely recognisable from the band's heights of fame, Dylan O'Conner hasn't changed much at all. Older, but not the worse for it. The boy-next-door charm comes off him in waves.

I point to the trail leading furthest right. 'Thank you. Ivy and Monet's room is through there. Number one, the most private of the accommodations as requested.'

Monet smiles. 'Thanks. Maman has some trouble sleeping.'

'You're in suite three,' I call after Dylan. He's heading down the path already but raises a hand in acknowledgement.

'Who's in suite two?' Monet asks.

'Your manager requested he be close to hand in case you need him.'

Something like revulsion flickers across her face.

Dylan returns in time to catch the end of the conversation and Monet's reaction. 'Since he's not here yet, any chance of a last-second switcheroo, or something? They need their space, from him especially.'

I consider the layout. 'Suite five is empty for the weekend.'

Ivy St Fleur claps her hands. '*Parfait*. It is settled; you will move him.'

'That shouldn't be any trouble,' I say. 'I trust you'll find everything you need within your suite, including information about the estate. It's a family property, my husband and I being the fourth generation of Harpers here. Please enjoy the cold welcome drinks in the mini-bar or the tea and coffee in the nook by the balcony. And the freshly baked chunky-choc cookies are from a family recipe that Bruce's grandma made back when this area was nothing more than a paddock. Or there's a selection of fruit, if that's more to your liking.'

I've piled on every luxury I could think of, but they show no sign of being impressed. Oh, to live such a life.

The sting of my nails in my palms reminds me to relax my hands. My next breath is a little shaky, but they're too self-absorbed to notice.

'I'm suggesting we all meet around four, so I can show you the estate and where the concert will be held. I'll play some music through the intercoms in your rooms when it's time to gather. Until then, you may relax or, given the heat, indulge in a dip in the infinity pool around the other side of the house. Follow a signed path down to Hawk Bay for great beach swimming, and if you're lucky you might see some kangaroos or other wildlife we have on the island thanks to the national park area. However, please heed the warning signs for other beach areas. We've had recent great white shark sightings, a local swarm of box jellyfish and areas of the ocean are known for unexpected rips.

'Dinner will be served at seven on the deck,' I continue. 'I've put together a buffet selection, considering today's travel. Tomorrow we'll have something a little more formal.'

I don't mean to give them a choice in the matter, but I can hear the request for approval in my voice.

So must they, because Monet inclines her head like royalty. 'That sounds awesome. Whatever you're cooking over there smells incredible.'

'It does,' Dylan says. 'I'm starving.'

Ivy folds her arms and makes a face. 'Maybe to you. Some of us feel nauseous at the scent of flesh sizzling.' Her words are directed in a stage whisper to her daughter.

No one could accuse the woman of subtlety.

I force a pleasant smile. I'm sure I'll laugh about this when I tell Elsie. Or, almost sure. 'I promise you we have dishes catering for all dietary requirements.'

'And a great big pig on a stick for those of us with taste,' Dylan says.

Somehow, he's ended up at my side, and he nudges me good humouredly.

I look up and spot the figure at the side of the house, hidden by the trees. It's Bruce and he's staring at Dylan. The drummer is standing so close, our elbows are touching.

Bruce's gaze darkens.

Dylan is still talking, saying something that makes Monet laugh, but my amusement has quite disappeared.

Swallowing hard, I take a small step away, but there's no longer any sign of Bruce. That doesn't mean he's not watching.

'How do we contact you?'

I blink, trying to make sense of the question Dylan has just asked. 'Pardon?'

He waves towards the house. 'If we need something.'

'Of course,' I say. 'There's a bell in the suite. Ring it, and either myself or my husband will come.'

Internally, I wince. Did I emphasise the husband part too much? Dylan was just being friendly; it wasn't like he was trying anything on. Bruce has got me overthinking again.

'Thanks for everything,' Monet says. 'We should be fine from here. Are you sure changing Bugsy's suite isn't too much trouble?'

She's reminding me of the request, but considering I'd almost forgotten, I can't be irritated. 'I'll get on to it right away.'

'Much appreciated,' Dylan says.

He moves to pat my arm, but I wrench away. I don't look back, not wanting to see his confusion. Too bad, Mr-Famous-Drummer, it's for your own good.

It doesn't take long to rearrange the suites, but I linger. What did Bruce see? More importantly, how much did it piss him off?

Deciding to combine returning to the main house in company and getting another job off my list, I head for suite four. I knock. It takes so long for the occupants to answer, I begin to think they might have headed out to explore. Worry flutters behind my ribs. Telling people to stick to the paths through the bushland areas, to stay this side of the stage paddock and to be careful near the cliffs doesn't mean they'll obey.

But then the door edges open. I glimpse narrowed, beady brown eyes before the door slams shut.

I stand there, blinking.

That was the director's wife, Connie. She didn't say a word when I greeted them off the boat, quiet to the point of rudeness. And now she's slammed the door in my face. What the hell?

The door opens again, swinging wide to reveal a large, rounded, older man reminiscent of a pudgy De Niro, from the crooked nose to the deep creases around brown eyes. A thin black moustache feels like a pretentious reminder that he's the director and financer of the documentary side of this endeavour, Marco D'Angelo.

'Can I help you?' His heavy brows lift in question.

Adopting my most polite expression, I say, 'I have a few minutes to show you to the interview space, if you'd like.'

The addition of the director's requirements had me

googling 'good interview spaces' at two a.m. one night. He approved the pictures I sent a week ago, but reserved the right to request changes. How we're supposed to change it if he has an issue, I have no idea, but the sooner I know what I'm dealing with, the better.

Marco darts a glance over his shoulder. 'Give us a moment.'

I nod, and I'm staring at the closed door again.

My watch tells me I'll be cutting it fine to greet the others, but he reappears a moment later, his wife at his side. They trail me back through the garden – with its gum trees and natives surrounding lush lawn areas, all of it kept green by tank and bore water – towards the main house, Marco's breath growing heavier with each step. In contrast, Connie is completely silent.

'That's the way we came from earlier, and that route leads to the kitchen area,' I explain, pointing. Pride flares in my chest at how we've transformed the old house into a restaurant and tasting area as well as our private quarters, not visible from here. This side shows off the old stone structure, with its wide verandas that keep out the blazing Australian sun, which morphs into the glass-and-wood modern luxury of the side that looks out over the water, capturing the stunning sea views from the edge of the cliff. A view echoed in miniature from each of the private suites. 'Please come this way.'

I've chosen a room for the interviews in the huge sprawling homestead, away from the dining room where we will come together as a group to indulge in the best food and wine of the area – and take in those views. It's a secluded area originally designed for us to be able to have a retreat from guests, connected most closely to our private area of the house.

Inside, there's a lounge with a few chairs, an imposing old-fashioned desk, and on a small table sits an old-style turntable with a box of vinyl records picked up from a vintage shop. The room can be accessed through a small but neat courtyard sheltered by vines.

I open the French doors wide, and Marco steps in after me. Connie scurries behind. The woman is beginning to remind me of a rodent.

I wait, holding my breath, for Marco's verdict. I already explained the set-up in an email, but it's all I can do not to repeat it. Elsie always says I turn from clam to chatterbox when I'm nervous.

And as the seconds become minutes, my good intentions desert me. 'My husband, Bruce, brought up the gear you sent ahead and there are plenty of power points. Outside too.' I point to the carefully piled gear against the wall that I'm guessing is lights and microphones. 'I know you'll be wanting to see the stage area too. I don't know what you do for sound, but be aware the concert guys won't be here until the day of the show. I thought if you put a note on the door when you're filming, it would keep the others away. If there's anything else you need, just ask.'

Marco looks down to Connie. She murmurs something I can't hear and he nods in response. 'It will do,' he says. 'Leave us now.'

I do as I'm told. Not for the first time today. I knew taking orders from guests would be part of running a place like this, but I didn't know they'd be quite so imperious about it.

Nor how much it would grate on my nerves.

Adam – Friday

I'm in the bathtub when I hear music. I tilt my head, trying to make sense of it through the pleasant fog from the hot water. Then I remember – the chick said they'd ring the suites for the stage tour.

I sit up fast, sloshing bubbles and water across the tiles of the huge bathroom and knocking the glass on the wooden bath shelf onto my lap. Four balls of ice and the last drops of the Three Chains Distillery's signature gin fall right onto my junk.

Oh, that's cold.

The icy blast gets me lurching out of the bath. I wrap myself in one of the huge fluffy bath towels while using another to roughly mop up the water. The tiles are cool beneath my feet thanks to the tasteful whirr of the air-conditioning.

Man, it has been a while since I've experienced this kind of luxury, but the show will change all that.

Relatively dry, I pad out of the bathroom to the bed, where I left a fresh pair of black jeans and a fresh T-shirt. It's not that I care about the way the kid's nose wrinkled as she passed me, nor about impressing Ivy, but it feels good to be clean.

And the gin has taken the edge off.

If I never have to get on board another boat, it will be too soon.

'Wait 'til you get a rough trip,' Bugsy had chortled.

Bent over the side, parting ways with everything I'd ever eaten, I'd hated the bastard even more than usual.

I drag on my clothes outside. The suites are designed so that even naked on the balcony, I can't see even a hint of other human habitation. I could imagine I'm the only one on the whole island.

Figuring the director guy, Marco something-or-other, will be on the tour with his camera, I comb my hair back and divert past the bathroom mirror to make sure there's nothing too gross in my teeth and no nose hairs have grown in the last five minutes. Man, no one told me that about getting old. My reflection isn't Adam Rake from when The Cedrics Band was on the cover of every magazine, but he'll do. Particularly with sunglasses.

A minute later I'm outside and I'm ready as I'll ever be to be documentarised.

A sudden ring of laughter and a call of 'Come on, Maman' shatters the illusion that each of the suites is isolated.

My stomach drops. I turn back to the door and take out my card to unlock the suite.

'You're not missing this.' Bugsy's order comes from behind me. 'So turn back around and pretend you're not a complete pussy for once in your life.'

I turn. The calm I'd found from the gin Bugsy directed me to has totally disappeared.

'I have a headache,' I say. It's not a lie, there's a background pain that gets stronger every time I picture the kid's face. Jonny's kid. Ivy's kid.

'I don't care. There's no way off this island.'

'What?'

He smirks, showing one canine tooth that sticks out at an odd angle. He's never had it fixed, says it's from a fight at an exclusive bar in LA. But I heard him admit once a cow kicked him when he was a kid. An actual cow.

'There's no way off this island for you. What did you think I meant?' He shakes his head, snorting through his nose. 'You are basically trapped here until the show is over, so you might as well get used to it.'

My fists clench that a guy like Bugsy can stand there with his cow-tooth, wearing a stupid striped suit – doesn't he know it's like a billion degrees? – and tell me what to do. I want to tell him where he can shove his orders, so bad, but I want the chance he's dangling in front of me even more.

I mean, money's great and all, but that moment on stage when the fans are screaming back the words you're singing and kids are picking up guitars because they want to be you? There's nothing like it. *Nothing.*

So, we both know I'm not going back inside.

'I don't know how this happened,' I grumble as we head for the meeting point. 'I had everything.'

'Let me remind you,' Bugsy replies. 'Firstly, when Jonny died you weren't the front man and being a dead guy's brother only gets you so far.' Bugsy is holding up a skinny hand, gold rings flashing as he lifts a finger on every point. 'Second, the songs you chose for your solo releases were shithouse. Third, you could have at least tried to act like you were grieving.'

My teeth grind together.

'Fourth, you pissed away the money you did earn and screwed up any sympathy credits you might have had by being late or drunk or both.'

I kick the ground. 'You gotta live the life, man. What's the point if you're not rock and roll?'

He doesn't bother to answer as the gardens between the suites and the main house come into view. The others are gathered on the lawn up ahead, and I can't help but notice Bugsy increases his stride. Now he has me trailing along like a good little boy, he's obviously keen to concentrate on more important matters.

Like Monet St Fleur.

I have no idea how someone like him got his greasy claws into a talent like that, but he's not going to wreck it by associating with the likes of me. There's so much mystery surrounding this kid, and it only adds to the buzz.

Early videos caught by fans from when she joined her mum on some tours as a little tacker suggested she could become a voice of a generation, but then they dropped off the radar – apparently, so she could have a 'normal' childhood. All anyone's properly seen of her since are a few blurry clips on social media released in the last year, teasing the voice of an angel.

The idea to launch her first single in this reunion set is pure genius.

Which means I'm certain it didn't come from Bugsy. Someone else is pulling the strings, and if I'm going to get through this weekend with some kind of career resurrection, I need to work out who before it all blows up in my face.

Adam – Friday

I have strolled into packed stadiums, awards shows and presidential offices confident whoever's waiting would hang on my every word, but stepping out into the garden knowing everyone will be there has the gin I didn't drink enough of burning the back of my throat. Noticing the unmanned camera on the tripod pointed towards the group waiting in the shade, I'm surprised the whole entrance isn't more orchestrated. Because I reckon, left to our own devices, we won't make for exciting viewing.

Dylan's there, standing between Monet and Ivy like he belongs with them. Then there's Edward and a blonde lady. He got married and quit music, if I remember rightly. He was a nerd when we were kids and nothing's changed. Right now, he has the pained look of a man heading for a vasectomy rather than someone about to be part of a music doco watched by millions. Although his woman's just about jumping out of her skin, she looks so excited. She's actually not bad looking, which puts her way out of old Edward's league.

There was a time I'd have thought about showing her what a real star can do, but it's all a bit too much effort these days. I'm more worried about whether he still remembers how to play the keyboard than if he's playing his wife often enough.

Thankfully, I get away with just nodding to the group in general as I walk up.

Edward nods back. No pretend 'great to see you' from him at least. Like Dylan, he was Jonny's friend, not mine. They all were.

'Hi Adam, I'm Lara, Edward's wife. But you probably knew that.'

'Um, hi. Nice to meet you.' The woman who had been alongside Edward seems to want more. 'At last?'

'It's great,' she says. 'Isn't it super great to have everyone here?'

'Yes?' I shoot Edward a look, because every time I step back she seems to take a step closer, and I reckon she's only a few more excited questions away from having me up against a wall.

But it's not Edward who saves me.

Lara's attention is caught by the moustached director crossing the lawn to lift the camera from its tripod.

I take the opportunity to edge away, so Bugsy is between me and the others. He's busy talking with the host chick and the director, now with a camera on his shoulder, about what he wants for the shots. The old dude says something about cameras, plural, and it's only then that I notice the tiny grey-haired woman at his side.

Florence claps her hands together once to get everyone's attention, then steps back, leaving old-dude to speak.

'Welcome to Sparrow Hawk Island. Consider the weekend and the documentary to have officially begun. I'm Marco and I'm in charge. Other than during the interviews, which will be primarily conducted in the main house, I'm looking for candid shots of the weekend: you all being back together, and then getting ready for the show; and of course, during the actual event. Nothing posed. Genuine interactions.'

'So we should, like, act really natural?' The chirpy voice belongs to Edward's wife.

I try to send him a sympathetic look about annoying women, but he's staring straight ahead like he doesn't know any of us. Fine, it's not like we were ever buddies.

'Pretend we're not here,' Marco says. At a nudge from the little woman, he adds, 'Remember, though, you've all signed media agreements to be filmed the whole weekend. No saying something and trying to take it back. My vision will only work if we're uncensored.'

'The suites are private, though, aren't they?' Monet interjects with authority.

I keep my gaze from her or her mother.

For the first time, Marco looks flustered. 'Yes, of course.'

Bugsy chortles. 'What he's saying is that all of you need to be on your best behaviour.'

Ha, as if I don't know who that's directed towards.

We're held a few minutes longer so the director and his wife can go ahead to better shoot our approach to the stage area. I haven't been involved in much screen stuff, but this all seems a bit amateur. I thought there would be sound guys, tech people, the works. However, it does fit with what I read online about Marco D'Angelo. He's known to be a bit eccentric, and I'm not going to argue when 'genius' was used more than once. My career can use a bit of genius.

I'm watching for the cue to get going when I hear my name.

'Adam.'

Just my name, only two syllables, but from her it's goddamn music. I read once that her voice can make a grown man cry, and I remember nodding along with the words. There's something about Ivy St Fleur that tugs so deep, it's like she could split you open and you'd thank her for the service.

Throat dry, I turn. And she's there in front of me, so close I could touch her.

God dammit, how I want to touch her.

I cross my arms. 'Ivy.'

I manage a shuddering breath, like a schoolboy around a crush, but all that does for me is hit me with her scent. In the years since I've seen her, she's turned her preference for warm vanilla and chocolate scents into a signature perfume line entwining the two that has the power to stop me dead when I pass a chick on the street who's wearing it.

Ivy is sporting dark sunglasses and the same wide, floppy hat as earlier, but this close I can see a hint of her eyes and the sincerity in them when she asks, 'How are you, *mon ami?*'

I fight a sudden urge to spill the truth. 'Not bad.' I shrug. 'You?'

Has my voice always sounded so needy? This whole thing is so fucking inane, but it's not like I can avoid her all weekend.

You've managed it for nearly eighteen years.

My thoughts taunt me.

'Did everyone get all your instruments across?' Dylan asks loudly, before Ivy can answer. 'Adam? I know you were bringing yours as hand luggage.'

He says it all innocent like, but he saw my guitar, and I saw the kid whisper something before he spoke. Dylan's not the type to be making sure of the details. Mr Big Shot guest drummer doesn't need this gig at all. And I know for a fact that Edward tried to pull out of this event. Now I've met her, I reckon the wife was the keen one. And Bugsy's definitely

46

not in charge. I'd thought maybe Ivy, but fuck me if it's not the damn kid who's running this show.

'I've got it,' I say.

And in that moment of distraction, Ivy moves away.

Right then, Monet catches my gaze. One eyebrow lifts, and the sight of it is a gut punch, because that expression could be Jonny. And because of that, I know exactly what it means.

She wants me to know who's in charge.

And she wants me to know she doesn't want me talking to her mother.

Lara – Friday

At Florence's direction, we head away from the house. Edward and I are at the back of the group, me following where we're going on the map that was provided in the suites. A glance around suggests I'm the only one who brought mine with me. The big meeting-the-band moment was all a bit anticlimactic. If I hadn't googled the director and found his recent awards and the promise of the big networks lined up, I'd wonder if the bloke knew what he was doing.

'It's not the way I would have done it,' I say softly.

'Lucky you're not in charge then,' Edward replies.

The St Fleur women lead the way, walking with the hostess. Edward didn't introduce me to them, and I couldn't quite get up the nerve to go over and say hello. They shine with effortless star power. Ivy is smaller and more beautiful than she was all those years ago, and her daughter is all the best bits of her and Jonny.

It doesn't matter, there's time.

First, we head up a winding path – away from the cliff edge and not too far from the main house – to a locked-up building labelled on the map as the distillery. The building, which I'm guessing could have once been the stables, is smaller than the huge house but with some sections made from the same stone in between newer iron-and-timber sections.

'Here's where we make the gin,' Florence explains. 'The one you'll find in your suites that will be officially launched, along with the lodge, at the concert. There were some limitations in setting up, as we wanted to use this old building as the starting point. Then we had to consider plumbing and distribution, and even how we'd bottle the finished product. It was a lot of planning, research and hard work, but we're proud of what we've made.' She smiles fleetingly.

Inside, the amber still shines glorious in the light streaming in from the large windows. The pipes are polished to a marvellous gleam. Barrels line a far wall and there is a large workbench with various ingredients to flavour the gin.

'We use mostly native botanicals, giving the gin a real Australian characteristic,' she says. 'There are dangers in the process, of course. We use highly volatile and flammable substances and take pride in doing so with the utmost safety.'

'Do you have distillery staff?' I ask.

Florence blinks like she didn't expect any questions. 'The set-up is small enough for Bruce and me to do small batches. However, once the lodge is open properly for business, we'll have help from the mainland.'

'Must have been tricky getting it over here,' Bugsy says.

She nods. 'The winery production took a hit with the fire and we wanted to try something new. Fiction Distilling, run by some people I met at a book event, shared their expertise.'

'What are the other buildings?' I add, bored with the gin talk. I point from the map to the shapes of sheds mostly hidden by trees and shrubs with vines snaking between. According to the map, the house and distillery are surrounded by dozens of acres of bushland containing the stage area within it, and also a quarry, before it opens up to farmland.

'Storage, mainly,' Florence replies – *none of your business*, in her tone.

Her dismissal makes me bite back a query about the neighbouring farm shown on the very edge of the map, as well as the area I know to be preserved as a national park taking up more than half the five and a half thousand acres that make up the island.

We're about two minutes down a winding trail on the far side of the distillery, heading deeper into the island, when Monet stops and says something to Florence. It's too soft to be heard from where we are thanks to Edward, who's slowed to re-tie the practical walking shoes I couldn't dissuade him from wearing.

'Are we walking or not?' he'd countered when I suggested something more on trend.

The pretty white sandals I chose are fast becoming an unpleasant dusty brown, and I reckon I've felt every single rock through their thin soles. However, I daren't complain.

I'm about to ask how much further when the three women in the lead turn off to the right. When the rest of us make to follow, Florence waves us along. 'Just follow the track and turn left at the sign. You can't miss it. We'll catch up.'

'See you there,' Dylan says immediately.

I'm pretty sure Monet mouths something like *Thank you* in his direction. There is a story there, I'm sure of it.

Dylan's quick acceptance makes it impossible for the rest of us to argue, but I look long and hard at the path they chose. There's nothing to see but more trees and more vines. It's like they've disappeared.

I would have guessed the stage set-up would be close to the main house, but we trudge along a narrow dirt track for long minutes. There are vines among the bushland either side and some towering gums, but they don't give much relief from the temperature. It's like the heat actually comes off the gravel beneath our feet.

There's going to be cameras filming us, could be already for all I know, and I can feel that I'm flushing. I was going to bring a touch-up makeup kit, but Edward practically shoved me out the door. I glare sideways at him now, pleased his pale skin is fire-engine red.

He's grumbling and I hope there are no microphones close enough to catch it. A quick scan of the trees, fences and trail-side bushes shows nothing but boring nature. I'm surprised they're not using drones to get some overhead shots. But maybe it's part of the director's style to be all old-school.

'You could at least pretend you don't hate this,' I whisper.

'You'd know all about pretending, wouldn't you?'

I turn so quickly my toe catches a rock and I wince. 'What's that supposed to mean?'

'Nothing.'

He ups his pace so I have to trot to keep alongside.

Any thought of developing camaraderie with Adam or Dylan is spoiled by the fact that the manager guy is reminiscing about back when he was in a band.

'I really could have been someone,' Bugsy says to Dylan.

Dylan grunts. 'Let me guess, if only you'd had a manager like yourself.' He laughs. 'Everyone thinks they could have been someone special.'

'Not me,' Edward says.

Adam smirks. 'Good that you know your limitations.'

'Pity you've never known yours,' Edward fires back.

Anger sweeps across Adam's face, and I resolve to remind Edward about playing nice. Doesn't he understand that these people are important?

Bugsy is still going on about himself. 'They used to say I had a tone that could melt panties,' he says with a look at me. Then he reaches over and pats my arm, his hand damp with sweat, his touch a beat too long. 'Excuse the language, my dear.'

I smile, because the man does have power, but edge away.

'But my true calling,' he continues, 'was a life of service, and I had to follow that path.'

Dylan snorts. 'Forget it, Ian, just because you've managed to lure Monet to the dark side doesn't mean I'm going to follow. I'm not joining your little stable of wannabes. No offence,' he adds in Adam's direction.

Adam acts like he's not listening.

'This heat,' Bugsy mutters, huffing with every step.

'It's awful,' I agree. 'I didn't realise it would be so hot. And all these flies. Yuck. I totally hate flies. They spread disease, and did you know they can actually taste with their feet? Do you think Florence has a spray to keep them away?'

No one bothers to answer me.

People think I don't realise when my babble irritates them. I do, mostly. But I don't care. I've learned that it's hard for someone to ignore every question – eventually, they'll respond.

At last, the path opens up and there's a sign with the distinctive Three Chains logo of three loops entwined. I snap a quick picture, making sure I catch Adam and Dylan in the shot. Beyond the sign, there's a wider path curving away beneath more gum trees – but no stage.

Bugsy is wrestling with the chain on a wide gate, with an impatient Adam about to elbow him out of the way, when there's a rattle from behind us.

We all turn to look and see Florence driving Ivy and Monet on one of the carts. They must have disappeared to get one and taken a different route. They pull to a stop and Florence walks past us to deftly open the gate.

Adam blocks her path. 'If there was a road, why the fuck did you make us walk?'

Lara – Friday

I probably wouldn't have sworn at our hostess with the possibility of cameras lurking, but my poor feet and ruined sandals agree with Adam asking why we were walking if there was an alternative.

Next to me, Edward folds his arms. His sunglasses have slipped down his nose and he's glaring over the top of them.

Florence's smile is encouraging. 'I thought you would all enjoy the opportunity to explore.'

'But not them?' Edward spits, hooking his thumb at Ivy and Monet.

Adam's eyes widen at the source of his backup but he folds his arms in solidarity. However, when he does so, it's in quite the different way to Edward. On Adam it's all moody rocker, and for the first time, standing there all pissed off, he reminds me of Jonny.

Florence looks to Monet with a silent question. But the girl gives an almost imperceptible shake of her head. Something is definitely going on there.

I snap another photo, catching the St Fleur women this time.

'I sincerely apologise,' Florence says. 'I will make sure we have transport to return you to your suites, and I hope the stage set-up makes up for any inconvenience.'

It's quite the humble apology, but partway through there becomes something strained about it. She's looking past us through the gate, and when I follow her gaze I see her husband. He's big and broad and kind of rough looking, and he's not even trying to hide his scowl.

Some women like that kind of thing, I guess.

Not me. Although I'm all for tortured, I prefer the poetic rather than the brutal.

Florence's smile is brittle. 'Hopefully, this doesn't spoil the big reveal. Bruce, if you'd like to show our guests the way?'

Bruce turns on his heel and strides underneath a vine-covered archway that forms a gorgeous living tunnel of dark shade. We all follow, Adam and Edward dropping their tough guy stances without protest. Ivy and Monet join the rest of us on foot and Florence trails behind with Bugsy.

Bruce is well out of the way when the group reach the opening of the tunnel. It means that Dylan, Adam and Edward step out first, followed by Ivy and Monet.

The camera on the scaffold in the distance appears pointed at the group ahead as I take a quick snap from behind. Luck, or were we shepherded in this way? Maybe this director knows what he's doing after all.

Then I'm out of the tunnel and I can't help but gasp. 'It's stunning.'

We're at the top of a slope that forms a natural amphitheatre around a huge stage at the foot. Beyond it there is the ocean on the horizon and vines in the foreground. It's so green here compared to the dusty trail, and I catch the scent from the smattering of yellow wildflowers.

Perched up on the scaffold, Marco captures the band as they head down towards the stage. I don't see his wife, but I'm guessing she's shooting from a different spot.

'The sun will set over the ocean during the evening and form a backdrop of an orange glow when you guys take the stage,' Florence is explaining, but I lose the rest of her words in the rustle of a breeze through the trees.

I realise I've been left alone at the top of the hill, everyone else more interested in the details of the stage set-up than the scenery.

Florence is pointing to the caravans lining the far edge of the paddock, with menu boards offering the signature gin, the Three Chains wines and other refreshments. I think she says something about extra workers manning them during the concert.

Pretending interest in the chairs and loungers set out that will allow groups of fans to picnic and relax in intimate groups, I capture a few more pictures. I'm guessing they can comfortably accommodate a couple of thousand attendees, but I think I read it will be closer to half that to keep it exclusive. Turning the little map to orient myself, I register the wider track Florence must have taken with Ivy and Monet and the fork leading to the docks. That must be the way they'll come from the boats for the concert.

I wander the stage area, trying to picture it as it will be on show day, but I'm more interested in watching Edward. My hope that being around the band would bring out some of the man I met fades when he checks his watch and asks when we're heading back.

'If you're ready to return to the house, Bruce has brought two more carts down and we should be able to get you back in comfort,' Florence says.

'Sure,' Adam says.

'We'll have a play tomorrow,' Dylan says. 'Get a feel for the acoustics.' He nudges Monet with obvious affection. 'Just wait until you hear this angel sing.'

Her cheeks go pink. 'I'm just hoping to do the band's songs justice.'

'You will, *ma chérie*,' Ivy assures her.

Edward nods, agreeing to anything if it means we can leave.

On that note, we begin the short walk up to where the carts are waiting.

Suddenly, Ivy sags at the knees with a soft cry.

Monet reaches out, taking her mother's weight just in time, then supporting her until they reach one of the nearby small loungers.

This is my chance to shine. A glance over my shoulder shows Marco and his wife coming this way, and they're filming.

'Don't.' It's Edward. His hand grips my arm. 'I know what you're thinking, but you haven't been a nurse for more than a decade.'

I suppress a flinch. Where have the years gone? 'This isn't brain surgery. Some things don't change.'

He lets go.

I hurry to Ivy. 'Excuse me,' I say.

Monet gives me a look that's a polite version of *who the hell are you*, while Ivy immediately dismisses me as nobody.

Inside, I squirm, but my smile doesn't falter. *No one is better than me.* I mentally repeat the mantra I've clung to since age six, when I overhead Mum asking the teacher why I couldn't read yet and muttering to Dad that I'd have to hope my looks lasted.

'I'm a nurse,' I say. 'I can help.'

Monet moves aside – take that, Edward! – and I study Ivy's features, taking in the sweat on her skin, and how she's swaying.

'Dizziness?' I ask. 'Nausea?'

Ivy nods.

'She said she thought she was going to faint.' Monet's voice is small, reminding me that for all her natural presence, she's still a child. Jonny's child.

'Do you mind?' I ask, lifting my hand.

When Ivy murmurs her acceptance, I rest my palm against her skin, feeling first the cool dampness of her forehead then moving to register the fast, weak pulse at her wrist.

'It's likely heat exhaustion,' I say.

'Do I need to call a doctor from the mainland?' Florence asks. The question's not grudging, exactly, but I guess this isn't the kind of headline she was looking for, and if Ivy leaves the island, Monet might follow. Show over.

I hesitate a beat. Every eye is on me now, including the cameras. It's my starring moment.

'No need for a call to the mainland yet,' I pronounce. I offer a comforting smile to Florence and the audience. 'We just need her to rest and cool down. If you could get the cart and maybe some water?'

I study my patient. She's already wearing a light loose dress so there's no excess clothing to remove. Monet is fanning her mother with her hat, and I nod approvingly.

Florence ducks into one of the small caravans and returns with a few bottles of water.

I take one from her and open it, before handing it to Ivy. 'Sips,' I warn.

The others have stopped a few feet away in some shade. They take drinks as well, murmuring appreciatively. I lick my dry lips. I'd love a cool drink, but getting one might lose me my position at Ivy's side. I try to send Edward a mental message, but he's slouched on a lounger further up the hill.

Then Dylan presses a bottle into my hands. 'Don't want the doc to pass out too.'

I should totally correct him on my qualification, but I'm too busy drinking. 'Thank you.'

Ivy is looking at me with a crease across her brow. 'You seem familiar.'

My stomach lurches. Impossible that she could remember. 'Probably from earlier, or maybe back on that awful concert day. Or you've seen someone like me somewhere, I've always been told I have a common face.'

I hold my breath as she nods slowly.

'*Vraie*,' she says, staring at me hard. 'That must be it.'

My heart hammers like a truck just missed hitting me head-on. 'Let's get you back, shall we?'

By the time we're back at the suites, Ivy's feeling a lot better. Their suite is similar to, but definitely bigger than, ours. The view is a little more far-reaching, everything a little more fancy.

'Rest and you'll be fine,' I say once she's on the bed. 'However, please do let me know if you feel worse.'

Monet walks to the door. 'Thanks. You don't know how much we appreciate it.'

Having seen the little pill bottles placed discreetly out of the way, I'm pretty sure I do. 'Glad to help.'

Edward is at his computer when I enter our suite. He looks up. 'I bet you loved that, didn't you?'

I say nothing.
He thinks I can't keep my mouth shut.
Shows how little he knows.

Florence – Friday

The fire that destroyed so much of our end of Sparrow Hawk Island coming up two years ago was a tragedy, but as I'm preparing for the first night's dinner, I can't help but feel proud of the result of the long rebuild. Thanks to firefighters who came by boat from the mainland, we were able to save most of the family homestead. However, it needed a complete gutting and refinish.

Bruce insisted we 'spare no expense', and I didn't need telling twice. After all, we'd never have got this event here with ordinary.

The main living and dining area, with its huge wall of glass, is furnished with plush loungers and scattered small tables for intimate dining that can seat up to forty, enough for if the suites were at capacity and day-trippers were visiting from the mainland. However, tonight the tables are being used as a buffet to display the finest produce from our region, and the intimate guest list means only myself and Bruce are on hand as staff. Marco requested we keep outsiders to a minimum, until required for the big show, and I assured him that by careful planning of the menu and meticulous preparation we'd be able to handle it ourselves. Local, freshly caught seafood, barbecued meats and vegetables, colourful salads and an array of exquisite sauces and dressings. And, of course, the carvings from the pig that's been slowly roasting in the kitchen courtyard.

The one that so offended Ivy St Fleur.

There are vegetarian and vegan options, but Bruce is particularly fond of his roasting pit and I couldn't deny him the opportunity to use it.

Marriage is all about compromise.

It's important to know the other person as well as you know yourself, to allow them the small wins that keep them happy. If I've told Elsie once, I've told her a thousand times. Bruce is just like a giant teddy bear once you get to know him.

One with a violent streak that almost matches his desire to please.

Unlike earlier, when we toured the stage set-up, everyone will have to interact tonight. My skin is tight, like the buzzing anticipation inside me is trying to break free.

The Cedrics Band together. At my – okay, technically all this belongs to Bruce, thanks to the prenup I had to sign – table.

I check the time. There's just enough for me to change. One last critical look around the room shows that everything is in its place. The outdoor setting, with its discreet overhead fans, looks like a pamphlet for luxurious, casual dining. I take a deep breath and turn towards the hallway.

I stop, sniff again. Is that... smoke?

I suck in air like a woman chasing her last breath. Memories roar to life. Sparks flying. Animals screaming. Everything around us being swallowed by flames. This isn't the friendly warmth of the pit, but something else. Something stomach-clenching for anyone who's ever lived in the Australian bush.

But when I try to work out where it might be coming from, it's gone. Now I can't smell anything but the native flowers artfully arranged throughout the room.

It must have been my imagination.

Because none of my guests smoke. I know that from the detailed questionnaire that warned me Ivy is vegetarian and about Edward's allergies. Only Jonny was known for the menthol cigarettes he tried to hide from his fans.

And he's dead.

I shake myself. I need to keep my mind on the dinner and not on imaginary fires. We have alarms, foolproof systems. Everything is under control.

I'm three steps into the narrow hallway to the main bedroom when I notice Bruce waiting for me. There's no way to easily pass him. Not if he won't let me.

'You've been avoiding me,' he says.

I shake my head, not trusting my voice. He sounds mad.

His mouth twists. 'This isn't the time for games, Florence. We both know that even now your precious guests might be making their way across to the house. Perhaps the first of them is in the dining area already.'

I think I hear the sound of the door.

Bruce's gaze flicks in that direction, showing I'm not the only one who noticed. And he knows how much I need this to go well.

As usual, I am at his mercy.

'You've been avoiding me,' Bruce repeats.

In the shadows of the old hallway, his eyes are darker than ever, his frustration palpable. His scent, earthy and masculine, is almost overpowering.

Heat pools inside me.

I nod.

One large hand comes out and grips my upper arm. He pushes me up against the wall. Not rough, exactly, but purposeful. His hands rest either side of my head and his lower body pins me in place.

'He was looking at you,' Bruce growls.

I don't need to ask who he's talking about; I knew there would be fallout from that moment with Dylan. 'He was simply being friendly,' I say quickly. 'Not every man I interact with wants to bed me.'

Bruce's laugh is a low, enticing rumble. 'That's where you're wrong. Just being close to you is enough to make a man lose control.'

I know better than to keep arguing. Before Bruce, I never felt particularly attractive but now, with his lower body against mine, the evidence that he wants me is unmistakable.

I can't help arching towards him.

'This is not the time,' I manage.

He leans close, so close his breath is warm on my damp skin. 'Tell me to go,' he whispers right into my ear, the stubble on his jaw scraping against my cheek. 'I'll leave you alone, you only have to say.'

I want to. The part of my brain that has worked so hard to pull this thing together, the part with the secrets – yes, even from Bruce, who knows so much of my darkness – is screaming at me to get the hell out of this hallway. But I can't. I can't get the words out. Instead, I moan. A little sound of pleading.

I feel his smile as he captures my mouth with his, plunders it, kisses me so hard I know my lips will be red from the contact.

In this moment, I don't care. I kiss him back. The hunger for my husband impossible to ignore, maybe stronger because it goes against every logical, thinking part of me.

His hands find my hips, draw me flush against him, and I grind even closer.

'Please,' I whisper.

I don't know what I'm asking. But Bruce does. Now we're hard against the wall and our bodies are fused into one and I can't tell if it's my heart or his, but the thudding drowns out our ragged gasps for breath. He smiles and kisses me again, somehow deepening the intensity until I'm nothing but sensation.

'Excuse me?' a man's voice says.

Two words, like stone shattering, slam me back into the reality of my guests and the band and the dinner I'm supposed to be serving.

What am I doing?

Instinctively, I try to pull away, but Bruce is too strong, and with the wall behind me there's no place to go. He lingers, his lips hard on mine for a long, deliberate, possessive moment.

I don't fight it.

And not only because the heat of the kiss is still slicing sharp and sweet through my veins. If a moment of civility with Dylan earlier made him mad, then rejection now might push him over the edge. And that's not where I want him.

Not yet.

Bruce lifts his head, breaking the contact between us, and smiles a slow smile. He steps away, then doffs an imaginary hat to our interrupter and strolls away, closing the door to our rooms behind him.

His little show allows me to gather my composure. When I turn to face the man, I'm my usual self, hopeful the dim lighting of the hall disguises my ravished skin. I tried every avenue I could think of to get this event happening, but it was the tenuous connection of the record executive who'd attended Bruce's fancy private school being owed a favour from Bugsy that got us over the line.

He's here to repay a debt, but he acts like we should be grateful for his attendance.

I will not be sorry to never see him again after this weekend.

He's standing there, smirking, a fine sheen of greasy sweat on his skin, something lascivious in his gaze. There are people who would have looked away if they'd interrupted such a private moment, but I felt Bugsy's beady eyes on me.

'Did you need something?' I ask.

He snickers. 'Couldn't make it to the bedroom, huh?'

With the band here, Bugsy no longer matters. However, I keep a polite smile in place. 'Not brave enough to say that with Bruce still here, huh?'

His eyes narrow. 'Don't push me, lady.'

I can't help it, I laugh. I'd disliked Bugsy by reputation, but that pales alongside my disgust for him in the flesh. He's the kind of man who'd throw you into the path of an oncoming train for the mere possibility of self-gain. And what is with those stupid braces? Does he think he's some kind of 1920s gangster?

His cheeks flush pink, the red veins prominent, and he steps towards me. After Bruce's massive size, all the movement does is highlight Bugsy's weedy stature.

'I could take this event off this island right now. One word, one click of my fingers.' He does a weak snap for emphasis. 'And this will be over for you.'

'Really?' I'm glad I sound as bored as I feel. I move closer, forcing him to look up to meet my gaze. 'How about you run away with your empty threats, and I'll forget you tried, and we'll both get back to making this show a brilliant success?'

His jaw works and then his chest deflates. He's not completely stupid. 'I wanted to tell you we'll be ready to eat soon.'

It's a surrender and we both know it.

Still a little off balance from my interactions with Bruce and that smell of smoke, I don't have the energy to rub in his capitulation. 'Excellent. Please make yourself comfortable – there are drinks in the bar. I'll be with you in a moment.'

He hesitates and then responds in kind, all rancour gone from his rat-like features. 'Thank you. It sounds divine.'

A STORYBOOK LOVE:
THE CEDRICS BAND FAN BLOG

10 December 2021

Greetings friends, fans, *fam*.

I am here at last, and let me tell you, the air in this coastal town is literally humming with the excitement of the show being only a couple of days away. Accommodation in Port Este is so full, people are bunking down in nearby farmers' sheds so they can be certain not to miss the boat when it comes on Sunday.

Until then, we're making our own fun. There are impromptu dance parties, catch-ups and lots and lots of old songs on repeat. I don't think my spine has stopped tingling since I arrived because when I stand out on the dock, I can literally see Sparrow Hawk Island.

Picture it with me. I'm talking stunning cobalt waters with gentle waves, and a cerulean sky with the distant greens and browns of an island meeting at the horizon, all warmed by the kind of bright summer sunshine that lends the whole world a cheerful glow.

I have it on good authority that the band is already over there.

I know you guys need every detail, so I have made it my mission to befriend everyone in this place, and I mean everyone. From the girl working at the café here to the surly boatman who took them across. And the old Ricky charm has not failed me.

I have heard some things already.

Things you know I will share with you.

However, remember that I am simply a messenger and take no responsibility for the truth or not of these rumours. You may have noticed all involved with the show have gone quiet on the socials. Not only does this make us all even more desperate for the show to come – hello, just about peeing my pants over here – but there was a whisper that it was a condition of the event and the documentary that they share nothing. Hello, anticipation!!

So, any of you girls out there hoping to stumble across Adam doing some pre-show swiping on the apps, you'll need to give up, because he's out of contact.

A little birdie told me that not all the band were happy to part with their links to the outside world. I'm not naming any *red-haired* folks, but make of that what you will.

I know you are all wondering how they're getting along being back together again after all this time and I am glad to say that although we're not talking BFFs or anything, relations have been civil.

So far.

We all remember what happened at the memorial, and we're hoping time has healed those wounds. Not getting ahead of myself, but this could be the beginning of a new special chapter in the story of the band. We know the magic when they play together, and we're all hoping this event is not a one-time thing.

Speaking of new music – don't get too excited; not The Cedrics Band, but something we're nearly as excited about – Jonny's girl and her imminent debut song. I get chills when I think about it dropping mere days from now.

Not surprisingly, she is fitting in with the band so well. I know wherever he is, Jonny's watching over her, and I know she would be making her dad so proud. Just between you and me, it's worth noting that it's good for that girl to have the band all around her. The old saying of 'it takes a village to raise a child' and all. Ivy St Fleur has been even more reclusive than usual these last few months, and I don't want to worry you all unnecessarily but I'm concerned that the young girl could all too easily become an orphan.

Yes, it would be a tragedy in our time, but the world showed with the loss of our Jonny that it can be a cruel, cruel place.

Now, on a brighter note, someone is playing 'Slow Dancer', and you know I can't miss a singalong of my fourth favourite song.

Don't forget to follow the link below and sign up for more detailed news as well as actual sound bites from the band performing* for only a small fee. I wouldn't be here without your support.

> 'Sway in time, let the beat control.
> Because you know I'm a slow dancer.'
> SLOW DANCER – The Cedrics Band

Ever gratefully yours,
Ricky
The Cedrics Band Number One Fan

* Videos of the show may not be available until I'm back on the mainland, depending on internet access on the island.

Monet – Friday

There's a lull in dinner conversation on the outdoor deck as Florence and her husband excuse themselves to clear the dishes.

'Dessert won't be long,' Florence says with a smile. 'In the meantime, feel free to help yourself to another drink.'

As we wait, I'm not the only one to find a sudden fascination in the gorgeous view of the orange sky over the dark ocean. The silence around the table is punctuated by persistent rustling from the garden of unseen small creatures, although the citronella candles burning around the deck's perimeter stop mosquitoes from feasting.

My light floral dress sticks in patches to my damp skin and I'm thankful for the overhead fans creating a breeze. Florence comes outside to offer tea and coffee, prompting Adam and then Lara to escape inside to the bar and refill their glasses of beer and bubbly respectively. The bottle of the Three Chains signature gin they're launching at the concert that was on the table is empty, something I feel is more to do with its alcohol content than it being particularly good.

It's like everyone here has exhausted their capacity for superficial conversation. And no one wants to go any deeper.

We've done the weather, the sea crossing and the stage set-up – something I had to agree was better than I could have imagined, given the isolation. The view was discussed in more detail than anyone wanted when we first sat, and commenting on the delicious food occupied the meal.

The questions I've waited all this time to ask want to burst free, but I don't ask them, instead fiddling with my glass. It's not the right time.

Will it ever be?

I shove the needling doubt from my mind. I have a plan and I'm not going to falter now. After feeling for so long that it was running out, now, finally, time is on my side.

I worried a little that there would be questions about Maman not joining us for dinner. But it seems her little display about the smell of the pig roasting is enough that everyone assumes it's some kind of tantrum.

Refusing Florence's offer of help, since I'd rather not have her exposed to Maman's current mood, I took across a tray earlier. The child in me wanted to put a slice of the pork on it just to annoy her, but I resisted. She probably hasn't touched anything anyway.

I'm not sure the director and his wife even noticed we are one short. After informing us the filming was for flavour montages of the weekend, Marco suggested we act like the cameras aren't even there.

As if any of us are going to do that. We've all been caught out by unexpected paparazzi. Well, except maybe Edward's wife, if the way she's spent half her meal fixing her hair, adjusting her posture and staring at the camera is anything to go by.

As expected, both the director and his wife are seated such that they're always out of shot.

'Dessert is ready inside,' Florence announces.

I trail the others beneath the twinkling fairy lights hung above, and in through the wide-open stacker glass doors. Adam scampers ahead; his avoiding me is hardly subtle. Again, I feel the press of time ticking by, but distract myself with sweets. He can't keep this up all weekend.

Spying a tray of Maman's favourite custard-filled, chocolate-topped profiteroles, I resolve to take her a plate of them when I return to our suite to try to tempt her appetite. It seems our host has done her research with the inclusion of a few French dishes. Not even I know for sure where Maman was born, but she adores all things from France. Even with the hard-to-ignore cameras set up at the perfect angle to capture me stuffing my face, there's just no way I can resist an apple tarte tatin. And the sweet and tart flaky mouthful I sneak on my way back to the table confirms my choice is a good one.

'This is so yummy,' Lara says, giving voice to my own sentiment a few minutes later, when Florence joins us outside.

There's a murmur of agreement around the table.

'Are you sure *this* is actually gluten free?' asks Edward loudly, gesturing with a spoon at his crème caramel. He practically had a fit when he discovered the crunchy noodle salad he'd heaped on his plate had soy sauce in it. Might as well have accused Florence of trying to poison him.

Florence's smile in response to Lara's compliment falls away. 'I'm sure,' she replies.

Even though there are three people between me and Florence's husband, I swear I can feel him bristle at Edward's tone. Florence shoots him a look that clearly says, *Leave it*.

It's like he's her guard dog.

Oblivious to the tension, Lara laughs. 'I've made poor Edward sick more times than I can count. Doesn't help that he seems to develop new intolerances every five minutes. I'm sure he'll be fine.'

I wince. Is she trying to make this more awkward?

'This apple tart is so good,' I say, hoping to change the subject. 'What kind of apples are these?'

'I use a combination of Granny Smith and Pink Lady apples grown just over on the mainland. I like the balance and the way they maintain their shape through the cooking process.'

'Interesting,' I say. I mean, it *really* isn't, but at least Bruce is no longer snarling.

Down the other end of the table, Adam gulps the rest of his beer. Not that I'm meaning to count, but I'm pretty sure that's his seventh bottle. When he stands to head inside, however, it's on steady legs.

I jump to my feet and follow.

He's so focused on the drinks fridge that I'm pretty sure he doesn't notice me behind him, not until he turns, beer in hand, and discovers me blocking his exit. I swear I actually see him consider jumping the low stone-topped bar. Instead, he holds the bottle in front of him like a shield.

'Beer, huh?' I say.

I have played this out in my head a million times, and never once was that the opening of the first ever private conversation with my uncle. *Beer, huh?*

He looks at me and then looks away like it hurts. 'Yeah.'

'Cool.'

Think, Monet, say something. But I've got nothing. Maybe I should have let him continue to avoid me. Heat prickles in my neck despite the cool provided by the air-conditioning.

'I wanted a drink,' I blurt.

Again, no prizes for scintillating conversation, but at least he nods at this.

'You're in the right place then.'

We stand there for seconds that could be centuries. Until finally he uses the bottle to point outside. 'Well, yeah, I should be getting back.'

'Cool.'

I step aside and he darts past me. I don't watch him go, I'm not yet that pathetic. Instead, I pour myself a drink and head back outside. At least our next conversation can't go any worse.

I've barely sat back at the table when Lara looks across at me. 'Where's your mum, then? Is she sick?'

I blink at the stranger with the lipstick staining her teeth. 'What?'

'After her turn earlier? I hope she's not any worse.' The woman's smile is more vulture than caring.

'Ah, yes. Earlier. The heat.' I'm blaming Adam for my inability to structure proper sentences. 'She just wanted a little more rest. Thanks again for your,' I say, finally sounding almost like my normal self.

'I'm just glad it wasn't anything more serious,' Lara says brightly.

Too brightly?

I study her face, but it's completely blank.

I'm saved from having to say anything more by Dylan rising to his feet.

'Can I have your attention?' He waits until everyone is looking his way, then takes a deep breath. 'I know we're all thinking about Jonny, but I think it's time to bring him out to play.'

Unease ripples around the table.

'Not literally,' he adds. 'Unfortunately, that's impossible, although I reckon he'd love to show up unannounced, stir up some trouble. I can picture him striding out those doors, a smoke in one hand, a drink in the other, saying "surprise".'

Grief and sadness mix in his tone as we all look towards the empty doorway. For a second I think I smell the smokes Dylan mentioned, but then it's gone.

Dylan's the only one I know who'll talk about Jonny the friend, the joker, the man, instead of some tragic story.

And I should know. With Maman recalcitrant at best to talk about my father, I've scoured every corner of the internet – from the fan blogs to the opinion pieces about electrical safety after the authorities found it was a fault in the wiring that caused the explosion. So, I know the blast, impacted by the nearby high-strength, flammable cleaning liquids, left little of Jonny to identify.

To most of the world, Jonny was a brooding star or a warning of what can go wrong, but to Dylan he was a mate. His best mate. And that's obvious in the waver in Dylan's voice when he lifts his drink. 'I know you're here in spirit and in all our hearts. To Jonny.'

Adam doesn't meet anyone's gaze but slowly reaches for his drink, lifts it, and echoes, 'To Jonny.'

Then he finishes the whole thing.

When he sits again, Dylan grins at Adam. 'So, bro, tell us the news. You were doing that reality programme or something?'

The question lands like a lead balloon.

I know Dylan. Is he charming? *Yes*. Always able to read the room? *Not so much*.

I'm not the only one at the long table who tenses. For all that he's an A-grade creep, it seems Bugsy isn't completely awful at his job, because he clears his throat and says loudly, 'Florence, what did you say this fruit was called again? It's delicious.' He takes a huge mouthful to underline his point.

'Native finger lime,' Florence replies. 'Nature's fruit caviar. I'm partial to the crimson for the drama but there's yellow, green and pink varieties too.'

Her explanation peters out, and Dylan is still staring at Adam, waiting for an answer.

I pride myself on being able to defuse any situation, but my brain seems to have stopped working. I'm not sure if it's finally being here with The Cedrics Band or the cool fresh glass of Three Chains Sauvignon blanc that no one questioned me drinking.

Or maybe it's just because I want to hear Adam's response.

Without looking up, he stabs at a piece of chocolate cake. 'It was nothing.'

'No,' Dylan says with a laugh in his voice. 'I remember, it was some castaway island thing. With votes and everything. Mate, if you were that hard up for cash, you should have called.'

Despite the soft lighting, it's not hard to see Adam's hand tightening around the fork.

I kick Dylan under the table.

He holds up his hands, the picture of innocence. 'I'm only teasing my old friend here. You don't mind a bit of teasing, do you?'

Adam exhales hard. 'Give it a rest.'

'I haven't upset you, have I?' Dylan's smile doesn't reach his eyes. 'I'm joking. I know that Adam can take a joke.'

I look to all the adults around the table, but not one of them moves. Out of ideas for subtle, I reach out to the man who's been part of my life ever since I can remember, but Dylan shakes off my hand.

His whole focus is Adam. 'He should be familiar with comedy, I reckon. I mean, the guy's whole life is a joke these days. Maybe it always was.'

Adam – Friday

I stand so fast, my chair flies backwards, hitting the ground with a clatter. There's a buzzing in my ears and the lights on the edge of the deck pulse around Dylan's stupid face.

'Seriously?' I can't help slurring. 'You think I'm a joke?'

'Pretty much,' he says. 'We only have to listen to you speak. Just how much have you had to drink? Get a hold of yourself, bro. It's embarrassing.'

'I'm not your bro,' I grind out.

The talk of brothers has me thinking of Jonny. He might as well be right here at the table. He's better than me, more interesting, and sure as hell not become freaking old.

'You're right,' Dylan says. 'You're not my brother. But yours did always think he was unlucky with the one he got.'

'Why don't you come here and say that?' I growl.

No one speaks.

Every muscle in me bunches, ready for Dylan to move. He's bigger than me these days, but I don't care. It wouldn't be my first fight.

I glare around the fancy table with its fancy linen and the fancy flowers floating in bloody jars. I meet gazes, sneer as they look away. Any sign of anything, from anyone, and I'm ready to take a swing.

There's the softest of clinking sounds from my right. Bugsy, no doubt. He positioned himself so he can run interference between me and everyone else. Adam-the-fuck-up can't be allowed to ruin anything.

Then he coughs quietly, but within is a muttered, 'Cameras.' Message received.

I'd forgotten they were filming this whole thing. Down at the other end of the table I'm pretty sure the director guy is grinning. I've met his type, they twist everything you say or don't say, ask leading questions, end up making you look a fool.

Well, tonight I've gone and done half his job for him.

All thanks to Dylan.

Some of the tension seeps from my stance. I make a point of uncurling my fists and ignoring the amusement on Dylan's face. How I'd like to wipe that superior smile right off. But there are conditions on my contract, strict and detailed, and fuck knows I've messed up contracts like this one often enough.

One of them specifically mentions that there will be no repetition of an incident like when the guy came at me in the hotel pool two years ago. Fucking Sampson's Creek, in the butt end of nowhere. Me thinking I could relax, floating in the water, only to have some chick run her mouth off about Jonny and her wannabe big man take a swing. I had to protect myself.

How Bugsy found out about what happened in that shithole, I don't know, but I don't want it public. It's already hard enough to sleep at night.

I can feel Bugsy's rat-gaze on me and force my muscles to relax further.

Avoiding Dylan brings the kid right into my line of sight. Her big eyes are so damn like her mother's that it twists my gut. And there's something in the way she's watching me.

Something different to everyone else. I saw it back by the bar when I realised that I pretty much have no vocabulary left these days for talking to women I'm not trying to screw.

Monet St Fleur is reserving judgement. Unlike everyone else here, who shows they already know what a loser I am.

I want to tell her right then and there that she's making a mistake. I want to lean down the table and say it right in front of her so there can be no misunderstanding: I am not a nice man. Aren't kids practically wired into the net these days? Fucking hell, look me up.

Uncle Adam is exactly the piece of shit Dylan is making him out to be.

The fight goes out of me. I walk over slowly, pick up my chair and return it to its position at the table. I manage to force out something placating. 'I'm not here to argue with you about the past.'

Dylan takes a long sip of water. 'Because you'd lose.' Another sip, a smile to everyone else and especially at the cameras. 'Because he's a loser.'

'Please, Dylan,' cries the kid. 'Stop it.'

But she's wasting her breath, because I'm not arguing.

I use the chair I'm still holding to keep myself upright. 'Thank you for dinner,' I say, almost managing it without a slur.

I nod my head at the table, but I don't actually look at anyone's face.

Adam Rake, the loser in the family. Wish you'd died instead of your brother.

I've heard it and read it so many times from 'fans' of the band online and in real life that the sentiment lives rent free in my brain. What they don't know is I would have gladly traded places if life only bloody worked that way.

'Goodnight, all. If you don't mind, I will take my nightcap to go.'

And then, without waiting for permission, I head for the bar, grab the first full bottle of spirits I find, and head out into the darkness. The bright, almost-full moon above renders the decorative lights along the path secondary, and once I adjust it's easy to see where I'm going. It's somehow cooler away from the lights, and the others, but still hot enough that I could use a drink. I fumble with the top of the bottle. Great, I managed to get one still sealed in plastic. I pick at the edge.

'Open,' I growl. I can't go back there. The big walk out fails when you have to skulk back in for a drink.

Standing there, wrestling with the tiny scrap of plastic, swaying with the heartbeat of the world, a hint of breeze stirs the hair on the back of my neck. I taste a hint of menthol smoke in the air.

Jonny?

I lift my head, heart cartwheeling in my chest as tears blur my vision.

There's a scrape of shoe on stone behind me.

I turn, almost letting the bottle slip from my grasp. Not Jonny – of course not, that would be impossible – but Bugsy, and he's pissed.

'Go to bed,' he says, poking a finger hard into my chest. 'You're lucky I'm not firing you on the spot.'

'Lucky?' I laugh. 'It's not a reunion if I'm not on that stage. You'd be fucked then.'

He steps closer so he's right up in my face, and I smell the breath mints that must explain the menthol I thought for a drunken, stupid second was Jonny.

'Make no mistake, you are expendable.'

The rasp of my breath is loud in my ears. He's not the first to tell me this but, God, he's done it enough times that the clench of my hand around the neck of the bottle is so tight I'm shaking with it.

I hate him.

Like Jonny did. Like we all did after the rush of being discovered faded and we realised we had to work with him and how much he took from every bit of success we had.

If I had a choice, I'd never see him or his braces again.

The enlarged black pits of his rodent eyes stare right into mine. 'Go. To. Bed.' A poke into my chest with each word.

I could swing. One decent heave of my arm would send this bottle on an arc. An arc that would end with the most wonderful of thumps into the side of Bugsy Malone's ugly head. Then he'd never get to tell me what to do again.

Once I think it, I can't think of anything else. It would be so easy. So wonderfully, satisfyingly easy. Every single nerve in my body tenses with the possibility of finishing this once and for all.

But he takes a step back.

Maybe my thoughts are on my face because he's moving further and further out of reach.

'Or go fall off a cliff,' he says. 'I don't care.'

Then he's gone. And as the plastic tears free from the top of the bottle and the lid comes off at last, I know only one thing. There's no way in hell I'm going back to my suite now.

Lara – Friday

Not surprisingly, Edward heads for his computer the moment we walk back into the suite from dinner. After Adam's dramatic departure ruined the vibe, Edward jumped up, said a general 'Night, everyone, thanks for dinner', and began walking. It would have looked strange for me to linger. As it was, I had to scramble to thank our host and follow.

I managed to keep quiet on the walk back, but when he powers on the laptop and looks more intently at some spreadsheet than he's ever looked at me, I can't help myself.

'This was supposed to be a break.'

He doesn't lift his head from the screen. 'And yet you continue to prattle.'

I retreat into the bathroom and go through my night-time routine on autopilot before changing into a new shorts and tank set I bought for the trip. It isn't sexy lingerie, but if I'm caught on camera it's kind of mum-cute. I think.

'We should have stayed longer,' I say when I return to the room, where Edward hasn't moved from his laptop.

'I wasn't stopping you.'

'You don't think it would have seemed strange for me to stay on without you?'

This at least gets me his attention. 'I don't really care. If you want to squander more of your evening out there, then you go right ahead. The conversations were monotonous at best, and the food mediocre.'

I bite back on suggesting he get over the soy thing. It's not like anyone was deliberately trying to poison him. 'I thought it was nice.'

'You don't know these people. They're not your friends.'

I know them better than he thinks, but I'm not going to start down that path. 'They were yours, though. You were part of one of the most iconic bands of this century. Doesn't that mean anything to you?'

His lips thin. 'It wasn't all fun and games. Not everyone out there is like the persona they present to the world.'

As much as I've pressed over the years, Edward has been expert in avoiding talking about his times with the band. 'Then tell me,' I beg.

'Why?'

'Because I'm your wife. However much you say it's a closed chapter of your past, it's a part of you. And that means it's important to me.'

His gaze meets mine.

Am I getting through at last? Is he finally going to tell me all about the band?

But then he's shaking his head and closing the laptop. 'You're a piece of work, you know that?'

'I don't understand.'

'That makes two of us then.' He heads for the door, brushing past me.

'Where are you going?'

'Not back to the deck, if that's what you're worried about. I feel a sudden need to stretch my legs.'

The door clicks a moment later, telling me he's gone. A

minute ago, he was ready to sit in front of his computer for the next who knows how long. Now, he suddenly wants exercise. What a surprise... he'd rather wander the wilderness in the middle of the night than spend time with me.

But tonight, I don't have it in me to care. At least this way I get some privacy.

Edward thinks I'm an open, if rather shallow, book, but he doesn't know everything. And what he doesn't know won't hurt him.

Because if he found out... I don't know what he'd do. I've never seen Edward jealous, but then again I've never let him believe he has reason to be. It's been getting harder lately though, not to let something slip.

Despite having heard the door close when he left, I make sure it's shut. I even peek outside just to be sure he's not close by.

The place is deserted. I'm finally alone.

After checking the curtains across the huge windows are closed, I make short work of lifting out my clothes and then opening the seemingly sealed bag of sanitary items. With a shake of my wrist, I let the contents of the one place I'm certain he'd never look tumble out onto the bed.

There it is: my link to the world off this island.

The ad that led me to the compact black satellite phone promised rugged durability and global coverage from their first-rate satellite network. If it works as advertised, it will be worth every penny it cost.

I check over my shoulder more than once as I log on. The rush of adrenaline when the device finally connects to the outside world is worth all this risk. I read the messages and then type quickly, hands steady, only letting myself smile when I press send.

Then I don't delay in returning it to the bag of women's products.

The satellite phone was a necessity, just as Edward remaining oblivious is one. Because if I'm not careful, I could lose everything.

The rattle of the suite door has me shoving my things back into the suitcase, my hands clammy. I zip it closed, and by the time Edward enters I'm on the couch with my book.

'Nice night for it?' I ask.

'I'm going to bed,' he replies.

'Already?'

'It's past midnight.'

'And we wouldn't want you turning into a pumpkin.'

He doesn't crack a smile.

Resigned to his imminent snoring, I pop my sleeping tablet on my tongue and swallow it down with some of the bottled sparkling water left in the mini-bar. Without looking at Edward, I sit on the edge of the bed. I don't really have trouble sleeping. More, it's that I have trouble with dreaming of the past. Combined with a tendency to mumble in my sleep, it's a recipe for disaster.

There are things I dare not risk talking about where Edward might hear me. So, every night before bed, I pop a blackcurrant-flavoured sleep aid and drift into dreamless slumber. Unless Edward is away. Because a woman can let herself dream sometimes.

His bedside light is already off, and he has his back to me. The brittle lines of his bony shoulders through his thin top and the lack of heavy breathing tell me he's still awake.

'Did you slide the chain across?' I ask, thankful for the

expanse of the luxurious king-size bed that means I'm basically on my own over here.

'I'm not an idiot.'

I make a face at his back then catch his eye in the reflection of the glass cabinet. 'Neither am I.'

He says nothing but he doesn't have to, the raise of his eyebrows is enough.

I tug at the sheet – Egyptian cotton and high thread count, I can tell – and turn away from his superior expression, flipping the switch for my light. My side would give me an amazing view if it wasn't dark and I hadn't made sure to draw the curtains across. It means I'm instead staring at blackness with just a hint of ambient light seeping around the edges.

If Edward was different, if our marriage was different, maybe we'd leave the curtains wide open so we could wake together in the dawn light, enjoy the view and each other.

As if on cue, Edward begins to snore.

I squeeze my eyes closed and pray for the tablet to kick in.

Lara – Friday

Sometime later, a faint, repetitive *tap, tap, tap* – like the sound of a stick lightly running along a metal fence – lures me from the thick black of oblivion. Eyes closed, fighting temptation to sink back into unconsciousness, I strain to hear between the regular bleats of Edward's snores.

Nothing.

It must have been a fragment of a dream. Or maybe a small animal running over the roof. We are out here in the middle of nature.

I shift out of the damp patch on the sheet, shoving the top layer of material away to allow the blast of air from the system humming resolutely above to cool my skin. However, moving only gives temporary relief from the heavy heat. I'm sure I turned the air conditioning to its coldest setting, but maybe I could get up and check.

If Edward was a gentleman, I could nudge him and he'd investigate for me. If he really cared, he'd have checked it himself before getting into bed.

He snores extra loudly, as if in response.

Eyes open now, and brain foggy from the tablet I took, I try to muster the energy to get up. Slowly, I swing my uncooperative-from-sleep legs over the bed. I sit there, blinking a few times, trying to adjust to the low light. Then I sigh and heave myself up, onto my feet.

And that's when I see it.

My suitcase is open. I zipped it closed earlier when I heard Edward returning. I'm sure I did.

Tap, tap, tap.

In my head I hear again the sound I put down to a dream. Could it have been my suitcase being opened? Was Edward going through my things?

Next to me – but as far across the bed as it's possible to be without falling off – Edward continues to snore. The rhythm of it unbroken, the beat so familiar from our years of marriage it's impossible to fake.

He's asleep.

But if not Edward then… who?

As my brain struggles to make sense and my heart rate jumps, a breeze stirs the curtain by the huge sliding doors leading to the balcony. It flutters in and then out, through the open door.

The door is open?

I stumble towards it, catching the scent of menthol and smoke in the air.

Jonny?

It can't be. I open my mouth to call to the ever-snoring Edward, but nothing comes out. My tongue is large and thick, and it won't cooperate with the instructions. My voice has never failed me before. So many report cards with: *if only Lara would talk less and listen more.*

I try again.

Something snags my foot. I fall forward. My hands don't come up in time. Landing snatches a cry from my lungs, cut off as my head hits the ground. The thud of it echoing inside my brain. The room wavers around me.

There's a rustle and a blur of darkness moving rapidly across the room.

I try to move, to follow the shape, but now I'm seeing all kinds of blobs of black and bright lights. A person? A ghost?

Then there's only the hush of the sliding door closing and a click as Edward sits up in bed. He flicks on the light and slides on his glasses. He stares down at me, lying on the ground, his frown disapproving. 'What are you doing on the floor?'

'There was someone in here.' But the explanation comes out weaker than I mean it to, thanks to the throbbing in my head.

'Where?'

I wave at the sliding doors. 'They went out that way.'

As Edward goes over to where I pointed, I drag myself up to a sitting position, my hand going to the tender spot on my head.

He checks the door. 'Locked,' he says. He slides it open and looks out on the balcony. 'There's no one there.'

'I saw them.'

His gaze takes in my hand on my head. 'Or you imagined you saw something after falling.'

My vision is fine now. It doesn't take my nursing background to know it was probably affected by me hitting my head. But I'm sure there was someone there.

And my suitcase is open.

Not only that, but I'm sure I didn't leave out anything for me to have tripped on. Scanning for a possible culprit, I can't miss the yawning expanse of the gap under the huge bed.

'Someone was in here, and they hid under the bed when I woke and reached out to trip me up to make their escape.' It sounds fantastical aloud, but it's the only explanation.

Edward is already back in bed. 'Of course they did. And then they jumped over the balcony and disappeared into thin air.'

'Really nice. I'm concussed and you're being an arsehole.'

A brief expression like pity crosses his features. 'Do you want me to call someone up at the main houses to get you an ice pack? Do you need a doctor?'

I picture the call, the conversation, all with Edward not bothering to hide his doubt.

I know it's what he expects me to do, and part of me wants to. I can see it playing out as a scene in the documentary, giving me the starring moment that I deserve. Surely the director would come running with his camera. There could be a manhunt, and I could be brave and inspiring on screen as I insist on joining those looking for the intruder.

But the longer I'm awake, the more improbable the story seems. I'd look a fool, and if someone *was* in here... they'd know I saw them.

I manage to stand. 'My head is already feeling a bit better.'

The only people to call are those most likely to have access to that locked door and until I know what they might want, the best way forward is to play dumb.

It's worked pretty well for me in the past.

I pout. 'I don't want to cause any trouble.'

His eyebrows lift. 'If you're sure?'

Okay, so maybe causing trouble is usually exactly what I'd want to do, but this is different. I have things in that suitcase that could ruin my life. 'I'm sure.'

As I replay in my head the moment I fell, trying to determine what really happened, I know one thing: I need to watch my back.

Monet – Saturday

Before the sun is more than an orange smudge on the horizon, I leave Maman asleep and slip out of our suite. It's barely past five and already stifling outside, even though I wear only running shorts and a light sleeveless hoodie over my sports bra. The other suites are in darkness, probably sleeping off all the drinks from dinner last night, and reflections hide any movement in the main house.

Right now, even the prospect of talking to Dylan is too much.

And when it's all too much, I run.

I've covered a lot of kilometres around our huge estate these last two years, ignoring the mags' speculation about my supposed fad diets to keep in shape, followed usually by some less than flattering camera angle to imply some kind of resultant binge. It's all rubbish. I'm lucky – thanks to my parents' genetics, my weight doesn't change much, but I also got their dodgy-at-best headspace, so I run to keep ahead of the demons snapping at my heels.

After yesterday and the dinner that sucked every last drop of energy from my bones, I thought I'd crash and wake feeling better, but my eyes are gritty from tossing and turning into the small hours. It's too late for second thoughts now. I have to finish what I started.

I need to clear my head and get my brain right for today. My chest flutters, anticipating the sound check on that gorgeously set stage, of playing with the band for the first time. It might not be the goal of this thing, but my heart doesn't care about plans.

Today I'll play with my father's band.

Cap pulled low on my head, I set out at an easy jog. The map Florence provided suggests the best open-trail route is to head back towards the jetty where we arrived yesterday to avoid the heavy bushland or ending up on the neighbour's farm or lost in the huge expanse of the national park. I keep quiet through the gardens and then past the sprawling main house where we had dinner last night. I'm sweating before I hit the top of the path we came up on the carts yesterday. It's easier going down and I run a little faster. Creatures scurry through the undergrowth around me, and it's easy to imagine their little squeaks and rustles like the creatures from my favourite Disney films.

As my eyes adjust to the low light, I see bigger shapes as dark shadows, hiding deep between trees and vines. Their eyes watch me at heights much closer to my own. I ignore the skitter of fear across my skin.

It'll be the kangaroos Florence mentioned.

Everyone else is tucked up safely in their beds, and there can't be paparazzi on an island. At least, not until we ship them over tomorrow.

I try to recapture yesterday's feeling: when the plane landed and Bugsy met us, full of details about what would happen over the weekend; when we were hurried through the airport past screaming, adoring fans calling my name along with the band's; when we travelled across the water in that tiny boat and the wind caught my hair, and despite the strange looks from the boatman, I laughed with the joy of knowing it was all coming together.

Why does it feel now like it's all out of my control?

I'm breathing hard when I reach the docks. Solar lights show the path to the small jetty where we docked from the mainland. A couple of sheds squat nearby, their padlocks obvious even from this distance. The tang of the sea fills my every breath, and the lap of the waves hypnotise. I turn away from the water, even though my sweat-dampened skin begs me to wade in.

In the 'enjoy our island but don't get yourself killed' lecture Florence gave us on arrival, she said Hawk Bay – the next around – was fine to explore, so I head that way. The trail is narrow, and in places it forces me to climb up and over rocks. A few minutes in and I'm pretty sure the main house is somewhere above me, but it's hidden by a steep wall of jagged rocks, interspersed with clumps of saltbush and a few straggly swamp gum trees.

I'm negotiating a difficult section when my foot slips. I grab at an outcrop, wincing as rock scrapes against my palm to take my weight. Tiny stones, loosened by my scramble, fall down into the black water. Sucking in a breath, I stare after them.

That could have been me.

I can picture the headlines: 'More Tragedy for The Cedrics Band', or maybe 'Did She Really Fall?'

I walk on, taking more care. Despite my slow pace, the nature of the trail has my muscles protesting by the time I descend to a wide gentle beach. Hawk Bay, I presume. The one visible looking down from the suites. White sand stretches into the lingering darkness, the expanse broken only by clumps of seaweed. Here, a mix of lemon and eucalyptus overlays the scent of the ocean.

By the time I reach the far end of the bay, the sky glows orange. The dawn light will soon expose me to anyone who cares to look.

The warning signs and chain-link fence across the track leading towards the next bay along confirm my recollection of the area being out of bounds – all the better not to be disturbed. I step over the metal links.

And even before I get to the next bay, it's worth the detour. Towering gums allow the darkness to linger as the path weaves into rocky tunnels sculpted by nature's hand. At times, I have to squeeze to get through, and the rocks touch over my head.

My breath catches but it's not so narrow it brings the dark thoughts, not close enough that the trapped feeling in my chest outweighs the need to keep going. And then, finally, what's become more of a tunnel than a trail opens out to a rock pool in a cave deep enough that the light from the opening at the top doesn't penetrate the gloomy shadows across the water. Sharp edges of stone jut from inky black depths, the air above it thick and rank, like something has died and rotted here for centuries. Despite the smell, my breath comes easier here.

Finally, I am properly alone, and I can't resist sliding my contraband from the pocket of my sleeveless hoodie. I listen, but there's nothing beyond the thud of my heart and the faint lapping of the black water against slime-covered stone.

With trembling hands, I wait for the device I bought online with all its promises of 'anywhere, anyplace' to find signal, only exhaling when it finally connects. A heartbeat later my second, private phone lights up, thanks to the hotspot created by the satellite link. Relief floods me, hot and sweet.

I log on, knowing that if anyone could see me, I'd be grinning like a fool.

Being online comes with a price for someone like me; however, that's only if I'm myself. You can be anyone you want on the internet, and if you're clever enough you can find almost anything.

I need to see what's happening out there, need to make sure this weekend will all work as I've planned.

But no one can find out.

Even here, hidden away, I don't dare risk being online too long. I type quickly, and then slip the device into my hoodie pocket before the day has begun to brighten.

Needing to get back, I scan my surroundings for the way out but I've been so absorbed in my phone I can't remember which way I came from. Two tunnels on opposite sides beckon and I take the one with the sand most disturbed, but I'm only a little way in when it narrows much more than the way I came in, so my hands can touch the rock either side and there's no sky above.

And I can't breathe.

I can't breathe.

I can't breathe.

The thought of being lost, trapped down here where things have died, shrinks my skin on my flesh. I stumble back on trembling legs, catching the sobs before they can start.

I'm not stuck. But I find myself hurrying along the other path. This one is relatively open with glimpses of sun and sky, and I realise I should never, ever have gone the other way.

Focused more on the getting out than the twists and turns in front of me, I am almost upon the figure before my brain registers what I'm seeing.

Connie D'Angelo, the director's wife, is standing right in

front of me. Her leathery skin, grey hair, faded black T-shirt and washed-out khaki shorts blend her into the shadows.

Until she speaks.

'You're the child.' Her voice weaves softly into the cracks and crevices of the rocks around me. 'Monet.'

'Yes,' I reply. 'It's a beautiful morning for a walk.'

'And yet,' – her mouth curves – 'you were almost lost in there.'

She was watching me? I hope the flicker of unease doesn't show in my expression. 'I don't love tight spaces.'

'But you wanted privacy.' She pauses. 'Don't worry, dear, I won't tell anyone what you were up to. I know young people need to forge their own path. I'm a mother, you see. My boy... well, safe to say that I understand.'

Whatever she saw isn't something I want as a bonus extra in their little film. Maybe I should have orchestrated the reunion gig without the film, but I feared it wouldn't be enough to get everyone here. It's too late now.

Making nice is my only option. I smile politely. 'You couldn't sleep either?'

She shakes her head. 'I don't sleep much these days.'

'Is it because of the pressure of filming?' I ask. 'Lots of people are excited to see what you'll produce.' I try to edge past her, but there's no way through. We'll be making conversation for as long as she wants to.

She responds with another tiny shake of her head. 'Not work. Family. You know what it's like.'

I don't, not really. I have Maman, and maybe Dylan, but that's it. Maybe I'm just not cut out for family.

I make a sound that could be agreement. 'Is it something with your son?' I ask, recalling her mentioning a boy. 'Is he in the movie business too?' I add when I think she might not answer until we both become actual stone.

'He does do a lot of pretending.' She sighs. 'It's not easy, you know, given everything that he's done, but I love him. A mother always does.'

I nod. It's beginning to dawn on me that I am effectively trapped here with this woman, no one knows where I am, and I'm not sure she's all there. I could probably overpower her, but then I'd be the celebrity who beat up a frail old lady.

What are my chances she doesn't have a camera hidden away somewhere?

I inhale and catch a hint of her perfume, the kind of old lady roses-and-powder scent that makes me feel like I'm breathing through cotton wool.

Connie straightens. 'I'll let you get on then, dear. And I shouldn't dally. Marco worries about me out by myself – he's a bit old-fashioned like that. Likes to look after me.'

Control her more likely, I think, having seen him ordering her around the day before.

'Be careful,' Connie adds. 'It's barely light and there are always dangers lurking.'

It feels like a threat.

'You too,' I say.

Then I'm past her, adrenaline humming like I've had a narrow escape.

Florence – Saturday

When my phone buzzes, it's still mostly dark. I've already been up for an hour, not that I slept much after clean-up last night and preparations for today. I needed to ensure the three bread makers I had put on a timer will be ready for breakfast, which I have scheduled for eight. Then there's the fresh fruit and the different cereals, as well as the hot food, some of which will be kept warm in the oven – but some will need to be made on request.

The timings of this last day before the concert have gone through my mind so often that I've begun to dream them.

There's another buzz before I get to where the phone rests on my bedside table, and then another. My stomach constricts. Something has happened in the world of The Cedrics Band fandom.

The firewalls in place for the rest of the property don't apply to my phone, and it's configured with a number of alerts centred around this weekend's event and the band. I cannot have any surprises before the show.

I swipe to open my phone, and facial recognition does the rest.

'Fuck.'

Bruce is out doing something on the property, and Elsie doesn't reprimand me for my language.

'Fuck.' I say it again, louder, for good measure, knowing

that here in the main bedroom of the huge house I'm far away from any of the sleeping guests. I sway on my feet as my breath catches on the fear cutting through my chest.

This is bad.

'Exclusive Pictures as The Cedrics Band Reunite' screams the headline on some dodgy celebrity-gossip website. And right below the words are pictures from the tour of the stage area yesterday afternoon.

Fingers trembling, I zoom in on the pictures one by one. Only one has all the band members in shot, not surprising considering how careful they all were to keep their distance from each other. And in that one, Adam is so hunched over he's barely recognisable, and Edward's face is obscured by his annoying wife.

His *well-placed-for-not-getting-a-good-shot, annoying wife*, I mentally amend.

'What's wrong?'

I was so caught up in my phone screen that I didn't notice Bruce come in. I choose to focus on the genuine concern in his voice rather than the dirt he's just tracked in via his work boots.

'There's a leak,' I say. I hold my phone out so he can see.

He squints. 'That's bad?'

I take a breath to try to keep my voice level. 'Yes, it's bad because we have a leak. But it's not as bad as it could have been.' I'm thinking as I'm talking, trying to guess how this will be received. As I think, I pace.

Bruce watches me.

'Maybe,' I say eventually, coming to a stop, 'this might actually end up working in our favour. They aren't great shots, and they might build hype, plus they've mentioned the lodge and the gin.'

He nods, although I know this kind of thing doesn't really matter to him. 'Wasn't there that blog thing that you found was posted yesterday afternoon? It could be the same culprit.'

I didn't discover the conjecture by some Ricky person about what might be happening here until after last night's dinner. 'It didn't say anything that couldn't be guessed from one of the fans across the water on the mainland. I don't think that person is on the island,' I respond.

After the blog, we'd decided we needed to keep a closer eye on our guests, as giving up their phones is no guarantee of them behaving. But this is next level.

'These pictures were definitely taken yesterday, but by who?' I study the angles again and who is present in each picture. It seems to clear everyone immediately associated with the band, except maybe the director and his wife. They would have had high-definition footage if they'd wanted to make such a move, so it doesn't make any sense that it's them. 'Could the media have sent a drone across from the mainland?'

Bruce shrugs. 'Unlikely, without us seeing it. No, I reckon we've got a rat on the island.' His eyes are bright. 'And I think I have an idea who. I'll handle it.'

Something flares deep in my belly, something like excitement. 'Don't do anything silly,' I say, despite part of me wanting to encourage him. This event is too important to indulge in the games Bruce likes to play. 'We can't have anyone getting hurt.'

He's almost bouncing on the spot. 'Trust me.'

'You forget, I know you.'

If what happened with Bruce hadn't happened... If he hadn't done what he did... Well, knowing how little I brought financially into this marriage and his family's wealth, I would never have asked him for something so ambitious as this launch. But he owes me for staying with him. Most women wouldn't have after what he did, but I'm not afraid.

He pulls me close and presses a kiss to my neck. 'Come on, that's all in the past. I'm a reformed man. You know you can trust me, babe.'

'Do I?'

He nuzzles into me, but I can tell from the fact he's not edging me back towards our bed that he's already thinking about whatever it is he plans to do about his rat suspect. I should ask him. But sometimes ignorance really is bliss.

I pull away. 'Promise me you won't do anything to risk the event.'

He cups my face and kisses me long and hard before grinning. 'I promise.'

When he lets go, I feel like I have the imprint of his rough calloused skin still on me. It's not like I haven't thought about the power in his large hands. I saw the reports, I insisted on it when he begged me not to leave him. I will not deal with an unknown. Mistakes are one thing, even if they're of the murderous kind, but I won't be ignorant.

That doesn't mean it needs to work the other way. There's no way I can tell Bruce everything, not if I want to keep him under control.

He strides from the bedroom, all purpose and excitement.

I hear the click of the door to the outside closing behind him, and I return to scrolling through my phone.

Yes, this will work out fine as long as there are no more leaks.

After tomorrow, there will be very different headlines. And I will be the one responsible for them.

Adam – Saturday

I slowly stir to consciousness.

Soft lips brush my forehead, the gentle touch overriding the pounding in my temples. Despite my splitting headache, my mouth curves into a smile, and I ease onto my back, opening my eyes.

'What the actual f—'

The sheep standing over me takes the opportunity of my open mouth to investigate further, with its damp nose bumping into my teeth and cutting me off.

I shove a hand in its face and perform a crab-like scramble backwards, trying to get to my feet. Squinting into the already hot sun and keeping the sheep in front of me, I try to make sense of the long grass, dilapidated fence and the other sheep dotting the paddock.

I spin slowly in a complete circle. No sign of the huge house or the luxurious suites overlooking the ocean. There is ocean, however – a distant blue horizon beyond more paddocks and some thick bushland at the end of the valley. How the hell did I end up here?

The curious sheep *baas* loudly at me.

'I don't speak sheep, man,' I tell it.

But the dumb animal has kind of given me the answer, because behind it, up a hill, there's a fence, and the fence looks like someone has pretty recently tried to fight it.

At the sight, a memory slams into me from the night before.

Pain.

A shock I received that has me wincing now just recalling it. Must be an electric fence.

I rub at my chest, remembering the agonising seconds trying to catch my breath after landing, winded from the stupid thing throwing me off. I'd thought that was the end, that I'd die out here on this island in the middle of nowhere without even getting to play on stage one last time. I'm not ashamed that I'd nearly cried.

Nope, I'm not risking that again, but surely there must be a gate.

I head up the hill towards it, every muscle aching with the movement, and my head the worst. There's a new rip in my jeans and some dried blood, but no broken bones, so I'll take the win. I'll get back to the suite, shower, find some painkillers and I'll be sweet. It's not like I haven't done worse.

More of last night begins to filter back in.

The argument, storming off with the bottle of cognac – a drink I usually can't stand – stumbling along a trail and finishing the liquor in burning gulps right from the bottle. Happy with myself for walking away like a mature adult instead of wrecking Dylan's pretty face.

I see in my head Bugsy's superior sneer as he told me to go to bed.

'I'm not a child,' I mutter with a kick at the ground that hurts my toe.

Okay, so maybe a properly functioning adult doesn't drink so much they half kill themselves scaling an electric fence, but I didn't fight a human, so the prick can't use it against me.

I wipe at my mouth, feeling my fat lip. Ouch. I think that one came when I tried to stand too quickly after the shock and fell face first on the rocky ground. It should be fine by showtime.

Closer to the fence-line, the signs warning about the thing being electrified become more obvious, but there's no way I'd have noticed them last night. Besides, what's with the Farmer Joe set-up anyway? I thought this whole island was part of the resort.

The bird in charge had said when we checked in to make ourselves at home while we are on the island. Well, I don't have electric fences in my backyard.

I'll be having a word with her when I get back. Could have bloody killed me.

'What do you think you're doing?'

The question is barked from behind me and I freeze, mid scratching my balls. That's no sheep.

'I asked you a question.'

Dropping my hands to my sides, hoping I look less lost-vagrant than I feel, I turn. I'm hoping it's the bloke, maybe Bruce, the one who grunted at us when we arrived and didn't add much to the dinner conversation.

It's not.

The stranger is standing only a few feet away, and he's holding what looks rather like a rifle. And his easy grip suggests a familiarity with the weapon and a willingness to use it that has last night's drinks climbing up the back of my throat. His long-sleeved red and black flannel shirt has its collar up despite the biting heat, and his jeans are more patch than denim. Combined with his wide-brimmed hat, sunglasses and long bushy beard, the man's age is hard to place.

What is clear is the anger radiating from him.

And the rifle. Can't forget the rifle.

'I'm from the band.' My voice is more squeak than anything, and he shows no reaction. I want to back away, but I can't seem to make my legs move. 'I didn't mean to end up here. Seriously, I got lost.' I hate how pitiful I sound, and at the same time I'm terrified it's not apologetic enough.

The man's mouth twists and the hand with the rifle twitches.

My stomach heaves. Unable to do anything but ride the wave through my body, I spin away, bend over and puke into the long grass. The force of it puts me on my hands and knees, the acid smell and recognisable colour of the chocolate cake from dinner making for another wave of sick just when I thought I was finished.

When I'm finally done, I drag in a few shuddering breaths, hoping the fact the man hasn't taken this chance to shoot me in the back is a good sign.

When I manage to clamber back to my feet, the bloke looks disgusted as well as angry. Who cares? As long as he's not shooting.

'Look,' I say, making a weak effort at kicking dirt over the mess. 'Just point me towards the Three Chains estate, and I'll be on my way.' I'm glad I've remembered the name of the place.

This time it's the hand without the rifle that moves, and it's towards a gate. As he does so, I recall a dim memory of a map and the chick in charge saying something about a farm and some kind of park. This must be the farm.

'Thanks, mate.'

A utility vehicle rumbles over the ridge on the other side of the fence before I can take more than a couple of steps.

The burly guy from the estate – definitely Bruce – climbs out of the ute and shoves on a hat as he approaches. With his muscles bulging from a khaki short-sleeved shirt, he might as well have stepped off the front of a hard-man's workwear catalogue. 'Morning, Willie,' he says cheerfully. 'I hope you're not bothering one of my guests.'

'It's all fine,' I say. 'I was just leaving.'

But Bruce isn't looking at me. And for all that he's smiling and the tone is cheerful, it's like there's more bristling electricity between the two men than on the fence.

'He shouldn't be on my land,' Willie says. 'He's gone and damaged the bleeding fence. Who's going to pay for it? Him? Or you?'

Bruce is still smiling. 'Not sure why'd you be thinking anyone should be paying. Unsurprising though from a Tucker, generations of scammers. You're one like your father Harry was before you. Seems to me, this is as much your fault as anything. He would have harmlessly slept off his big night if you had a normal fence there. Why do you need an electric fence for sheep?'

'It's not just about keeping them in,' Willie replies. 'It's also what you keep out. There's all kinds of vermin – some on four legs, some on two.'

Despite the old wrap-around sunglasses, I swear I can feel his gaze flick over me as he speaks, but I'm not stupid enough to argue with a guy carrying a gun. Not sober, anyway.

Bruce snorts laughter. 'Didn't work, from the look of things.'

Puffing out his chest, Willie moves closer to Bruce. 'You laughing at me?'

'Don't know,' Bruce says, scratching his cheek. 'You being funny?'

My stomach is knotted. Does Bruce not appreciate Willie is probably borderline psychotic and definitely armed?

'I warned you,' Willie growls. 'Warned you this whole concert thing would get out of hand, but you didn't listen. Just like your Pop never did. You Harpers always think you know best.'

It appears I've landed in the middle of a generational feud. As if this wasn't bad enough.

'Too bad,' Bruce says. 'Because it's happening. You seem to have trouble remembering that you don't own the whole island. And not for the first time. We have council approval. The band is here, the fans will come teeming off the boat, the noise will travel all the way to your pathetic little hovel, and there's not a single thing you can do about it.'

Willie passes the rifle to his other hand and back. 'Don't be so sure about that.'

It's Bruce's turn to step forward, all fake friendliness gone from his rough features, a scar on his jawline showing white in his flushed face. 'Are you threatening me?'

'Not at all,' Willie says. 'Warning you, I am. I have rights to deal with trespassers, you know.' He rubs at his beard. 'Been quite a bit of trouble around here with foxes. When a man's livelihood is at stake, he tends towards a shoot-first, ask-questions-later policy.'

I am definitely on the wrong side of the fence. I edge towards the gate.

'Don't push me,' Bruce says.

He's not mucking around, the tone giving me chills as I finally work the chain holding the gate free, open it and scarper through. My hands slip with sweat as I fumble to get it closed and secured again, but I'm not going to risk pissing Willie off more.

It's all I can do not to run the few feet through the long grass to the safety of the ute, only breathing properly again when I'm settled in the passenger seat and the door is closed.

When I dare look over, Bruce has moved even closer to the fence-line.

Whatever he's saying to Willie has the other man lifting his rifle.

I shrink back into the seat, but Bruce doesn't flinch. He stares Willie down, then casually walks away. He takes his time, not at all concerned about the gun barrel trained on his spine.

He slides in and his nose wrinkles. 'You might want a shower when you get back.'

It's the exaggerated politeness in his tone that has me turning towards the window, shame churning in my empty gut. It has me thinking he'd have left me to the farmer, if given the choice.

And Willie watches us leave, gun in hand.

Florence – Saturday

Just how Bruce plans to deal with the rat leaking pictures to the media niggles at my brain through the morning as the guests trickle in for breakfast. He wouldn't do anything stupid, would he?

The director and his wife are first to arrive in the dining room, a little after eight a.m. After setting up a small camera to capture the room, they talk quietly between themselves at a private table. Monet and Ivy choose a spot well away from the others after Ivy thanks me for the food sent across for dinner last night.

'My pleasure,' I reply, although it was barely touched when I collected the tray.

When Lara and Edward arrive, she scans hopefully, but they sit alone when no one makes eye contact with her.

After the way dinner ended, it is not a morning for conversation.

Marco requests a complete fry-up, but the others are happy with the selection of fruits, cereals, breads and pastries.

After the guests finish, I clear the tables and begin lunch preparations without any sign of Bugsy or Adam. I stand for several long seconds in the doorway, trying to decide whether I should see if they want anything.

Bruce's ute approaches. Maybe I'll send him over to deal

with them. I glare at the suites. How hard is it to either show up for breakfast or let someone know?

The ute stops behind the house. One door slams closed almost immediately, followed by another. Bruce did not come back alone.

My stomach drops, the apricot Danish I scoffed while loading the dishwasher churning uncomfortably. Please let Bruce not have actually caught someone spying.

A moment later, Adam Rake appears around the corner, head down, looking like he's been dragged through the bush backwards. There's blood on his knee and he has a fat lip.

My eyes close. *Bruce, what have you done?*

'Sorry about breakfast,' Adam says.

That sounded like genuine contrition. I open my eyes, appreciating now that he's wearing the same clothes as last night.

He lifts a hand and pushes a lock of greasy hair back from his face. He must catch a whiff of himself in the process because he grimaces. 'I got a bit lost, had an altercation with a fence. Your husband found me.'

I breathe properly again. Bruce found him like this.

'There's plenty of food left over from the buffet. Or I can cook you something fresh, if you like?' Relief makes me more amenable than I have time for.

Adam picks grass off his clothes. 'I think I should probably shower and catch up on some sleep. But, thanks.'

He hurries away. At the sound of a door opening, he breaks into a jog, ducking out of sight mere seconds before Bugsy appears. Apparently unaware of just missing Adam,

Bugsy hooks his thumbs in his braces and offers me the kind of smile that makes my flesh creep.

'Not too late for breakfast, am I?'

'Unfortunately, I've packed most of it away. However, there's some bread that can be toasted and a bowl of fruit. The pastries by the coffee machine are fresh and delicious.'

Irritation pinches his features. 'I was hoping for bacon and eggs.'

'Then I'm sure you'll be on time for breakfast tomorrow. Excuse me, there's a lot to do and Bruce is waiting for me in the kitchen.'

I head back inside without waiting for a response, aware he won't follow me and risk bumping into Bruce – although, when I reach the safety of the kitchen, my husband is nowhere to be seen.

With so much to do, I don't have time to look for him. Through the morning, I know Bruce is around, because we have a huge master list of jobs that need to be done on a whiteboard in the pantry and ticks appear next to things. I stay close to the main house so I'm available should one of the guests require assistance.

On an errand to freshen up about half an hour before lunch, I pause in the hallway just along from where Marco is doing an interview. It's the drummer's turn. The director wasn't happy with sharing his schedule, but I insisted I needed to know. And the location lets me wander past often through the day. It's quiet here, but it's not particularly well soundproofed. And if I happen to linger outside as I pass by... well, there's no one around to see me.

There are the security cameras too, discreet, almost invisible through the house, but always recording. Because it would be a shame to miss the best bits while the cucumber needed to be prepped for the salad or some such.

'If you're ready,' I hear Marco say.

There's a rustle that I imagine is Dylan settling into the chair in front of the bright light and camera lens. 'As I'll ever be.'

'Please state your name and occupation for the camera and tell us why you are here.'

'Dylan Samuel O'Conner, and I'm a musician. A drummer. I'm here because I played drums for a while in The Cedrics Band, and we're going to play together again this weekend. Oh, and because I couldn't get out of the interview.'

There's amusement at his admission. Although not reclusive like Ivy, from what I can work out Dylan hasn't exactly chased the spotlight in the years since the band split. Is he here for the money or some other reason? I make a quick note on my phone to check deeper. He seems successful, but he could have drug or gambling issues.

'Tell me about the band,' Marco says.

'Sure,' Dylan says. 'What would you like to know?'

'Start at the beginning.'

Dylan chuckles, clearly comfortable with the story of the band getting together, one I've read myself more than once online and even in old magazines.

'It started with Jonny,' Dylan says. 'We were friends from school. Him and Adam lived with their grandparents a little way out of town. It wasn't far from their place to the big smoke, but it felt almost country. His pop had this shed, and the boys had done it up as a teenagers' retreat. We hung out and jammed, talked big about how good we were.

'Jonny wanted to do more than talk about becoming famous. He drove the whole thing, really, got Adam properly involved, convinced Edward who we knew from music class to play keys. Let me tell you, that part was not easy. Edward's parents thought rock music was a waste of his classical piano lessons. We played a few places in our area, at our school dance, and people seemed to have a good time. Covers mostly at first, but when Jonny started writing his own stuff, things changed. You know it, everyone's heard "Storybook Love".'

Storybook Love.

Out where I'm standing, it seems like the title of their biggest single echoes off the ceiling. The saxophone sample borrowed from a jazz legend, the catchy melody and then Jonny's voice on the opening line, *I read it in a storybook, I heard it in a song...*

I lean back against the wall, my knees weak. It's one thing to read about how they began on a screen, another to hear the affection in Dylan's voice. This is his life.

I try to focus on Marco's voice. 'Where did the idea come from?' he asks.

My nails bite into my palms as I wait for Dylan to reply.

Dylan sighs. 'I don't know, really. Maybe some girl dumped him, although he didn't talk about anyone special at that time. Never stayed with anyone for long. As far as song-writing goes, he inhaled everything, from the Beatles to Joni Mitchell to some of the jazz greats, but he was always a bit different. You'd find him lying on a hay-bale with a poetry book, just thinking.'

'Did Jonny come up with the band's name, too?'

'Nah,' Dylan says. 'That was an accident. Jonny was doing all he could to get us a bigger gig, but not even his charm could get us spots on nights booked months in advance. But his pop was at drinks with a mate when he heard about a cancellation for that night at the bar. It was this huge talent night and somehow his pop got us in last minute because he knew someone in charge. But the old bugger couldn't remember what we were called. They just put Cedric's Band, and we've been that ever since.'

Marco makes a strange noise. 'That was his grandfather's name?'

'Yeah, before that we were like Super 5, which is pretty bad in comparison. It didn't really fit that night anyway, because Peter couldn't make it, said he had a throat infection.'

'Peter?' Marco asks. 'Are you saying you had another member?'

'Not really. He was another guitarist from school, called Peter Trafford. Pretty average player and he sang some of the backing vocals too for a few gigs, but the guy wasn't reliable. He'd bail on us at the last minute, or just not turn up at all. It wasn't like we really needed him, anyway. Jonny and Adam could handle the guitar, and the guy was just a hassle in the end.'

'What do you mean by that?' Marco asks, the question sharp.

'The guy told Jonny he was sick, but I know he was at a party that night with some older guys we'd gone to school with. Rough guys. We didn't need someone who'd rather be high stealing street signs than showing up for a show. I think he ended up in jail.'

Florence – Saturday

Jail?

Dylan's so casual in announcing that one of the original band members is an actual felon that it takes a moment for me to register he's actually said it for the world to hear. This isn't something that's on any of the fansites, and certainly not on the band's own media releases.

Dylan's still talking. 'Anyway, that night was the first night we played "Storybook Love". It was so new I don't think Peter had even heard it or been there for any of the practices. The song was a bit rougher back then, less pop than the tune we eventually recorded, but the heart of it was there. Ian heard us. And the rest, as they say, is history.'

'You mean Ian Malone, the manager known as Bugsy? He signed you up on the spot?'

'It sure felt like it. We didn't have a chance to think about it, which is probably part of the way they get young talent to sign their life away.' Dylan laughs but sounds annoyed. 'Take that as a warning, if any aspiring musicians are watching this. People like Ian promise kids the world and rarely deliver.'

'But it worked out for you, didn't it? You got everything you could possibly dream of.' Again, there's an edge to Marco's commentary.

I sneak further forward but can't properly see the reclusive director's face. I can't help but wonder whether Dylan has noticed Marco is sounding anything but impartial. The director of something like this should at least appear to be respectful, if not an actual fan.

'It didn't work out that great for Jonny,' Dylan says.

Him I can see, and he's frowning at the direction Marco is taking the interview.

'Would you have made it as a band without that night?' Marco asks.

The location of the carefully placed hallway mirror allows me to edge forward and steal a look in the room. Dylan lifts a hand and pushes his hair back even though it's shorter now, maybe an unconscious motion reminiscent of when he was long-haired and baby-faced.

'That's impossible to know,' he says. 'Jonny wrote the song, but even more than that, when he sang, he had a way about him that made people feel like he was talking just to them. And Ian *was* there. The Cedrics Band was formed.' He hesitates. 'But if you really want to know… I think, yeah. Jonny would have made it. There was a light in him the world didn't even know it was waiting for. It's because of him that we're here now. He's the only reason anyone gives a shit about the rest of us.'

'You've since had a successful career as a drummer.'

Dylan shrugs. 'I'm a good drummer. But I'm no star. Everyone wanted to be Jonny. They still do.'

'But he's dead.'

'It's only made them love him more.' Dylan's wistful.

'You were jealous?'

'No.' He laughs. 'God, no. That kind of attention wasn't for me. But you could see Jonny fed on it. Perhaps he'd thirsted for it his whole life. I'd rather be in the background, do my job decently and not be stopped by screaming kids on the street. But I miss him.'

'As a bandmate?'

'He was my best friend long before we jammed in that old shed. I've never met anyone like him, before or after.'

'What about the rest of the band? How did you all get along?'

There's a long silence before Dylan answers. 'Like any band on the road, there were good days and bad.'

Interesting. Maybe Dylan isn't quite as easy-going as he wants everyone to think.

I peek into the room, unable to resist attempting to see both interviewer and interviewee. Dylan's arms are crossed. He must realise in that instant how he'll look on screen, because he quickly relaxes and adopts a warmer tone. 'We were like family.' A grin. 'And sometimes families disagree.'

'Sometimes they do a lot more than that.'

Marco's reply is so quiet and his face so expressionless that I immediately doubt not only that he spoke at all, but also the inference of something dark in his tone. There's no denying there is hatred in his voice, though.

I'll have to watch him.

Someone knocks at the outside door, and I duck back out of sight before the new voice speaks. 'Oh, sorry. I'll come back later, yeah.'

I don't need to look to recognise the speaker. It's Adam Rake.

'You were supposed to be here two hours ago,' Marco snaps.

Two hours ago, Adam was only just arriving back from wherever Bruce found him, in no condition to be in front of a camera.

'I can go—' Dylan begins.

'I'm beginning to get the impression you don't want to speak about the band, Mr Rake,' Marco says to Adam. 'Or maybe it's one band member in particular? Your brother?'

'The band is more than just Jonny,' Adam is quick to retort.

Dylan snorts.

'Look, we'll sort out another time,' Adam continues. 'You have my word.'

The door slams, and it's impossible to tell whether the mumble of doubt regarding the value of Adam's promise comes from Dylan or Marco.

There's a hint of a shadow by the door frame, then before I can register what I'm seeing, it slides fully open. 'Can I help you?' Connie asks.

I muffle a yelp. 'I was, ah, just passing on my way to my room. Hope I didn't interrupt anything.' My practised excuse comes out all garbled.

'Really?'

The soft question and the accompanying glance at the mirror I've been using to look into the room lodges just beneath my ribs. *Sprung.* How long has this woman been watching me listen in?

I don't have to fake embarrassment, but the gushing is something I've worked on for a moment just like this one. 'You must think I'm silly, but I have been such a fan of the band for so long that I couldn't resist listening in. I know I could just ask Dylan questions, but I don't want to be like some groupie bothering him.' I look down at the floor. 'I hope I haven't messed anything up. That would be just so terrible.'

I hold my breath.

I'm pretty sure I read once in a magazine that there is a

significant percentage of the female population of around my age that would still call themselves fans of The Cedrics Band. This woman has no reason to doubt that I'm one of them.

'Let me know if you need anything,' I say and flee for the kitchen, forgetting until I'm out of the hallway that I said I was on my way to my room.

Lara – Saturday

I knock on the open door. 'Hi, I'm Lara, Edward's wife, and I'm here for my interview.'

'Where's Edward?' the director snaps.

'He's been unavoidably detained with work, but he sends his apologies.'

In actual fact, when I reminded him for the fifth time about the interview, he'd growled, 'If you care about the stupid interview so much, you do it.' So, I left, with his taunts about checking under the bed for monsters following me out of the suite. I'm not as sure about what happened last night in the bright light of day, but I stand by the fact that there was very possibly someone going through my things.

'Come in then,' Marco says with a sigh. 'What are you waiting for?'

I sit in the only vacant chair in front of a simple lighting set-up and alternate between staring at the camera lens, watching me like some alien eye, and pretending it's not there. I cannot mess this up. This documentary is going to be huge. It's going to be seen by all kinds of important people. While I might be a little older than your average new screen talent, this could be my break. I could be a TV presenter, a weather girl, or something.

No one is better than me.

This is my chance to make an impression. I've researched interviews and chosen an outfit to negate the camera's ten pounds. Even checking the blue dress for any embarrassing lines or rolls. My makeup is heavier than usual to account for the lights, and my hair is in a sleek knot and sealed with hairspray to avoid stray fly-aways on close-up shots.

'Where would you like me to look during the interview?' I ask. 'I read most interviewers prefer you look at them, but I wanted to confirm your preference.'

Marco doesn't look up from his tablet screen. 'Either should be fine.'

There's a soft sound, and it's only then that I notice his wife behind him. Connie leans close to her husband and whispers something I can't make out.

Marco looks to me. 'Connie asked if you could stop making that face.'

That face is my usual expression. 'I'll try,' I say. I put on a smile. 'Is that better?'

They share a look. 'Never mind,' he says. 'Who are you and what is your connection to The Cedrics Band?'

I can't see any tell-tale red light, but I assume the camera is on. I'm ready, but I take a moment before answering because I once read a brief pause adds poise. 'My name is Lara Jan Murphy, and I'm married to the keyboardist from The Cedrics Band, Edward.'

Marco looks down at his tablet again.

Deliberately, I still my hands, forcing them to relax in my lap while wriggling my toes to release the nervous tension in my body. *Do not fidget on camera*, I remind myself.

'So, Lara,' he says after what seems like hours. 'Tell me, and of course the public, how you and Edward met. I understand it was around the time of Jonny's death.'

I sit up a little straighter. This is my favourite story to tell. I've told it so many times I have it down to an art. Back in the beginning, I'd have Edward at my side chiming in at all the right places, but that stopped a long time ago. 'Well,' I begin, leaning a little into the lights.

And in my head, I'm back there on that day. Standing in the cold, which in itself was exciting, because the wind chilling me was European. The snow was melting in the gutters from the weak sun in the blue sky above.

'It was my first overseas holiday. I travelled from Australia with a few friends because my parents didn't want me there on my own.'

I can see Mum shaking her head the night I told her about the trip. 'Don't go getting yourself in trouble,' she'd said. 'You know those foreign men will only want one thing.'

I push her out of my head before I can be distracted.

'I did a tour through Spain, seeing wonders I had only read about in books, and then discovered I was in Paris at the same time as the band when someone at the hostel I was staying in – another backpacker – was giving away their tickets because they had to fly home suddenly. I figured we might as well go, as it was cheap.'

The story flows with the smoothness of repetition, if not complete truth.

'You were a long-time fan of the band?'

'I think you'd have to have been under a rock not to know The Cedrics Band. We'd eaten at a café near the stadium and were heading back to the hostel to get ready. We detoured past where we'd need to go later that night, not wanting to lose our way, being in a foreign city and with limited French between us.' I allow a faint chuckle in my voice but get nothing from the man behind the camera. I dare not look around to see where Connie is and just hope she's not capturing the loose skin beneath my jaw.

'Go on,' Marco says with a hint of impatience.

'There were already people lined up waiting to go inside. We stopped to debate whether to stay rather than go back to the hostel. I hadn't done my makeup properly and had planned to wear a different dress, but—'

'Then you heard the explosion?'

He's cut me off. He's actually gone and cut me off.

My lips press together, and in my head I count backwards from five. I will not let my annoyance show, but I will tell my story how I want to tell it. 'We approached the front of the line,' I continue. 'Where it was cold in the sun, it was freezing in the shadows of the huge stadium. I remember I couldn't stop shivering. I thought it was just the temperature, but now I wonder if I didn't sense something. I've always been quite sensitive in that way.'

'Why get to the show so early if you were just a casual fan?'

'I explained that we were getting a feel for the area. I've always organised myself to make sure where I am is where I want to be, to be organised.' My voice catches, that did not come out right. 'Can I try again?'

He looks at me then. 'You want to change your answer?'

I don't like his tone, but I don't want to put him off me. I smile sweetly. 'I simply want to give you the best material for your documentary.'

'I'll be the one who decides what that is. So, there you were, outside with all the other desperate fans—'

'I didn't say that.'

'Sorry, of course you didn't. You just happened to be there. Was it any of the band that would do, or did you have your sights set on Edward in particular? Or was it that all the rest were taken and the quiet, less charismatic keyboard player was – what might you call it? – low-hanging fruit?'

Lara – Saturday

My mouth opens and closes at the casual insult, and I almost say it then, almost correct what is clearly a whole range of assumptions this director has made about Edward and about me. But I'm on camera. I swallow back a few pertinent facts I'd like to shove down his throat and manage a grim smile. 'I don't like the direction you're taking these questions. I thought you wanted me to tell my story.'

'You agreed to be interviewed.'

I stare down the camera. 'I did not agree for you to make fun of me or my husband.'

'So, you two are happily married, are you?' Marco lifts one corner of his mouth. 'Be careful how you answer, the camera sees everything.'

Mum always said I have a tendency to have my thoughts all over my face, but I'm no longer that little girl so desperate to please. 'We're fine, thank you very much.'

'No dark secrets?' Marco asks, eyebrows lifting.

My chest cramps. He can't possibly know. No one can.

I think of Ivy's frown, her comment that she'd seen me before. I think of the things I brought that are even now secreted away in a package of sanitary products. But every marriage has its private moments.

'Well, how about that, it seems I've hit a nerve,' Marco says. 'The viewers and I are all wondering what it is you have to hide.'

'Nothing,' I snap. But it's too late. For all my preparation, I've let this get out of hand.

'Can you finish your story, or shall we talk more about your marriage?'

'Yes.' I compose myself. 'I was outside the stadium when I heard and felt the explosion. Instinct kicked in and I ran. I was a trained nurse, and it's always been my passion to help people. No one from security tried to stop me. Thankfully, because I might have been too late for poor Edward.'

'And where was your friend?'

It's an excellent question, and one I really hoped wouldn't come up. I learned years ago when telling the story that I sound so much cooler with a friend than describing the same situation with me alone. That starts to look more... desperate. More... questionable. Begins to make other details less solid.

And I did prepare for this, but I find under the glare of the bright light the answer I practised has completely vanished. Marco is waiting, tapping his fingers impatiently. There's a scrape behind me. Connie capturing my inner panic in close-up, probably.

Dampness breaks out in the small of my back. You'd think they'd have the aircon on in here. 'He was detained by security,' I blurt.

'He?'

I scramble for a name; my friend has been female any other time I've been asked. Why did my brain have to choose now to fail me? *Better hope her looks last because there's not much else there.* Mum's voice echoes in my brain.

'Ricky,' I say quickly. 'He tried to follow me when I ran inside to help but security must have realised that they'd lost control and they did their job, preventing most people entering the stadium who weren't emergency personnel.'

This is better. I'm back in my flow now.

'Fate guided my steps, and I ran, unerring, through the twists and turns until I found myself emerging from the darkness into the light.'

For the first time, Marco looks interested. 'You were actually in the concert space?' He looks over my shoulder – at his wife, I'm guessing. 'Did you get all the way to the stage?'

The guy just can't help wrecking my story.

'Yes, I came out onto the grass right at the back and I stumbled closer and closer. And that's when I saw him.' I slow to take a breath, allow my voice to choke up a little.

'Was it Jonny?' Marco asks.

When I tell this story it's hard to stop the memories from playing like an old movie reel in my mind but always, *always*, I remember that, in my head at least, I'm in charge. I get to choose where the camera focuses, and it's never the middle of the stadium.

But now he's said it I'm back there in my mind. I'm slowing, staring with my jaw hanging open at the place where the end of the stage used to be. And I know no one will ever see Jonny Rake again. My head drops into my hands. He died that day, and I was right there.

I blink and the first drop runs down my cheek.

Think about Edward. Do not think about Jonny.

'I saw Edward,' I manage. 'He was on the ground, between some rows of chairs, a good distance away from the main explosion site. He must have been thrown from the far edge of the stage.' I sniff on the last word, try to dab prettily at the tears I can't seem to stop. My delivery not as smooth as usual, but hopefully it comes across as emotional. 'He was unconscious and not breathing. My training allowed me to save the man I would go on to marry. I gave him the kiss of life.'

Usually, I finish all attractively misty-eyed, but the memory of that horribly empty middle of the stadium has opened the floodgates, and no amount of blinking is helping.

'What else did you see?' Marco asks.

His tone is insistent, and I frown at the camera. 'Stumbling upon my husband-to-be's prone body isn't enough?'

'Of course, I'm not downplaying that, it must have been traumatic for you.' Marco's voice is coaxing now. 'But your experience is unique, and I am sure everyone who sees this production will want the full understanding of what you went through. It's obviously an important part of the band's story.'

I sit a little straighter. 'I guess so. You really think it's that important?'

'I'd say pivotal.'

Me, pivotal to the documentary. Warmth flushes my body. I knew it.

Tears forgotten, I try to think back. 'There was a hive of activity, all centred around the end of the stage, the worst point of the explosion.'

He leans forward, vulture-like. 'Did you see him? Did you see what was left of Jonny?'

My voice catches in my throat. I can't speak.

But Marco keeps pressing. 'Tell us. Was he dead?'

Monet – Saturday

I've read about screams splitting ears, shattering chandeliers and curdling blood. But the one I hear coming from inside our suite as I'm on the path returning from the main house is a hook grabbing at my intestines, threatening to loosen everything inside.

'Maman?'

I stumble on legs I can no longer properly feel towards the door.

What's she even doing back at the suite already? She and Dylan were both reading in the sunny garden when I went across to delay my interview until after our main rehearsal.

At the door at last, I fumble to get it open, hands slippery with sweat. I hold the card in place, but get only red lights and an unapologetic beep in response. Stupid card.

'I'm coming,' I call.

The only response is the beep of the card reader. Again, it flashes red. I shove at the door. 'Why won't you open?'

A pale hand pushes mine. It's Florence with the master card. This time the door swings wide.

'Maman?' I cry, stumbling into the suite. 'Maman?'

It takes only moments to make my way to the combined bedroom and living part of the suite but long enough for me to second-guess every detail of my plan.

I knew there were risks, but I assumed they were all on me. I should have known this was a mistake, should have known Maman was vulnerable, should never have…

I stop dead where the hallway opens up into the rest of the suite. 'You're fine?'

It comes out as a question because Maman is sitting perfectly at ease on the couch near the huge glass windows. Her white jumpsuit shows off her golden skin and the stunning view provides a gorgeous backdrop.

I lift my hand to my chest, where my heart is still hammering. 'Why the scream? I thought something terrible had happened.'

Acutely aware that Florence has followed me inside and that others may follow, including those with cameras, I say nothing more – but my jaw aches with wanting to.

Sometimes, I'm not sure which one of us is the parent.

Maman sniffs, but on her it's a pretty sound of distress. 'Take a look at the bed, *ma chérie.*'

Behind me, Florence gasps.

I turn slowly towards the beds, having skipped over the space in search of Maman.

At first, there's only red. Red spreading before my eyes in the middle of the once bright-white sheet on Maman's bed, the furthest one against the far wall. Scarlet smeared in horrifying stretches over the mountains of fluffy white pillows piled right at the headboard. A few drops of crimson dripping remorselessly from the side of the soaked mattress onto the floorboards.

So much blood.

The back of my throat convulses. I cover my mouth, taste acid as my stomach heaves. Eyes closed, I spin away before I add to the mess.

'You see,' Maman says. 'I was not so much being overdramatic, was I?'

When I find my voice, it comes out small. 'No, you weren't.'

Without looking back at the damage, I make my way to perch on the other end of the couch from where Maman sits. It's not visible from here, but not being able to see it isn't helping much. My brain won't stop flashing images of what's up there back at me.

Florence trails me down the few steps, hands wringing together. 'This is appalling, I am so sorry.' Her pale skin is positively white with distress. 'Did you see anything?'

'No,' Maman says. 'It was like this when I returned. Dylan accompanied me to the door, but I was alone when I discovered the mess.'

'Has anything else been disturbed?' Florence asks. My face must give away my thoughts because she quickly adds, 'Not that this is not terrible enough. Again, please accept my apologies that such a thing has happened. We pride ourselves on providing a luxurious experience for our guests. If you were paying, I would insist on providing a refund. However, perhaps another bottle of our gin or our sparkling wine would help soothe the situation.'

She moves towards the mini-bar, and I force myself upright to block her path. Can't have her seeing what is stored in the fridge. 'Thank you, but that won't be required.'

She inclines her head. 'Then I can only offer my assistance in the move.'

'What move?' Maman asks.

'To the empty suite next door. I presume staying here is the last thing you'd want to do. We'll gather everyone together and insist that the culprit reveal him or herself.'

I share a look with Maman, registering not only her irritation but the dark hollows around her eyes and the jut of her bones beneath skin, stretched and thin.

Moving from here suggests we're scared, and that won't please Maman.

'Leave us,' Maman says. She stands, rising to her full height, which barely brings her to our host's shoulder. But eyes alight and head high, she's imposing nonetheless. 'My daughter will strip the bed and leave the sheets outside the door. You will return with fresh bedding and not mention this to anyone. I will find the culprit, and I will make them pay.'

Florence bows her head. 'As you wish.'

I try to keep my expression neutral. Maman could have at least let the woman clean up the mess. It's not that I think I'm above such things, but more that I'd rather the disgusting blood-soaked sheets be dealt with by anyone but me. But arguing with Maman will only get me in trouble. And the truth is that I haven't seen such life in my mother for a long time.

Maybe this is worth it to actually get her fired up about something.

'Where can I put all the dirty linen?' I ask.

Florence nods. 'Follow me.' She strides back along the hallway to a slimline panel in the wall that, when unlocked, reveals a cupboard I hadn't noticed. Within it are huge garbage bags and plenty of fresh sheets and pillowcases to make up the bed. 'Would you like me to stay and help?' she asks.

'We'll be fine,' Maman calls from the living area.

'Thanks, but we'll be fine.' Hopefully, my annoyance isn't evident in my voice. What is Maman playing at?

'I'll leave you to it,' Florence says.

When the door clicks closed, I wait a beat to make sure we're alone and then flop on the couch next to Maman. 'Now tell me what is really going on.'

Her eyes are shining. 'We need to leave.'

'Didn't you just insist on staying here?'

'Not the suite, we should leave the island now, while we have the chance, before something worse happens.'

I take a breath so I don't snap at her. And I smell nothing. Nothing offensive that I'd expect from the carnage on the bed sheets. I sniff again. There's Maman's perfume, some wine from a bottle Dylan opened last night and something sweet. Could blood smell sweet?

'Our safety?' I ask, distracted.

'Yes.'

'Because of a prank?' The longer I'm in the room with the desecrated bed, the less scared and more annoyed I'm becoming. It's a bad cliché from a horror movie. If someone really wanted to upset us, they should have at least been original.

Maman crosses her arms. 'It is one thing for you to chase some fairy-tale family dream but another to put our lives at risk.' As usual when she's passionate about something, her accent is thicker. But other than the scream, she doesn't appear all that frightened.

'How do you propose making this happen when you just sent away the one woman who can get us off this island?' I ask. 'Unless you have plans to swim.'

'Dylan will help.'

'He can't get us off the island. We're effectively here at our host's pleasure, at least until the boats come with the fans. We can't leave yet.' When her shoulders droop and she doesn't argue, I know I've won. I have to be on stage for rehearsals in a few minutes, and I need to prepare, but I can't leave her with all this. 'Who do you think is responsible though?' I ask, knowing she'll have a theory, and I'm not in a hurry to start the clean-up.

'That Florence, she does not like me. Most women do not like me. I cannot trust her.'

I don't point out that her efforts with her fellow females aren't exactly great. 'But Florence came running to let me in. Would she have done so if she was guilty?'

'Yes.' Maman nods. 'It's the double trick.'

'You mean double bluff?' There's a shortness to my tone that, predictably, Maman ignores. It's infuriating that she insists on the pretence that English isn't her first language, even with me. I was ten the first time I screamed at her that we weren't even French. She walked out and returned with our passports showing our citizenship.

End of conversation.

When Ivy St Fleur doesn't want to engage, she simply doesn't, and no amount of tears, threats or tantrums will change her mind. In these last few months, she's softened a little – the fact that she's here at all shows the huge change, when I've been stonewalled about my father and his family for my entire life.

'What about Adam?' I say, just to put it out there as I make my way to the mess.

Her eyes flash. 'No.' Her denial is immediate.

I want to press her on her certainty, but given the stresses of the day and her health, I don't want to upset her more. The eternal battle that I know she's not above using to her advantage.

'The husband didn't like me complaining about meat,' she says.

Him I can picture with blood on his hands. 'All this because you're a vegetarian? Seems extreme.'

'You laugh now,' Maman says with a pretty yawn. 'But the world is a dangerous place. Bad things can happen without any warning.'

The spectre of my father rises between us. It's a message I've heard my whole life, and it stops my teasing.

I turn to say something comforting but while I took a moment to think about what to say, her lunchtime medicine caught up with her and she's curled into the corner of the couch, asleep.

Noticing she's still wearing her sandals, I return to her side and gently remove them, then cover her with a light blanket, because despite the heat she often wakes with chills. I brush my hand across her cheek, my heart so sore it's hard to breathe. There was a time she'd have argued with me until she'd got us off this island by sheer will.

As I place the sandals on the small mat by the door, a drop of red smears from the sole. I sniff it. Red wine? Tomato sauce? A mixture of both?

I take the stairs back up to the bedroom level. Up close and without the shock of earlier, what I thought was blood appears to be thicker and tinged purple.

It's the same combination as on the sandal.

Maybe Maman stepped in a drop. Or maybe she thought I'd be so horrified I'd agree to her plan to leave. Could she have done this herself to get us off the island?

The more I think about it, the more it makes sense with her lack of real fear, but there's no way she'll ever admit to such a thing.

With a sigh, I peel the first dripping sheet from the bed. This is so not what I thought I'd be doing right before I play with my father's band for the first time, but thanks to Maman, I don't have a choice.

Monet – Saturday

Thanks to needing to clean up, I arrive down at the stage a while after everyone else. My suspicions about Maman's involvement in the 'blood' that wasn't blood were heightened when she insisted on staying in the suite alone to rest. As expected, she acted shocked when I revealed the mess was some mix of sauces and possibly jam.

I slow, heart racing, and hitch my bag over my shoulder as I climb the steps up onto the stage. Playing with the band wasn't the reason I put this whole thing together, but it's something I've thought about.

Something I've dreamed about.

And the three of them are waiting for me. Adam with his guitar held close, like he's afraid someone might snatch it from him; Edward in front of the keyboard that I organised to be shipped in when he professed not to care about the instrument he'll play; and Dylan flipping a drumstick up in the air absently.

'We'll open with "Storybook Love",' Adam says, before I can even say hello. 'Give the fans what they want.'

Although she's busy with something over by one of the caravans, a good distance from the stage, Florence looks up at Adam's words. She might act reserved, and more focused on the event than the actual music, but there aren't many people in the world who don't have a strong opinion on the band's biggest song.

I've seen it on top ten best *and* top ten worst songs of all time lists, which is quite some feat. The stupid thing has been the bane of my existence. It's not easy when most of the world think one of the biggest songs of the early 2000s was about a fight between your mum and dad.

I know from Maman that Jonny wrote that particular song ages before they met. But every time the band play it, they show her grieving after his memorial rather than the cheesy video clip that was released originally. Which pretty much makes me the 'storybook love child'. Yes, that was an actual headline after I was born.

Talk about cringe.

Dylan and I already talked about getting that song in particular over with because of my lifelong embarrassment, but now he shakes his head. 'I think we should save it, build some momentum and then play it at the end to bring the show home. The end lyrics work – "Our happy ending in a storybook love".'

I glare at him, which is kind of useless since he's refusing to meet my gaze. At this point I think Adam could say the Earth was round and Dylan would disagree out of spite.

'I think maybe—' I start.

'Who was it about?'

We all turn towards the voice that cut me off. Florence is no longer over by the caravans, but right by the edge of the stage.

'Who was what about?' Lara asks from a spot perched off to the side. I was so intent on the band I hadn't noticed her – surprising, given her bright yellow spotted sundress.

'Who was that song about?' Florence is looking at Adam, at Dylan, at Edward in turn, an intensity burning in her pale features that's almost uncomfortable to witness.

Adam blinks and frowns, obviously not having picked her for a fan. 'I don't know.' He shrugs. 'There were lots of girls back then, and afterwards.'

Dylan and Edward shrug too.

From the purse of Florence's lips, that was not the correct answer.

'Does it matter?' Lara asks brightly. 'The lyrics in it speak to everyone and could be about anyone. It's that universal, timeless quality that everyone loves all over the world.'

Florence shakes her head. 'I guess not. It was different anyway before.'

'How do you know?' I ask.

Her cheeks flush. 'I don't. Just a guess. I figured all songs morph and change.'

But she'd sounded certain.

'Or maybe I read it somewhere years ago. Lara's right, it doesn't matter.'

But there's something about the way she says it that suggests it matters a lot. Before I can question her, she hurries back to what she was doing.

'That's decided then,' Dylan says. '"Storybook Love" to finish. When did you want to play your new song?' The latter is said to me almost apologetically. He's throwing me a bone for going against what we talked about.

Lara claps her hands. 'Oh my gosh. I can't wait to hear your song. And the others, of course. Does anyone else think it will sound strange with a girl singing them?'

Everyone looks at me as her prattle rambles to a close.

My song.

And me singing Jonny Rake's lyrics with his band. It's not like I haven't had every word memorised practically since I could talk, but as annoying as she is, Lara has a point. They're designed for a male voice, and some of them simply don't work as well with me.

I mentally apologise to Dylan and then blurt it out. 'I think Adam should sing.'

'No,' Dylan snaps.

Right at the same time as Adam sputters, 'What?'

My mouth has gone dry, and I wish for the water bottle I left back at the suite. 'Some of them need a male voice. I'm not being a part of this if we sound crap.'

Dylan glowers. 'I won't sound crap.'

'No,' I say quickly. 'Look, I've got some ideas. If we can work through the set list, I'm open to discussions.' I raise my eyebrows at Dylan. 'Reasonable conversations about how best to showcase each song. And if we're closing with "Storybook Love", we can open with mine.' I fumble for my bag, wishing I had the time to go back and rework the music and the lyrics, but knowing there's no amount of revision that could make this any less terrifying. 'I know I said I'd perform it with just my guitar, but I'd really love it if you all played it with me. It's not too complicated.' I'm glad my hands don't tremble when I hold out the music I prepared.

I've only ever played for Maman and the record execs who were frothing so hard at the thought of signing Jonny Rake's daughter I could have shown them anything.

The band thumb through the photocopied pages. No one speaks.

My stomach somersaults. 'Maybe it will make more sense if I play it.'

Somehow, my knees keep me upright for long enough that I can make my way across to one of the three guitars I had sent over. I pick up my favourite electric acoustic, instantly more myself with its glossy black body in my hands.

'Hey, you play a Rake guitar,' Adam says, approval in his voice.

'Of course she would,' Lara chirps. 'I can't believe I am actually here for this momentous occasion. This is so cool.'

I try to tune her out as Edward shushes her, try to pretend none of them are here and there aren't filmmakers with cameras watching my every move. I pretend I'm playing in my studio at home, alone, like always.

I cough a little to clear my throat. 'It's, ah, it's called, "Finding Me", and it goes something like this.' I breathe out, close my eyes and allow the hint of breeze swirling down from the surrounding trees to cool my overheated skin.

Then I begin.

Adam – Saturday

'She's good, she's really good.'

'You sound surprised,' Bugsy replies.

I hadn't meant to speak aloud, letting my guard down as I'd moved away from the others to grab a drink, my whole body humming from what I'd just experienced. After Monet finished her song, we all clapped and congratulated her, and I tried not to show just how much it affected me. So much for worrying about how I'd fake it if she was no good.

After that, we moved on to the band's catalogue. Singing those songs with this girl who is like a mix of both her parents' best bits reminded me of why I let Jonny talk me into the whole band thing in the first place.

That feeling of making really good music. There's nothing on this planet like it.

I was so wrapped up in the high of jamming that I hadn't noticed when Bugsy arrived. Now he's sidled up next to me and seems to be waiting for a response.

'The kid hasn't sung in public for years. Not since she was a little tacker on one of Ivy's tours. I didn't know what to expect,' I explain.

He's bouncing up and down on the balls of his feet. 'She's going to be a goddamn star. I knew it. This, Adam-my-boy, is my big ticket back.'

'She's a person,' I mutter.

But he's not listening, probably already counting the dollars she'll make him.

His hand suddenly grips my arm. His eyes are bright in a way I know all too well. 'Look, last night I was maybe a bit hard on you. Come by the suite after this, before dinner, and we'll chill.'

Chill? Ha. I don't need what he's really offering spelt out for me.

'Nah, man,' I say quickly. 'I told you I'm not doing that anymore.' I don't know what stuff he has, but I know I can't go there. Even if I want to. Even if I'd give just about anything to find that promised oblivion.

But if I've learned one thing it's that I'm no casual indulger, and the only way it will end is in destruction – mine or somebody else's.

'Come on, Adam, don't be a killjoy. I'm only talking about having a good time.' He nudges my shoulder with a knowing smile. 'Relaxing a bit before we have to make nice with everyone around the table. I'm trying to do you a favour.'

I step back and let some of my annoyance show. 'Ask someone else.'

There will be takers, there always are. But not me, not today. Sure, I'll drink myself blind, but I lost years to the rest of it.

Bugsy sneers. 'Didn't expect you to have become soft.'

'This isn't about being soft, man. I'm going to launch something from this show.'

'Suit yourself.'

He stalks away and I go back to the drink that suddenly tastes a lot like why-did-I-do-that? I gulp the water and wish

I'd brought the bottle of gin I noticed had been replaced above the shelf in the mini-bar. I wander back towards the others. The sooner we get through this rehearsal, the sooner I can get back to my suite.

But I can't bring myself to pay attention to what the others are talking about. Instead, I squint up at the distant trees, shielding my eyes from the sun's glare. There's something red up there, something jarringly out of place, even from this distance.

'Adam? Hello? Do you have something more important to do? It's not like we have a huge show tomorrow.'

Edward's tone, when it registers, is unusually firm. Possibly because it's quite obvious I'm not listening to him at all. This isn't the first time – it's not like the guy has ever had a lot to contribute. Back in the day, he was always whining about needing to wrap up the jam session so he could do his homework.

Nerd-alert.

But the drone of his nasal, annoying voice is enough to make anyone zone out, and I'm about to tell him as much when Monet sighs.

'Can you guys stop bickering so we can get this done before I literally melt?'

'Sorry,' I say. 'I'm all yours.'

'What are you all wearing for the show?' Monet asks. Clearly, she's given up all pretence that she's not the one driving this thing.

Edward looks surprised that his current outfit of beige-on-beige might not work for such an important show and Dylan simply shrugs. Probably because he looks good in everything, the way he's all jacked with muscle these days.

But I bite. 'We were never a band that really catered to a particular... what do the kids call it?' I don't give anyone a chance to answer, although Lara lifts her hand like a student in class. 'Aesthetic.' I drawl it out. 'We were real musicians.'

'Really?' Monet asks.

'Really.' I'm on a roll now. 'And we're not going to compromise the legacy of the band just to get a few more likes or shares or whatever it is.'

Monet smirks. And again, despite inheriting so much of Ivy's gorgeous features, she looks so much like Jonny it hurts.

I look away fast.

And the red I noticed before is moving at walking pace. As I stare, it stops, mostly hidden behind the silvery trunk of a tree. I concentrate on the place I last saw it, trying to make it out.

I block out everyone around me.

Maybe it's my age, but it's a bit like needing to turn down the radio to park the car, I have to stop listening so I can look properly. I'm no animal expert but I can't think of a single red one big enough to be spotted in those trees from here. Let alone one that would sit there watching a band rehearse.

But creepy farmer guys with rifles would.

The more I think about the incident this morning, the more I think there's nothing more that Willie guy would like than to hide up there, line us up through his rifle sight and pick us off one by one. Clearly, he doesn't want this event to go ahead, and he hates anything to do with Bruce's family.

Could one of us right now be in the rifle's sights?

Adam – Saturday

'Is there a problem, Adam?' The question comes from Monet. She's holding the tablet and looking at me like she's actually interested in the answer.

However, a quick glance up to where I think I last saw the red figure shows nothing but bushland. Monet might have an open mind regarding me, but it's not like anyone else will believe me.

If I speak up, and we go up there for a look and find nothing, it will give Dylan more ammunition.

I swallow my concerns and give her my full attention. 'I'm good.'

She holds out the tablet towards me.

I squint at it, trying to see properly. When I do, I squirm. She's found a picture from when we were some tiny music festival's banana ambassadors. The yellow and black suits were not flattering – not even Jonny made that cool.

'Ouch. Well, that explains the smirk-face,' I say. 'Not fair, with no signal here you had that already. You trapped me into saying all that so I'd look like a dick.'

I look around, but the ever-present cameras, well, aren't. Both Marco and his ghost-wife are quite some distance away. Getting wide shots, I guess.

Monet laughs. 'No, that was all for my own personal amusement, wanting to see how far your rant would take you. I actually didn't think outfit planning would make great footage.'

She's right. Man, this kid is smart. Edward and Dylan lean over to look at the screen and guffaw. I think it's the first time they've agreed on anything since we've been here.

Dylan shakes his head. 'What were we thinking?'

'That we'd do just about anything for a buck,' I say. 'Fine, maybe we weren't always so principled.'

'Maybe,' Monet agrees. 'But my aesthetic matters to me and I've worked out something I think you'll all like. I mocked it up from this.' She scrolls through her photos and shows another picture from a photoshoot for a magazine cover about a month before that final show we never got to play.

We gather around Monet's screen to see and it means that all three of us are standing shoulder to shoulder. We're so close I can smell Dylan's fresh aftershave and that Edward reeks like an old person's laundry. And I realise it's probably the closest we've been to each other since our last gig with Jonny. He loved to do that thing where you all link arms and get pumped together before walking out on stage.

I suck in air, because out of nowhere his absence gapes like a hole's been shot out of my fucking chest.

My throat aches and I blink, and the others are talking, but I can't pull myself together enough to listen. I close my eyes. *Get a grip, Adam.*

Why did he have to be the one to die? He always thought he was better than everyone else. Maybe if he'd just… Maybe if I hadn't…

There's a touch on the back of my hand.

My eyes fly open. I look down. It's Monet. Jonny's kid. And the pressure of her fingertips pulls me back into the present. I look at her face, but she's not even looking my way.

Then she's gone, disappeared backstage. And Dylan, Edward and Lara all seem unsurprised at the development, so I wait as though I too have a clue what's going on. But I don't have to wait long, because she pushes a hanging rack out onto the stage.

There are garment bags with each of our names on them. Talk about preparation.

'This isn't set in stone or anything,' Monet says. And for the briefest of seconds, she actually looks a little nervous. 'The sizes should be right.'

I'm past being surprised by her planning, instead checking out what she's put in there for me. Might as well look, it's not like she can force me to wear it.

As promised, the clothes are inspired by that shoot. Basically, tight black tees and denim. But updated to fit on more mature shapes. And with allowances for Edward's lack of a single rock-and-roll bone in his body.

'Not bad,' he says, holding his black shirt and jeans up against his frame. Which considering his constant whining about everything is a fair compliment.

I don't hate mine either. I've worn enough black T-shirts over the years to appreciate the softness beneath my fingers. I'm glad there's no price tag because I don't want to know how many weeks' rent the – I count three – tops in here would cover. And the jeans are exactly the kind I like.

'What about you, Monet? What are you wearing?'

The question comes from Edward, but from the unconcealed curiosity on his hovering wife's face I reckon she's made him ask it.

'Seems only fair that we know,' I add.

Monet bites her lip, nods, then disappears backstage again. When she returns, she has one of those see-through costume bags. In it is a dress, white and soft. A simple summer thing that's gossamer light, yet with plenty of fabric.

If the world didn't already ache for Jonny's daughter, they will when they see her on stage with her father's band in this.

'What do you think?'

Again, I sense a little vulnerability. For all her apparent confidence, she's still just a kid. I look up and meet her gaze. She's looking right at me, and if she's deliberately doing that hopeful nervous thing she has happening in her wide eyes, then the girl should be an actress, because I would swear she desperately wants my approval.

I've been pretty shit as far as uncles go, but for this I don't need to try to be able to do the right thing.

'It's perfect.'

And her smile feels better than the high Bugsy offered me.

We play through a few more of the songs, but no one is really feeling it. There comes a point where everyone knows what they're doing and *practised* is in danger of becoming *bored*.

Dylan must recognise that we're getting a bit stale, because he stands, stretches and announces, 'We'll play the bridge of "Touch of Colour", then one more time on Monet's song, and I reckon we'll call it done for today.'

'No.' The word is quiet but slices across the stage. Edward clears his throat, puts his glasses straighter on his nose and says it again. 'No.'

I don't reckon my jaw drops open, but the feeling is the same. Edward never argues. Whines and complains, yes, but never argues. But maybe it's more correct that he never argued with Jonny. Not like me and even Dylan. All of us came to blows at one point or another. We'd disagree and things would escalate, and we'd wind up wrestling on the floor, knocking over mic stands. We all had opinions, and no one ever wanted to back down.

Except Edward.

It seems he's grown a spine. And I'm not sure if I like it.

Dylan's jaw tightens. 'What do you suggest, then? Something fiscal, I presume, since that's your speciality, as opposed to the rest of us who are actual musicians.'

'He's right, Edward-lad, you're not really here for your good ideas,' Bugsy adds.

Edward pushes his glasses up onto his nose again and although he takes a deep breath, when he speaks his voice is strong. 'We should go through "I Know What You've Done" again. The timing between Adam and Monet was awful on the chorus last time through, and it should be one of our best.'

Dylan stares him down.

I consider arguing just to piss Edward off, and I would if it was any other song. Part of me almost tells them then. Tells them *I* wrote that track in a whiskey-infused rage after a girl whose name I can't even remember broke my heart by asking me to introduce her to Jonny. I'm listed as a co-writer, but most people think the credit was Jonny feeling sorry for me.

Before I can say anything, Monet nods her head and flashes me a grin. 'He's right, it did sound a bit crap. We'll do the others first, and then let's tell that two-timing tramp in the song what we think of her.'

Lara – Saturday

'I Know What You've Done' has never been one of my favourite songs, but when they play it through I have to admit it's never sounded better. It's like Adam and Monet have sung together for years.

It's so good it leaves me a little uncomfortable, although no one notices. I feel like screaming at them that Edward wouldn't even be here if I hadn't forced the issue.

The manager guy invited me to go for a walk with him and while I don't know exactly what Bugsy was offering, Edward was glaring my way.

'Later,' I'd suggested.

Bugsy's beady gaze made my flesh constrict but I kept my smile in place when he leered, 'I'll keep you to that.'

A loud sigh breaks me from my mental debate about whether Bugsy's possible connections that could make me famous outweigh his creep factor.

Monet is the source of the noise, standing in the wings of the stage with her head bowed.

'Are you okay?' I ask.

She blinks at me in surprise – *yes, I am here, I exist* – and her face softens. 'This is what I wanted but… It's hard to explain.'

'Try me.'

The things I know about this girl. From her star sign to her bikini size, all of it has been written about online. Along with her lack of having seriously dated anyone male or female and her following in her mother's footsteps in rarely venturing from their estate.

Like her mother, though, being around Monet St Fleur in the flesh is altogether different. She's more ordinary than the air-brushed pictures from the tabloids would have me believe, with a small pimple on her chin and a love for activewear without designer labels. But at the same time, she shines like her father.

'I'm worried that it will completely crash and burn tomorrow, and everyone will discover that I can't measure up to the late, great Jonny Rake,' she says. 'But even more than that, what if it all goes perfectly?'

I nod. 'Success can be as terrifying as failure.'

She grins. 'You do get it.'

'That's because I'm old,' I admit. I feel Edward willing me not to embarrass him, but anything I say will do that. 'I've been married almost as long as you've been alive.'

'Did you go all out or, like, elope?'

I can tell from the wistfulness in her tone at the end which she thinks is more romantic. Easy for her to fantasise about escaping the eyes of the world when just by existing she's the centre of attention.

'We had a huge party with just about everyone we knew, and I had the princess dress of my dreams,' I tell her. 'Edward was my Prince Charming that day, all dapper in a suit with tails and a waistcoat.' Looking at Edward now, even near the keyboard and with his hair a bit mussed and some spark in him, it's hard to imagine. 'It was seriously the best day of my life. Other than when the kids were born, of course,' I add quickly, in case she thinks I'm heartless.

It wasn't all perfect.

Having to face my family when everyone realised the band weren't coming wasn't much fun. Suddenly I'm back there again, feeling about the size of an ant.

'Are you just about ready to head back up to the house?' Dylan asks Monet.

While we've been talking, the boys have sorted out what needs to be packed away, ready for tomorrow's quick sound check before the show.

'I was just saying what a pity it was that none of the rest of the band could make it to the wedding,' I blurt, loudly enough that Adam lifts his head from where he's crouched next to an amp.

I don't look at Edward. He can get mad all he wants. It's been nearly two decades and it's time to call these people on their bad manners.

Dylan's forehead crinkles. 'What wedding?'

Adam heaves himself to his feet. 'Weddings aren't really my scene, but I don't remember anything about it. First I heard about Edward getting married was when I saw some pictures somewhere in a magazine.'

The somewhere he's talking about was only an exclusive shoot with a leading women's magazine.

'I guess you all had better things to do than be there on Edward's special day,' I say.

'Enough,' Edward shouts. He closes his eyes like just looking at me pains him. His hands are clenched to fists. When he finally looks at me again, it's with a despairing shake of his head. 'God, Lara, just shut up, will you? For once? I have begged you to move on from this, but you just couldn't let it go.'

'What do you mean?' I ask.

There's something in his eyes, an expression I've never seen before. This is past being annoyed and way past angry. He takes a step towards me, and I have to catch myself from flinching back. This is Edward, my harmless, ineffectual, accountant husband. But my heart is suddenly knocking against my ribs, and there's a rushing in my ears.

The rest of the world around us disappears.

'I didn't invite them, okay? They didn't come because I didn't invite them.'

'But we—'

'I know what you wanted, I was there, remember? You don't need to talk to me like I'm some kind of imbecile. Adam and Dylan and everyone else you put on my list didn't come to our wedding because their invitations were never sent.'

'Never sent?' It comes out a pitiful echo.

He nods. Then, as if he'd forgotten the audience we have, he forces a weak smile at the others. 'Sorry. I thought it was better to have it a private occasion, you know.'

Clearly relieved at the change in tone, Dylan bobs his head. 'No worries.'

'Yeah,' Adam agrees.

I don't see anything else. Eyes stinging, I don't wait for whatever Monet might say. I'm on my feet and heading for the stairs off stage before she has the chance.

'Lara, wait.'

Edward catches up with me by the shelter of the trees. Remembering – far too late – the cameras, I don't pull away when he grabs my hand, but his damp, sweaty skin against mine feels like that of a stranger.

'Why?' I ask, without looking at him.

'It wasn't The Cedrics Band you were marrying. It was me.'

I tug and he lets my hand go. 'You lied to me all this time. Why not just say that from the beginning? You made a fool of me in front of everyone I knew.' I have to force the words out past the lump in my throat. 'You let me believe it was the band, let me blame them, when all along you knew the truth. Why?'

His arms are folded. 'Maybe you should ask yourself that question.'

Things are strained between us all the way back to the suite. I do my best to pretend that everything is fine, making myself join the others in the carts for the ride back up the trail when I want to storm off into the bush and never see any of them again.

Although by the time I'm alone with Edward once more, I'm almost beginning to believe it might be okay. It means I wasn't rejected. And he's right, it should be enough that it was our special day.

'Do you want to use the shower first?' I ask as I close the door to the outside world. It's an olive branch of sorts. He knows how important it is to me to look nice for dinner and risking a delay is a big concession.

He lifts his arm and sniffs. 'I guess I could use one.'

I smile, relaxing. He's usually one to fight a shower and a change of clothes, claiming it's a waste of time, so he must be looking to smooth things over. His eyes are shining, and his cheeks are flushed, but it's not sunburn – it's the electricity of having been on stage. He's practically vibrating with it, and it stirs a rush of remembered attraction.

'You had fun up there, admit it.'

He huffs a breath through his nose, and the light in his eyes vanishes. 'I've never pretended not to like music. Give me a good arrangement of a Beethoven sonata or a Cedrics Band original and I will find enjoyment. It doesn't mean we're all besties.'

The edge in his voice twists my belly. 'Why can't you enjoy this? Is it because I want you to be here? Is that what we've come to?'

'What we've come to?' He scoffs. 'I think the real question you – or maybe I – should be asking is whether there was ever anything more?'

And like that, the tentative truce is shattered. 'You're the one who proposed.'

'Yes,' he says. 'I'm the fool who asked you to marry me, and I'm living the consequences of my actions.'

'You make it sound like a prison sentence.'

He doesn't deny it. 'Let's just get through the weekend. We'll play the show and we'll go back to our lives. I mean, it's not like Jonny is going to magically appear.'

'Jonny?'

'That's probably what you were hoping. No full body found at the explosion site and all. Then you'd get the full groupie experience. Unless you've already had that. You claim to have been a casual fan, but you've never actually said whether you ever saw the band before you lined up outside the stadium on that day. Perhaps you'd already met one of us?'

This is dangerous territory. 'I don't see what that has to do with anything.'

He raises his eyebrows. 'Don't you? You can't possibly be this clueless.'

My eyes well up. With Edward, tears have always sent him scurrying. I sniff and then blink a few times.

'It doesn't matter what I do, you're the same as my family.

I'll never be enough for any of you.' The words spill out. This isn't my first time on this particular path. 'Sorry that we can't all be super clever. You of all people...' I cover my face with my hands. 'You said me not being book smart didn't matter to you, then you call me clueless. You promised I was enough just the way I am.'

There was a time when a performance like this one would have had him desperate to make things right. But the fact that it has him stalking out of the suite will have to do.

I get what I wanted: conversation over.

A STORYBOOK LOVE:
THE CEDRICS BAND FAN BLOG

11 December 2021

Not to alarm anyone but the band performs tomorrow.

TOMORROW!!

Okay, I admit it. I am alarmed. And I am amazed and grateful about the support I received after yesterday's post. Those buy links for exclusive content were humming all afternoon. I promise you will not regret it.

In fact, as a sneak peek for those of you not sure whether to sign up or not, I intend to go live tomorrow when I arrive at the island so you can be the first to see the gorgeous place where they will play.

And, in even better news, I'm hopeful of arranging an exclusive early tour of the stage set-up.

And this will all be free. My thank you to all of you for your support.

I can't give you a time just yet, but keep checking back to catch the stream when it happens. It won't be long, thanks to the security conditions, and my sources only have so much power to get me close to the band – but it will be the very first stage glimpse for all of you.

The whispers are saying that the stage arrangement is going to be the very definition of a picturesque, intimate experience. Imagine bushland and the setting sun, imagine a gentle slope with happy groups of concert goers and a roped-off section at the front for the VIPs. It's the stuff of dreams.

I need to tell you guys something.

Just between us, because I know you will understand. Right alongside the excitement and anticipation, there is sadness too.

Because Jonny won't be there.

I know I'm not the only one who still thinks of him, who dreams of him, who wishes somehow that it was all a horrible mistake. If I'm completely honest, and I know I can be with you all, I'm nearly as nervous for tomorrow as I am excited. Can they still be the band I loved without Jonny front and centre?

His smoky voice caressing the lyrics, his soulful eyes staring out into ours. The way he'd not exactly dance, but allow the music to move his lithe body. He was more than just the images in the magazines. He was the rasp in his voice during the first song after a break, thanks to the three smokes and bourbon he'd have sucked down.

The way his ribs showed skin almost blue when his T-shirt rode up as he'd sing the chorus of 'Light the Soul'. And the way his left hip jutted out more than his right when he'd lean on the mic stand.

I miss Jonny more than ever tonight, and I'm sure I'm not alone.

'It's been so grey with missing you, even though there
have been others.
Now's the time for me to shine, to paint a touch
of colour.'
A TOUCH OF COLOUR – The Cedrics Band

Yours,
Ricky
The Cedrics Band Number One Fan

Monet – Saturday

'Tell me about your childhood.'

It's not the first time an interviewer has asked me this exact question, but the tone is new. Sitting behind the camera, draped in shadow, acclaimed director Marco D'Angelo is undoubtedly, undeniably, unmistakably bored.

As the child of Jonny Rake and Ivy St Fleur, I've been followed by cameras ever since I can remember. I've been told I light up any stage. Maman has refused more offers for me to be on the screen than I can count. Strangers and reporters have taken on, and lost flesh to, our Dobermann guard dog, Artemis, just to catch a glimpse of me. And when anyone asks me a question, they don't simply listen to the answer. They hang off my every word.

But not this man.

When I showed up, still high from singing with the band and the progress I think I'm making with Adam, it was to an empty room. He was late and he didn't even apologise.

I don't care, not really. I'd intended to let a couple of media people into the inner sanctum to help build hype and ensure the whole band bought into the event. Bugsy's suggestion of Marco fitted well enough when I saw he'd won awards.

But now I wish I'd never agreed.

It's not like I'm one of those fame-hungry types, but, although I'm only seventeen, I do expect a certain level of respect.

Instead of continuing my story, I say nothing. I sit, poised and completely comfortable under the bright lights with the camera on me, and I do not say a word. I smile to myself; I can do this all day.

As I sit, straight but relaxed, my thoughts return to the odd way Dylan stopped me when I was walking over here. He'd been waiting outside when I closed the suite door quietly so as not to wake Maman. In fact, I was so distracted about whether I'd made a selfish mistake bringing her to this island and into this unending heat that I almost walked into him.

'Dylan, you scared me,' I'd said.

He'd gripped my shoulder to steady me. 'Where are you going?'

'To my interview.' I didn't add, *not that it's any of your business*, but it was there in my tone.

'I'll sit in. Make sure they don't take advantage of you.'

I'd shrugged free. 'No, this is something I want to do for myself.'

Walking away, I'd had the strangest feeling I'd disappointed him. When I'd looked back, he hadn't moved but he'd seemed a stranger. An angry stranger.

A good minute passes of my wondering what Dylan's problem was before Marco lifts his head. 'Whenever you're ready,' he says. Then he goes right back to not paying me attention.

'No.' I say it low, but firm.

'I beg your pardon?'

'No. I will not speak to someone who has no interest in listening to what I have to say.'

There's a rustle behind me. I somehow manage not to flinch or let my relaxed smile slip as I realise that Connie's here. Has she always been here, or did she sneak in? The woman moves so quietly and seems to blend in with the furniture. In my annoyance with her husband, I'd not considered she might be standing there silently in the shadows, watching on.

Has she told Marco about our meeting near the cave this morning? She said she wouldn't share what she saw, but she scuttles to Marco's side and says something in his ear.

I don't move. Don't react. Don't bother straining to listen. I simply wait.

Marco shakes his head, then sighs. As Connie melts back into the shadows, he looks at me properly for the first time. 'If I seem a little distracted, it is because I have a lot on my mind.'

It's not an apology, but it is an admission of sorts.

'I appreciate you're working, but so am I,' I say. 'Tomorrow, I launch a single that will likely go straight to the top of the charts but will also be analysed and compared and measured against the work of my father. A man who I have never met, who I know little about and who died before I was even born. Honestly, Mr D'Angelo, I am terrified, but I am here because I have agreed to be a part of this and I pride myself on my word. If you don't want to listen to what I have to say, if Jonny Rake and Ivy St Fleur's daughter isn't required in your documentary, then trust me, I'll be glad to walk out of here right now.'

He considers.

And that alone just about has me out of there. If not for having a few things I'd like to share with the world, I'd already be back in the suite.

But then he nods. 'Please, go ahead, I'm listening.'

I give the spiel, the one I've learned to say about appreciating Maman's attempts to shelter me from public life, about wanting to continue my father's legacy. Stuff that can be found in a billion places online. But this time Marco is paying attention.

'And I can't wait to share my debut single with the world.' I allow my smile to show some vulnerability, because God knows the world doesn't like its young women too confident. 'Hope you all like it.'

'There have been rumours,' he says.

'You'll have to narrow it down. There's lots of them.' I shrug. 'It comes with the territory.'

'Would you say that the legacy you mentioned before is a good one?' he asks instead of answering.

This is unexpected. Jonny Rake has practically been canonised within the music industry. A talent, a prodigy, a pioneer. To even ask such a thing suggests there's doubt.

'No one is perfect,' I say carefully. 'But the music lives on. The Cedrics Band means a lot, to a lot of people.'

'So you're saying it doesn't matter who got hurt on the way, because they sold a few records?'

The gasp to my left is so soft I'm immediately uncertain I heard it at all, but considering Connie has been silent before now, it's practically a cry.

My answer matters.

I can feel it in the weight of their gaze, their sudden interest. The problem is, I don't know what the right answer is, not for them and not for those who'll be watching. He said 'they', so he must have meant rumours about my father and the band then, but which? The conspiracy theories that he's not dead? That he cheated on Maman? That they could be arseholes?

Think.

I'm taking too long. Whatever I say now will appear calculated at best. It's like I've been riding a whale and suddenly it's remembered that it's about a million times bigger than me and I'm surrounded by water deep enough to drown. All I can do is hang on.

'I think my father changed the world just a little with his music,' I say, non-committal. 'And that's an incredible thing.'

Marco's arms fold and his already shadowy eyes go black. Clearly not the right answer.

'I'm sure they never set out to hurt anyone,' I add.

'Are you?'

'I think so. I wasn't even born back then.' That reminder might be a bit of a cop-out, but the energy in the room has turned. I need to look after my reputation.

Note to self: make sure I have veto on the film before it's released.

'Speaking of your childhood, you were home-schooled, weren't you?' He looks to his wife as though checking something. 'After an incident at the boarding school you attended?'

My stomach cramps as memories of the friends I thought I'd made threaten to shake my composure. Cate Fionnan and Lily Kirsten. Sold their stories to the tabloids, which began my focus on learning IT. I vowed never to rely on anyone else to get a story wiped from the internet.

How does he know?

Marco is staring at me and I realise I haven't answered.

There's no sympathy in his gaze when he asks, 'Have you ever made any real friends?'

'I wouldn't presume to speak for anyone,' I say, a slight waver in my voice betraying the thudding of my heart. 'There are many people I value.'

'Really?'

The door is right there. I could run now, get some kind of injunction to stop this ever seeing the light of day, but it's too late.

I have to ride this out.

'What's wrong?' Marco asks. 'Did someone at school say mean things about your dad? Did they dare to question Saint Jonny?'

I breathe out hard, trying to keep my frustration from showing. This has gone far enough. He wants a big story, well, I'll give him one. After all, it's half the reason I'm here.

'Enough,' I say. 'You're not asking the right questions.'

'Really? I must have missed, young lady, when you released a documentary to critical acclaim.'

'Let her speak.'

It's the first time Connie has actually said anything, and it seems to surprise her husband as much as it does me. He gives her a long, hard look.

'Go ahead,' Marco says to me.

I swallow. This is it; this is my chance. 'You haven't asked me about that concert where my father died.'

'Perhaps because you weren't even born.'

'But it's the defining moment of my life. I have spent months, years, looking for answers about what really happened that day.'

'And what did you find?'

I pause, let the moment build, then I lean forward and stare straight down the camera lens.

'My father's death was no accident. It was murder. And I know who's responsible.'

And then I tell them everything I know.

Lara – Saturday

Edward has been avoiding me since the crying episode. Thankfully. We haven't spent this much time together for years. In theory, we still share a bedroom at home, but Edward usually ends up sleeping in the spare room.

He returned to the suite in time for the quickest of showers before dinner. At least he changed to a more formal outfit of unimaginative black slacks and a green shirt that I bought him last Christmas. I thought it matched his eyes, but it makes his pale skin even more pasty.

He didn't even bother to say I looked nice, but considering I saw him disappearing down the trail to the beach with Bugsy less than an hour before we needed to be over at the main house, I was just glad he showed up at all. I let myself imagine Bugsy was trying to talk him into a tour, and then that the manager had interest in me – professionally, rather than the sleazy looks.

We walk into the huge glass-walled room and when I stop to admire the gorgeous lights strung overhead, Edward keeps going. I don't care, it's not like I want him to babysit me. But he's grinning like an idiot as he starts talking loudly to Dylan about something, waving his hands with more enthusiasm than I've ever seen from him.

If we were currently speaking, I'd tell him, *I told you so*. I knew that being on stage would revitalise him. He's so excited he can hardly stand still, and when Bugsy joins their group in a pale-blue suit with a pair of matching trademark braces, Edward slaps the other man on the shoulder and then practically gives him a hug.

I try to ignore the pang in my belly that he's never happy like that with me. Ever.

This is my chance to make my own band stories, since Edward has always shared so little. I've taken and treasured the few details he's let slip of pre-show rituals and early days jamming until they fell asleep in the shed. Over time, I've moulded these into stories wheeled out with new people like the best silver or the good wine. But I'm not going to need to live on Edward's scraps anymore.

Last night's intruder won't be one of the stories. In my time alone in the suite I was able to check for my hidden link to the outside world, and the device wasn't disturbed. Maybe it was some kind of hallucination, but I won't be admitting as much to Edward.

'Would you care for a drink?' Florence asks, appearing at my elbow. She's holding out a tray with a selection of filled crystal glasses.

'Thank you,' I say. I choose a glass of bubbly and allow myself a long sip, the cool liquid not distracting me from how good a time Edward seems to be having. I force my attention to my host. 'The way you've decorated this room is incredible. It was nice before, of course, really nice. But this is, like, really classy.'

'If you don't mind,' Florence says, 'I should keep moving.'

I don't watch her go. I'm not that desperate. Not yet.

As though in answer to a prayer, Monet walks through the door right at that moment. This evening she's accompanied by her mother, who's barely left her suite all weekend. After what I saw in there when accompanying her after her fainting spell, I'm surprised Ivy's here at all.

When Monet, gorgeous in a dark-green spaghetti-strapped jumpsuit, leaves her mother to head for the bar, I use the excuse of checking on Ivy's health and make myself approach the couch where she's sitting.

No one is better than me, I remind myself, but my knees are shaking. We're both wearing black dresses, but hers is somehow more – more on trend, more flattering, more classy – and it's all I can do not to high-tail it back to my suite and count down the hours until I can return to suburban life.

'Good evening,' I say.

She glances past me. I hold my breath, tense up. Here comes the brush-off. But then her smoky-eyed gaze settles on me. '*Bon soir* – Leah, was it?'

'Lara. And I'm glad you're feeling better.'

'I am.' She smiles, a lazy curve of her full lips. '*Merci, mon amie.* It is because of you. If you had not been there yesterday, I do not know what I would have done.'

It's been written in magazines that the warmth of Ivy St Fleur's smile could melt the polar ice caps, and I'm not immune. Her thanking me feels like a benediction.

'I am just happy I was there to help.'

Monet returns with a glass of sparkling water for her mother, and a smile for me, and then moves away again to speak to the hostess, offering her help. She really is a lovely young woman. The tabloids have her all wrong.

As Ivy sips her drink, her gaze lingers on my face, the tiniest of lines forming between her brows. 'You really do seem familiar.'

'I don't know,' I say. 'There are lots of blondes, and you've travelled all over the world. Oh, and I do have a sister, maybe she went to one of your shows.' It's a weak suggestion, considering my older, clever sister doesn't even look like me.

She's really staring at me now, the warmth vanished. 'No, that's not it. I can almost remember, it's right there. I'm sure I'll have it soon.'

An invisible hand squeezes my throat. This, I should have planned better for, but I did not think someone like Ivy St Fleur would possibly remember that brief interaction we had all those years ago. Standing there beneath the twinkling lights with a glass of fancy champagne in my hand, I discover that I'm quite out of explanations.

I step back. If I can get away from her and this conversation, she might stop searching for an answer to the question. 'Let me know if you remember,' I say brightly. Too brightly for the circumstances, but it's the best I can do.

'Wait,' she says. It's a command. This is a woman used to having people like me do as she asks.

I waver, my scrambling brain stuck, like what I suddenly recall Edward moaning about when his computer flashes and whirrs in protest. A death spiral or frozen loop, or something that means I could well stand here forever and not be able to decide what to do next.

Ivy's gaze meets mine and there's a flicker there. She's beginning to remember.

It breaks the cycle in my head. I am not the only one with something to lose. In fact, now I can think again, I'm pretty sure that she'd want to complete the full course of this conversation even less than I do.

The realisation drives me to move. Not away from this gorgeous woman who I'd longed to properly meet and dreamed of becoming friends with, but towards her. Close enough that when – smile still pasted in place – I murmur, 'You might want to take a hint from me and stop before you give voice to any memories you've just uncovered,' I'm able to artfully shield what I'm saying from any lurking cameras.

She arches back a little; the warning in my tone was unmistakable. 'But—'

'If you think of where you were when you think you might have seen me,' I say, 'or more importantly, *who* you were with, you might appreciate that it's best we assume we met yesterday when I kindly helped you.'

Her head tilts in question. There's a pause forever long, and then she nods slowly.

I straighten and smile again and ignore the sting in my palm from where my nails have drawn blood.

When I move away, I lift my head, and Edward is staring at me from a small group including Dylan and the director. There's an intensity to him that draws me closer. The thrill of the stage doesn't account for the way Edward is acting. If I didn't know better, I'd think he was high.

And as I close the distance between us, he continues to stare. Mum's voice is there in that look. In the disappointment. *Pretty just isn't enough.*

The others are talking about whether to split the encore into two.

I take a breath and join in. 'I think that maybe—'

'Seriously, Edward,' Bugsy says, interrupting me. 'Can't you keep her quiet? Invest in a muzzle or something?' He chortles like it's a joke.

And I know what I'm supposed to do here, I'm supposed to laugh and go along with it, because if I don't, I'm being difficult. But my hands are clenched, and I'm not sure which of the snickering faces I want to punch more. The sleazy manager who's tried to grope my arse or the man I married whose face says he wishes he'd said it.

I feel eyes on me. Florence is staring this way. Understanding on her face before the polite hostess mask returns. It's enough to remind me I'm not alone.

Next to me, Edward wipes his hand under his nose, sniffs and stares until I can see the dilated pupils in his wide eyes before he turns his back, leaving me standing in the middle of the room, my neck hot, empty glass in hand, deliberately excluded.

This is not the Edward I know.

Monet – Saturday

Maman surprised me by agreeing to join the rest of us across at the main house for dinner.

She's always loved to do the unexpected. Waking me at midnight one random Wednesday when I was nine to fly across the world to be at Disneyland for a private night-time opening. Declaring the eighth of June ice-cream day when I was four and celebrating it by eating nothing but my favourite cold, sweet goodness every year since on that day, despite having a typical parent's obsession with me eating my vegetables every other day of the year. Letting me leave school without me needing to beg.

Even I caught my breath at how gorgeous Maman looked when she stepped out of the bathroom and announced she was ready. She's lost so much weight these last months, but her makeup skills corrected her pallid skin tone, and the simply stunning dress fitted to her body in a way that disguised how wasted it has become.

'Don't look so surprised,' she'd teased. 'I still have it in me.'

I hadn't been able to say anything, trying hard as I was to stop the tears stinging my eyes leaving mascara tracks down my cheeks. But when I gave her a hug, I felt her hold me tightly against her for a few beats longer than necessary.

We both know how this is going to go.

Now we're just playing out the time we have left.

Maman's transformation and unusual enthusiasm to socialise is just the distraction I need to stop thinking about what I said in the interview. The satisfaction of having seen the smug director's eyes widen and his jaw drop throughout the rest of our conversation doesn't make up for the worries that I've pushed too far too soon.

There is still nearly a whole day until the concert, and nearly two before we are off the island and truly safe from any repercussions. But I didn't risk everything to falter in my plan at this stage, even if I'm afraid Maman suspects something.

'Be careful,' she'd whispered in the suite before she let me go, something so often said with her protective ways but with heavier emphasis than ever before.

'I will,' I'd promised.

But I'm better with computers than people, and the doubts are beginning to creep in.

Thus, my futile offer to help Florence when we arrived, and Maman seemed to be settled talking to Edward's wife – her name keeps escaping me – in an attempt to keep occupied.

'Thank you, but no. Please, relax and enjoy yourself,' Florence said with a frown. 'You're our guest.'

Shut down, and not wanting to approach Dylan as Connie is right behind him sipping on something amber, I instead wander over to the fireplace mantel as if I've never seen anything more fascinating than the styled items. I seem to remember Florence saying she decorated herself, and the woman has taste. The décor is the match of any of our rooms at home, and there have been whole magazines devoted to my mother's sense of style.

I lightly touch a finger to the design's centrepiece. A decorative blue and white vessel of such delicate beauty that it absolutely belongs in this space, despite not strictly following the deep woods and crisp white of the rest of the room.

And the whole time I'm aware of Connie's gaze on me. I kind of wish I could go back to before, when I didn't notice her presence in a room. I have given this strange little woman too much power. At any moment she could spill to everyone what I said in the interview about Jonny's death, or that she saw me going online early this morning.

I sneak a glance her way. She catches me looking and smiles a neat little satisfied smile.

A hand rubbing against my bare shoulder has my glass of sparkling water slipping from nerveless fingers. It hits the edge of a rug and bounces, before rolling with an attention-drawing tinkle across the floor.

'Bit clumsy, isn't she?' Bugsy – the owner of the clammy hand – says with a loud guffaw.

'Not usually,' I say through gritted teeth. And then, 'Keep your hands to yourself.' The latter is low but clear. If he thinks I'm going to let him paw me then he's in for a shock.

Florence appears with a towel and mops up the mess and replaces my drink in one deft move. I take a sip, appreciating she noticed what I'd been drinking.

Bugsy uses Florence's appearance to edge away. Obviously, whatever he wanted from me wasn't worth me daring to stand up for myself. At seventeen, I walk the line: still young enough to appeal to a certain type who like girls rather than women, but with adulthood casting a shadow over everything.

From across the room, Maman beckons for me to join her, pride on her face. 'What did you say to that horrible man? He looked like you'd slapped him.'

'Just told him what he could do with his wandering hands.' I know she worries for my future, and I'm glad she's beginning to see that I can look after myself.

She shakes her head. 'Men!'

'Not all of them,' I say as Adam enters. I'm hopeful he'll be different.

But I'm not the only one who noticed the new arrival. Maman is so busy pretending she's not aware of Adam Rake that she hasn't heard a word I've said.

'So, then I said how I'm feeling bored,' I continue. 'And I told Bugsy despite the fact he makes me want to hurl that I'd meet him outside for some sex in the garden. Sometime between dinner and dessert.'

Maman's head snaps around. 'You said what?'

I laugh. 'Just making sure you're paying attention. I thought you said you couldn't have less interest in Adam Rake if he was the last man on earth.'

'He's no one,' she says fiercely. 'No one.'

'Well, he's my uncle, and he's over by the bar alone. Seems a perfect time to get to know him. Do you need anything?'

Her arms cross and she glares. 'I need nothing from him.'

That isn't really an answer to my question, but it's telling nonetheless.

But just as my approach to Adam is cut off by Florence calling everyone to the gorgeously set table, I'm starting to wonder if I've completely misunderstood my mother's hatred of this man.

Along with the others, I sit at Florence's direction.

'Tonight's meal will be four courses using primarily locally sourced ingredients,' she informs us as she tops up drinks. As if on cue, her husband appears for the first time this evening.

His black shirt, a few sizes too small, stretched over his bulging muscles as he carries a tray in each hand.

'Dietary preferences have been taken into account – however, if you have any questions, just ask. We begin with a cauliflower panna cotta, with leek on a mushroom soil.'

A small slate serving board is placed in front of me by Bruce's large hand. The white substance on it wobbles, although the force of it landing is surprisingly gentle. I wait until everyone is served before tasting, noticing that Florence and Bruce aren't seated with us this evening.

The food turns out to be cool and fresh, with a surprisingly agreeable tang. Despite cauliflower rating in my five least favourite vegetables, I know better than to refuse to try it. Connie is sitting directly opposite me, and I don't need to give her any further scoops.

Polite murmurings about the food and the heat and the success of the rehearsal and expectations about the show tomorrow last through until the second course – of either seared scallops or, for those who don't like seafood, a burnt butter, sage and white carrot gnocchi – is being cleared.

Dylan starts in on Adam, as I should have guessed.

'Not to brag or anything, but I could get work in any band I wanted. And Edward here, he's apparently doing great things in the financial world.' He raises his nearly empty glass of clear liquid – his third glass of the to-be-launched-tomorrow gin – in Edward's direction.

Edward laughs way too loudly for the compliment – quite the contrast from last night's sullen demeanour – and his wife sinks into her seat.

But then Dylan focuses again on Adam. 'Not you, though. You've just been so unlucky. In work, in love, in life. It's like you're destined to be miserable.' Dylan chuckles and smiles at Adam like the high-school mean girl who disguises her barbs with humour, daring Adam to take offence.

A pulse beats in Adam's jaw.

Bugsy watches, ready to step in.

'It's almost,' Dylan says, 'like it's karma.'

There's a viciousness about him, a side I've never seen before. He's enjoying watching Adam squirm.

I remember I was about eight when I first found Adam on the internet. At my mention of his name, Maman took to her room and ordered me to forget he existed. I tried asking Dylan. His face twisted at the question, and for the first time in my sheltered, privileged life, I was afraid. 'He's no one,' Dylan said with the kind of finality that kept me from asking again. At least, for a while.

Adam is trying to ignore Dylan. He's not drunk as much as last night, and although his eyes flash with annoyance, he doesn't respond.

Dylan leans over the table. 'I said it's karma. As in, you've got exactly the life you deserve.' This Dylan isn't the one I know. Even his voice is different, like Adam's mere presence has wound some internal screw into his vocal cords.

Adam stares down at the table.

My heart is thudding. Dylan is supposed to be someone I can count on. He promised he'd do this for me, but when I beg him with my eyes to stop, he's not even looking at me.

'What's wrong, Adam?' he asks. 'Can't you take a joke?'

Adam – Saturday

'What's wrong, Adam? Can't you take a joke?'

Dylan's words are heavy with meaning. It's not the first time he's said it this weekend.

Suddenly, I remember. It's clear as day in my head. But it's not him talking, it was me, back when we were kids. I'm maybe fourteen, so that puts Dylan at eleven. He'd come home from school with Jonny and was being picked up for his dance lesson from our place. He was in the lounge all decked in his tights and singlet and I walked past him and said to Jonny, with a nod in Dylan's direction, 'Who's your girlfriend?'

'Please,' Jonny begged. 'Leave him be.'

But I'd had a shit day at school and didn't need telling how to behave by my kid brother. The kid that I'd been compared to and found wanting by some turd-for-brains music teacher not an hour earlier.

'Sure, I'll leave you girls to it,' I said.

I shoved the little coffee table hard as I passed, laughing as a glass of juice tipped and the sticky orange liquid flooded Dylan's bag.

He'd said nothing 'til then, but that made him jump to his feet. 'I hate you,' he cried. 'Those jazz shoes cost a lot of money.'

I looked down at his skinny little arms and his pretty little face and smirked. 'Can't you take a joke?'

It echoes in my head. That small face superimposing on the man in front of me, all twisted in rage. An unexpected cold sweat drenches my skin. I'd completely forgotten that whole thing, but I doubt it was the only time I would have acted that way.

And like someone's opened the general admission doors before a concert, the memories rush in to fill my head. Not just Dylan, but Edward too. Or 'the girl and the nerd' like I used to call them. Like being female or smart was the worst insult I could come up with.

My eyes close. I'm sick with it. How could I have forgotten this?

When I open my eyes, Dylan is glaring at me and suddenly the animosity he's held on to for all these years makes sense. The guy must hate me, and with good reason.

But I was a kid back then. I have done far worse since and this successful man with his easy grin and respect within the industry can't begin to hate me more than I despise myself.

Besides, he has Ivy.

Without breaking eye contact, I lift my bottle of beer and drain it in a few gulps before standing and crossing the bar to get another. All my good intentions of not overindulging haven't even lasted until the main course.

'Manage to make your interview, Adam?' Dylan asks when I'm back at the table. 'Or did you flake out on your responsibilities?'

A quick look to Marco shows him straighten at the question.

'I'm sure there'll be time later,' I say.

'I don't know, it's a pretty busy schedule with the show and all.' This comes from Lara. Great, just what the world needs: input from the clinger. She must notice my annoyance because she quickly adds. 'At least, that's what I'm guessing.'

Marco folds his arms. 'She's right.'

My jaw tightens. It's not like the guy has been trying hard to get me to talk. Probably just wants to join in on the 'kick Adam while he's down' club.

'We can make time in the morning,' Monet is quick to interject, flashing me a smile. 'The fans don't get here until one, and we don't go on until after six. I didn't fit in mine until just before dinner, and Maman hasn't done hers yet.'

At the other end of the table, Ivy inclines her head without looking at me.

'There you go,' I say to Dylan. 'There's plenty of time. Anyway, it's not like the world's going to end tomorrow.' Dylan looks like he has more to contribute, but I keep talking. 'What is it with the early start for the gig anyway? Is it that some of us don't want to be up past their bedtime?'

Monet's head drops so her hair falls across her face, shielding her expression, but not fast enough for me to miss that there was hurt there.

Why did I say that? I want to explain that I was having a dig at Edward, and I didn't even think of her as a kid, but that will probably only make things worse. One day I'll stop fucking everything up, but clearly today is not that day.

'It's not like anyone watching this documentary will believe anything you say.' This comes from Dylan, still on about the interview. 'Wouldn't trust Adam as far as I could throw him,' he says to the table in general. And the cameras, don't forget the cameras. He flexes, smirks, looks around. 'Poor analogy, maybe, since he's pretty lightweight compared to me, but you get what I mean. The guy's a snake.'

Dylan's words play to a captive crowd. Strangers might have pretended interest in things other than our little spat, but there is too much history here, too much hurt.

It's the fact Dylan's right that sucks most of all. I'd say anything to look good, always have. I want to defend myself, but nothing comes out.

Like a predator sensing an imminent kill, Dylan's face lights up.

'Leave it.' Ivy's soft command stops Dylan. 'We're trying to enjoy the meal.' Her tone softens. 'Please.'

As silence falls, I'm not stupid enough to miss that she hasn't disagreed with what he's said about me though. I should hate this woman. But instead, I close my eyes, and I'm back there all those years ago – looking up at her above me in the dawn light – and I would give my left testicle just to hold her again.

It's been hard enough to pretend everything is fine with her hiding out in her suite, but her sitting there all soft lips and that signature vanilla scent makes it damn near impossible.

Since the moment she walked in tonight, I haven't been able to concentrate on anything else.

And she's acted like I'm a stranger.

It's that damn ache that gets me lifting my chin, gets me refusing to let her decree defuse the situation. Anyway, Bugsy's so off the planet after the indulgences he clearly enjoyed without me that I could start a punch-up and he probably wouldn't even notice.

'Really, Dylan?' I sneer. 'You're singling me out for a few stretches of the truth? Because everyone here is all about openness and honesty. Every bloody person around this table is full of secrets. Everyone here has something to hide. Even you.'

Ivy averts her gaze.

'Besides,' I say. I can hear desperation in my voice. 'Does what I say really matter? It's not like anyone wants to hear the shitty truth of my life.'

Ivy exhales softly. 'Adam.'

It's only my name. A soft plea for I don't know what, but it lodges deep in my chest, where my heart used to be. I have spent nearly half my life trying to avoid this woman, but being forced to be this close has unleashed something in me, something basic.

'Well, look at this,' I say, bright, forced, so loud it turns every head back towards me. Everyone but Ivy, of course. 'You actually realise I exist.'

She doesn't speak, doesn't say a word. But she does that thing where she huffs a small, dismissive sigh through her nose.

I am so fucking tired of this woman dismissing me. I am so tired of what she does to my insides. I'm sick of the hold she has on me.

'I'm sick of it.' It slips out. And out of context from the thoughts flying around like jacked-up popcorn in my head, it probably makes no sense at all. Except maybe to Ivy.

She looks up at last. 'Then stop,' she says.

'Stop what?'

'This. This whole self-destructive, *stupide* path that you are on.'

I don't know whether to be glad she gives enough of a shit to know how messed up I am or be ashamed. The shame wins. Shame I've carried for so many years. Ever since that night, my heart aching from Jonny's death, when I went to her only to be ordered away like some peasant.

'Oh baby,' I sneer, lifting my beer in a sarcastic toast. 'I'm just getting started.'

Florence – Saturday

Ivy's staring at Bruce, horror distorting her features, as he finishes a story he launched into, presumably to stop Adam starting any major altercations. 'You kill them?'

Although the sighting of the majestic kangaroo hopping out in the garden and Bruce's story helped defuse the tension, I now wish the creature had stayed away. Ivy's is not an uncommon reaction from a foreigner. She's not grown up here the way everyone else has. Although I'm sure as hell she's not French either. Small-town America, I'm guessing from what I've read on the internet discussion boards on the topic. I don't blame her – a woman sometimes needs to bend the truth to get what she wants, and her mysterious air certainly helped get her noticed.

I take charge. 'Sometimes the kangaroo population density becomes such that some humane culling is required. The measure is taken to prevent them starving to death, and only by a government-issued licence holder.'

When Ivy looks at me, it's hard to look away. 'You shoot them?'

Something like shame bubbles within me. 'I don't personally, no.'

Bruce leans back, his mouth curving into a grin. 'That would be where someone like me comes in.'

Ivy's luminous eyes shine with a hint of tears. 'There must be another way.'

'No,' Bruce replies. 'There isn't. I get my gun, head out in the dark before dawn, and set up near a dam. It's a favourite spot of theirs. They go there to drink with their babies as the sun rises.' Those around the table lean forward as he speaks. 'It's a beautiful location. Good open land, good light.' He laces his fingers together across his hard stomach and leans back, satisfied. 'Makes for easy pickings.'

Ivy pales. 'Not the young, too?'

'Yes ma'am.' Bruce's grin shows discoloured teeth.

He's enjoying this, I can tell. If I don't do something now, he'll be describing in detail how the animals are skinned.

'Enough,' I say, ignoring Bruce's frown. 'It's not an issue here on the island, as the national park protects them.' I stand. 'Would anyone like another drink? More dessert?'

No one answers immediately and in the silence it's clear Ivy is sniffling. When I cry, I tend to go red and pathetic, but as her full lips acquire a pretty tremble and her eyes drip a couple of restrained tears, it creates quite the beautiful image.

Dylan clears his throat. 'I'd love some more of that gin with tonic, if you're getting one.'

I shoot him a grateful smile. One not missed by my husband. I mentally kick myself.

Bruce eases to his feet.

I freeze, I can't help it. I've cut off his story, then shown the drummer, who he was already jealous of, my appreciation. Why didn't I think first? It's not like I've sipped anything but water tonight.

But he doesn't shout. Doesn't storm out. Doesn't come around the table to claim what's his. Rather, he approaches Ivy, surprisingly light on his feet for such a big man. The hunter from his story not risking startling his prey. He crouches beside her and murmurs something.

She lifts her head, looks at him. Really looks at him. And it's clear as her eyes widen, and she lifts her hand to play with the ends of her hair, that for all her fame and money, she's no better than any other woman he's tried to charm. Mostly, he doesn't bother, but when he does… the animal in all of us, the primal core, simply can't resist.

At the lightest touch of his hand on her arm, she rises. He leads her away from the rest of us to a spot on the couch, where he says something that has the effect of a shot of whiskey. Her limbs relax, a smile spreads over her features.

He's not looking at me, but this is deliberate. I know it is, but my every cell is on alert. Jealousy doesn't allow for rational. And that's what makes it so dangerous.

Damn him. Bruce and I have been here before and it didn't end well.

I drag my gaze away and grit my teeth. I have worked too hard to be distracted by stupid games. But when I look again, I can't miss the way he's leaning in close. And she's responding to it. For all he's rough and unpolished, the chemistry of him is impossible to resist.

I'm shoving my chair back and heading over to them before I can make the conscious decision to do so. He's won this round and we both know it. Bruce might be a loose cannon, sure. But he's my loose cannon.

He rises to his feet and moves to meet me. One large hand reaches out and cups my cheek, the touch releasing whatever had me about to make a scene. 'Darling,' he says, 'would you like me to organise the cheese board?'

I close my eyes, inhale, quickly reach out and squeeze his hand in thanks for saving me from myself and his power plays. 'I would really appreciate it.'

'I know,' he says.

As the guests finish their dessert and then attack the cheese board like they've never seen a brie or Persian-style feta, I busy myself with drinks and clearing some of the mess. Eventually, only the director and his wife remain seated, with the others – even a glowering Adam – drawn to the lounge area with Ivy.

I survey the table. On my last trip to the kitchen, Bruce was stacking the dishwasher and could probably fit in a few more items. But first, I'll offer coffee.

As I turn, clammy fingers brush against my arm. I recoil from Bugsy, who's drunk enough red wine that, combined with whatever else he's taken, he didn't even notice my reaction.

He frowns. 'Tell me again how we ended up here?'

I dart a glance around, but no one is paying us any attention. 'By boat, I believe.'

'You can't trick me with your clever words.'

I raise my eyebrows; it was hardly high-level wit.

'No,' he slurs. 'How was it that we ended up holding such an important event right here? I mean, it's nice and all, but there are lots of nice places in the world.'

My belly lurches, but I keep my expression polite. I'm starting to wish I'd told Bruce about what Bugsy said in the hallway yesterday. He'd be unable to speak today if I had.

He's studying me. 'You people are old money. But not even old money can sway some people. There must be something else.'

I don't try to hide my disgust. The man's a walking parasite. I saw him earlier with Edward's wife. I can tell she felt the same.

But my tone is light. 'Remember, I went to school with the band. I wasn't in the same year, though.'

Nothing was that simple, of course it wasn't. Not when you want The Cedrics Band with all their fame and baggage. There were favours, and I don't dare even think about the details of what I had to do with that record executive to make this happen. Not when my husband is nearby. Sometimes, I fear Bruce can read my mind.

'Right place, right time, and a bit of luck,' I add.

Bugsy blinks like he's trying to bring me into focus. 'You have a secret.'

My laugh is choked. 'Don't we all.'

One of Bugsy's slimy fingers pokes into my chest, probably marking the bodice of my white silk top. 'You shouldn't keep secrets, it's bad for your health. I should know.' He chortles to himself.

I edge out of his reach, but hesitate. If I walk away now, will he think he's on to something? If he even hints at what that record executive wanted from me in return for setting this up... the power in knowing he'd had Bruce's wife...

If Bugsy knows about the deal I struck to get the band to our island, it could destroy everything.

Florence – Saturday

Breathe, I remind myself, as the walls close in. Bugsy doesn't know anything.

Edward is suddenly in front of me, pushing his glasses up on his nose. 'School, huh? I don't remember you.'

Like Bugsy, he's far from sober, but his wife behind him has barely touched her wine and is watching on with curious eyes. Just my luck. I'm caught like one of the mice Bruce carried out from the trap in the pantry an hour before dinner.

Say something.

But my brain doesn't produce a single thing. Now, they're all looking.

Bugsy leans close and his finger hooks a stray lock of hair from my cheek to behind my ear. 'Were you a naughty girl at school?'

I taste bile, but he's saved me. *This*, I can handle. 'Keep your hands—'

'*Oof.*'

The slam of something huge into Bugsy's side sends the small man flying over the back of the couch and sprawling onto the coffee table, arms and legs spread like one of the starfish that sometimes wash up after a storm. His glass hits the floor, shattering at my feet. Red wine pools like blood on the floorboards. Spatters of it instantly spread on the back of the couch.

Bruce straightens from the shoulder charge, grins, and stalks around the long way, his stride eating up the distance between them as Bugsy moans and struggles to sit up.

'What did I do?' he whimpers.

Bruce lifts him off the table with one hand gripping the front of his shirt. 'Don't. You. Ever. Touch. My. Wife.' He emphasises each word with a sharp shake that has Bugsy's head rattling.

Bugsy blusters unintelligible defence, but Bruce isn't listening.

Then, in the age-old move of desperate men, Bugsy's head comes forward. *Thud.* His forehead lands square on Bruce's nose.

Bruce grins as though given permission and punches the smaller man hard in the stomach, releasing him as contact is made so Bugsy stumbles again, doubled over.

'You don't want to do this,' Bugsy cries. 'You don't want to mess with me. I work for powerful people.'

Bruce just pushes him harder.

It happens then, in slow motion. As Bugsy flails to keep upright, he bumps Adam, whose beer flies from his hand. The bottle lands with a plop on the rug at Dylan's feet, the golden-brown liquid inside spilling all over his white sneakers.

The drummer is on his feet and in Adam's face in a heartbeat. While I've been looking the other way, Edward is now bending over Bugsy, snarling at something he said, while Lara is trying to pull him off, with Bruce waiting above both of them to get another clear shot at the manager. There's the smack of flesh against flesh, and then Adam and Dylan are locked together in a careening dance across the rug, bouncing off the wall.

Monet leaps aside to avoid them, her outstretched hand doing nothing to separate or slow their progress. Ivy's hands cover her face as she shrinks back out of the way.

Scents of sweat, alcohol and adrenaline combine in the air to overwhelm the candles so artfully placed and the expensive perfumes and aftershaves.

Bang.

Adam's head hits the mantel.

'No!' The cry is snatched from within me.

I throw myself through the throng, chest so tight I can't breathe, push Dylan aside and grab the blue and white object from the mantelpiece.

I hold it close, cradling it.

Backing up against the wall, I glare at the chaos of bodies, ready to swing. Just try and let them get close.

Adam or Dylan's flailing arm hits an angel figurine. It shatters on impact. I sink to my knees as though I can will it back together, but there are too many pieces and too many trampling feet, so I leave them there broken.

These absolute fuckers will pay for that.

'Stop!'

I clutch my precious container to my chest and turn towards Monet's command. The others do the same.

She eyes each of us in turn, giving the director and his wife a particular glare for watching on as the whole thing unfolded with undisguised glee, camera silent in the corner, capturing everything.

'We have a show tomorrow. Brawling isn't going to help. Everyone needs to at least pretend they're professional, unless you want this documentary to be titled *How The Cedrics Band Imploded: a Tale of Idiocy and Ego.*'

Silence hangs in the air for a beat, and then around me heads drop, limbs untangle and one by one, with mumbles of apology from some, the room begins to clear.

I yawn. It's late, so much later than I thought, and there is so much left to do. But I don't move from my spot on the floor, leaning back against the wall.

We're alone when Bruce notices what I'm holding. He swipes a hand at the blood dripping from his nose. 'Okay?' he asks.

I drag myself upright, careful not to drop my precious load. My reflection in the broken glass at my feet shows a virtual stranger with a feral tangle of hair, tame compared to the wildness in her eyes.

Bruce is waiting for reassurance I'm not hurt.

I nod.

Any idea that the band would use this time together to reconnect and find their way to each other has been smashed like the angel, the fragments so broken they're never going to be pieced back together.

This whole event has all the markings of a disaster in waiting, but when I look to my husband, I acknowledge the one truth none of us on the island can escape.

'The show must go on.'

ACT II

Florence – Sunday

'Today's the day,' I tell Elsie. 'And it's going to be a scorcher.'

Sometimes it still surprises me when she doesn't answer. Sometimes, I'll be standing in the kitchen as I am now, and I'm positive that if I just turn my head quickly enough, I'll catch a glimpse of her dark hair and big eyes.

I feel her encouraging response from the little blue and white urn I've relocated in here to be out of the reach of our guests.

It's show day at last. I imagine that this buzzing of anticipation through my veins is how the band must feel when they're getting ready to go on stage to play.

My guests have not yet arrived for breakfast; they must be nursing heavy heads and maybe a few bruises from last night. An all-out brawl wasn't the best way to end a dinner party, but I suspect there's nothing like an audience to turn the band into rock stars.

The rap on the outside kitchen door is so hard it shakes the old window alongside it, and the mottled glass shows a blurry figure outside.

'I'm coming,' I call. I cross to the door and open it. 'Oh, it's you.'

With his hunched shoulders and long, stained brown coat, the man fills the door-frame. He's wearing a wide-brimmed hat pulled low on his head, and he's frowning through his beard.

'Morning, ma'am,' our neighbour, Willie, says. 'Might I have a word?'

This man used every dirty tactic he could to fight us getting the council permissions to have the concert on the island. I should know, because I had to use even dirtier tactics to win. And now he's on my doorstep on the day of the show? This smells like trouble – and unwashed farmer.

'This isn't a good time. Come back tomorrow.' I move to close the door.

A large boot-clad foot stops the heavy old door. 'You see, it's about my missing sheep.'

'Sorry, but I have more important things to worry about today, as you very well know. Maybe you need to go home and count again.'

He tugs his hat lower and glowers. 'That boy took my lamb. I know he did.'

It takes me a second to realise the boy he's referring to is my huge lump of a husband. The husband who changed the menu on me yesterday at the last minute to lamb. The one who headed out yesterday convinced he knew who the media leak was and that he had a plan.

Willie's eyes narrow. He must be able to read my – well, Bruce's – guilt on my face.

'I don't know what you're talking about,' I say. Instinctively, I take a step sideways to block Willie's view of the three huge fridges lining the wall across the other side of the room, as though he could somehow see the leftover lamb inside.

He folds his arms. 'Ma'am, I think perhaps you do.'

I scan past Willie's shoulder into the still-deserted yard.

Small mercy that at least none of the guests seem to be up yet, and this door is pretty sheltered from a casual walk past.

Where is Bruce anyway? If he wants to play games with the neighbour, then he should be here to deal with the fallout.

'I'm sorry,' I say. 'Bruce isn't here right now.'

Willie chews thoughtfully on the edge of his thumbnail. Then he nods, drops his hand, takes a short stride across to the old stone retaining wall and sits. 'I'll wait.'

'You can't do that.' I can hear the desperation in my voice.

Obviously, I'm not the only one, because for the first time Willie looks almost happy. 'I think I can.'

It says something about my stress levels that I contemplate the firearm stored in a locked safe beneath our bed to convince him to move. But now is not the time for weapons.

Not yet.

'Please go.' I try for my most cajoling tone. 'I will send Bruce over to you the moment he returns.'

'No.' A fly lands on Willie's beard and burrows in. He doesn't lift a hand to wave it away. Another takes up residence on his nose.

I try to keep my revulsion from my face. 'Look,' I say. 'I'll pay you, replace the animal. Whatever.'

He's already shaking his head.

There's movement through the shrubs from the direction of the suites and the sound of a door closing. Willie sees me glance that way and stands.

'It's not Bruce,' I say quickly as I register Monet, in running gear, striding with athletic grace towards the path above the cliff. 'It's just a kid – no one you need to worry about.'

'Maybe I should ask her if she's seen my lamb,' Willie says.

The rumble of the ute approaching stops me telling him what I think of that idea. Our gazes meet.

It's Bruce. It has to be.

Willie heads that way, almost running. Knowing Bruce, he'll relish the chance at confrontation with his family's old enemy. He'd better make sure none of the unpleasantness spills over to the guests.

I'm drawn around there, like someone passing the scene of an accident who can't look away. But as soon as the two men come into sight, I wish I'd stayed in the kitchen.

'A gun?' I ask through gritted teeth.

Willie turns – the weapon that he must have concealed at the door now in his hand – with guilt pinching his features. 'It's a rifle,' he says, like that explains it.

'That you're waving around at my husband while I have guests staying here?'

The idea of them hearing a shot teases something in my brain. A noise before dawn, loud enough to penetrate sleep but from far away. A bang? Willie shooting something on our land? By the stage set-up?

But then the memory – if that's even what it is – is chased away by the confrontation happening in front of me.

The tendons stand out on Bruce's thick neck, and one hand is gripping a bunch of Willie's coat, but when he sees me he's more a naughty toddler than enraged man.

This cannot happen. This stupid feud will not derail my day.

Willie must register the fury in my expression, because he hangs his head much like Bruce.

'I don't know nothing about no lamb,' Bruce mutters. His ears are pink, and he might as well flash a sign saying *liar*.

Willie doesn't reply, but the message in his planted feet, lowered brows and tense shoulders is obvious: *we're not done here.*

'Sort this out.' I hiss the order at Bruce.

'It's fine,' he says. 'You don't need to worry.'

A shriek splits the warm morning air.

Before I can properly make sense of what I'm hearing, it cuts off. Eyes wide, I spin towards the front of the house where it came from. Next to me, I sense the two men move in unison in the same direction, then I see their jaws hanging open like two machines in the clown game at the fair.

'Did you hear that?' Bruce asks.

I hold up a hand to silence him, as – carried on the softest of breezes – there comes the clatter of the glass door into the main dining room opening. I head that way at a run, the men following. We're almost to the open door when she emerges, stopping us cold.

Monet is pale, almost grey, and her eyes are so wide they're virtually bulging. She's gasping huge, shuddering breaths. Her hands extend towards me, shaky and pleading. 'You have to, you must... Please, you need to—'

'What's all the fuss?' My tone is sharp.

Monet gulps. 'There's someone down there.' She doesn't point or move her head to suggest where she might mean. Rather, her gaze is fixed on me, begging.

'Where?' I speak slowly and carefully. 'Who?'

Her lip trembles and she draws in another of those juddery breaths, swaying a little. 'On the trail. They didn't answer when I called, and they didn't move. Oh God, they haven't moved at all.'

'You did the right thing coming to the house,' I say. I sneak a look to Bruce, but there's nothing in his face to suggest he knows what the girl is talking about. This is not part of today's plan. I try for gentle. 'Show us. Someone's probably sleeping off a big night. I'm sure there's nothing to be worried about.'

Monet nods and then she catches her lower lip between her teeth, turns, and leads the way.

Monet – Sunday

As I lead Florence towards the trail, I know what we'll find. I knew as soon as I spotted the shape, despite the distance and the rocks obscuring the view.

But I can't say it.

My brain will not even think it.

As though by sliding away from this terrible thing I've seen and avoiding putting it into words, I can somehow make it not true.

I focus on the uneven path, carefully placing each foot. I listen for the breaths of those following. Florence's is comfortable and regular, but the breaths of the two men are harsher, the stranger's almost a wheeze.

For all my not thinking and not looking ahead, I stop exactly far enough from the thing on the trail for me to point at it but also keep it out of my line of sight.

'Wait here,' Florence commands.

It's not like I was planning to follow, but the two men obey as well, their close proximity filling the air with the scent of sweat. Acid burns the back of my throat, but I can't bring myself to take a step away and take me closer to what's on the path.

I gag. Their huge shapes are penning me in.

I can't breathe.

I can't breathe.

I can't breathe.

Scrambling over rocks and bushes, sending gravel spraying behind me, I clamber off the trail, up and around them, until I'm on the other side and several feet away. The hint of acid becomes bile, and then the pain au chocolat I grabbed from the pastries basket for breakfast is in my throat and out of my mouth and splattering into a small shrub. I heave and heave until my belly is empty, then I suck in air, tasting the fresh spray of salt from the water far below.

'You could have just asked us to move,' Bruce grumbles.

But he's wrong, too wrong, and too unfamiliar for me to begin to explain, as I wipe my hand across my mouth.

A muffled yelp from Florence has them turning away from me. She's further down the path now, at a spot that must be right where the figure lay. Her knees sag and I don't want to look but now I am, and I can't stop, and I know what it is there and then her hand covers her mouth as her already pale skin turns practically white.

She staggers close enough to us that her wild gaze can find her husband. 'See the girl inside and get rid of Willie. Now. Then bring a tarpaulin.'

Bruce nods in a way that's practically a salute.

'What is it?' the stranger asks. 'I'm not going anywhere.' He's got two hands out, trying to get past Bruce, but the bigger man doesn't let him. He forces him back up the path.

'You can't do this,' the stranger grumbles.

'And yet I am,' Bruce retorts.

They keep arguing as I trail them, but at a gesture from Bruce I turn off at the deck outside the main house. My legs almost fail me before I reach the closest chair, but then I'm sitting, and I whimper my gratitude that I no longer need to keep myself upright.

'Wait here,' Bruce orders.

I nod.

And then I'm alone. The grumble of their voices disappears around to the back of the house. I think of going to Maman or Dylan, but I can't make myself move. It's like my bones have softened into the shape of this chair, beneath this shade, under this sun, and they will not carry me all the way across the cobblestone path to the door of our suite. Besides, I can't picture actually forming the words to say what has happened.

Making it back up here and showing Florence was enough.

This is her place; she will know what to do. She can tell everyone what is down there on that trail. She can answer their questions.

As time blurs and my head falls onto my hands and my eyes close against the bright, hot sun rising higher and higher, it's tempting to cry. To throw my head back and scream. To put my foot to the ground in a stomp and squeal that *I will not have it*, like a spoiled toddler given the wrong-coloured crayon. But it's not really my style, Maman has never indulged such behaviour. And now more than ever I know it won't help.

No amount of wanting this to not be true will make it so.

Edward – Sunday

The low chime playing through the intercom feels like it's skipped my ears to set up an echo within my auditory cortex. With a low growl, I slam the lid of the laptop closed so I can no longer see the pages of numbers that refuse to remain in their allotted positions thanks to the throbbing in my head.

I glare at the speaker built into the wall panel. What is this fresh hell? Good-morning music? An alarm to make sure we're all up and about?

Next thing they'll have us doing group yoga or some equivalent nonsense for bonding. It's bad enough we have to play nice on stage and over meals. That fight last night after dinner was always going to happen. Put a group of people with more secrets than sense in a room and it's like setting a fuse.

At least I'd had something to take the edge off.

Despite the pain in my skull, I can't help a smile. Feeling a bit under the weather today is a small price to pay for last night. Best night of my flipping life.

The chimes stop and the small speaker crackles. Then Florence's voice rings out. 'Attention all guests. Could you immediately make your way over to the main house and gather on the deck outside the dining room? Please don't be alarmed. However, it cannot be understated that your presence is imperative at this time. Do not delay.'

Fear licks a hot, sharp shiver up my spine.

'Why?' I say out loud.

But the speaker doesn't answer my question. I stagger to it on legs made of Styrofoam. Hit the small buttons below it with my palm. Then, when nothing happens, I do the same with my clenched fist.

'Why?' I say again.

There's nothing but silence.

I squeeze my eyes closed and force the tightly strung nerve endings firing nonsensical signals to settle the *flip* down. No one could know what I've done yet.

Most likely there's some minor glitch in the event schedule, like we're needed on stage earlier. An event I could have told Florence would be a huge waste of time and money for her. Around ninety per cent of start-ups fail, and a large number within the first year. They should have invested more in making these suites genuine quality instead of taking the short cuts on details and finishes that are apparent to anyone with a brain. The gin is good, I'll give them that, but they've risked too much on this show. On a band that anyone can see is more likely to self-combust than blow everyone away.

That's the flaw with this whole event. Certain properties of relativity theory make time travel a theoretical possibility in some space-time geometries. However, not by this lot and not here. The Cedrics Band should remain in the past where it belongs.

If this isn't about the schedule, then maybe there's been an accident. That's it, they'll be getting us all together to warn us away from the docks because some dumb schmuck has run a boat full of fans into the side.

Or it could be that we're needed on stage earlier...

I shake my head so hard the pain doubles. *Idiot*. I already thought of that.

Am I thinking straight?

I try to probe my own thoughts for logical progression but find myself staring again at the silent speaker. What I need is more of whatever I had last night. Bugsy must have more, and that means I should be able to get my hands on some if I play these next few minutes right. Because last night I wasn't just thinking straight, I was on top of the whole flipping world.

I find my glasses – so that's why the numbers on the screen wouldn't stay put – and hope I'm not taking too long. I don't want to draw attention to myself arriving alone long after the others.

The others...

It doesn't hit me until I'm at the door of the suite that opens to the outside, my hand on the handle. They'll all be there. I have no idea what time it is, but I'm pretty sure given the angle of the rising sun and the racket being made by some offensively enthusiastic birdlife that it's well and truly past time that everyone should be up.

Leaning forward, I let my aching head rest against the cool door and try to think – something that seemed so easy to do yesterday afternoon and right through to the early hours of this morning, that now feels like the mental equivalent of trudging through thick mud. Not that I've ever done much of that. This faux-luxurious set-up is close enough to the great outdoors for my liking and it doesn't even have decent Wi-Fi.

This is fine. I'm boring Edward, they probably won't even notice me. There's something to be said for being the quiet one. Overlooked in a room, walked past in a corridor, unobserved at the side of a stage. They always treated me like I wasn't there. And in doing so practically handed over their secrets gift-wrapped. Back then I went along with everything, didn't complain, grateful like a patsy to be carried along on Jonny's ride, but I'm not a nerdy kid anymore. I'm not here to make friends.

Bugsy's the only one who's noticed that I've changed. We'd never have partied together back then the way we did last night.

I pull the door open and step outside, head high, ready for anything. Whatever was in those pills opened my eyes, and I have no intention of closing them.

Monet – Sunday

The wood of the deck creaks.

Someone's approaching.

I jerk my head up, my hands out in front of me to ward off I don't even know what, but it's only Florence and she's standing a safe distance away. Her husband's not with her but I refuse to think about what he might be doing.

Bring a tarpaulin.

Although the flicker of Florence's gaze appears to take in my raised hands, she gives me a beat to drop them before she speaks. In that moment is the shared understanding of what we've seen, of what she's left behind on that trail. 'Don't tell me Bruce has just left you here alone?'

I nod, unable to get any words out past the lump in my throat. Unwilling to think about the hot slick fear slicing through my belly. Because the thing on the trail was definitely, unmistakably, a body.

Someone is dead.

And from what I saw, it was no accident. Someone killed them.

Florence tuts. 'He's a foolish man. I'm so sorry, you must be upset.' Her gushing sympathy is a marked change from the annoyance when I interrupted her earlier. 'Do you want a drink? Water? Something stronger? You must want your mother. If you're okay here, I'll go and call everyone over.'

Again I nod, but this time I manage to croak, 'Water, please.'

She brings me a full glass before disappearing inside again, and I remember there was some kind of intercom system that she called us on that first day to tour the stage.

Oh no, the stage, *the show*. This cannot be happening.

I take the glass and it rattles against the table from the tremor in my hands. The cool of the water soothes a little, but after a couple of sips I place the glass down and wrap my arms around myself. The trembling that took over sometime on the trail now becoming a shiver.

'They're coming,' Florence warns softly as she steps back out onto the deck.

I swallow. 'You'll speak?'

She lifts her hand as though she's going to reach out, but then she lets it fall to her side without touching me. 'Of course.'

The murmurs of conversation as the others approach, all questioning what's happening, all still so bright and even annoyed that their morning has been so interrupted by the hostess without any warning, are muffled and distorted. It's as though I'm hearing it from a cold, calm patch on the sandy floor far beneath the ocean's surface.

They're all still bobbing happily above.

Even Maman's high-pitched cry of concern – '*Ma cherie*, what is wrong?' – when she rounds the corner can't really penetrate. I register the concern on her face and although only minutes ago I wanted her arms around me, now I can't bear the thought.

I drop my head forward, unable to meet her gaze, and certainly unable to answer any of the questions that are already spilling from her lips. 'Why are you over here already? What has happened? Are you hurt?'

I remain stiff as she tries to wrap her arm over me until she straightens and breaks contact.

Florence is here. Florence can tell them.

'What's going on?' Marco asks. 'I have a lot to do this morning.'

'Yeah,' Edward echoes from the back of the group, his arms folded across his sunken chest and his glasses reflecting the sun, making his expression unreadable.

Adam smirks at him. 'Got to go and do your makeup, do you? Can imagine that takes a while.'

Florence raises her hands for silence. 'I understand that this is a very busy day, and I wouldn't have called you over if this wasn't important. Very important. It really isn't something that I could put off sharing, nor is it something I wanted to have to say individually. It's much better that everyone hears this as a group.'

'Get on with it then,' Maman says. 'Whatever it is, my daughter is clearly upset.'

Florence doesn't reply immediately, and I understand that for all her apparent confidence, the words to explain what was on the trail aren't quite coming to her lips. It turns out that even for someone much older than I am, it isn't an easy thing at all to actually say.

'I don't have time for this,' Marco grumbles.

'Show a bit of respect, the kid is clearly upset,' Adam says.

'Well,' Marco replies, 'Connie used to get a bit emotional that time of the month, but it doesn't mean she had reason.'

I ignore the old director's sensitive contribution. We hardly need another corpse.

Despite the impatience from the others, Florence continues to hesitate.

Thinking back to the kangaroo conversation at dinner, I reckon her husband wouldn't have such qualms. But he isn't here, and I don't want to think about exactly what he might be doing.

The silence stretches. I can't bear it.

'Bugsy's dead,' I blurt.

Two words that explode across the group. Every head turns to me. Mouths open to speak but nothing comes out.

'No,' Connie whimpers.

I didn't plan on saying it, didn't in fact think I could. But the pressure of knowing meant that I just couldn't keep it inside any longer.

'She's right.' Florence has found her composure. 'He was on the trail leading down to the docks – the more challenging way around the cliffs. I'm no expert, but given we were all here last night, I'm guessing it must have happened last night or early this morning. Monet found him and came to me, and I've confirmed that he has passed.'

'How did this happen?' Maman asks.

With my head down again, I feel as she goes to embrace me and decides better of it. That allows me to make myself look at her and try to say I'm okay with my eyes, even if I don't know that it's true.

'Did he fall?' Edward asks. 'If it was that dangerous, there should have been signs, surely.' He's stepped forward and while he was unreadable before, he's now clearly incensed. 'This man was important to everyone here and this is a terrible tragedy. You invited us here as guests, and our safety is your responsibility.'

I expect an echo of outrage from his wife, but for the first time I notice she isn't by his side. Or anywhere else for that matter. I wasn't really paying attention – maybe she took herself inside at the shocking news.

Dylan frowns at Edward. 'Chill, bro. She hasn't even said how it happened.'

Florence clears her throat. 'As I said, I'm by no means an expert, but there is little doubt that this wasn't an accident.'

'How can you be sure?' Marco interrupts her to demand.

'Because he was found on an easy stretch of track. There were no signs of him having fallen.' She sets her shoulders. 'And one of his light-blue braces was looped tightly around his throat.'

As she speaks, my hand lifts to my chest, my fingertips slide along my sweat-damp collarbone. Whoever did this, their hands would have rested thus, they would have had to as they held the ends of the braces tight until he stopped struggling at all.

I imagine that the killer, in the glow of dawn or under the silvery light of the moon, watched the life sputter from his eyes. I was too far away to see properly, but I think the whites of them were red, like they'd nearly burst from the pressure. Also, his lips were like a swollen advertisement for bad fillers, and there were dark markings where the braces rubbed against his neck.

'He was strangled,' Florence says.

Questions echo in my head. Did the killer hesitate? Did they think about stopping and then decide they'd gone too far? Did Bugsy beg them to let him live, or did he rail against what was being done to him with rage and fire?

Why didn't I stop sooner when I saw the figure ahead? I got too close, way too close, and now it's like my brain has zoomed in on the details and I don't even know if they're actually true or a mix of every bad TV show I've ever seen.

'Did he have family?' I whisper.

'Ian?' Dylan asks. 'Doubt anyone would hitch their wagon to that.' He's dismissive.

'But you don't know,' I counter. 'He could have a partner, a child who'll have to go on without him.'

Dylan shrugs. 'I think only other rodents will miss him.'

Edward steps forward but not close enough to be within Dylan's reach. 'Have some respect, the man is dead.'

'Being dead doesn't change the kind of person he was,' Dylan says. 'And I'm not going to pretend otherwise. He was a parasite who got rich from other people's hard work – like this show.'

'The show is in a few hours.' My stomach flips at the thought. 'Will we be expected to go on stage as though nothing has happened?'

I see the moment the realisation of what's ahead ripples around the group.

The director is the first to speak. 'The cameras are all down there ready from yesterday and the networks have record audiences waiting. Not to mention the in-person audience.'

'God,' Adam mutters. 'They could arrive by boat any minute.'

I might have pulled the strings to get everyone here, but as far as the logistics and the schedule goes this is Florence's event. She's in charge here, so it's her that I turn to with the biggest question of them all.

'Are we supposed to act like a man hasn't lost his life this morning? And, more than that... what if the murderer is someone here?'

Florence – Sunday

Every single person gathered on the deck looks to me for answers. Answers I absolutely can't give them. Because there is a dead man on the trail by my house and millions of dollars resting on this band streaming a live show in about ten hours' time.

So, even as I'm trying to work out what this means for the Three Chains launch and everything I've put in place for today, I do what event planners and accommodation managers have been doing since the cavemen first visited each other's fires.

'Everything is under control,' I lie.

Not one of them believes me. Monet is perhaps the exception, but hers is more a desperate suspension of disbelief than any real conviction.

Edward pushes his glasses up higher onto the bridge of his nose. 'What do we do now?'

'We need the police,' Dylan says.

'Of course,' I agree. 'Contacting them is my next task, but I wanted to talk to all of you first and make sure you were all comfortable.'

'Comfortable,' Ivy cries, her hand flying to cover her mouth. '*Mon dieu*, he is dead.'

I force something I hope is a sympathetic smile in her direction. 'I understand this is all rather distressing. I meant that I wanted to keep you all informed. We have links directly to the nearest mainland police station and once we're done here I'll be contacting them immediately. In the meantime, we would appreciate none of you wandering that way.' I point in the direction of the trail, where Bugsy lies dead.

Ivy appears mollified by my explanation, relaxing into the chair Dylan has pulled over for her. The cynic in me wonders if it was just a way to get some of the attention, because she doesn't appear all that distressed.

I grab another chair and drag it to the group, but no one sits, so I stand behind it, my hands lingering on the back, using its bulk as a kind of a shield between me and them.

'You're preserving the crime scene,' Edward says knowingly.

I try not to make a face. 'Yes. Although the man was basically a stranger to me, I'm still shocked. I understand some of you were closer to him, and I want you to know that there's no need to be alone with your grief if you feel you need to talk to someone.'

I can hear my own words like they're some trite social worker character in an old TV sitcom, but I don't have any experience in what to say in a situation like this.

'It's not like he slipped,' Adam mutters, shoving a hand through his hair. 'Someone did this. Who?' He stares around at the group like the culprit will just leap out if he glares hard enough. 'I mean, he pissed off pretty much everyone here at some point, which makes it hard to narrow down.'

'I'd rather keep the speculation to the professionals, but it was an interaction that required some strength.' Despite my not wanting to talk about it, instinct has me pointing out that I couldn't have overpowered him and held the braces for as long as it took for him to suffocate.

Adam considers. 'That doesn't rule anyone out. Could have been more than one person. Not that I'm accusing anyone,' he adds quickly.

I'm not surprised we've reached this point, but I'd hoped it wouldn't be quite so soon. My chest is tight. If they knew what Bugsy had been saying to me. If they knew what I've done to make this weekend happen.

Unbidden, I think of Bruce in the early hours of this morning, sliding over in bed after we were sated, the adrenaline of the fight in the main room bringing us together even more violently than usual. He'd nuzzled my neck, his large arms around me, holding me in place. 'What did he mean?'

My stomach lurched, but I held my body still, aware of my husband's full length against me. 'Who?'

'That manager, Bugsy, when he touched you. He said something about secrets.'

Bruce doesn't do casual at the best of times. I should have realised how much he wanted to know, how unlikely it was that he accepted the issue as finished.

Now Bugsy is dead.

And it seems like there's a whole gang of amateur detectives within the band looking for answers.

I'm not going to ask Bruce about it. Nor about the hours he's been missing from our bed. Not with the strange noise I'm now certain I heard in the early hours. I'll know if he lies, and if it's happened again then I'll have to do something about it. Either way, this is my problem. It's my fault. Like it was the last time Bruce lost his temper.

I push the memories back and return to focus on my guests. This is a setback; it's not game over. It can't be. Get through today and everything will be worth it.

'Well, there appears to have been a struggle before he died,' I say.

'What do you mean?' Adam asks, when everyone else appears too stunned to say anything.

I hope I don't regret this, but I've started now. 'There was something caught under his nails. Possibly from the material that was around his throat. And his fingers are marked with cuts and abrasions. I'm guessing that he tried to fight off his assailant.'

Edward huffs. 'You sound like a crime drama and the whole struggle thing isn't exactly Sherlock-level stuff. He's hardly going to have been strangled to death willingly.'

My hand tightens on the back of the chair, and for the briefest moment I let myself imagine lifting it into his arrogant, doughy face. Instead, I keep my tone steady. 'I'm just saying that whoever did this might have injuries.'

At my pointed comment all eyes turn to Adam, but he doesn't flinch. He stares each of us down in turn, his head high, aware of the mark on his cheek. 'You all saw Dylan hit me last night, remember?' He points at the drummer. 'He's got a scratch on his neck. I keep my nails short for guitar, pretty sure I didn't give that to him.'

'Hold on,' Dylan replies, stepping towards Adam. 'You'd want to make sure you have some kind of evidence before you start making accusations. I'm not the one who argued with Ian in the yard after the dinner that first night. Yeah, I saw you.'

'I didn't touch him,' Adam growls.

Dylan gives an exaggerated shrug. 'You would say that.'

'It's not like you've ever liked the guy,' Adam is quick to reply. 'Only person in the world that called him Ian, wanting to show how not friends you are.'

I push the chair forward so it's between the two men. 'Now is not the time for accusations. I have to contact the police, and I'd rather there wasn't another incident needing to be reported.'

After a heavy pause, Adam takes a step back.

In response, Dylan makes a show of being relaxed. 'I'm not going to do anything that might hurt poor little Adam's feelings.'

Marco puts an arm around Connie and holds her against his side. 'There is more at stake here than you two bickering.'

'We can't be expected to play, can we?' Adam asks. 'The guy is dead.'

I've had longer than all of them, except a stunned Monet, to think about this – longer to try to reconcile what the dead man means for all the work I've done arranging this event. And I pride myself on being able to adapt. This is not going to wreck my plans.

But there's only one response that makes sense.

'When I alert the authorities, I expect they'll cancel the boats with the fans and the media and bring boats to transport each of you to the mainland as soon as possible.'

'What?' Edward is wide-eyed.

Monet wraps her thin arms around herself but when she speaks there's a strength in her voice that I can only admire.

'We have no choice,' she says. 'Whether the authorities insist or not, the show must be cancelled.'

Edward – Sunday

The director puffs up, his arms folded across his chest as he frowns at Monet's announcement that there will be no show.

'And who made you the boss, little missy?' he says with a sneer.

I sigh. These people really aren't particularly bright. 'There has been a death, likely suspicious. The child is not making some huge call on this, she's stating the flipping obvious.'

Monet shoots me a grateful look and it's tempting to point out to her I never wanted to do any of this anyway. Cancelling is no skin off my nose. In fact, getting off this island can only be a benefit. Ideally, our evacuation proceeds in a timely manner.

The girl is like a puddle of disappointment over the whole thing. My sympathy's limited. As much as I'm not into commercial music anymore, she doesn't need a gimmick to launch her song. It would be a success even if she wasn't who she is. She's more of a musician than the rest of these hacks.

Dylan's thoughts on the matter are impossible to read as he's crouched over, comforting Ivy, who seems to be exaggerating just how much she's affected by the whole thing if you ask me.

'Cancelled,' Adam mutters under his breath with a shake of his head.

With the manager gone and the show off, I reckon I'm watching the last ember of his career be snuffed in front of me.

He catches my eye. 'Are you smiling?'

I rearrange my features. 'Shock is a strange creature,' I reply, to avoid having to explain. The guy's a bomb waiting to go off.

I stare at him, blank faced, until he looks away.

Kaboom.

I can practically hear it and fight to control a giggle that comes out of nowhere. Little does he know.

'I'll let you know what the authorities say once I have made contact,' Florence is saying. 'Hopefully, after I speak to them I'll know some timings regarding boats and any other next steps. In the meantime, would anyone like some breakfast?' She makes the offer way too perky, too loud, too everything for the circumstances.

I guess there's no how-to-deal-with-a-dead-body chapter in the Host 101 manual.

No one takes her up on the offer of food, and she turns to go inside. I'm not surprised, it's not the kind of news that builds an appetite. Although, upon thinking of it, I find myself hungry and wondering if it would look strange if I followed her in.

Like he's heard my thoughts – maybe I'm not the only one after all – Adam calls after her, 'Wait.'

She stops and looks back towards us.

'What are you going to do with him?' he asks. 'With Bugsy.'

Okay, not what I was thinking.

Florence frowns. 'Do?'

'It's only going to get hotter, and you said it could be a while before the police can get here. And well, things...' – he gulps – '... can spoil quickly in the sun.' He's clearly trying not to gag.

Monet's face blanches.

Adam exhales hard through his nose. 'Do you need help with the body?'

'He's covered for now,' Florence says. 'I'll make sure I speak to the authorities about whether preserving the crime scene or other matters are more important. Thank you for the offer.'

For all that Marco told off Adam and Dylan for arguing about who might have motive to kill Bugsy, the moustached director barely waits for the door to close behind Florence before beginning to speculate.

'If she's right about the cause of death, then it's most likely to be a stranger, I reckon,' Marco says. 'Everyone here wants the show to happen, and this will certainly be some kind of disruption.' With a nudge from Connie that doesn't take an expert to read as *tell them*, he adds, 'I saw a bloke up by the main house getting hustled away by Bruce only a few minutes before they called us over.'

Monet inclines her head. Her arms are still wrapped around her waist, but she's less pale than she was before. 'Marco's right. There was a stranger up there when I went to Florence to tell her what I'd found.'

'What did he look like?' I ask.

She shrugs. 'I don't know. The full stereotype outback farmer, complete with hat, long coat, bushy beard.'

'That will be the neighbour, Willie,' Adam says. 'He has a gun and seemed like he knew what he was doing with it. He's the only other resident on the island as far as I can tell.'

'He's a friend of yours?' Dylan asks, not bothering with any subtlety in implying the two of them could be in it together.

I'm not the only one who looks to Adam for his response, the verbal ping-pong between the two men hard to ignore. I'd bloody get popcorn if I could. About time someone held Adam Rake accountable for being the biggest neanderthal arsehole on the planet.

Adam shakes his head. 'No, but he certainly seems to have a grudge of some sort. Still, him killing Bugsy? From what I saw, I can't imagine him bothering. The way that whoever did this... well... it seems pretty personal to me.'

Monet's gaze on him is intense. 'You think it was one of us.'

Dylan sneers. 'More accusations?'

'No,' Adam replies. 'Just saying Bugsy wasn't exactly Mr Popular.'

'Neither are you and you're still here.'

I can't help a smirk at Dylan's retort and wish I'd thought of it.

'The killer could be any one of us,' Monet whispers, visibly distressed.

'But most likely none,' Ivy says quickly, her tone gentle. 'You mustn't be afraid.'

Connie eases away from her husband. 'No one is going to hurt you,' she says quickly, then ducks back behind Marco's bulk.

Monet gives her a small smile in return.

'Well, we don't actually know that is true,' I can't help pointing out. Even as I say it, I'm realising it's going to draw attention my way, but I can't seem to stop the words tumbling from my mouth.

'Any one of us could be next.'

Adam – Sunday

I don't know if it's the feeling I have that none of this is real, but I'm not afraid. Despite Edward's blunt announcement that we're all possible targets.

No one else seems too worried either. The mood is more curious, like we're talking about the latest episode of a hot new TV mystery.

Not that any of this is happening to us.

Not that a man we all know is dead.

Even the usually anxious Edward doesn't appear too fussed. I guess it would be hypocritical to sob over someone nobody much liked, but I swear the guy's almost happy. He's bright-eyed and strangely bouncy. It takes me a second to notice what's different about him from yesterday, but then it hits me – he's alone.

'Where's your wife?' I ask.

He blinks at me like I'm speaking a foreign tongue.

'Lilah? No, Lara,' I correct. 'Sorry, I'm not always that great with names.'

Edward looks around. 'I'm pretty sure she was just here.'

'No, she wasn't,' Marco says in that authoritative tone that makes my teeth grind together. 'I noticed you came out alone when Florence called us all over here. That's right, isn't it, Connie?'

She nods obediently.

'I meant,' Edward says quickly, 'that she was intending to come over here the last I saw of her. She said for me to go on ahead since the message from Florence sounded urgent. Maybe she needed to change her outfit or something. She does a lot of that.'

'Huh? Change her outfit because someone's been killed?' I'm trying to understand, but he's lost me.

'No, you simpleton. Not because of Bugsy, she doesn't know about any of this.' He over-pronounces each word so it's clear. 'Because she didn't come over here with me. She's back at the suite.'

'But didn't she want to know what all the fuss was about?'

He shrugs. 'I'm her husband, not her keeper.' Then he glances back in the direction of the suites. 'Although, she probably should have come by now.'

'A man has been killed,' I say. It's petty, I know it, but I copy his slow tone. 'Shouldn't you perhaps go and check on her?'

'Why do you care anyway?' he snaps. But then he seems to realise that my confusion over the situation is echoed on everyone else's faces and a familiar grimace returns to his expression. He pushes at his glasses and sighs. 'Look, I might not have been entirely honest.'

'About what in particular?' Dylan asks.

Edward exhales in a miserable sigh. 'The truth is that I don't know where she is. She must have headed out before I woke up. That's if she came in at all.' He lowers his voice to a mumble. 'I thought maybe she'd found somewhere else to sleep.'

'Like where?' Marco fires the question.

But Dylan doesn't give Edward a chance to answer, instead shaking his head at me. 'You just can't help yourself, can you?'

'I haven't seen her,' I say.

'You sure about that?' Dylan presses. 'I mean, she's female and you have a reputation for not exactly being discerning. No offence.' The latter is directed at Edward, who doesn't seem like he's even listening.

'I'm sure.'

I can feel all the others watching me for a reaction. They're judging, I know it. And Dylan's right, I do have a pretty bad reputation with women, but they all should know that not everything published online is the truth. And besides, I've always been straight up about what I'm offering.

'Come on,' Dylan says, mock cajoling. 'This isn't some game, just tell us.'

My hands clench, and it's only Ivy and her kid's presence that stops me taking a swing to shut his stupid mouth. No matter how many times I promise not to bite at one of his digs, he just keeps pushing and pushing.

I deliberately keep my voice even. 'We all get what you're trying to say. And I repeat, in case you didn't hear me properly the first time, that I haven't seen her.'

Not that she wouldn't have been receptive. The woman didn't so much flirt as radiate a pathetic kind of sexual hopefulness. Like she'd engage with you, if you gave her half an opening. That typical groupie who'd latch on to anyone in the band. Just being near her made me uncomfortably aware of how often I've taken up one of those offers. But I'm past wanting to be with anyone who's not interested in me alone.

Dylan puts his hands out, palms up, the picture of a good guy trying to do the right thing. 'You might as well just tell us.

Put poor Edward out of his misery. Maybe we could go look in your suite?'

Frustration propels me forward. 'I don't want you anywhere near my things. The chick isn't there, okay? Can you get it through your thick head?'

He's so close now I can't miss the amused lift of his eyebrows. 'You're sounding pretty defensive for an innocent man.'

I lunge, pushing the empty chair aside, but a slender hand on my chest stops me dead.

Monet stands between us, glares at us each in turn. 'This male posturing isn't helping. You're supposed to be grown-ups.'

I let her nudge me backwards with the slightest of pressure. 'Male posturing?' I repeat.

'Look it up,' Dylan says. 'Maybe if you'd bothered to see your niece, like, ever in her whole life, you'd know that she's damn smart as well as extremely talented.'

Monet's hands are on her hips and she raises her eyebrows at Dylan. 'Seriously, not helping.'

But she doesn't need to worry about me losing my temper anymore. I deflate like one of those festival tents being taken down when the show's over. Dylan's right. It was one thing to follow Ivy's order to keep away, but it's clear I've missed out. The kid found a body a few minutes ago and she's the one calming us down? Impressive.

She's the only family I have left, and she's a virtual stranger.

'You could know all this,' Dylan says, clearly unable to resist rubbing it in.

My arms fold across my chest. Classic defensive pose, yeah, but I can't seem to stop myself. 'And you'd have let me hang around?'

Dylan laughs, looks at Monet, then Ivy. 'You reckon I'd have had a say in the matter?'

He's right. These women are not under any man's control. I hesitate, unwilling to share the promise I made to Ivy that terrible night. The one that now – of all the things I've messed up – seems like the one vow I really should have broken.

'I was doing everyone a favour,' I say. This at least is true. 'You all know the kind of guy I am. A screw-up, a failure. No one needs that in their lives.'

'I did.'

Monet's words are soft but unmistakable, and they land so hard in my chest that it's all I can do not to bend double.

Dylan shakes his head. 'You weren't involved because it might have been all a bit hard for you. Because you couldn't handle responsibility.'

I suddenly remember a time when Pop told Jonny off for something. He covered his ears, closed his eyes and ducked his head in an attempt to disappear.

But there's no escaping this.

I drag a hand across my eyes. 'I didn't have a choice.'

Finally, Ivy meets my gaze and the pain in those gorgeous eyes sucks the breath from me. 'You always had a choice.'

'I don't know why we're talking about this,' I say. 'We can all join in with our theories on how I've failed everyone later. Right now, we need to remember a man has died.'

Monet – Sunday

At Adam's reminder that Bugsy's dead, Dylan and Marco return to theorising about what happened to him.

'I knew I should have been recording,' Marco says.

'Now that would make some interesting footage,' Dylan agrees.

I want to scream at both of them. *A person is dead, it's not entertainment.* But I'm more concerned about Edward's wife.

Maybe Lara was annoyed with him last night and stormed off, but the longer we're all together and she stays away, the stranger her absence becomes. She didn't seem the type to want to miss out on anything.

Edward doesn't seem worried that his wife hasn't appeared, but I bring my hands together in a kind of clap that gets everyone looking at me. 'Maybe Lara saw something.'

Edward lifts his head at that. 'Like what?'

I wave towards the trail. 'Like maybe she saw what happened down there.'

I don't know why I have such trouble saying the words, when my brain is ringing with them over and over. *Bugsy is dead.*

'We need to find her in case she knows what happened.' I feel like I'm speaking to myself.

But then I feel Adam's gaze on me. 'Why don't we all check our suites?' he says. 'Then after Florence is done talking to the police, we can check the house.'

I flash him a grateful smile and look to the others. 'Please. Then we'll know she's fine.'

There are a few grumbles, but everyone separates to check for her.

In only a few minutes, everyone is back on the deck, and there is no Lara to be found in the suites.

'Florence is still inside,' Maman says.

She was the one to wait in case Lara showed up here.

Edward does a pompous little cough to get everyone's attention. 'You know, I didn't want to mention it before, but Lara said she woke and thought someone was in our room the first night.'

'Do you think it could all be related?' Dylan asks.

'I figured she was imagining things,' he admits.

Despite the sun on my back, already hot enough to burn, I realise I'm still shivering. A slight trembling through my whole body I can't seem to control. Sheer will stills one hand, but it's like the rest of me vibrates all the more to compensate.

Bugsy is dead.

But Lara is only missing.

Missing is something I can wrap my head around. It's *home late and forgot to call*, it's *been too busy to get in touch*, it's *wandered off into the bushland and can't find her way back*. It's not dead.

Missing is also something I can do something about.

'I'm going to look for her,' I announce. 'Properly search the place. We all should. If we work together, we can get it done fast.'

'How would we know where to start?' Maman asks. 'Isn't it dangerous? We should wait for the help.'

I know the question is more about her own physical limitations and fears for me – *be careful* – than a lack of sympathy, but internally I flinch at how it must sound to the others.

'We'll pair up and spread out,' I reply.

The alternative is to sit here and wait for help and allow something truly terrible to happen.

Something else.

The swish and clunk of the door opening announces Florence returning.

'What did the police say?' I ask before anyone else can speak.

'They'll be on their way as soon as possible, along with a boat to return you all to the mainland, but in the meantime we have a small problem.' She takes a breath. 'I'm really sorry, but the power has just gone out.'

Now she's said it, the absence of the air-conditioning hum is obvious.

Marco sniffs his dismay. 'Surely, in such an isolated locale, you have contingency plans for such an occurrence.'

'Yes,' Florence is quick to assure him. 'We have back-up generators, but they can be temperamental in the heat. Bruce is heading out to restore things now.'

'We have a problem, too,' I say. 'Lara is missing.' When Florence appears confused, I add, 'Edward's wife. He hasn't seen her since last night, and neither has anyone else. We were just discussing going to search for her,' I explain.

Florence frowns. 'Now?'

I'm on my feet, ready to get moving. 'Now's as good a time as any.'

'Do you think she's in danger?' Florence asks.

'No,' Edward says.

Just as I say, 'Possibly.'

Florence looks from one of us to the other and seems to decide Edward would know best. 'It's not that I'm not concerned,' Florence says. 'The safety of all my guests is highly important to me. However, there are things I must attend to.'

'We understand,' I say. 'But the rest of us can look.'

'You're right, it has to be better than sitting here.' Adam's support is as welcome as it is unexpected.

'This is nonsense,' Marco says. 'We don't even know this silly woman. Chances are she's busy looking in a mirror somewhere and has lost track of time.'

'Steady on,' Dylan says, when it doesn't seem Edward will defend his wife. 'I'm sure she's not trying to cause any trouble. She doesn't know Ian is dead, and we can't rule out that whoever did that is still here somewhere.'

'Which is the reason we need to find her.' My voice cracks.

'I'm not jumping because a child says so. If there's danger, we should stay together.' Marco gives me a fake-kind look. 'Clearly, finding the body has been quite the shock, and you are not thinking straight right now.'

'What?' I sputter.

'It's obviously distressing, but that doesn't mean we should all pander to your whim.' He looks around him for support.

I think of Connie when I was alone with her at the cave, talking about how he's old-fashioned. She sounded almost scared.

He doesn't scare me. 'I don't understand what you mean.' I sugar-coat each word. 'Please explain.'

He frowns. 'It's obvious. You're rather sheltered with your upbringing and the cosseted life you lead, and it's not hard to see that you're quite... delicate. We can't be expected to follow along just because you say so.'

'I'm what?' From somewhere behind me, Maman snickers. 'Listen here. You don't know me at all. You can take your misogynistic judgement and shove it up your—'

'Excuse us.' Connie tugs at Marco's arm and draws him away.

The anger in me feels good, better than the hopelessness of before. I watch as she whispers in his ear.

Connie practically shoves Marco towards me a minute later.

'We'll search for the missing woman down at Hawk Bay.' He makes the announcement like he's been on board the whole time.

I'm about to suggest other areas when Maman interjects. '*Excusez-moi*, everyone, you seem to be ignoring the possible danger.'

'No, it's all the more reason for us to find her,' I counter. 'If she's hurt then every minute might count.'

'Wait, this might help,' Florence says. 'I don't know.' She's holding out a tablet of some sort. 'It's the security footage,' she explains. 'Our system is mostly for the possums and isn't reliable, but it managed to capture something last night.'

We gather around her, all of us close enough – thanks to the small screen – that the tension radiating from everybody builds to an almost tangible thing coated in the scent of nervous sweat. I brace myself and hold my breath as she presses play.

It's night and the footage is blurry, but the figure that resolves as it gets closer and closer in the darkness is unmistakably Bugsy. The time stamp in the corner shows three a.m. He totters across the screen, gait unsteady but moving with what appears to be a clear purpose. A few seconds later he turns off towards the cliff and then he's out of shot.

Breaths are released around me, the relief universal. It's clear I'm not the only one glad not to see anything more.

'Is that it?' Marco is scathing. 'That tells us nothing.'

'Wait,' Florence says.

Like the others, I return my focus to the screen. Another figure appears. They move in the same direction as Bugsy, then turn onto the same trail.

'They're following him.' Adam more breathes than speaks the words, but I think he's right.

The person striding after Bugsy is wearing dark clothing, maybe jeans and a hoodie, and they have a cap pulled low on their head. Way too much for the heat unless you are particularly trying to disguise yourself.

In the last moment, the figure turns back towards the house. Towards the camera.

'It's Jonny,' Dylan cries.

And I feel my heart stutter in my chest.

Edward – Sunday

Dylan has officially lost the plot. There's no way the grainy, pixelated figure on that cheap screen is Jonny. No way at all. He's too tall, too pale and, most importantly, far too alive.

'Get fucked,' Adam says, jerking away. 'It is not. You're fucking dreaming.'

I've rarely found reason to be in agreement with the older Rake brother, but on this occasion I think Adam's right. I don't know who that is, but it's not Jonny. It can't be Jonny.

Florence has stopped the footage on the clearest shot of the man's face. Ivy leans so close to the screen her breath makes little fog patches, Dylan at her side only a little more restrained.

'*Non*,' she says eventually on a choked whisper, lifting her head with tears in her eyes. 'It is not him. It is a stranger.'

At her mother's words, Monet sags a little. 'Now we know what the guy looks like, we can keep an eye out for him.' She looks to Florence. 'Was there any other sign of him?'

Florence shakes her head. 'It looks as though he didn't come back this way.'

'There you go,' Monet says. 'Most likely he did what he came to do and probably left the island.'

No one argues.

She straightens. 'As planned, we split up and look for Lara, while taking all reasonable precautions to be safe. We should report back within the hour, and make sure no one is left vulnerable.'

'What about me?' I ask.

Around me, eyes widen, blink. Had they forgotten I'm even here? It wouldn't be the first time.

'It's nice and all that you are deciding what should happen in this search for my wife, but none of you have thought to actually include me.'

There's more blinking. At least Monet has the grace to look shame-faced, and she's probably suffering remnants of shock.

I would know how to diagnose her symptoms. The voice of my tell-everyone-she's-a-nurse wife is so loud in my head, I actually sneak a glance behind me, making sure Lara's not standing behind my shoulder like she always does. Always with something to say. Often some made-up nonsense about the band, but failing that, a medical opinion with more bravado than expertise.

Her appearance would cut all these do-gooders' searching short, quick smart.

But there's no Lara.

Monet gives me a sympathetic look. 'Do you want to wait at your suite in case she comes back?'

'No,' I blurt.

Immediately, I second-guess myself. Would it be better if I waited there? But it's too late, the words are out, and backtracking will make me seem strange. It's hard enough as it is to act normal with the comedown from whatever Bugsy gave me last night still flaring through my system.

Lara could probably give me a medical lecture about that too, if she was here.

The discovery of Bugsy's death has made it decidedly more difficult to get hold of more of those pills. However, unless he had his whole stash on him, it's not necessarily impossible.

'What do you want?' Monet asks.

More drugs, I think.

That would shock them all. But I don't say it. Chemical improvements to my mental state will have to wait until this whole search-and-rescue thing is over.

'I want to get out there, even though, as I said, I'm sure there's nothing to be worried about. Maybe I could check the stage area?'

Dylan and Adam share a look that I can't read. Since when do they have unspoken communication? They hate each other, don't they? Adam was awful to both of us back in the day. Being the mature, logical one, I figure his clear failure in life has evened the score, but Dylan's not so logical.

They're looking at me now. Did I say something out of place?

My usually infallible brain function is just not up to scratch, and it's making me doubt everything I say. I'll have to remember this for when I'm off this godforsaken island and back with my boys. I imagine sharing with them a – modified – version of this moment, with the conclusion: *And that is why you don't take drugs*.

I stifle a laugh at the idea, covering it with what I hope passes for a sound of distress, as I realise they've kept talking and I've missed it.

Oops.

'What did you say?' I ask. 'Sorry, maybe I'm more worried than I realised.'

'That's okay,' Monet says. 'I can only imagine how you must be feeling.'

'I'll stay with Ivy and Monet, and we'll search the building here,' Dylan says. His tone suggests no argument.

Which makes me want to argue. Adam, too, appears less than thrilled with that leaving us as a team.

'Maman needs to stay close because of her sunstroke,' Monet says.

Ivy sighs and nods. 'It's true, I'm still feeling some effects.'

My argument dies in my throat.

'However, I have a solution,' Monet continues. 'Adam and I will head for the dock we arrived at on the first day. Marco and Connie can cover the other bay as they suggested, and you can join with Dylan and Maman to look around here and up behind the distillery. If that's okay with you. We'll assign the stage when we return.'

Stay here? Possibly get a chance to search Bugsy's room for more of those pills? *Halle-flipping-lujah*.

I pretend to consider. 'I guess.'

Dylan looks like he has something to say.

'Edward needs to be somewhere central,' Monet insists. 'Unless you want Adam to go off alone?' She dares him to argue with a look.

'I'm fine alone,' Adam says.

Monet glares at him. 'No.'

'That sounds good,' I interrupt before more arguments can start. 'We probably shouldn't waste any more time.'

Dylan frowns at me.

Did I sound too keen then, when I wasn't in a hurry to search before? I swear he mutters something to Ivy that I can't hear. Now she's looking at me, too.

I wish I'd never spoken at all.

'I'm not sure this is such a good idea,' Florence says. 'Maybe you should all wait in your suites until the police get here.'

If I could be honest, that sounds like a great idea to me, but from the shakes of heads around the group it seems Monet isn't the only one too amped up to sit around.

'No,' Dylan pronounces. 'We'll head out, but we'll be sensible.'

'Speaking of the suites, Florence, why is one empty?' Monet asks.

Florence doesn't frown so much as blink her annoyance. 'I don't understand.'

'Wouldn't it make sense to have it used? By media, or a VIP.'

Florence holds the tablet against her chest like a shield. 'Marco insisted on it being exclusive.'

'No, I didn't,' the man himself replies.

'Then there must have been some miscommunication,' Florence says. Her tone is level but there's such venom in her look that I'm surprised Marco is still upright.

Monet looks thoughtful. 'Can those staying close to the house have the key card to check in there?'

'If you wait here, I'll get the card for your search.'

This just got interesting. Maybe this is the opportunity I need to wipe anyone's head of anything I've said that was out of place. I might not be thinking at my best but it's better than any of these schmucks. Florence is an unknown, and I get the impression she doesn't think much of me. She might regret that.

'That was... odd,' I say thoughtfully when she's gone. 'Guilty conscience?'

Adam shrugs. 'Maybe the whole thing is getting to her. I still can't believe Bugsy's dead.'

'Maybe,' I agree. 'Or maybe she has something to hide.'

It's like one of the science experiments I used to do so well at school that Adam would ridicule me for. But in this case, it's my words I set off, and the effect is the ripple of reaction around the group. They're considering it now, thinking she might be concealing something. No one is thinking about my behaviour anymore.

They're suspicious of Florence.

Sometimes it's almost too easy when you're the smartest person in the place.

Florence – Sunday

Despite the old, thick walls of the main house, the heat is already beginning to seep into the kitchen. It's closer here, more demanding than in the city where you're never too many steps from air-conditioning, in the knowledge that we're one power failure from being stranded at the mercy of the relentless sun. Only the nearby sea keeps that knowledge from overwhelming me.

Now, without the help of the air-conditioning, every movement creates more heat and unpleasant friction. And all my good intentions to ignore what the temperature might be doing right now to the body on the trail are failing me.

It's Adam's fault. If the washed-up guitarist hadn't brought up the idea of rotting meat, I'm sure I wouldn't be thinking about it.

Maybe I should have had Bruce move the body to the cool room, but it is a crime scene. I'll talk to Bruce about it when he gets back. If he ever gets back. I don't know what's taking him so long.

Bugsy's death has changed the schedule for today and my plans must adapt.

I'd laugh if it wasn't so dreadful.

There's an old saying in the event-planning world: 'You can't plan for a vicious personal murder on the day of the show.'

Okay, there isn't any such saying. And standing in front of

the half-prepared salad – that no one will eat – knife poised in my hand, I recognise the hysteria threatening to break through my ever-shredding control and breathe in deeply to try to calm it.

I can't let the guests see how rattled I am.

At least I'm not the only one. Everyone's been thrown by Bugsy's death. It's one thing to wish him dead and another to see his braces wrapped around his neck.

Then there's the missing woman.

The husband seemed rudderless, like he doesn't know what to do without her direction.

In the brief time inside, away from the others, I'd snuck a look at the news headlines. After the pictures on the gossip sites of the band together, I figured the source might want to break such a huge scoop.

But there's been nothing.

With Willie knowing at least something about what happened – and I'm still not sure how Bruce convinced the man to leave – if it was him, the news would be everywhere by now, wouldn't it?

I even checked the fan blog that Bruce pointed out by the Ricky character in case they actually had some real inside information, but the stupid thing wouldn't load. A crashed website isn't going to do much.

Today is salvageable. It must be.

And if I focus on what needs to be done, then I can avoid thinking about the flies already circling the manager's body. Ever-present on this remote island, their plump black bodies, spindly legs and glassy eyes are drawn primarily to areas of moisture. Eyes. Mouth. The flesh wounds where he struggled to stop what turned out to be unstoppable.

I drag my thoughts into the present and the salad ingredients piled around me on the bench. I begin to chop. The knife glides through the flesh of the cucumber like it's not even there. Bruce has a thing for sharp blades.

Steps sound in the hallway.

I swivel towards the door, expecting Bruce, but it's not him. A sudden hot sting blooms on the end of my finger. I look down and my stomach rolls.

There's so much blood for such a small nick.

I stand, unable to move, as the bright-red liquid seems to pulse out of my fingertip with every thud of my heart. It drips onto the plastic board, runs in small rivulets where it finds the moisture from the cucumber. Eventually, it stains the pale-green flesh of the nearest piece pink.

'Are you okay?' Dylan asks. 'That looks nasty.'

He's right. The blood is spreading. I grab at a nearby tea towel and wrap it around the injury.

'It's just a scratch.' I switch to hostess mode while cradling my hand against my chest. 'Can I help you?'

'Ivy's feeling the heat and could use some cold water.' He frowns because I'm still staring. 'Are you sure you're okay? You look like you need a shoulder to cry on.'

I study him.

With Jonny dead, Edward retired and Adam lurching from one disaster to another, it's Dylan who the fans have held closest to their hearts. I guess his dull kindness might have an appeal for some.

I straighten. 'I'm fine. Nothing a bit of organisation can't handle. There's a bottle of water in the fridge that should still be cold.'

I cross to the fridge but let him carry the large bottle of

water. You'd think he deserves a medal from the way he acts like he's done me a huge favour. Then I lead him back out to the main dining area.

I wince as I enter the large, rapidly warming space. Somehow, after what happened with Bugsy and then with the power going out and the search, I forgot to clear away the largely untouched breakfast things. The fresh fruit has begun to soften and weep at the edges. The pastries, once crisp and plump with fruit, now shine with congealing fats.

'I was just about to sort this out,' I say.

'Do you need a hand?' He doesn't mention that I was clearly already trying to prepare food for later.

'No, you look after Ivy. I'll get a Band-Aid for this and get to it.'

I notice Ivy is out on the deck, under the shade, presumably waiting for him to bring the water. None of the others have returned.

'Where's Edward?' I ask. 'Wasn't he with you?'

Dylan shifts his weight. 'He wanted to keep searching.'

'Alone?'

He lifts his chin. 'He's a big boy, and he was pretty determined. I'm sure he won't be long.'

Interesting. On the surface, it makes sense that he'd be more driven than the others to look for his wife; however, Monet seemed to be the main instigator of the search.

'I'm sure he'll be back soon,' I agree. 'Is there anything else I can do for you?'

'No, that's fine, thanks.' His relief that I'm not calling him on his disregard for Edward's safety is obvious. He scans the space, registering the bare mantel. 'What about the damage from last night? At least let me help with that.' He gestures to where they broke the figurine. 'How much?' Dylan asks with the certainty of a man who has discovered everything has a price.

For a second, I think about asking for cash. The money could be useful. But instead, I shake my head. 'No. We'll sort it out with insurance.'

His smile crinkles his eyes. 'If not, make sure you bill me.'

'Oh, you can be sure I will.'

After cleaning up lunch preparations, I escape to check the suites, aware the next sweep of the area could be by the authorities and knowing I need to salvage something from today.

When I leave Bugsy's suite, Edward is outside. He freezes at the sight of me.

'What are you doing?'

'Nothing,' he says. Then, as though realising he needs more, 'I thought I should check if Lara's in there.'

'There's no one in here,' I say. 'And I'm sure the authorities would prefer we don't disturb anything.'

'Of course.' But frustration twists his features. 'Speaking of the authorities, is there any update?'

'The power is still off, making ongoing communication difficult, but we're certain they're on their way.'

We walk side by side towards the main house.

'Shouldn't you have backups in case of emergencies?' he asks. 'Battery power, for example?'

'We are doing our best.'

'Maybe your best isn't good enough.'

I stop, narrow my eyes. 'Perhaps you'd like to let this go before I start theorising exactly what happened to your wife.'

It's a stab in the dark provoked by annoyance that he won't

let this go and his odd behaviour. It lands, with the colour draining from his face.

On a roll now, I lean in close. 'You know,' I say conversationally, 'we have more than one security camera on the property.'

'Really?' It's strangled.

'Really.' I fight a smile at his discomfort.

His eyes dart around. 'Where?'

'Wouldn't you like to know?' I murmur.

Before he can ask anything else, the others return from their search for his missing wife.

Monet – Sunday

The glasses of cold water Dylan poured when Adam, Edward and I joined him and Maman on the deck are all gratefully emptied before anyone puts the obvious into words.

'There's no sign of Lara anywhere,' Adam says. He seems to be looking particularly hard at Edward as he says it, but I can't tell if it's worry that he'll react badly or something else. Adam didn't try to hide his surprise when Edward explained he'd gone to search alone. I, too, didn't think the accountant had it in him, but people do strange things when their loved ones are threatened.

Florence left us with the promise that the generator would be working soon. Apparently, Bruce is close to fixing it.

'Maybe Marco and Connie have had better luck in looking for Lara,' I say.

They haven't returned yet, and I can't say I'm that sad about it. When we split to look for Lara, Connie made sure to tell me as she passed how she was looking forward to interviewing me about finding Bugsy. The threat if I refuse was implicit in the way she squeezed my arm too tightly.

Hopefully, the police will get here soon and make talking to them impossible.

'I fear something else terrible has happened.' Maman's suggestion is a whisper. 'These things come in threes, you know.'

I shoot Dylan a questioning look. Not because of my mother's tendency towards the dramatic, but at the weak, thready nature of her voice.

His shrug is almost imperceptible, but then he mouths, 'She says she's okay.'

Part of agreeing to her coming to the island, given everything the doctors told us, was that she promised not to lie.

If she says she's okay, then she must be.

'How long do we give them?' Edward asks.

Then they're all looking at me, and it's all I can do not to tell them to ask an adult. I wish I was still preparing to play. I think of my white outfit, such a contrast to my current sweat-soaked activewear.

Tendrils of hair are plastered against my neck, and I'm pretty sure my ponytail is hanging limp down my back.

'Five minutes,' I say, more decisively than I feel. 'If Marco and Connie haven't returned from their search in five minutes, then Dylan and Edward can go looking for them.'

I glare around the small group, daring one of them to argue. If they're going to make me decide, then they can do what I tell them.

Edward sputters but says nothing.

The five minutes pass with Dylan getting more water, along with a plate of crackers and dips, from inside with an apology from Florence, who says she will report to us about the next steps as she knows anything.

With time up and a promise to be careful, Dylan and Edward head for the trail down to Hawk Bay, where the older couple said they'd be.

'Maybe I should have gone instead of Edward,' Adam says as soon as they're out of sight.

Maman is as far away from him as it's possible to be without being in the sunshine, and her face remains blank at his words.

I sigh. 'Yep, like you have my whole life, pretend he doesn't exist.'

Apart from a small thinning of her lips, my sarcasm doesn't get any rise from her. It's not that I wanted to force her to interact with him, but it's partly why I sent the other two away.

Adam is doing a good impression of not noticing our side conversation.

'They'll be fine,' I say loudly.

When neither Maman nor Adam reply – I think she's asleep again – I stalk over to the far edge of the deck, sit on the ground, dangle my feet and, with a glance to make sure they can't see me, slide the device I swung past my suite to get out of my pocket and stare at the screen. It all made so much sense before I came.

'What's that?'

I jump at Adam's question and move to cover it. 'None of your business.'

He flops to the ground beside me. 'That's me.' He leans over and peels my fingers back gently, so I could snatch them away, but I'm too tired to bother covering the links that basically encapsulate Adam's electronic footprint. 'Why do you have all that information?'

I can't tell him everything, so I settle on a part-truth. 'I was curious. It doesn't matter anymore because I thought I might be able to contact the outside world, but the part that let me go online has been taken from our suite.'

'You really should—'

I jump up and growl, 'You forfeited the right to have a say in my life when you turned down every invitation Maman sent and ignored all the letters I wrote.'

'But…' He trails off, unable to offer a defence. He pats the deck beside him. 'I'm here now.'

I want to run and want to sit. So I do neither. 'You want to talk all of a sudden? Tell me, was that my father on that security footage?'

He hesitates and stupid hope fills my chest so I feel I could burst.

But then he shakes his head. 'No.'

I sag and he's up in front of me, his hands keeping me upright. 'It's not so much that I really think he's alive or have any proof he didn't die, apart from the limited DNA material they found,' I say. 'But Dylan seemed so sure. I don't know. I just think if he is alive…'

'Then he wouldn't miss this reunion,' he finishes for me.

The return of Dylan and Edward breaks what I think is my first real connection with my uncle, and we hurry back to now-awake Maman's side. Dylan's already talking before he reaches the deck. 'Marco and Connie aren't down there. In fact, it doesn't look like they went that way at all. Did any of you see them?'

I shake my head, and Adam and Maman do the same.

'He didn't even want to search for Lara,' Edward points out.

'What are they up to?' I ask.

'That's what I'm going to find out.' Dylan is already heading for Marco and Connie's suite. He's banging hard on the door before the rest of us get across the courtyard area. Even Maman walks across. Whether she didn't want to miss the action or didn't want to be left alone, I don't know, but she seems a little brighter.

'There's no answer,' Dylan says. His hand goes to the lock.

'You can't just go in there,' I argue, a sick feeling in my belly. With what Connie knows about me, I don't want to piss her off.

Dylan isn't swayed. 'Watch me.'

My touch on his shoulder halts him. 'Are you planning on breaking the door down? Maybe we should find Florence and get the master key or whatever it's called?'

'With the power off, the door should just open, shouldn't it?' Adam asks.

'Unlikely,' Dylan says. 'Usually, this kind of card-reading lock is battery powered.' At Edward's puzzled look, he adds, 'I've experienced a hotel or two with a power outage.'

There's the click of heels on the path. It's Florence with a purposeful expression on her face. 'I wondered where you'd all disappeared to.'

'We need to get into this suite,' Dylan says.

Florence hesitates. 'I'm not sure I can really—'

'You unlock the door all civilised like,' – Dylan's polite tone makes his words more unsettling – 'or I break the door in. They should have been back by now, and I'm pretty sure you don't want to be responsible for more casualties, do you?'

Monet – Sunday

Florence hesitates, looking from Dylan to the closed door, then swipes a card across the lock. 'Please,' she says as it clicks. 'Remember they are not as young as the rest of you. We don't want to frighten them.'

I trail the others inside the older couple's suite and stand back to absorb the scene. The open laptop. Piles of camera equipment stacked haphazardly in corners, on surfaces and in the middle of the lounge. Clothes scattered around the room like there's been a laundry blizzard and it's snowed old people's underwear. A pair of greyish high-waisted undies actually hangs off the light fixture. I hear again Florence's words from earlier about Bugsy: 'There appears to have been a struggle.'

A frisson of nerves sets the fine hairs on the back of my neck to standing.

What the hell happened in here?

'There are no bodies in the bath,' Dylan says cheerfully from behind me. 'Nor the shower.'

I lean against the wall to give him room to pass. It's like since finding the body on the trail the whole world has compressed into me, and I can't seem to get enough space. I breathe in, trying not to gag on the scents of cheap laundry powder, rose perfume and not-quite-clean human.

Maman's gaze is on me, and there's understanding in her

eyes. It's been the two of us for so long, she knows how I'm feeling. But two isn't enough. Two can far too easily become one.

'There's no one here,' Florence says. 'This is a waste of time.'

While everyone else is stunned into stillness, Dylan strides over to investigate the bench over the bar fridge. He picks up a bottle, sniffs it. 'This juice is still cold, so it can't have been out too long. They must have come in here and had a drink – the question is, was it before or after they searched Hawk Bay?'

Adam points to the single cup on the table. 'Only one of them.'

'And there was no sign of them down at the bay,' Dylan says.

'Do you think someone broke in here and hurt them?' I ask.

'Maybe the guy who got Bugsy,' Edward says. 'He waited for us to separate to search for Lara and then took down the oldest and weakest members of the herd.'

Spots of colour flare in Florence's pale cheeks. 'I'm sure there's a reasonable explanation for all of this.' But she isn't fooling anyone.

A surge of sympathy flows through me for the slightly strange woman. She's worked so hard to put this together and can't do anything but watch it spin out of control. The prospect of the show happening ever, let alone today, is getting further and further away. I'm no financial expert, but I'm guessing her livelihood is hanging by a thread right now.

Over by the huge TV at the end of the bed, Edward is waving around a USB. 'The Cedrics Band,' he reads off a taped-on label.

That gets Dylan's attention. 'Do you think it's about us?'

Edward snorts. 'No, I think it's a complete coincidence that they've spent the weekend filming us and interviewing the band and there's a USB here labelled with the band's name on it.'

'Put it in,' Adam says. 'It might tell us something.'

It's all right for him, he's avoided his interview.

'No power,' I remind them.

'I have the tablet,' Florence says.

Maybe it's background footage that they intended to combine with what they shot over the weekend. I can't come up with a reason to stop this, and then I'm too late. Edward has already plugged the small unit into Florence's tablet.

She clicks on a file, and the screen flickers to life.

Chords from 'Storybook Love' crackle through the speaker, and then it's Jonny singing on stage. I know this, it's Berlin and the second-to-last big concert they ever played.

I exhale. It's old, it's fine.

And then...

Dylan's on the screen and Marco is speaking. 'How did you all get along?'

An ugly emotion twists Dylan's features before he gets them under control. 'Like any band on the road, there were good days and bad.'

More music, shots of happier times, and then a close-up of Adam, seedy and snarling outside the interview room. 'The band is more than just Jonny.'

Stills from the shoving-over dinner.

Dark looks.

Clenched fists.

What must be every hint of disagreement and tension over the whole weekend is on a high-speed mix of misery, caught on film and displayed such that none of us could come across any worse.

Until finally, when I think maybe I've escaped, my face is up close in the interview room. My belly contracts as my expression shows a desperation I don't recognise.

'My father's death was no accident. It was murder. And I know who's responsible.' A pause where no one in the trashed suite even takes a breath, and then I add the fateful words. 'Ian "Bugsy" Malone had him killed.'

What I said echoes through the suite. The video flickers to a stop.

'You thought Ian was responsible.' Dylan puts his hand over his mouth as though he didn't mean to say it aloud.

Edward points at me. 'She killed Bugsy.'

And how can I defend myself? I've thought enough about how a timely accident to the man responsible for the death of Jonny Rake would give him the payback he deserves. The ceasefire in speculation after Florence shared the security footage is suddenly forgotten.

'*Non*, never.' Maman crosses to my side, like a bear defending her cub – a mock-French, tired and sickly bear – and stares the others down. Then she tugs at my arm and stretches it out. 'She does not have the strength to do such a violent action. It is not possible.'

I stand there, wooden and unmoving. I can't deny that I wanted him dead. But I'm not the only one.

'There's a trail,' I say, when it seems I have to say something. 'Bugsy was in debt to some dangerous people. People behind some of the world's biggest record labels, people whose names and faces aren't known to the public. They didn't want The Cedrics Band to succeed. There are traces online.'

Maman frowns. 'But Jonny's death propelled the band to finish the year on top.'

I shrugged. 'It confused me too at first. But then I found something else, and it all made sense. Jonny Rake was not the one who was supposed to die that day.'

Next to me, Maman recoils like I've punched her.

It takes a minute of silence, but Adam is the one who nods first. 'Killing Jonny made the star a martyr. Assuming you're right—'

'I am,' I interrupt. 'The payment trail is not that well hidden. No one thought of examining Bugsy's dealings, because they believed Jonny's death was an accident. That's why no one has ever looked properly before. These people Bugsy was involved with don't need to worry about evidence – they're untouchable.'

Adam waits for me to finish. 'That means it should have been one of us.' He looks at his remaining bandmates.

Edward yelps. 'That's ridiculous.'

'No,' Dylan argues. 'It makes sense. Compared to Jonny, any one of us could have kicked the bucket and it would have barely caused a headline. Sure, some fans would have been sad, but it wouldn't have made the hype.'

'Nor destroyed Bugsy's primary ticket to the big time,' Adam agrees. 'It would have been a setback, not a wipeout.'

Edward folds his arms. 'You want to take this on the word of some kid barely old enough to drive?'

'A kid you thought old enough to kill a grown man a few minutes ago,' Adam reminds him with a sneer. 'Make up your mind.'

'It all seems pretty convenient,' Edward says sullenly. 'It's not like we have any proof.'

Florence clears her throat. 'And we still don't know what happened here.' She gestures to the dishevelled room and its lack of occupants.

Maman makes her way to the sofa and sinks onto it like her legs can no longer take her weight. I'm about to tell her she should go and lie down when she holds a laptop out to me, the one I noticed when we first entered the suite. 'This might tell us something.'

I shake my head, take a step back, beg her with my eyes not to do this. Marco and Connie could return at any moment.

Edward sniffs. 'Even old people like Connie and Marco know basic password protection.'

Maman is ignoring him. The device shakes a little from the unsteadiness of her hands and I know I'm going to give in before she even asks the question.

'Can you access it?'

Florence – Sunday

I fully intended to make my excuses and depart once the lynch mob discovered the suite belonging to Marco and Connie was empty, but two things keep me there: first, the film showing the band's true awfulness, and then the insistence in Ivy's voice when she asks Monet to investigate the older couple's laptop.

If they're going to do this, I need to be present.

I take the laptop from Ivy and assess Monet, with her movie-star looks, youth and the easy confidence of wealth and privilege.

In my planning for this weekend, I didn't spend much time researching Monet. I hope I haven't made a mistake. I try to picture her wrapping the braces around Bugsy's throat, but I just can't see it.

Her theory that Bugsy had Jonny killed makes a strange kind of sense, but everyone here already wanted Bugsy dead, so it doesn't really change anything.

'You can get through whatever passwords they have set up?' I ask.

Monet bites her lip and nods. 'Probably.'

'She's like a computer genius,' Dylan says.

I can feel them all watching me for what to do. For now, I still have some control over the proceedings.

With one guest missing and another dead, I can't ignore a

chance to find out more about what might have happened to the two who are absent. Two who, of everyone here, should not be going off half-cocked today. They have just as much skin in this game.

I shove the laptop into Monet's unwilling grasp. 'Please hack it... or whatever it's called. I'd hate to think we had the answer right here and ignored it.'

Monet takes the thin silver computer to the small table and opens it. I hover behind her, watching as her fingers fly across the keys.

I will her to hurry as the others gather around me. Bruce will be up at the house, wondering where I am. He won't like to be kept waiting, but if I can find out what's happened here then the delay will be worth it.

I don't even realise how tense I am until the screen flashes and a tidy desktop with a few small icons appears.

'I'm in, but there's not much here,' Monet says.

I don't know what I expected, but this is just about the best-case scenario. 'We've checked the device,' I begin briskly. 'And now we should probably respect their privacy—'

The soft double tap of Monet's finger on the keyboard cuts me off.

I register the name of the file a moment before a window opens on the screen.

HELP.

A beat passes then Connie's face appears, close to the camera.

At first, there's nothing but the sound of the computer whirring.

'Turn it up.' Edward reaches out, but Monet is already moving.

Connie has a way of fading into the background, but

the lens of the laptop acts as a spotlight, and her lined face filling the small screen draws every eye as she leans closer to it. Although the top of her head is cut off, what remains is shown in high definition, complete with wrinkles, dry patches and age spots accentuated in the bright light. The necklace at her throat shines, a small gold circle linked with a much larger silver one.

Each breath she takes is a ragged sound into the microphone.

Monet taps something, and the breathing gets louder.

'My name is Connie Trafford,' she begins, 'and I'm at the Three Chains Distillery on Sparrow Hawk Island. I don't have long. He could return at any moment and I'm afraid of what might happen when he does. You need to see this, it explains everything.'

Ivy's hand covers her mouth. 'I knew he was a bad man.'

I roll my eyes but bite back on pointing out how everyone's an expert in hindsight.

On the screen, Connie's eyes dart from left to right. Her hand passes through the corner of the picture. Is she holding something? Whatever it is, it's there and gone too fast.

She's so close now her tonsils fill half the picture. 'It's too late. There's someone coming. Please, if you're watching this, I'm afraid what happened has caught up with Marco. He's not behaving rationally.' She gulps a sob. 'It's because of Peter, I think. I thought he'd moved on, I thought this weekend would bring closure.' She wipes a hand across her eyes, leaving a trail of wetness on her papery skin. 'I'm scared.'

The video stops.

'There must be more,' I say. This doesn't make any sense.

Monet presses 'play' again, but it stops in the same place.

The small bar at the foot of the screen shows the video has reached its end.

Ivy is sniffling. 'He's done something to that poor woman.'

'And Bugsy,' Edward pipes up. 'Probably. The guy has lost the plot. Maybe he's hurt Lara too.'

'Hang on, a minute ago you thought Monet hurt Bugsy.' I give her an apologetic look. 'We don't know anything.'

Adam's eyes flash. 'We know that little old lady was terrified and now she's nowhere to be found.'

'Hold up,' I say. 'She's maybe sixty, sixty-five. Hardly end-of-life scenarios, and I'd look awful in that light too.'

'But you're not missing, having made a cry for help,' Adam replies.

I can't argue. For all I know, this is exactly what it seems. For all I know, Marco has hurt his wife.

We'd already searched the suite, but with Connie's plea ringing in our heads and her face frozen on the laptop screen, we look again and replay the clip. We pause the video as her hand passes the corner of the screen. It appears she's clutching one of the rocks from the garden, as though preparing to defend herself.

While the others work without any apparent plan, I try to think about what we saw. I'm sure that she was in this part of the suite and that her gaze, at the very last moment, went to the huge glass sliding doors.

While others look around the bedroom space and the bathroom, I cross to the doors and open them.

I feel someone follow me outside but don't look to see who because I'm too busy scanning for anything that fits with Marco somehow dragging his wife out here for some nefarious purpose. I look down to the rocks of the cliff that pepper the incline towards the escarpment edge proper – where it falls away to more rocks and the crashing ocean far below.

Something glints just below the balcony. My heart stops, and I stare so hard my eyes stream watery tears. I lean over the rail, trying to get a better look. It's possible for someone to climb down there, but the going is rough.

'It's her necklace,' Edward says with pompous certainty from uncomfortably close beside me. 'She was wearing it in the video.'

He's right.

Now I know what to look for, I can see that as well as the long chain, there's the silver circle and the smaller gold one linked to it.

'He's done something to her,' Edward announces loud enough to bring the others running.

Again, he's right. And further, as my hands tighten, I notice there are marks of a struggle on the rail, only noticeable if you're looking for them.

I had plans. I know it's selfish, but I can't help the thought.

'Clearly, she's gone over the edge here,' Edward says. 'I'd bet the body has already broken up on the rocks below. It's probably shark bait.'

'I never liked him,' Ivy announces.

I want to argue, want to go back in time and never let them into the suite. I need to talk to Bruce.

This changes everything.

'I should return to the main house,' I say into the charged silence. 'We all should. Hopefully, Bruce has the generator fixed, and we can inform the authorities about these developments. We have to consider the fact that this, too, might now be a crime scene.'

'But where's Marco?' Monet asks, her voice surprisingly level given the shock she must be feeling.

'Probably long gone,' Dylan answers, placing a comforting arm across her shoulder.

Ready to lead the guests back to the main house, I go to pick up the laptop, but Adam's hand on it means I'd have to tug it free, and I don't want that kind of confrontation. Not yet. Not while Bruce isn't at my side. I clench my jaw, not to show the seed of fury lodged hard and small inside me.

'I was thinking we need to bring that somewhere safe,' I say instead. 'The police will want to see it.'

He nods. 'I will.'

I'm the last one out.

Then, with the shake in my hands the only thing revealing the panic in my head at time running out, I pull the door closed, hearing the lock click into place.

The hard seed inside me is almost ready to bloom.

Adam – Sunday

As we troop out of Marco and Connie's suite, I'm trying to make sense of what we found there. Could Monet be right? Could Jonny's death have been a mistake? A murder intended for someone else?

I've always been a dead-is-dead kind of guy and tried not to think too hard about if there's some grand plan to life, but murder, by definition, is a plan, and it means that someone – Bugsy, if Monet is right – wanted one of us dead. And it could have been me, instead of the brother the whole world mourned.

The happiest times of my life were on stage with Jonny. And it didn't matter, despite how twisted everything became, that Jonny was the star, because he took us along for the ride.

I'd accepted his death as a terrible accident, but what Monet said changes everything.

We'd argued on that last day. And I'm not talking a casual disagreement – this was one of those no-holds-barred explosions where everything you've never said gets brought up.

I can still hear my voice shouting at him as if from a stranger. *She is not your property.*

And the lazy, infuriating smile he gave me in return. *Well, brother, she's certainly not yours because you've never had anything worth having and you never will.*

When you're fighting with a sibling, when you're cutting them as deeply as you know how, you don't stop and wonder if it will be the last thing they'll ever hear you say.

I'm so caught up, I almost walk into Ivy. Has she waited for me?

After my talk with Monet, part of me wants to berate Ivy for that stupid promise made so long ago. But that's not what comes out of my mouth. 'He never even liked art.'

Her mouth tugs down at the corner. 'I don't understand.'

'Her name. *Monet*. Jonny only cared about music. I even gave him the chorus for "Touch of Colour"; the guy wouldn't have known one end of a paintbrush from the other.'

She doesn't answer for the longest time. 'I know.' Two words, quiet and with the musical lilt that Ivy St Fleur is so famous for.

'But they always link it with that song.'

She shakes her head. 'It's too late for this.'

'What do you mean?'

But I'm directing the question to the beautiful curves of her back as she's walking away.

I find myself instead walking next to Edward, trailing the others, trying not to stare at Dylan walking with Ivy and Monet. I know I maybe should have realised this about seventeen years ago, but it hits me that's where I should be. Without Jonny, Monet is the only relative I have left.

'Put your tongue away,' Edward says with a snicker. 'You're drooling.'

If the guy's wife wasn't missing, I'd be tempted to take his tongue and knot it. Instead, I keep my tone level. 'How are you doing? You must be worried about Lara.'

'I'm fine.' He takes a few more steps. 'I was never enough for her anyway.'

'She said that?'

'Not in words,' he says. 'More in her disappointed glances, muffled sighs, suggestions on how I could be improved. You don't need to improve someone you're happy with.'

'You could have just told her.'

'Could I? You can tell you've never been married. I didn't want anything to happen to her, but I couldn't keep her there if she didn't want to stay. You get that, don't you?'

He's pausing as though waiting for me to agree, but I can't. It says something for how fucked all this has become that I've lost my ability to bullshit Edward.

Nor can I say the things I want to say to him. Maybe things weren't great between them, but he should have raised the alarm sooner, especially once Bugsy was discovered. He has to take some of the blame if something has happened to her.

'The band is bigger than any of us, except maybe Jonny,' he continues. 'And she was obsessed – not with me, but the band. With him. Obsessed.'

When I don't say anything, he huffs and pushes his glasses into place, giving me one of those looks that always pissed me off, and made any promises to Jonny not to give the little snot a hard time impossible to keep.

As I look at him, something flashes through my head. A memory?

I close my eyes to focus. In my head, I can feel the breeze of the night; the world is filed off at the edges, the way it is when I've drunk enough to numb the pain. There's something nagging, and maybe it's important, but then Edward is huffing and I'm back in the present.

'You don't comprehend anything, do you?' he sneers.

'You're wrong,' I reply. 'I heard your little whine fest, and I understood perfectly well what you were doing.'

'Really?' He crosses his arms. 'What?'

'You're trying to absolve yourself because she's missing and you're shit-scared. You're not as intellectually superior as you seem to think you are.'

'I don't think I'm—'

'Yeah, you do.' I cut him off. 'It's a flaw, man. Makes you act dumb, make mistakes.'

I walk faster, my focus on those ahead who are going into Ivy's suite rather than over to the main house. I'm not going to let that door close and have to knock. Knocking gives them the option of not letting me in, and I'm sick of being on the outside.

They're almost at the suite door when Dylan says something to Ivy and nudges her shoulder gently. She looks up at him, mustering a weary smile. The familiarity of it slows me in my tracks. It might have taken two days of me not being able to see anything past raging jealousy, but now I realise there's definitely more brotherly affection than fuck buddy in the touch.

They're not together.

I feel it deep in my gut with a sudden certainty that's stupidly exciting. Just because she's not with him doesn't mean she's available, and even if she was single, she wouldn't look twice at a guy like me. But the persistent images that have haunted me about the two of them together dissolve under the summer sun.

Edward and I reach the door a moment after the others, just as Dylan is about to close it. He sniffs the air, his eyes narrow. 'What's that smell?'

'I don't know what you're talking about.' I try not to breathe in his direction – so much for the fresh minty breath of the gum I picked up.

'You've been drinking.' It's not a question. 'Christ, Adam, it's barely afternoon.'

'It was one shot of the gin.' I drag my hand across my face, let him see how hard I'm trying here. 'He's dead. I needed something. Please,' I say. 'We have a lot to talk about.'

Adam – Sunday

Dylan considers whether to let us in and I wait, despite every bit of me wanting to insist. Instead, I give him a chance to choose to let me in. After all, he's the one who's been there for Monet and Ivy all this time.

The hand of his that's not holding the edge of the door is cradled oddly across his waist, holding something bulky beneath his fitted T-shirt. And it's me looking there that seems to decide him.

'You probably should come in,' he agrees. 'You'll want to see this.'

'See what?' Edward asks, but he follows me inside.

I allow Dylan and Edward to go ahead because my heart is stuttering in my chest, and not because of what happened in the director's suite. It's the primal reaction to breathing in a space filled with Ivy's scent. It's knowing that she sleeps in here.

I'm not proud of my body's reaction, but I can no more control it than I can undo every stupid mistake I've ever made.

A mental run-through of every fuck-up, the long line of which is never far from my thoughts, lets me walk further into the suite and through Ivy St Fleur's bedroom without a hard-on.

And I don't let myself look at Ivy, who's reclined on the couch, her dark glossy hair spread across a pile of pillows, over near the closed curtains.

But, of course, I know exactly where she is.

Dylan moves to the centre of the space and takes a breath. 'I found something in Marco and Connie's suite,' he announces. 'I didn't understand what it was at first, but then it clicked and, well, you guys should see it for yourselves.'

He pulls something out from where he'd secreted it against his body. It's plastic on one end and hairy on the other. He's buzzing with an odd kind of excitement as he makes a gap in one end of the thing and then slides it over his head. With a few tugs, it settles into place.

'It's the man from the security footage,' Monet cries.

I squint at the smooth plastic features and dark hair of the mask and imagine it grainy, but I already feel she's right. No wonder Dylan thought it was Jonny – there's something in the nose shape and the stubble that makes me wonder if whoever made it copied a picture of my brother for inspiration.

'Does that mean Marco was the one who…' My voice trails off. For all that I fantasised about ending Bugsy's blight on my existence, I still find it difficult to put into words the finality of what's happened.

'Of course,' Edward says. 'He killed Bugsy. He's certainly big enough to have held the other guy down.'

I edge past Edward to take a closer look at the mask. It does look like the one in the footage.

'But why?' Monet asks.

'You saw the film he'd put together. He must have some kind of grudge against the band.' There's a thread in the folds of the latex near the ears. I pull out the long line of light blue that matches the colour of the braces Bugsy was wearing to dinner last night, and place it across my palm. 'And Bugsy in particular.'

'I've got it,' Monet says. 'Connie mentioned her son to me the other day and then in the video she said something about Peter. And she didn't call herself Connie D'Angelo or whatever Marco's surname is.' She's talking so fast the words are tripping over themselves.

'Peter Trafford,' Dylan says slowly. 'Marco asked me about him in the interview.'

I'm about to ask who they're talking about when I remember. The loser who'd never turn up for a gig, who missed the night that changed our lives when we were discovered by Bugsy. 'What happened to him?'

'Jail,' Edward says. 'I thought there was something familiar about her. She's Peter's mother.'

'Really?' I say. 'You reckon you recognised the pimply faced teen you knew nearly two decades ago in that tiny mousy woman?'

His jaw juts out. 'You don't know what I think.'

Dylan's pacing. 'This means he probably doesn't have anything against Lara. If she's hidden somewhere, she's probably safe.'

Edward's face is blank, but then he realises that Dylan is waiting for a reaction. 'That's good.'

'We need to search for her again,' Dylan concludes. 'Or for Marco, let him try to take on someone his own size.'

'But the authorities are coming,' Monet says. Her voice is pleading but her eyes suggest she's not even fooling herself. 'They'll be here soon.'

'And what do you expect them to do?' Edward snarls at her. 'That's if they're even coming.'

I frown at him. She's just a kid. But at the same time, I'm glad I'm not the only one thinking this way. The blind trust in our hosts is getting thin. I'm not sure how long it's been since Florence first disappeared to call the authorities, but something should be happening by now.

'What does he mean?' Monet's looking at me.

I sigh, there's no way to sugar-coat this. 'I'm not saying Florence lied, but there's been something a bit panicked about her since Bugsy was found, and with the power going out as well. Maybe she wasn't able to contact them but can't admit it.' I hate to do this here, but I add, 'And she'd have the best access to this suite if someone snuck in and took your satellite link, more likely than Marco.'

'Her what?' Dylan turns to Monet. 'Your what?'

For a moment I catch a glimpse of ordinary teenager in Monet's eye-roll. 'They're like practically giving them away online. It wasn't that hard to get one.'

Ivy's forehead is creased in a frown. 'But yours, it is missing?'

'Yeah,' Monet says. 'I hoped to call for help.'

Ivy's features seem to slacken, and she sinks back into the cushions. 'So, we're stranded here?'

'I don't know,' I say. 'We can't count on anything or anyone.'

Edward is antsy. 'We should find Florence. Make her tell us the truth. The husband has been doing something with the generator, but there's no sign of any power returning.'

Dylan shakes his head. 'I'm just not seeing it. I think the woman is under a heap of pressure, and she's probably losing her mind about what to do. I agree that we need an update on when the police will get here.' He looks to me. '*If* they're coming. But there's no need to threaten anyone.'

'This is ridiculous,' Edward says. 'You people don't know anything. We're standing around here chatting when we need to be doing something.'

'Calm down,' Dylan says, reaching out a hand towards him.

Edward whirls away out of reach, eyes wild. 'Don't touch me.'

I dart a look at Dylan. He's still no friend of mine, but I can't be the only one who registered the unnatural squeak of Edward's voice. Come to think of it, he's been acting strangely all day.

Dylan's eyebrows lift enough to show I'm not alone. We move in casual unison, putting ourselves between the keyboardist turned accountant and the couch where Monet is perched at her mother's side.

'I see what you two are doing,' Edward whines.

'We're not doing nothing,' I say.

'Which means you're doing something, you idiot.'

I reel back from the snarled disdain in him. Not so much stunned at this different side of Edward, but instead wondering if this is the real man, plucked skinny and vicious from the true depths of him.

There's a loud click.

We turn as one towards the door we came in through. I feel a sinking sensation deep in my gut even as Edward scrambles up the stairs and along the short hallway towards the front of the suite. He swipes the lock with the card in desperation, tugs at the handle, shakes it.

The air in the place seems to evaporate as my blood chills and thickens.

'They've locked us in.'

Edward - Sunday

I try the door a few more times to make sure, but it's not budging. 'They've locked us in,' I repeat.

I feel Dylan beside me and move aside for him to try. Not that I think he can make a difference, no matter how many steroids he's been taking, but rather because he clearly isn't going to take my word on the situation.

'It's locked,' he agrees.

I bang on the hard surface. 'Let us out.' But I don't even know who I'm yelling at.

'I reckon it's the husband,' Dylan says, striding down the small hallway. 'But why do they want to keep us in here?'

'For our safety,' Adam suggests. He's up at the huge glass sliding doors leading out to the balcony, the open curtains now letting light and more heat stream in. 'Locked too,' he says.

A small flare of satisfaction fills me when Dylan bodies past him and checks that door too, obviously not believing the loser guitarist any more than he believed me.

Yes, because given the fact there are dead bodies on trails and people missing, we're going to fool around about this.

I bite down on the urge to point out the obvious. I'd thought Adam the weakest link, but Dylan must have taken a few too many protein shakes.

He rattles the door hard, turns the internal lock a few times and rattles it some more. There's a sheen of sweat across his frustrated, meaty features, and veins show on his forearms from the effort.

'Maybe Florence was worried we'd risk more trouble,' Adam says.

Dylan shakes his head. 'Then why not just ask us to stay put? There's no way I'm staying in here now.'

He has a point. There's nothing like a locked door to make you want it open.

'Just breathe, *ma petite*.' A glance over to the couch shows Ivy murmuring the comforting words softly on repeat to Monet, her slender hand brushing the girl's hair.

I look away, feeling I've intruded on a private moment, then look back because it's not like I asked to be stuck in here with them. Seriously, from the glassy sheen of panic in the kid's eyes, you'd think we were about to run out of oxygen.

'...and I think that will be the safest,' Dylan finishes.

He's looking from me to Adam, and I have no idea what his plan was because the melodramatic kid in the corner distracted me, but I nod because it's not like I have a better option.

Anyway, it's not rocket science. With the front door well locked and made of solid wood, the logical way out is through the back.

As Ivy and Monet edge back from the glass door, Dylan grabs a towel and wraps it around his upper body, then picks up one of the chairs.

'Wait,' I say. 'You're going to smash it?'

Dylan frowns. 'That's literally what I just said.'

'Try using your brain first, it's likely tempered glass.'

'Which means?' Adam asks.

'It's not going to break easily.' I sigh, grab a knife from a dinner tray and cross to the sliding door. Dylan stands aside as I kneel by the corner. 'This is newer so it might not work, but some of these doors have a basic hook-style lock and because they're on tracks, you can just...' I insert the tip of the knife in the track and use it to lever the frame up. There's a click and the door moves.

I can almost feel the grudging respect of the others settling over my shoulders like a cape. I'm freaking Superman. I stand, drop the knife, brush my hands off and grab the handle.

It doesn't open. It must have an extra mechanism.

'You all heard it,' I say. 'You all heard it unlock.'

'Out the way,' Dylan says, chair back in his hands. 'I don't want you getting hurt.'

He doesn't say anything about my failed attempt to open the door, but the ridicule is there in his exaggerated concern for my welfare and then in Adam's cough that sounds like it's covering a laugh.

Fools.

I back away. 'Far be it from me to stop you hurting yourself.'

Dylan ignores me, steps up to the glass and swings the chair. It arcs through the air, and the corner of it hits right in the middle of the huge pane.

Spiderweb cracks appear and the whole thing holds in place. Before I can suggest clearing off the pieces, Dylan swings the chair again and it rains glass shards.

Automatically, I lift my hand to protect myself, despite having moved far enough away to miss getting hit.

Dylan grins, eyes wide, fine specks of glass in his beard and tiny cuts on his face turning red. He kicks the last pieces out the way then drops the chair. 'That'll do it.'

Monet picks her way past him outside, sucking in air like a drowning person.

'So, what now?' I say.

'We could climb down and get around that way,' Monet says, pointing off to the side of the balcony.

The rest of us follow her out, except Ivy, who's probably waiting for someone to come and carry her like Cleopatra or something. The girl's right – thanks to the way the ground slopes up towards the distillery from this first suite, it's not even that difficult a climb.

From here the main house is hidden by trees and bushes, but I stare that way anyway. 'Whoever locked us in would have to have known it wouldn't hold us for long.'

'Maybe it was Marco?' Adam says.

Monet wraps her arms around her waist and her gaze goes to the water, probably thinking about Connie's untimely end. 'There's something we're not seeing.'

'I'm pretty sure of it,' I mutter.

'Then tell us what's going on, smart boy,' Dylan says, then huffs in derision before I have a chance to say anything at all. 'Yeah, thought so. You don't got nothing.'

Which means I have something.

But I don't say it, because the something I have isn't for sharing. Not with these idiots.

Although I didn't speak, I must have shown something in my expression because now Dylan's staring at me, eyes narrowed. 'Maybe you're not the quiet introvert we always thought you were.'

Something lurches in my stomach. 'Which means?'

'You're the one who's lost track of your wife and don't seem all that cut up about it. I've never had one, but it's not like they're a guitar pick or a drumstick.' His eyes narrow further. 'And now there's the possibility that Jonny's death wasn't an accident. Maybe everyone's been looking in the wrong place, maybe you weren't such a nice guy back then either.'

My skin prickles. He can't know. No one does. I never even told Lara, keeping the terrible truth inside even in the flushing glow after sex those early times when I thought she was my soulmate and I would have spilled anything, had she asked.

She never asked.

My cheeks get hot. They're turning red, I know it, but the more I think about it, the hotter they feel. I scurry back inside, out of the sun, annoyed when the others follow and Dylan still seems to be waiting for a response.

'I didn't have any reason to hurt Jonny,' I say.

'And I did?' The challenge in Dylan's voice is unmistakable.

Suddenly, I've had enough. I step right up to him, uncaring if he grabs me or hurts me or whatever. I'm so sick of being the pushover, the quiet one everyone thinks they can ignore or use. I know things about everyone here. 'Do you really want to do this?'

He smiles. 'I have nothing to be ashamed of, so you go right ahead and put your little theory out for everyone.'

'You're gay.'

Edward – Sunday

'Duh,' Monet says, tossing her hair over her shoulder to dismiss my big announcement.

Dylan's laugh has a dark edge. 'I'm bi, actually,' he says. 'But I don't expect someone like you to appreciate the nuances.'

I hate the way they all think I'm so nerdy and don't get what's going on. But I do. There's more and he knows it, and so will everyone else, because he couldn't resist trying to put me in my place. Serves him right. 'And you were in love with Jonny.'

He swallows hard, doesn't look at Adam. 'Yes, I was.' Then he meets my gaze and the usual beefcake arrogance is missing, revealing a raw chasm beneath. 'And I will miss him every day for the rest of my life. What of it?'

'He rejected you and you were mad with him. You had a reason to want him dead.' It's my trump card, but playing it doesn't bring the satisfaction I hoped, not when big dumb Dylan looks like he's about to cry.

Even Adam looks sympathetic.

'If you must know, Jonny didn't reject me.' Dylan's looking at Ivy now. 'At least, not in the way Edward is suggesting. What he wouldn't do is commit to there being an *us*. He loved me, but he didn't love me the way I loved him. I am so, so sorry. I knew he was with you, and I should have stayed away, but I couldn't help myself.'

Ivy's eyes fill with tears. 'Oh, *mon ami*, Jonny wasn't a man to be contained.' She lifts her arms and Dylan crosses to embrace her.

It's sickening. 'Don't any of you care that he was screwing around on you with anything with a pulse?'

Dylan shakes his head, wipes his eyes, but not because he's ashamed of his weakness – more because he's annoyed with me and his tears might prevent him glaring properly. 'You just don't get it.'

'And I don't want to. What I want,' I say, 'is to get off this stupid island.'

'At last, a relevant contribution,' Adam digs. 'With that in mind, I'm going to head out, stay hidden and try and see what's happening, unless anyone has any objections?'

Again, he shares a look with Dylan, who nods. Without another word to anyone, he heads outside, climbs over the edge of the balcony and disappears into the trees.

So much for anyone requesting my opinion. Not that I have a better idea.

I head for the bathroom to have a few seconds alone, splash my face, pull my thoughts together and work out what I'll do when... if... Adam returns. The bathroom is cool and quiet, and I lean against the tiled wall and sink to the floor. Somehow, I'm going to get off this island and put this nightmare weekend behind me.

'You're crying.'

It's Monet, and she's standing just outside the bathroom. I look around but we're alone; she's talking to me.

'I don't cry,' I say. 'It's one of the things that drove... drives... Lara mad about me. She always said I had the emotional depth of a toothpick.' I didn't mean to speak in the past tense, but Monet doesn't seem to have noticed. It's lucky really because noticing might have led to questions, and questions... well, I don't know where that ends up.

But my eyes ache, and when I press my palms hard into them, my hands come away damp.

'No one is going to think you're less of a man if you're worried about your wife.'

'Maybe I'm a bit concerned.' I try for a chuckle and it comes out choked.

'You guys have been together for, what, fifteen years?'

'Seventeen,' I admit. My voice comes out all scratchy, probably because it's been a long time since I've talked as much as I have today. 'Our oldest son is just a couple of months younger than you.' It was a shotgun wedding. Of course. I'd never have thought of proposing so soon and not to someone like that if she hadn't been pregnant. 'So we didn't have a lot of time to plan anything, but Lara made it special. Chose a Sunday so it would be the 4th of the 4th. She thought I'd like the pattern because I always had a thing for numbers.'

Did I ever tell her that I liked it?

'There, see,' Monet says. 'It would be strange if you weren't upset.'

I don't have the heart to tell her that strange isn't exactly unusual territory for me. Always the odd one at school, always the nerd. And not ashamed as such, but my reward for helping Jonny with his maths was playing in the coolest band I knew.

I stagger to my feet and towards the sink as nausea climbs in my throat. I lean over the porcelain but don't let myself heave, breathing in and out until the urge passes.

'Sorry,' I say when I sit again. It's not Lara being missing
– *she's just missing*, I tell myself again, anything else is
hallucinations from the drugs, because I never planned
anything like this – that has me upset. It's the waiting and the
heat and the wondering what we'll do if Adam doesn't return.

'That's okay,' she says. 'I can't even imagine how you must
be feeling.'

Such empathy in a young person.

It's Lara's voice in my head. There's that tinge of sycophantic
awe. Monet is famous enough for Lara to credit her with just
about anything, but I see through it. Always have. The girl's
not kind, she's conniving. She wants something. They all want
something.

I walk to the door and spot Dylan bent low over Ivy.

Again, I hear Lara's nurse voice in my head. *That really
does look like more than sunstroke. There's something going
on there.*

But then Monet's hand on my arm is turning me away
from whatever they're doing. She's smiling at me, distracting
me. 'Tell me more about you two.'

'There's not much to tell.' I'm hoping she takes the shortness
in my tone as anxiety.

'Everyone has a story. How did you meet?'

'At the stadium. In France.'

Her eyes widen as it sinks in. 'You met the day he died?'

I nod. It's hard to find the words when Lara was the one
who was always so excited to tell this story. 'She was
one of the first on the scene, coming to help when she heard the
explosion because of her nurse training. The shock of it had
thrown me back. I stumbled and fell off the stage, colliding
with a speaker. It knocked me out and I woke to her face

above me, in a halo of sun.' I'm speaking too fast; the faint widening of Monet's eyes suggests my behaviour is ringing some kind of alarm bell, but I've started now. Stopping will only make it worse. 'I thought she was an angel.'

'How sweet,' Monet says.

There's sympathy there now, but if she knew everything, she'd judge me. Women are predictable like that. I could try to explain about the drugs, but before I can say anything, there's the sound of Adam's voice from outside the suite.

'The whole fucking place is deserted.'

Monet – Sunday

'The hero returns,' Edward sneers at the sound of Adam's voice.

'Hardly a hero,' I reply.

'Some think so. Like your mother. You haven't noticed, have you?' Edward asks. 'That your mother and your... Adam have a thing.'

'Yes, she avoids him wherever possible because she can't stand him. I had to beg her to even come here.'

Edward's laugh holds more than a hint of ridicule. 'Oh, child.'

'Don't make fun of me. If you have something to say, say it.'

'Look at them. Look at them properly.'

Leaving the morose Edward in the bathroom – the guy can't seem to decide whether he's sad or mad about his missing wife – I head out to where Adam has come in from the balcony. It's only now he's back safe that I realise how scared I was that something might happen to him.

'There's no one up at the house. Just an abandoned golf cart.' He catches his breath before continuing. 'But that's not all. I thought I could smell smoke.'

Jonny. We're all thinking it – his smoking wasn't much of a secret.

But then he adds, 'The bushfire kind.'

I sniff the air but can't smell anything over Maman's perfume. And I can't help myself, I'm studying the two of them. Most people move gingerly in Maman's orbit. She appeared breakable for so long before she actually was that everything she's been through the last few years hasn't precipitated much change.

Adam does not move gingerly. If life was a china shop, then he seems to make it his business to smash into as much of it as possible.

And Maman... she's different with him here. How did I not see this?

'A fire?' Dylan asks. He drags a hand over his face. 'We need to get off this island, which means we need a boat.'

'Maybe Florence has gone to get help,' I say. 'They must have worked out about Marco too. Maybe they've gone after him. And the police will be here soon.' I don't really believe it anymore, but I say it anyway.

Adam gives me a long look in reply. 'Maybe,' he says as Edward snorts derision from the hallway. 'But I think we need to assume we're on our own. There's nothing at the docks – I noticed when we were searching for Lara – and the place is bigger than it looks from the way we came in. Although that could be a good thing, because any fire will take time to spread. I reckon the neighbour must have either a boat or some kind of phone. Getting to him has to be our best bet.'

I look from Maman to Dylan, share with a glance at him the realisation that she's not up to a trip across the island. Even with me having occupied Edward so she could take her medication – why she still cares about anyone knowing, I've no idea – she's weak. We need to bring the boat to her.

Oblivious, Adam continues. 'I walked a decent stretch of the civilised parts of the island after the first night. There are dangers. A quarry. Cliffs. Easy places where someone could get lost or injured... or worse.'

'We should wait here,' Edward says. 'Someone will come.'

'But they might take too long.' Dylan's pacing again, something he does when he's trying to think. Then he stops right in front of Adam. The macho bristling between them is there but it's different somehow. 'You know the way?'

'I'll get help,' Adam says.

Maman beckons me to her. 'You go,' she says.

'What?' I feel Dylan tensing, about to echo my surprise, but Maman's raised hand stops him.

Her pleading eyes take in both of us. 'Go with Adam. Dylan will stay here with me.' She turns to Dylan. 'She should be with him.'

His jaw works, but he doesn't argue.

I'm not so easily cowed. 'What about sticking together? What about wanting nothing to do with him all these years?'

Maman bites her lip. 'This is for the best. You are the computer genius. And here we are, what do you call it? Sitting hens.'

'Ducks,' I snap. 'Which you perfectly well know.' But her expression is one I know all too well; she will not be argued with. And besides, if she hadn't suggested it, I would have begged to accompany him. If there's a device at the neighbours, I give myself the best chance of contacting the outside world.

We need to get help.

I lean in close, let her wrap her hands around my neck and hug her for a few precious seconds. 'You're okay?' I whisper the question.

Maman presses her forehead against mine so she's staring into my eyes and I can't possibly miss her next words. 'Be careful.'

I don't wanna leave you. But I only think the childish cry. 'I'll be careful,' I say instead.

There's not much to take. I grab my useless phone just in case, along with some water and chips that I can't stomach.

With Dylan on one side and Adam waiting below, I make a less than elegant descent over the balcony, and he helps me negotiate the rocks until we're on level ground. When I sneak a look back, Dylan's already gone inside.

I figured we'd be hiking to the neighbours, but when we make it around to the front of the suite, the abandoned golf cart Adam mentioned is on the path.

'Did they leave a key in it?' I ask.

'No.' He gets in and fiddles underneath for a minute before it sputters into life. 'Hot-wired,' he explains.

'Where did you learn that?' I ask as I take the seat next to him, trying not to compare this moment with the excitement in me on the day we arrived. This connection with Adam was what I wanted, but not at such a cost.

He sets the cart moving before he answers, and I notice that he's scanning either side of the trail intently, and I know it's for Marco or one of the missing women or even the hosts. 'It's not as cool a story as you might think. Pop thought we should know how to start his ancient ute if something happened on the property.'

The fondness in his voice overlays the tension of the situation.

The small engine complains, and I can feel he's pushing it to go as fast as possible.

We get away from the house and for the first time I catch the hint of smoke in the air. 'What if we're heading straight for the flames?' I say. 'Or for Marco?'

He doesn't answer, and I realise it's because he can't see any other option. If we don't try to get help, we could all die here.

Monet – Sunday

The realisation that we're all out of decent choices should be terrifying, but it just makes me feel less alone. There's relief in the knowing. The sense of dread in me since I found Bugsy has a face and a name.

'Marco D'Angelo.' I say his name softly enough that it's swallowed into the crunch of leaves beneath the wheels and the low growl of the cart engine. It fits that he'd do this, I guess. He didn't try to hide his horrible views. *Old-fashioned*, Connie had called him.

Connie. Can she have gone over the balcony down to the rock, like it looked at their suite? My brain can't seem to process it as fact, despite the necklace and the state of their room, but neither can I think of another explanation. Is it hypocritical to feel tears threatening for people I didn't like?

'Are you okay?' Adam's darted a look across at me, nearly driving us into a low bush as a result.

'The media is filled with teenagers rolling their eyes and defining cool, but here I am with all the fame and money I could want, and I'm struggling not to cry over a couple of strangers.'

'They haven't all seen a dead body.'

'But Bugsy was a douche. It's not like I'm sad about it.' But again, my voice wavers, and I'm seeing Bugsy's veiny cheeks, and I can picture too easily from Florence's description the marks at his throat and the deadness of those eyes. My throat is thick, and I have to force the words out. 'Tell me about Jonny Rake, how you remember him.'

There's a shadow on Adam's features. 'You really want to do this now?'

I make a show of looking around, sucking in a great lungful of smoky air – I think it's getting thicker – until I have to cough. When my eyes stop watering and I can speak again, I say, 'There might not be another time.'

'And if you're dead, will it matter?'

'It will matter to me.'

One of the few quotes I've managed to find online about my father that says more than the same old line of 'a brilliant musician whose life was cut tragically short' was from an interview with Adam. In it, he said that Jonny was the baby of the family with all that entails, even with their grandparents after their parents died. He said that when Jonny wanted something, it was really hard to say no. When some distant relative, feeling pity for their orphaned state, blew through town and gave nine-year-old Adam a second-hand guitar, Jonny cried because he wanted one.

And Adam gave it to him.

It was written as some sign of how Jonny Rake was destined to be a music prodigy. I read it and felt sorry for his brother.

'Fine,' Adam says. 'Ask whatever you want, but I'm not in the mood to sugar-coat this for you.'

We've reached open farmland, although there's no sign of any animals. I'm not great with directions, but I think we're well past the stage area. There's a closed gate ahead that must be the divide to the other property.

'He's always reported to have had this brilliant but tragic life. Is it true?'

Adam's laugh is pure pain. 'It's hard looking back. Growing up, I didn't ever stop and think, yeah, I'm the side note in Jonny's sad story. We were just kids getting by. Losing Mum and Dad sucked, but lots of kids grew up worse off. Gran and Pop were great, and we didn't miss out on any love, not really.' He's fixed on the trail ahead, his hands showing pale where they grip the steering wheel so tight he's shaking with it. 'Jonny in particular hardly knew our parents, he was so young. And everyone loved Jonny.'

'So, you're saying it's all bullshit?'

I think for a second he's going to correct my language, but he must realise how he'd sound.

'I didn't say that. Because in hindsight I can't help thinking something was always going to happen. He was too... much.' He gulps and keeps his focus on the shadows beneath a clump of gum tree overhanging the closed gate, but the wistfulness in his voice tells me almost as much about Adam as it does about Jonny. 'Jonny was too full of spark to keep burning that brightly.'

He's stopped the cart in the shade, the reprieve from the sun overhead a relief. If he realised how raw and obvious his love for his brother is, I don't think he'd be talking at all.

'You loved him a lot?'

I know as soon as I say it that I've said the wrong thing, because the vulnerability in Adam's face is replaced by the usual swagger of a failed rock star.

He jumps out and crosses to the gate. 'Yeah, he was family.'

And despite the change in him that means I know I won't get the answer I want, I open my mouth and call after him anyway. 'If family matters so much to you, why don't I?'

Without meeting my gaze, he fiddles with the chain and then the post. Frowning as he does so. He pushes the gate open and then returns to the cart, the passing seconds letting my words drift and fade into the trees, allowing him to avoid answering. 'There was a lock on the gate, but it's broken.' He points to a distant clump of buildings in the opposite direction from where we've come that must belong to the farmer. 'We might be too late.'

I blink and make sense of what I'm seeing. 'Smoke. It doesn't look like the chimney kind.' I don't know what I was hoping to find here, but this isn't it.

He scans the unblemished paddocks. 'We'll have to get closer to be sure, but it doesn't look good. I'm no expert, but that wouldn't explain the smell all the way at the other end of the island where the suites are.'

I follow his logic. 'Which means there's more than one area burning, and they're a long distance apart. Would be a big coincidence.'

His mouth flattens to a grim line. 'This is no accidental bushfire.'

Edward - Sunday

I regret being left behind with Dylan and Ivy about two minutes after Adam and Monet disappear. Not that I was given a choice. While the space should feel roomier, just the three of us means there's no one here to distract them. And makes it next to impossible to avoid the prowling Dylan.

'I shouldn't have let him go,' Dylan mutters, making like he's going to punch the wall then pulling up short. The cuts on his face from the glass have dried into tiny scabs.

Ivy's smile is coaxing but strangely weak. 'You know it made sense.'

'I can know that and still hate it.' He stalks out onto the balcony, seemingly uncaring of the sun beating down on him from above. It's like he's daring someone to come and attack us so he can fight with them.

Doing my best to blend into the wall is protecting me so far, but at some point he's going to remember I outed him, and it might be me he takes his frustrations out upon.

'Edward, can I talk to you for a second?' asks Ivy. We're alone for a moment, and I get the distinct impression she wants it that way.

'Sure.'

She picks at the edge of the cushion, and then she looks at me with something like fear in her eyes. And then picks at the edge some more.

Enough of this. 'Whatever it is you want to say, just say it.'

She sighs. 'It's just that I heard you.'

'Heard what?'

Another long pause. 'You fought with her and now she's missing. I was not well, but I am sure of these facts.' She takes a reedy breath. 'I think I know what it might have been about.'

Okay. I can deal with this. 'All couples fight.'

'They do, but this was serious. She was so upset, and I heard her crying and crying.'

My teeth grind together. Lara and her tears. 'She did that,' I say. 'Pretty often, in fact. Wear the wrong shoes to dinner, tears. Forget to pick up the tofu, tears. Anyway, if you heard all that then you heard that she walked away from our argument.'

'But you said...' She lowers her tone. 'That you'd had enough.'

'Did you ever think I might have been embarrassed? Look,' I barrel on, 'I got mad with her, but she deserved it.' I hate the pleading in my voice, but she needs to understand. 'She pretended she was a casual fan, but she wasn't. I recently found the blogs she'd created going back decades. She wrote post after post, all of them gushing, all of them written as some guy called Ricky.'

'A man?'

'Yes.' I grasp on to her confusion to back up my point. 'I think like short for Cedric. It's deceptive. You see? She lied about that, she lied about everything. I married an obsessed stalker.'

She's shaking her head. 'I'm not sure that's a good reason to—'

'She fucked him.' I bow my head as she flinches, but the woman wanted details, she can have them. It's the first time I've said it aloud but it's kind of freeing, so I say it again. 'She fucked your Jonny. Just like Dylan did, and like everyone wanted to. It wasn't like he was discerning, was it?'

Ivy hesitates. 'I don't know what to say. She was your wife, and one fling with Jonny before she even met you shouldn't change that.'

'You don't understand,' I choke out. 'None of you understand.'

My hands curl into fists.

I see her gaze swing to them and then look to where Dylan is, just outside. She's worried. Ivy St Fleur is a little bit scared. A sudden glow like happiness fills me, curves my lips. I think I'm baring my teeth, but I don't care.

That's right, you should be on the defensive.

They should all learn to speak to me with some respect, respect I haven't ever had in this stupid band. I don't mean to move, but suddenly I'm leaning right over her and she's pressing back into the cushions.

'Dylan,' she calls.

Guard dog that he is, he comes running. And she must have sounded panicked to him – I could barely hear her over the rushing in my ears – because he closes the distance between us in two huge strides.

His veins are out on his neck and he grabs my collar, lifting me up to eye level like I was made of candyfloss. 'Did you do something to her, Edward?'

'No,' I stammer. 'We were talking. She called me over.'

'You don't sound sure.' He turns to Ivy. 'Edward doesn't sound too sure to me. Did he do something?'

Her eyelashes shield her gaze as she looks away. 'I don't know.'

'There,' Dylan says, but he lets me go. I move back so fast I hit the wall behind and fall down it, my legs proving somewhat unreliable. 'I'm starting to think you might not be very trustworthy.'

'You know me.' I can hear the pleading in my voice, and I make an effort to calm myself. 'I played alongside you. I'm part of the band.'

I never wanted to join a band. My path was more university and academic success and a nice house in a nice neighbourhood. But if not for the band, I'd never have been with a woman like Lara.

The way Dylan and Ivy are looking at me squeezes the air from my lungs. They're judging me, and I can tell they're putting two and two together and coming up with five, because they're not bright enough for even simple maths. And I want to tell them that, but I know saying anything will make this worse.

'I know what I heard,' Ivy says. Dylan looks to her and she falters like she feels bad, but if she really did she would never have opened her stupid mouth. 'I heard Edward arguing with his wife.'

Dylan stands over me. 'You fought?'

My head lowers, trying to erase the memory of satisfaction in Lara's eyes when she admitted it.

You really want to know? Then yes, I slept with him. More than that, I let him fuck me against one of those huge speakers at the front of a stage after a concert in Berlin.

'Yes,' I say. 'We argued.'

'Then where is she?'

Edward – Sunday

Dylan and Ivy are staring at me, but I can't seem to find any words.

'Where is your wife?' Dylan snarls.

My wife...

My breath hitches and I'm blindsided by a memory from years ago. Walking through the front door and there she was, a pose straight from one of those naughty magazines I was never allowed to look at, reclining on the kitchen bench wearing nothing but an apron.

She was all my fantasies come true.

She always said our oldest son was conceived that night. All I know is that I whispered over and over into her hair and then the crook of her neck and then between her breasts that she was everything I ever wanted.

Something hot and acidic burns at the back of my throat. I gag. Swallow the liquid back down, disguising the movement as a cough. Vomiting is a choice, and I refuse to do it. Not with Dylan and Ivy already slowing to look at me like I'm acting strange.

'Okay, bro?' Dylan asks.

'I'm not your bro.'

'Where is she?' Dylan repeats.

I lift my head, let them both see the confusion that's been dogging me since I went past the ravaged stage area to check

302

if my memories from early this morning were even real. I didn't have much time to look but I couldn't see her. It must have been a fantasy born of my rage. 'I don't know, okay? I do not know. I will swear it on anything.'

He's still standing over me.

More acid rises in the back of my throat, and with it a bubbling in my stomach. Oh, that's not good. That's not good at all. And it's not fear or guilt or anything so abstract. It's a lot more insistent than that.

'I have to go,' I say, rolling onto my knees away from Dylan then using the wall to lever up to a stand.

'Go?' he asks. 'Where?'

'Bathroom,' I manage, bending at the waist, curling my arm across my stomach like I can hold everything steady with a bit of pressure and sheer will. I look up the very, very short hallway and think of them listening in. 'But not here.'

'Why the sudden rush?'

The symptoms are all too familiar. 'Gluten.'

One side of his mouth kicks up. 'You must have whinged to the hostess once too often.'

I haven't eaten since I grabbed a muffin this morning when everyone split off to search their suites, and the peach and apricot was definitely on the gluten-free table set aside.

'You think she'd do something like that deliberately?'

'I think we're stranded on this island in a possible fire with no communication and no help coming. So, yeah, it might be petty compared to doing a runner, but probably satisfying.' He holds his hands up in innocence. 'If you're that kind of person.'

Florence... That bitch. I knew she didn't like me.

I'm out on the balcony before Dylan calls after me. 'Will you be okay on your own?'

I don't bother to answer. Like he cares, like any of them care. Besides, my needs are far too basic right now to worry about anything but the scramble over the rail and stumbling to my suite.

I get inside and then crab-walk the few steps to the bathroom as the door clicks closed behind me. I'm so fixed on that shiny white toilet bowl that I don't look around. I'm pants down in relief as the spasms in my stomach at last have their way.

Finally, I'm spent, and I clean up and flush. I'm turning to the sink when I see it.

I know what you did.

The cliché of it, scrawled in Lara's favourite pink lipstick on the glass window between the bathroom and the rest of the suite, is a jab to the solar plexus.

The back of my neck prickles.

I spin, my heart thudding hard, and then search the small space, but I'm alone in the suite and there's not a soul to be seen from the huge windows. Unlike Ivy and Monet's suite, the cliff drops away here, so it would be more difficult for someone to get in or out from the balcony. Besides, the door is still locked.

But the words are unmistakably there when I return to the bathroom.

And there's a faint whiff of something over the stench. Smoke? Menthol? Suddenly, I can picture Jonny with the cigarette hanging out the side of his mouth like it always did. And he's laughing.

I shake the image away. Not Jonny. But the words are still there. Florence? Dylan? Someone else?

'It's not even original,' I shout.

But no one answers.

I grab the nearest towel and stride to the glass, where I scrub at the words. But even when most of the lipstick is wiped off, I can see the accusation every time I shut my eyes.

I know what you did.

My heart thuds so loud I'm sure they will be able to hear it in the other suite.

I'd brought a little something with me for before the show, just to make sure it didn't all go the way Lara wanted. A small echo of what happened to Jonny.

I hadn't even intended to confront her this weekend. Walking the estate with Bugsy looking for a private spot to indulge in the escape he'd offered yesterday, I'd literally stumbled over the ingredients required to turn the disruption into a statement. I figured it was probably standard stuff kept on a property like this.

As for knowing how to combine them – well, that was all Jonny. Years of obsessing over the accident that should never have taken him gave me more knowledge than I could ever need. The nerdiness they all sneered at meant the information stuck.

Then, on the wave of righteous, Bugsy-fuelled rage, I just had to lure her to the stage. It was almost too easy with the note about wanting to hear her sing, knowing how desperate she was to be famous any way she could. I woke up with the whole thing a blur of sound and fire and a flipping rush better than anything in my life. There one moment, gone the next.

She deserved it, anyone would agree.

Except, when I took my chance to go to the stage area and check during the search, she wasn't there. I didn't have time to fully comb the place, but where could she have even gone?

She's nowhere to be found.

And now I don't know if I hallucinated involving her at all.

Monet – Sunday

Adam and I make the rest of the short drive to the neighbouring homestead in silence. I'm scanning for signs of life, but there's only a couple of sheep, which run from our rumbling approach, and the ever-increasing smoke over a motley collection of old buildings.

'We'll try the farmhouse first,' Adam suggests.

Now closer, it's clear the small weatherboard building is ablaze. The empty windows glow red from the flames within, the grass around it blackened, and the closest trees catching with flames before our eyes. The rushing crackle of it punctuated by a bang from inside. I jump and hope that Adam didn't notice.

'There can't be anyone in that,' I say. But what I mean is no one alive. And I think of the neighbour I saw this morning and flinch again as a window cracks.

I'm so hypnotised by the spread of black and red, the smoke seeming to suck some of the sunshine from the sky, the heat in front a match for the one beating down from overhead, that Adam is disappearing around the far side of the structure before I realise he's moved.

'What are you doing?' I cry.

'Stay there,' he calls, his hand up.

But I'm already moving, giving the fire an even wider berth than he did, blinking away tears from the smoke that billows in clouds of muddied grey from the holes in the roof, almost like the building is exhaling its last desperate breaths.

He's looking for that man. I know it.

'Willie?'

His call from ahead confirms my guess. By the time I catch up, he's shaking his head. 'There's no one here.'

Again, my insistent brain adds 'alive'.

He points to the driveway that heads to a distant deserted beach further down the valley and a smaller dock not unlike the one where we arrived. There's a rough shed of some sort down there, and in it what might be the front bull bar of a vehicle sticking out.

'If I had to guess, I reckon there used to be a boat there. There are ropes hanging like someone left in a hurry.'

'Maybe he fled the fire?' I suggest.

'Impossible to tell. Either way, it's destroyed any kind of communication device we might have found inside. Unless your skills extend to reincarnating computers from ash.' He takes a few steps towards the front of the house, coughing at the smoke.

My mouth opens automatically to warn him. 'Be careful.'

And I'm back in the suite with Maman telling me to go with Adam in case there's some computer to be hacked, and I'm asking her if she's okay and she doesn't answer. Instead of the promise I was looking for, a murmured warning to 'be careful'.

It's not like I've ever run wild; impossible to do much of anything stuck out on our gorgeous estate with guards and security cameras and staff monitoring my every move under the guise of serving. Maman's ways of privacy and isolation have infected my relationships outside our little bubble.

Be careful.

Words said so often I can hear them at will in my head and they carry the inflection of her accent and the musicality of her voice. Implied, in her way, that those outside of our little unit of two are not to be trusted. A lesson I learned the hard way after I'd pushed so hard to go to that exclusive girl's school. I couldn't trust them, and I came back home knowing she was right. I always assumed Maman was protecting my virtue in a reaction to her own mistakes. But maybe it wasn't my body she was protecting all this time. Maybe it was something far more vulnerable – my heart.

An icy, creeping dread fills my chest. I stumble after Adam, grab at his shoulder so he turns to me. 'We have to get back.'

Adam frowns. 'I just want to—'

'No. We have to get back there now.'

'What's wrong?'

How can I explain that I came here looking for family, but I lost sight of the most important person. 'It's Maman.'

'You're worried about Marco? They're safe in that suite. Dylan will look after her.'

'Please,' I say. 'There's nothing here.'

He seems like he's going to force the issue, but then his gaze sweeps my face and whatever he sees there changes his mind. He strides to where we left the cart, waits for me to get in and then turns it back towards the way we came. We're through the gate and back onto Three Chains's property before he speaks again. 'Tell me something.'

I know a distraction technique when I hear it but I'm not averse to being distracted. I can't stop myself thinking the worst about Maman. Why didn't I pick up that she dodged the question? The doctors said she could deteriorate at any time.

'Like?'

He shrugs. 'I don't know. It's not like I've ever done this uncle thing before, but you got to ask me about Jonny. Tell me something about your life.'

It's like one of those bad dates in a romcom. Tell me about yourself. Well, I like long walks on the beach, music, and I'm definitely a dog person although kittens are pretty cute.

All that's true enough, but it's banal.

I'm pretty sure he doesn't want to know that I once walked up to a stranger on the street convinced the man was Jonny Rake, that I pretend Father's Day doesn't exist, that I used to wake at night and hear Maman crying outside my door.

Maman.

My throat aches and we're still so far from the suites.

When I don't say anything, he takes a hand off the wheel and rubs at the back of his neck. 'You got stressed when you realised we were locked in, like panicked. Why?'

I'm surprised he noticed.

'Just your everyday dislike of small spaces.'

'You're claustrophobic?'

'My therapist says we're all on a spectrum of claustrophobia. I'm sure you wouldn't like being buried alive in a coffin.' I spit it out fast so the image can't get fixed in my head.

'Guess I wouldn't,' he agrees.

And then, because he made an effort, I give him something. 'I was maybe five, and we were on tour. Well, Maman was, but I went everywhere with her, always.'

He nods. 'The Summer Sounds Festival.'

I'm good with numbers, but that was quick. Maybe he's paid more attention to us through the years than I thought.

He seems to realise what he's revealed because he clears his throat. 'I'm crap at all this, because I'm crap at most things. Doesn't mean I never gave a shit.'

'Okay, yeah,' I say quickly. 'I ran a bit wild. Everyone knew me and I understood not to go out with the crowd. There was music and summer air, and I was bought more doughnuts and candyfloss than I could handle. It was pretty sweet. Up until that night, anyway.'

I hesitate. Now I've started this I have to go on, but it's hard to talk about it and stop the cramping of my chest, hard to remember and not feel the warm air getting warmer as the oxygen vanished. That's what you get for growing older – I didn't even know about oxygen being replaced by carbon dioxide back then, but my brain's cleverly overlaid it.

'What happened?'

'It was just before Maman's set. It must have been dark by then as she was the last act, and I snuck away from my usual perch in the wings and crawled to a spot I'd found earlier up under the stage. In my head it was an adventure, a cosy cocoon in a smuggler's cave or something.'

'But?'

'I got stuck.' I swallow hard, trying to keep my voice from cracking. 'Yes, I know, how perfect for my therapist when I revealed the source of my fear. The woman hardly needed to go far to get to the poor little daughter of stars who couldn't be heard over the fans.'

I can hear my breath catch as I keep my mind from picturing what I'm talking about.

'How long?' he asks.

'Somewhere between five minutes and a lifetime. By her last song, I managed to hyperventilate myself into a faint, and when I came to the set was over and they were looking for me. Someone heard me sobbing.'

'Shit.'

It's a funny thing when he looks at me, because unlike that first day where his gaze seemed to bend around me and glance off to the side, now it's more like he's drinking me in. And I find I don't mind it. Don't mind at all being seen by the uncle no one ever wanted me to know.

'There's something else,' I say. 'That screen you saw on the deck with your name, it's because I've studied you. Like, a lot, and I'm pretty good with computers.' I blurt it out. He needs to know what all this has been for.

He nods slowly. 'You know about me and you still arranged all this?'

I sneak a glance at him.

Obviously, me pulling the strings hasn't been as subtle as I hoped. 'That's all just data. I wanted more.'

'Family,' he whispers.

'Family,' I agree.

'We're nearly there,' Adam says. 'The smoke doesn't seem any worse.'

He's right. The clamp of dread around my ribs eases. I allow myself to hope. 'Maybe the authorities have arrived while we were gone, and we made the trek for nothing.'

'Maybe.'

I adopt my best grown-up voice. 'I know. Don't get my—'

A sound from ahead rips through my words, snatching 'hope' from my mouth as the boom vibrates right through my chest, somehow throwing me backwards, tilting the world.

Maman?

Florence – Sunday

A flock of birds launch from the top of the tree canopy, their concern at the distant explosion a cacophony of shrieks that echo down over the rocks to the private bay I kept everyone from with a few shark stories and some well-placed chains. I can't help turning to look and picturing what might be happening out of sight up at the house.

But I don't linger. This isn't the time for speculation.

As I approach the boat, the sound of crying rises over the soft splash of the water against the hull. Heart thudding, I stop to listen, but there's nothing out of the ordinary. Could it have been my imagination?

If I'd brought Elsie with me, I'd ask her if she'd heard anything, but the urn with my sister in it is nestled carefully up at the house, ready for the final trip off the island. And I can probably guess what she'd reply.

Stop wasting time.

And she'd be right. I need to get moving. Warily now, I inch forward, my small steps not making a sound on the wood of the jetty.

There it is again.

Someone's crying nearby. I'm sure of it. And it sounds like it's coming from the boat. Chances are it's one of the group who's lost their way and ended up down here and they're terrified, given everything with Bugsy. But, just in case, I let my bags fall to my feet and grab the knife I brought with me from the kitchen. The huge one, with the blade so sharp my finger still pulses with pain beneath the bandage placed over where I sliced it earlier.

I hold the weapon ready in front of me. Edge forward some more. Lean down so I can see into the dark shadows near the helm where I'm sure the noise came from. Blink to adjust my vision after the bright sunshine overhead. There's nothing there. A scrape comes from behind me, on the jetty.

Thud.

My head jerks forward as light explodes behind my eyes. The edge of the boat rushes at me as I fall against the side of the boat, and my hands fly out to protect my face. I catch myself so close that my lips parody a kiss on the top of the gunwale.

'What the—'

I cut myself off, as reason catches up with the pain spreading from the back of my head. If there's one hit... I throw myself sideways, just in time to miss another blow. Something crunches into the hull as I stagger, trying to get my balance, shaking my head to clear it. *Ouch*, now it hurts even more.

But I've turned enough that I can see my assailant.

And I'm not certain the blow I did take isn't making me see things.

'But there was that necklace over the balcony,' I manage. 'The room was destroyed. Marco...'

Connie, somehow straighter and brighter and bigger than she's been these last few days, smiles and passes a block of wood from hand to hand. 'I will miss that necklace, but the foolish man snatched it from me and threw it when he realised what was happening.'

I gulp in salty air, trying to regain my equilibrium. 'What is happening? What is all this?' I make a show of rubbing my head, not needing to exaggerate my wince, while I step sideways so the knife I dropped is hopefully hidden from her view. 'We had an agreement. The documentary would forever rewrite the story of The Cedrics Band, expose them for what they really are.'

She shrugs. 'Things change. I remembered I've always worked better alone. Peter and I have that in common. It's probably why that awful Jonny kicked him out of the band, he knew my son could be a star that would threaten his own time in the spotlight.'

'And Bugsy?' I ask. 'We never said there would be casualties.' I can hear the frustration in my tone. We had an agreement. She gets access to the band that she needed to show the world the truth about them; I get them on my island for my own revenge.

'The interviews with the band confirmed what I'd always suspected,' she says. 'Ian Malone, as manager, made the ultimate decision to keep my boy from taking his rightful place in the band. He was responsible for what happened afterwards: the depression, the trouble. It's thanks to him that Peter will probably spend the rest of his days behind bars.' Her voice cracks. 'My boy needed that band, and they stole it from him.'

It strikes me that, from what Dylan said, the reason Peter missed that fateful night was because he was already off getting into trouble, but mothers aren't exactly rational when it comes to their sons.

'Anyway,' Connie sniffs, 'Marco promised to sort that out for me, and Ian paid for what he did. For all his faults – and, let me tell you, some of his attitudes towards women were simply archaic – my husband had his uses. Unfortunately for him, that usefulness ran out.' She hefts the wood again, stronger than she seemed all weekend, but not made of muscle or I'd be face down in the water. 'And between you and me, his documentary footage was average at best. We were never going to get our revenge through an unflattering movie.'

'You could have warned me,' I say, knowing that I haven't been entirely honest with her either but embracing my role as the betrayed.

Connie laughs. 'I have ached for nearly two decades, you do not matter.'

'You really hate them.'

'Yes.'

Meeting Connie and Marco all those months ago and learning they were as desperate as I was to get The Cedrics Band back together seemed like fate. Now it feels like a giant headache. Mostly because the mad woman just hit me.

She actually hit me.

So much for the others thinking of her as elderly. This woman has been playing the weakling and is far more dangerous than any of them.

Connie takes a purposeful step closer. 'As I said, plans change and so do alliances. It's nothing personal, I'm sure you understand. Now, with Bugsy punished, Marco dealt with and the band up there scampering for their lives, I'd prefer not to be caught in whatever else is happening here. If you'd like to hand over the keys to the boat, I'll be on my way, and no one else needs to get hurt.'

'You're going to leave me here?' I sway on my feet. The

acting is easy enough, because she really did not miss with that wood.

She sniffs the air. 'What, are you worried about the fire? You've survived fire before. I'm sure you can do it again.'

It's the dismissiveness that gets me.

This woman, who thinks her wayward child is as important as everything I've done to get here, that for him she can wipe away what I've planned, and I'll just accept it.

I let out a growl.

Anger and pain sound so much alike, really. It's uncanny. This woman might have done away with her husband – I'm thinking that single cup we found in their suite did have a hint of cloudy residue in the bottom of it – but she didn't hit me hard enough the first time. And I have no intention of giving her a second go.

Letting my legs give up their battle to stay upright, I fall to my knees.

Triumph lifts her features. I'm down and she hasn't had to raise her hand again.

The high-pitched whimper I emit covers my scrape for the knife. Then, familiar handle in my palm, and with my sister's beautiful face overlaying my blurred vision, I propel myself forward and up, up onto my toes, using every ounce of strength I have left.

The blade goes in. Smooth. Up and into the side of her neck, higher still, until it lodges in something and there's red coming over my fingers and her eyes are so wide, and her mouth opens but she only manages a thick gurgle. I yank the knife out, then slash that sharp blade across her neck until the wood she's holding drops onto the dock and she crumples after it.

I take a breath, consider the blood on my hands and the knife, then I kneel so I can lean over and rinse them off in the water. Tiny fish come to investigate as the murky drops diffuse into the ocean.

I've seen enough movies that I'm careful to roll the unmoving Connie off the dock into the deep water below the boat and take a few steadying breaths, watching for the shadowy figure to sink into the depths.

'Bruce really does keep his knives exceptionally sharp,' I tell her before turning back to finish loading the boat.

I don't have time to waste. My husband will be waiting.

Edward – Sunday

Boom!

I'm almost back to Ivy's suite when I hear it. I stop, pressing back under the pollen-filled shelter of a huge gum tree. My insides contract in a way that has me wishing I was back in the bathroom.

What was that? Where did it come from?

Don't pretend you don't recognise the sound of fuel and a spark.

Putting my hands over my ears doesn't block Lara's taunting voice in my head. She's right, and I'm guessing this particular sound is most likely the combinations of all those stores of combustible liquid I noticed around the property.

I do a slow turn, staying in the shadows, trying to listen, but at first hearing nothing. Could it have come from the path down to Hawk Bay? Or was it back at the main house?

A rumble of voices carries over the rocks and garden from the suite balcony. The fools that they are aren't trying to keep a low profile.

If I can hear them, then so can whoever made that bang.

I stare into the bushland as though, if I concentrate hard enough, I'll see through the trees to whatever lies beyond. That sound could have been a boat backfiring. It could be the sign that Florence did call the authorities and they've made it to the island and help is on its way.

A really large fucking boat?

I ignore Lara's taunt in my head as another explosion, further away this time, sounds through the trees, scattering birdlife high into the clear blue sky with flapping feathers and disgruntled squawks.

That was from the trails we walked to the stage. I'm sure of it.

Instinct has me backing away, then running from the suites, even as logic tells me there might be no reason to flee. I know through my aching head and churning stomach that staying with the others right now isn't safety in numbers; rather, it's making myself a bigger target.

Maybe it's the remnants of whatever it was Bugsy gave me last night still zipping through my body. Maybe it's because I've been called a coward too many times in my life, and I'm damn sick of it.

I'm the new Edward. I veer off the trail, heading up towards the distillery. I'm not going to risk being stuck in the suite when whoever is responsible for the explosions arrives.

'Wait.'

I think maybe someone cries out after me, but my breath is too loud, and I can't be sure who spoke. I break into an ungainly jog.

Oh look, the nerd's trying to run.

I shove aside a memory of one of the bigger bullies, probably Adam, calling out to me across the oval in late primary school during a compulsory fun run. Fun? Ha. It was the last time I made that mistake.

I catch a hint of menthol on the smoke in the air and my heart flips. I know it isn't, I know it can't be, but when it comes down to it, I'm just as pathetic as the most desperate fan.

'Jonny?' I whisper.

Part of me wants him to lope into view. Tell me it doesn't matter that the note he found that drew him to his death was actually meant for me. I should have been the one checking those cords. The faulty connection was for the keyboard, not the mic like everyone thought. I saw it before the explosion threw me off the stage for Lara to find.

For a while, after I found out the truth about Lara and her obsession, I thought I deserved her having loved Jonny first, deserved being her afterthought. Figured it was karma for what I'd done and the secret I kept. But my wild night on this island with Bugsy gave me clarity, and I knew I didn't have to accept what she'd done. That I could make her pay.

But someone wrote on that bathroom window. Someone knows what I did. Now there's someone following me.

Friend or foe?

I'm not waiting around to find out. I push myself harder, shaky legs threatening to give way at every step. The paths seem so different from that first day, with Lara's incessant chatter.

I didn't realise it would be so hot. And all these flies. Yuck. I totally hate flies. They spread disease, and did you know they can actually taste with their feet? Do you think Florence has a spray to keep them away?

Just thinking about it brings her voice back to my brain so loud that I jerk, slip and fall hard onto my knees. Only the last desperate bracing of my hands stops me tasting dirt.

With a shaky breath, I half roll so I'm sitting and stare down at the raw redness on my hands, and then at the tiny pinpricks of blood welling around the sharp stones embedded in my knees. I haul myself up.

Every rock or crack in the path is a possible tripping hazard. And the pounding in my skull tells me that if I go down where they can see me, whoever's following me will be upon me. And there's already dead people on this island – I won't be getting up.

Remembering the locks on the distillery, I run past it, keeping to the shadows as much as I can until, chest heaving, I reach a huge structure – big enough that I have to shield my eyes from where the sun hits the galvanised metal sides. The air-conditioning vents up near the roof are silent and still.

That's right – the power is off.

The heat sticking my polo shirt to my skin suddenly feels five degrees hotter.

The metal handle is hot from the sun. There's resistance. I almost laugh. Of course, it's locked. I'm going to be stuck here.

Then, as I taste the giddy relief, it gives beneath my hand. I swallow, my mouth dry, as the heavy, insulated door groans open. No power means no light. The darkness is thick inside the silent shed, and I want to let my eyes adjust, but I'm aware there's someone somewhere behind me.

My instincts register what I'm seeing before my brain puts it into actual thought.

Carcasses.

Several large hunks of meat hanging from metal hooks above.

I jerk to a stop, a hand's-width from walking into raw flesh. Sheep, from the size of it. I taste hot sick, then force it back. Placing my hand over my mouth and nose does nothing to disguise twin bleach and coppery-blood smells.

A scrape of steps on stone and a grunt of exertion somewhere behind me pushes me further inside. I'm way too exposed out on the path, and no one will come looking for me in this butchery. I pull the door, but not before I've registered the pristine metal workbench, the scabbards mounted on walls with knife handles protruding, the small handsaw hung to one side. Plastic on the other benches rustles as I push deeper into the room.

Hands over my face, in a fruitless attempt to keep the smell out and my stomach contents in, I'm tasting the warming carcasses with every ragged breath.

I stumble and catch my weight on a bench to keep from falling completely. My palms sting as the scrapes from earlier protest the landing on the warming metal.

There's the scuff of footsteps. Someone's definitely out there.

Any moment now they'll reach that doorway, open it and then they'll see me. I need to hide. Pulling aside the plastic covering hanging from the bench, I crawl under it.

Every breath I take seems to echo off the walls, only dampening where it encounters the fly-covered hunks of meat hanging from above. My legs twitch, threatening to cramp from pushing them way too hard given my depleted energy levels from the gluten attack. As if thinking of it reminds my insides, my stomach emits a long, purposeful rumble, the muscles around it contracting in far too familiar fashion. Thighs and underarms sting from the chafing of trying to run in this heat.

I press back against the wall in the corner. As my eyes adjust to the darkness, the butcher's knives in their safety scabbards seem to taunt me from across the shed. So close and yet so far. Why didn't I pick up a weapon?

Because you've never been very good with knives.

I hear Lara's voice in my head, the same affectionate tone she'd use as she reprimanded me whenever I'd manage to cut myself while carving a roast. She always worried for me about the little things.

Laughter skitters from my throat before I can stop it. I press my lips together but it's too late. It's far too late. There's no way the figure now clearly over by the door could have missed that sound. No way it could be mistaken for anything but a coward hiding in the dark.

I try to think of an escape, but all I see is her face in front of me, superimposed on everything else. Her blonde hair loose around her shoulders, her makeup set perfectly, and the bitch is laughing at me.

You thought you killed me, Edward, but you're not a killer. You're an accountant. I'm just outside, and I am going to tell everyone what you did. And about Jonny. Now he was a real man in every way.

I push my hands hard against my eyes until lights and colours brighten and blacken, but her face is still there. And she's still laughing. A giant fist wraps around my chest, squeezing until each breath is a ragged fight for air.

And now whoever is out there blocks the light coming from beneath the doorway. The door opens.

Edward – Sunday

As light streams in, the shadow at the door becomes a figure in a flowing summer dress, and she steps into the shed. 'Edward?' she asks. 'Is that you?'

'Florence.'

That makes sense, she's probably rounding up the guests, making sure we're all okay. That's why she followed me.

She blinks, comes closer, moves aside to let in more light. 'What are you doing under there?'

My mad panic seems so silly to say aloud, even sillier as I unfold from the cramped position under the far bench and try to stand on wobbly legs. 'We need to get out of here,' I say, swiping a hand across my face, hoping the tears I hadn't noticed falling aren't obvious. 'There were loud bangs before, and I think I can smell smoke.'

'Yes,' she says. 'You can.'

'Then we should go to higher ground. Or maybe to the bay, where the water can protect us. To a boat. Something.' It's only as I'm speaking in a garbled rush that I realise how entirely calm and unsurprised she is.

'Sorry, but I can't let you do that,' she says. 'Bruce will be back any moment, and then he and I must get going. There's about to be a rapid escalation of the fire on the island, and it's likely to raze the whole place to ashes. We wouldn't want to be stuck here when that happens.'

She sounds so certain.

'How do you know? Is it the wind? Can you be sure?'

Her mouth curves. 'I know all kinds of things.' Then her lips twitch. '*Boom.*' Her eyebrows lift as she whispers the mocking sound effect, an imitation of the one I created myself.

I see again the taunt in Lara's lipstick. 'Was it you?' I ask.

She waits, eyebrows raised.

'Did you leave me the message on the mirror?'

She flashes a hint of a smile. 'A nice touch, I thought. Anyway, it's been lovely, but I have places to be.'

'Wait, but Monet and Adam were down at the docks earlier looking for Lara and there weren't any boats. How can you and Bruce get off the island?'

'They were right,' she says. 'There aren't any boats.' She smiles and draws her hand from a fold in the pretty floral dress. Her long, delicate fingers, one with a neat bandage on it, are clasped around the grip of a small handgun. 'Not for you.'

'They're hidden.'

'Yes, we have a private dock and we'll be leaving from it soon. Then the real fun here will begin.' She sees my gaze on the weapon and rubs the back of her head. 'Ran into some trouble earlier and decided I should be better prepared.'

It's then I notice the red on the front of her dress isn't part of the pattern, and there are smears on her wrists and even her neck.

That's blood.

And I know, suddenly, with that same certainty I saw in Lara's eyes when her gaze met mine across the stage early this morning, that I'm not leaving this shed. Not alive. And this woman will be responsible.

She doesn't even have to say anything more. There's no need for threats. Because we both know that I am not a man who'll take on a gun. Christ, I'm an accountant. Maybe I could offer her money, help with getting rid of the others – there's not one out there I'd give my life for – but clearly if she's willing to let this place burn to the ground, money isn't an issue, and she has that hulking husband for muscle if she needs it.

I'm sure I've read about animals fighting for their lives until their last breath, but I find acceptance comforting. I sink back against the wall, the effort of holding myself upright on nerveless knees almost too much. I stop trying to erase the images of Lara in my head.

'But why?' I ask.

Florence's eyes light up and she quickly looks behind her as though checking whether she has enough time. 'So glad you asked. My sister, Elsie, wrote "Storybook Love".' She says it with all the dramatic flair of the big reveal.

'So?' I reply.

Her face falls.

It's not that I expected such a thing, but I'm not exactly surprised that Jonny might have claimed to have written something he hadn't. He was a charmer and a bit of a rogue. He always did what was best for Jonny. It was just that whatever that happened to be, it was usually fun enough to be around that no one cared.

Obviously, Florence cares. Her lips are thin, whitening at the edges. 'What you did to her ruined her life.'

I'm pretty sure any manual for About to be Murder Victim 101 would not encourage making the woman holding the gun mad, but I've moved quite beyond fear. It's there, in the background, of course – in the shaking I am not even trying to control and the suspicion that I'm one more wave of that gun away from loosening my bowels. But I've been on the other side of this.

I know when someone is going to change their mind.

Besides, I think I irritated her that first night complaining about the gluten in the salad, and that's enough for her to pull the trigger.

'Borrowing some lyrics ruined her life? How?' I ask, trying to understand why she's so mad.

'She should have had the credit and all that came with it for that song. Not having it destroyed her.'

The gun prevents my eye-roll. 'Destroyed' her life... seems a bit dramatic. 'There's always the courts,' I point out. 'She should have said something.'

Florence's laugh is choked. 'She did more than say something. She filed a suit.'

There's a tug at my memory. Maybe a meeting with a lawyer in that hurricane climb to the top? I was hungover – we all were. When Bugsy said this kind of thing happened all the time, I didn't have any reason not to believe him. There were dozens of people trying to ride our coat-tails to success. She would have been just another hand held out for what it could get.

'And?' Maybe this is some kind of self-preservation kicking in. Because although I ask, I really don't give two shits about the answer.

'It didn't get to court until after Jonny had died. The lawyers said at a stretch that even if Elsie's work was the unknowing – God, they were so damn careful not to sully Jonny Rake's memory – *unknowing* inspiration for the song, then she should take it as a compliment. They said, with a snicker, that many women would have loved to be such a brilliant artist's muse.' Her mouth twists. 'Called him brilliant. It was the final straw for her.'

I think I know where this is going. It explains all this effort in getting us here to the island, the certainty I feel that she is going to follow through on her plans.

But that stupid flicker of wanting to live, which I didn't think I had, sparks somewhere deep inside. It makes me open my dry mouth, makes me ask the question, tries to keep me alive for a few more seconds.

'What happened?'

She lifts her hand, points the barrel at me, her hand steady. 'Elsie couldn't live knowing what he took from her. Couldn't risk turning on the radio or TV and hearing that blasted song.' Florence's eyes close and when they open again, they shine with tears. 'My Elsie couldn't go on.'

'I'm sorry.'

'No,' she says. 'You're too late. Too late for that from any of you.'

'Please,' I beg, my voice quavering then breaking. 'I didn't know.' So much for acceptance. 'Not all of us are like Jonny. I'd never have allowed such a thing. You've seen what they're like – I was used as much as your sister. I'm not even part of the band.'

'That's true.'

There's a hint of sympathy in her tone. Maybe this won't end the way I thought it would.

'But you have your flaws like anyone,' she continues. 'Speaking of which, where is your wife, Edward?'

I feel the blood drain from my features and reel back. This looks bad, I know it. But looking bad doesn't mean anything.

Not in the end. Forcing my head to clear, I edge forward, intending to beg or plead or something. But my legs fail me, and I fall to my knees. Still I crawl closer, looking up but unable to see anything past the end of the gun. 'I don't know where Lara is, I swear. And I didn't know about your sister.'

'Now you do,' she says.

And fires.

Adam – Sunday

After we heard the explosion, I floored the golf cart, but it was an agonising journey back up the winding trail. Monet's hand showed white knuckles where she gripped the side, and I reckon she was close to leaping out and legging it.

At last, we reach the top of the incline. 'The air's a little clearer here,' I say hopefully.

The kid doesn't reply but gulps in oxygen in a way that sounds a lot like a sob. Should I reach out?

I choose to focus on trying to get her to her mother.

She's out of the cart before it's fully come to a stop and taking the now familiar route to the balcony and climbing over. By the time I get inside, she's next to Ivy, and Dylan is cutting off whatever he's been saying, because clearly he doesn't want me to hear it.

My jaw tightens. 'Willie's place was no help. Deserted and on fire. How are things here?'

Dylan shrugs. 'There were a few bangs and Edward left.'

I hadn't even noticed. 'Why?'

Something close to a smile crosses Dylan's features. 'Bathroom business.' Then the solemn look is back. 'But when he didn't come back, I went to his suite. He wasn't there.'

'I think he went to look for Lara,' Monet says. She's holding Ivy's hand so tight I'm surprised her mother's not complaining.

And Ivy... I can't look at her because the sheen of sweat on her face can't hide the dull lethargy of her usually bright eyes. And I want so damn badly to go over there and ask her what the hell is wrong, but it's not my place. It's never been my place. I'm the kind of guy who was fine for a bit of fun when Jonny wasn't around, luring me with whispers of forever, but ultimately she chose my brother. Even after he was gone.

The worst thing wasn't that I really believed we were something special.

No, the worst thing is that I'd still give my left nut for the woman if she asked.

'We have to get out of here,' Dylan says.

I look out to the water. 'It's not like I want to hang around, but it's a long swim.'

His hands are in frustrated fists. 'There must be a boat on this island somewhere.'

Monet is shaking her head. 'I've run there often enough, there's none by the docks where we arrived.'

There's something we're not seeing. Surely if this venture means anything at all to Florence and Bruce, they wouldn't have abandoned their guests, and if they're the masterminds behind this whole thing then why her confusion about Connie and Marco? Unless the woman is a better actress than any I've ever slept with – and there have been a few – then she was as shocked as the rest of us.

'We need to get into that house,' I say. 'There must be something up there that will tell us how to get off the island, or at least get help.'

'It could be dangerous – you've heard the explosions around the property. They're basic firebombs, rigged like Molotov cocktails on a timer.' Dylan must see my and Monet's matching *WTF?* expression. 'I might have done a little more than look for Edward. I stayed hidden and kept my distance from the fire sites, but there's no one around. Whoever did this wants the whole island to burn, and they might have set something up at the house.'

I frown. 'Like an ambush?'

He shrugs. 'I don't know.'

I catch myself from pushing further. 'I'll go and investigate,' I say.

I can see Dylan's surprise and hate myself that little bit more. I refuse to sit here while Dylan measures the situation and decides that he's the only one who can look after anyone else.

'I'll be back soon,' I say.

I head for the door and the balcony, and none of them call after me. I want to believe it's because they know I won't change my mind, but I fear it's because they realise I'm expendable. Like I've always been.

'Adam, wait.' It's Monet, stepping out onto the balcony, her eyes imploring.

'You can't stop me.'

She bites her lip. 'I'm not going to try. I just wanted to tell you to be careful.' There's pity in her eyes. 'We all have secrets.'

'You don't know the depths of mine. You might have looked, but the internet can only tell you so much.'

There's a lot about my life I'd rather Monet not know.

She hesitates and then says, 'You should know, about what happened at Sampson's Creek. That was Dylan.'

Her words thrust me back in time, to that pool in that godforsaken town. With the chick who said those things, who wouldn't shut up about Jonny, and then the guy appearing out of nowhere. Then those fists are dragging me under and I can't breathe, and I feel with sudden certainty that I won't breathe ever again, and I don't mind. At least it's over.

But survival kicked in and I lashed out and they called the cops. Fuckers so glad to catch a celebrity screwing up. I was looking at time – a long time – and...

'Adam?'

I find my way back to the present, following her voice. 'You know? Dylan knows?' I have to scrape the words out.

'He paid the bail. And more. He made it go away.'

'He wouldn't do that for me.' I shake my head. 'You must be wrong.'

'I'm not.'

'Look, fine, whatever. That's all in the past. We're not out here to rehash Adam's shitty life.'

She flinches and I wish the words back. I don't want to break this fledgling bond between us, but she should know by now, I break everything.

I leave before I make things worse.

As I keep to the bushes, ducking across the open spaces, the memories keep nagging me.

There's a distant crack, a bit like a branch snapping. My heart trips a beat and my feet follow, bringing me to my knees.

Was that a gunshot?

Adam – Sunday

I drag myself upright and try to listen but there's no repeat of the gunshot sound. Weapons are a whole different thing to the fire I was mentally prepared for, the one even now darkening the sky in the direction of the stage area and making each breath a challenge. I scramble around me in the dirt, find a decent stick and heft it. It's not going to do much against a gun, but it's better than nothing. In the shelter of a tree, I study the glass front of the main house.

It still looks deserted.

But if there's someone with a gun... It hits me that I could be shot and then left for dead here on this godforsaken island, and I'm not sure anyone would miss me. Unless you count the tabloids and gossip sites counting down to my next screw-up.

If I'd pulled out of this event any of the billion times I thought about doing so, I'd be in a bar right now, oblivious to all of this. My only worry deciding whether I'll watch the reunion.

But I'd have been bitter, and alone.

I wouldn't have met Monet nor realised what I've missed for the last seventeen years. Perhaps lost my only chance to ever see Ivy again. Better to go through all of this than miss what I've been able to experience these last few days.

Pushing myself out of the shadows before I lose my nerve, I cross to the deck where only a few hours ago we were told about Bugsy. The doors are locked, and there's no hint of life inside. I round the building, tugging windows, looking for a way in, or preferably a large note with directions to a boat.

The snort of laughter catches in my throat.

'You think this is funny?'

I spin, lifting the stick in front of me in defence. 'Shit, Dylan, you scared me.' The chair leg in his hand shows I'm not the only one thinking weapons. 'Why are you here?'

His face crumples like a smashed-in paper bag. For just a second it's all scrunched, but then the stoic exterior is back, and I'm left as disconnected as before. Except, I saw it. I recognised the panic I'm battling isn't far beneath his calm surface either.

'Because I couldn't wait there and do nothing.'

Suddenly, I need to know. 'Sampson's Creek. Was that you?'

I wait for the punchline, my body tense. If Monet's right and it was him, it can only be some sort of long game he's playing.

We stand there outside the kitchen door, and I'm not sure whether he's going to laugh or hit me with the chair leg. His expression is like one of those pictures that shows something completely different depending on the angle. Love and violence, both at once.

'Yes.' It's almost ripped out of him.

And suddenly I get that he might want to wring my neck, but some of that love in his face is for me. Because of Jonny. Because he loved my brother that much.

I swallow hard, trying to get rid of a lump of emotion in my throat that I know Dylan will not appreciate.

'He loved you too,' I say, needing him to know. 'Maybe not in the way you loved him, but whatever you think was between you, there was that and more. God, the way he'd defend you.' I shake my head at my bumbling attempts and put it simply. 'You were his best friend.'

His head bows, but not before I see the moisture in his eyes. 'It was Ian,' he says, his voice choked. 'Somehow, that bastard found out about me and Jonny. Told him it would look bad for the fans.' He spits the word. 'And Jonny backed off because Ian said so. I fucking hated that guy.'

I think of the tarpaulin that I didn't dare look at on the way in and can't muster much of a pang that he's gone. 'He wasn't my favourite person either.'

He grins. 'At last, we agree on something.' He gestures to the window next to the door. 'Let's get inside.'

I put my hand up to stop him, feel it collide with the hard wall of his chest. 'Tell me what they were talking about back there. Monet and Ivy. That's more than sunstroke.'

He shrugs me off and shakes his head. 'She's sick, you bloody idiot. Dying kind of sick. So sick she broke every bit of doctors' advice to come here.'

Part of me already knew, I think, but hearing him say it aloud almost brings me to my knees. 'Then why did she come?'

'For you. All because Monet wanted to meet you.'

No wonder he's been so mad with me. I look at him properly. We've sat almost opposite each other at a table the past two nights, we've been on stage together, even wrestled, but I haven't let myself really look at him until now. He was my brother's best friend, and Dylan without Jonny isn't something that I can observe without aching. Maybe that's why we've always clashed – we've always loved the same things, just not in the same way.

'You've had work done.' I don't mean to say it aloud, but I'm so surprised at the unnatural smoothness of his forehead and the perfect straightness of teeth I know were crooked for so long, and so oddly amused despite the circumstances.

'Yeah.' He shrugs. 'It's part of the business, you don't need to give me shit about it.'

'Your secret's safe with me.' And then, 'I should never have treated you like I did.'

He nods.

The rock makes short work of the stained glass next to the door and then of the handle itself when it can't be unlatched from inside. The deadbolt suggests some kind of premeditation to the whole thing.

The door swings open and heat billows from inside. Thanks to the huge windows and the lack of any power, the place has warmed like a huge oven.

There's nothing out of place in the living areas or any of the other rooms we scan through, but it's not like they're going to have left a detailed plan for how to escape the island in case of a fire and the hosts mysteriously vanishing. There's no electronics or phones to call for help.

'Where are you going?' I ask.

'Their bedroom.'

I hesitate.

'These people left us here stranded with who knows what tricks left to play out, and you're squeamish about their privacy?'

He has a point. Inside, it's all very sterile, with no more personality than the suites. Following Dylan's lead, I look in drawers and cupboards, but even the clothes left behind lack character. There's nothing here.

But Dylan is looking at something next to the bed.

'What's that?'

'It was in this drawer, and there's a spot on the wall that's not as faded that matches the size, like it was on display. Maybe it's something that was hastily taken down before we came.' He holds it out. 'It's the lyrics to "Storybook Love". Could it be some fan memento?'

I take it from him, hear the words I know so well play through in my head as I read the framed writing. 'No, it's similar, but there's different lines, and I'm sure that isn't Jonny's handwriting. Wait, it's signed by someone... Elsie?' It's familiar but I can't place it. 'What did Florence say about how we came to have this show here? Was it something about going to school with us?'

'I didn't really listen,' Dylan admits. 'Florence wasn't in your year or ours, she had to be years younger.'

'What about Elsie though? I think there was a girl called Elsie in a class with Jonny.' I mentally scan for the people I'd see him with, in the hall. 'She had a similar waif quality to Florence, but she was quieter. Always deep in her poetry and feelings, always winning writing competitions.'

There's a pause as the pieces slowly fall into place.

'You don't think?' Dylan begins, obviously not wanting to put it into words.

'I do.' It hurts to say that, like I'm sullying Jonny's memory, but it's the truth. 'Look, man, we both know Jonny was an okay songwriter, but he was no genius lyricist. Not until "Storybook Love".'

'So, you're saying he stole it?'

I hesitate. 'I guess that is what I'm saying. There was some lawsuit, way back when. I don't remember the details, but

Bugsy said it was part of being famous, people trying to ride your coat-tails and claim a piece of you. Guess he knew what he was talking about on that front. Poor bastard. Anyway, I'm sure that was something about song credits.'

'But seriously, all this over a poem?'

'No,' I correct him. 'Over one of the biggest songs of the last twenty years and all the money and success that came with it. We were nothing until that song.'

Dylan sighs. 'It must have killed her hearing it everywhere, knowing she wrote the words.'

Something spikes in my memory then, something that would explain Florence being behind all this. After last night's dinner, when things got a bit heated and the small blue vase with the white painted birds circling it in flight was almost knocked from the mantel. The flash of Florence's anger in response barely registered at the time, but it was her first real break in composure.

'What if it did?' I ask, stumbling over the words in my rush to get them out.

'What?'

'What if it killed her? That urn on the mantel could have been the sister. That would explain all of this. I know my brother dying messed me up. If she held us all responsible...'

He's nodding. 'Then there is no help coming.'

'We have to get out of here,' I say, already heading for the door. 'If we're right, we need to get off this island before the whole thing catches fire.'

He places the picture on the table and moves to follow me.

I'm almost out of the bedroom when I race back in and grab the old frame from the side table.

'What are you doing?' Dylan calls. Now I know about

Sampson's Creek, and I'm not so bloody defensive and assuming the worst, I can hear the concern alongside the annoyance in his voice.

'I'm coming.'

As I lift the wooden frame, something falls to the rug with a soft thud. It's a silver key with a note attached.

If you've managed to find the poem then you might deserve this.

Given the state of the island and the situation we're in, I'm not going to argue with any possible help, even if it's in a cursive script that screams 'Florence' to me.

I pocket the tiny metal object, and run.

Monet – Sunday

I didn't try to stop Dylan following Adam. It's not so much that I'm not scared – my stomach is doing cartwheels with every sound outside – but the smoke in the air tells me time is running out, and two can search much faster than one.

Maman's forehead is warm beneath my palm, despite the wet cloth I placed on it.

'Is there anything I can get you?' I ask her.

What I'm really asking is whether anything in those bottles of medicine can help.

She shakes her head. 'Someone's coming to help though, *non*?' Her voice is hardly more than a whisper.

It seems like Maman has aged in the last couple of hours, or maybe she's just not trying so hard to pretend she's okay. I mumble something in response, because I can't bring myself to lie.

I shouldn't have brought her here. I feel the weight of what I've done heavy on my chest. All because I wanted to get to know Adam at last. All because of my fixation on family.

And then Edward, of all people, opened my eyes to something I can't believe I didn't see before.

'Maman, please, tell me about my father.'

She doesn't answer. And it could be the cancer wreaking its havoc or the smoke filling the air, or it could be the same stubborn silence I've encountered every other time I've asked this question.

'I know babies can be made without love, but there must have been something between you.' I'm desperate now.

'There was love.' It's a reedy whisper but impossible to miss.

'You loved him?' I hardly dare push; she's never given even this much away.

Her eyes are closed. 'I did. When he looked at me, I knew I was the only one for him.' Her voice catches and a tear appears on her dark lashes.

I don't breathe in case it stops her talking.

'And you haven't lived enough yet, but that's an intoxicating thing for a woman, to know you can so easily bring a man to his knees. I loved him more than anything in the world.' A small smile. 'Until I had you.'

Before I can stop myself, I blurt the idea that has been floating in my head since Edward's sneers in the bathroom. 'And that man you loved... Maman, was that man Adam?'

A long silence. And then, 'Yes.'

I pull away. Stagger over to the window and press my head against it, although the glass is too warm for it to help cool my wild, racing thoughts.

Adam is my father. My father is alive.

'I'm so sorry,' Maman whispers. 'You understand, now, why I needed to keep you away. I thought I could shelter you from all my mistakes.'

'The fake blood on the bed, that was you?'

Her head lowers in admission. 'Some red wine, some sauce. I thought it was best.'

'You were wrong.' I can't tell her it's okay, because it's not. Everything she's done to keep me away from here makes sense now, but this lie she's lived should never have been. 'You should have told me the truth.'

'I know that now, but I didn't think we deserved to be together.' She takes a ragged breath. 'You deserve everything, even the truth. Adam is your father and I... I am from a little town near Austin, Texas. No family to call my own, just a dream. I just wanted... to be someone special.'

I've wished to know for so long, but her sharing this feels like goodbye. 'Tell me later,' I say.

A nod. 'I love you, *ma petite*... Be careful.'

There's something in her voice that has me back at her side in an instant. 'Maman?'

She doesn't reply. Her breathing is even but shallow, and when I shake her shoulder she doesn't wake.

My throat is thick with feelings. Tears sting, and when I wipe at my cheeks they're damp. She needs help. No matter what secrets she's kept, she's my mother and I brought her here.

I need to think.

Our hosts are gone. I'm certain of it. But how?

I've never seen a boat at the dock apart from the one we arrived in. There must be another dock that they can access. I remember when we were coming here I looked up the island. There wasn't much beyond the sketched map we were given, one not showing much detail, but there was another bay past Hawk Bay. Past the cave.

My skin is suddenly too tight. I jump up, walk out to the balcony and stare up at the main house. The smoke is thicker, and I can taste it with every breath.

I picture Adam and Dylan returning.

They'll argue.

I can't risk the delay. But I know one thing for sure. If I'm not here, then they'll come after me. They'll have to. Because we're family, and that's what family does.

I press a kiss to Maman's forehead, breathing in her scent, not letting myself think it could be the last time. There's no way I'd leave her in this state if I thought there was a better way. I write a note telling them where to find me and place it on the table where they can't miss it, then I go. Before I can change my mind.

Doubt niggles deeper with every step away from the suite. Am I certain that only Adam and Dylan are likely to find Maman? Am I doing the right thing? Will we get off this island alive?

Yes. It's the only possibility I will allow.

My jog down the trail to Hawk Bay includes more than a few inelegant stumbles, but I don't fall and soon I'm past the gorgeous open beach with its white sand and gentle waves and over the chain-link fence. The signs warning of 'hazards ahead' and to 'go no further' give me the impetus to up my pace. This has to be the right way, why else would they have kept us out of an area that on the map looked like a perfect docking beach?

Although I try not to think about Connie, I can't avoid the memories of the last time I was here, when she spoke of her son in that strange way. That poor woman. When we get out of here, I'll make sure they search those rocks and that Marco is caught and punished.

Then I'm in the cave, by the murky pool of water. Its stagnant smell overpowers the smoke from outside. With the benefit of knowing – at least, believing – what's on the other side, I can't believe I didn't properly notice the other trail last time.

They wouldn't be able to get much through here, but I don't have time to explore above the rocks and work out if there's another way around.

Entering the narrow way, I stretch my hands out on either side, letting them brush against the rocky walls. I didn't fully register the direction of the other passage last time. I step further in. It can't be far; I just need to keep going. Despite the pressure of minutes ticking by, my steps slow the deeper I get, and my breathing grows shallow. Soon I don't need to reach to feel the cool rock on either side of me. I have to duck to a crouch.

Then I'm crawling.

My eyes prickle, but I can't stop edging forward. If I don't keep moving, I risk letting the fear bubbling at the back of my mind take over.

This is in my head.

I can breathe.

'One…. Two… Three…' I count aloud, making myself breathe in and out on each count.

There's another turning, a fork in the tunnel I didn't expect. Frozen, brain jumbled, I try to picture the map and the direction the bay is likely to be. Blackness closes in, and I taste the smoke from up on the hill.

The thud of my heart hurts my cramped chest.

Can fire go through tunnels? What if it's all burning on the other side and I'm crawling towards the flames? What if I'm trapped here and I'll never, ever, ever get out?

My skin is slick with sweat but I'm shivering with sudden cold.

And I can't see.

It's all black. Everything around me. The world spins and

there is no up, no down, and I am going to stay here forever. I try to breathe, but there's something in my mouth. The tunnel is full of it, completely, and it's pressing in on me on every side and I can't move. Not forward. Not back.

I can't...

Monet – Sunday

Frozen on my knees in the tunnel, an image of Maman on the couch, her eyes closed, appears in my brain. She needs me. Dylan does too. And Adam... The father I'm only just getting to know. I take a single shuddery breath.

I'm still here.

I take another.

I grasp on to the lessons of my therapist, relax my muscles. First my shoulders, where they're bunched around my ears, then my chest, my legs. Deliberately, I reach my hand in front of my face, and there's nothing but air. I breathe again. Then I blink and the tunnel is almost in focus.

'It can't be far.'

My voice disappears ahead of me and as my gaze follows it, I see that the space opens a bit. I creep forward. Ahead, the tunnel widens even more. And more. And then I'm up on my feet and the dim shadows are becoming light ahead.

There is literal light at the end of the tunnel.

The giggle becomes a sniffle and then I'm out, almost falling onto a neat wooden jetty. I was right, it's deep water here, and the picturesque shore is well around the curve of the small, sheltered bay, making it a good place to moor a vessel. However, the ropes meant to keep the boat tied to the jetty hang slack into the water, twisting gently in the waves.

'No.'

My cry scatters birds from where they are flocked along the empty jetty, close to the far end. What they leave behind turns my belly. It's blood. So much of it that the liquid has pooled in a concave hollow in the wood and large smears of dark red turned brown trail off to one side. Like something was dragged over the edge.

I find myself walking closer.

Acid burns my throat. I think I can smell the iron tang of the dark puddle, but that should be impossible given the ash now falling like twisted snow from the sky.

Who was here?

It's fresh. It has to be, given the heat of the day. I try to picture a scenario, but I can't make sense of it. Only the hosts could have known about this spot. Although, Connie was exploring here yesterday, but she's back somewhere on the rocks, thanks to Marco. Maybe it was Marco and he came here, fought Bruce.

My mind shuts down on possibilities. It's all too much. I'll get out of here and then I'll process all of this, or I won't be any use to those I told in my note to meet me the other side of the tunnel.

My gaze follows the trail over the edge of the jetty, but it's impossible to discern if any of the dark shadows in the water are human shaped. Impossible to rule it out. I spin as my belly contracts, stumble away from the blood, fall to my knees and vomit over the other side.

Only just missing a small dinghy.

I keep heaving, unable to stop my body, even though there's not much to bring up, but at the same time I assess the gently bobbing small boat hidden away between the jetty and the rocks, with its complete lack of any motor. It's definitely floating, has two battered old oars, and could maybe fit all of us.

As my eyes close on the last violent exertions of my gag reflex, I'm already dragging myself upright. I get away from where I was sick and splash some salty water on my face, even rinse my mouth with a little before spitting it out.

I climb down into the boat, relieved when it stays afloat. A quick stocktake shows a metal box labelled 'EMERGENCY', but it's locked. Then I'm untying the rope holding the dinghy in place, and I'm using an oar to push off from the jetty.

Rowing is awkward at first, but the thought of Maman and the others on the other side of these rocks keeps me going, through the air now murky with ash and smoke. I don't let myself think about what I'll do if they didn't get my note. I have to believe they'll be there.

Instead, I focus on my stroke.

Forward and back, forward and back. It's not perfect but I'm moving. No wonder I didn't make the rowing team during my short time at fancy boarding school, but at least they taught me the basics.

Proving all the warning signs a ruse, the water is smooth and calm with no nasty rips or currents. It's just me and the oars and the distant roar of a fire that must be pretty much covering the island by now.

My eyes sting from fear and smoke, but I blink harder and keep rowing. Once or twice I kick at the lock on the box as I row, but it doesn't budge. In there could be a flare or a radio beacon or... something. That's as far as my marine knowledge extends.

My breath rattles in a wheeze as the boat rounds the small outcrop of rocks at last. My arms are already screaming in protest at the unfamiliar exertion and my hands sting where the oars rub against my palms.

Hawk Bay.

Where I told them to meet me comes into view.

I scan the beach as I pull at the rough oars, refusing to let my mind question what I'll do if it's empty after everything I've been through, when victory is so close to hand.

My heart leaps in relief at the sight of the small group around one of the golf carts on the sand by the foot of the trail. They're there. All three of them. Maman is in the golf cart, but even from here I can see that she's upright and conscious. Her hand lifts in greeting when she sees me.

I gulp back a sob.

'Over here,' I cry, then force myself to keep rowing the last little way as waves threaten to push me back out to sea. Hopefully, Dylan or Adam will take over once they're in the boat. Maybe they'll have something to smash open the emergency box.

As I get closer, I can see in Adam's face his pride in me. Dylan is the one who cheers though. He's practised at 'us', but for the first time I think I can see a time where Adam will be too. My father... a concept not as difficult as I thought to get my head around, but he's in for a shock.

'You're brilliant,' Dylan calls out. He lifts his hands in the air on a burst of triumphant adrenaline.

That's when I see it.

Despite the distance across the shallow lapping water. It's a thread hanging from his top, wedged underneath the sleeve opening, close to the skin. And it's the same distinctive blue as Bugsy's braces that wrapped around his neck.

My belly rolls.

There's a good explanation. He probably picked it up when he found the mask in Connie's suite, the one that proved that Marco was the figure on the security footage. Which makes sense, because Marco wanted to punish Bugsy for what he did to Peter Trafford.

We only know Dylan found the mask in there because that's what he told us.

I push the thought away and focus on bringing the boat closer to the shore. Even as I refuse to look at the scratches on Dylan's neck. Could they be defensive wounds?

No.

Now isn't the time for imaginings that have no basis in fact. Yes, Dylan hated Bugsy but so did all of us, pretty much. That doesn't mean anything.

What matters now is that the most important people in my world are alive and about to get into this boat, and then all of us will be able to get off this island.

We have a chance.

Florence – Sunday

From his position next to me at the wheel of the boat, Bruce is staring back at the island. 'They're all going to die.'

It's not glee in his voice, but neither is there a shred of regret. Perhaps the closest emotion is satisfaction, although I suspect he'd have liked to see every one of them prostrate before we left.

I ease my arms around his broad waist and pull him close. I know it won't be hard to distract him from the tiny, distant blur of white that even now I think I can see making its way from the docks at Port Este. A rescue boat, which should get there almost in time. By my calculations, there might be at least a couple left alive.

I've never been able to tell Bruce everything. Who really can say they share every part of themselves with another?

Because I wanted more.

More than revenge. There needed to be someone left who'll know the full truth about what Jonny did and why all this had to happen. My clues left behind don't require much insight, and if they fail, there's a backup plan.

Of course, once they know what happened, they'll know my part in it. An infamy I've planned for and will enjoy observing from the new identity I've arranged.

In the planning stages, Bruce asked why we couldn't cut corners on the renovations and the distillery set up, but when

I explained that there's no point half-doing a performance so grand, he bought in completely. I knew we were well matched.

One hand on the boat's wheel, Bruce is already nuzzling my neck, any thought of looking at the distant island retreating further and further with every second. He has his hands full, quite literally, with me and our vessel.

In my bag is the blue and white vase that contains the ashes of my brilliant, beloved big sister. Elsie deserved the revenge we have delivered, but as much as that, she deserves the world to know what has happened. When those few left alive share the story, they'll have to share the motive. And then all will know that what is considered Jonny's great legacy actually belongs to her.

'Storybook Love' is not The Cedrics Band's. Not Jonny's. It is Elsie's words describing her heartache as a vulnerable teenager. The poem that started it all. Written in the English class that Connie's poor Peter shared as well.

I wonder, suddenly, if he knew the truth about that song and if, perhaps, he didn't attend the show that night Bugsy discovered them out of some kind of moral protest. Then I remember he's currently rotting in jail somewhere. I guess it's unlikely he'd have such scruples, considering how his life unfolded.

'Hey, baby,' Bruce murmurs. 'I can't wait to hit land, too.'

My nails are deep enough in his tanned skin to have almost drawn blood. In thinking of Peter, I've thought of his mother and the way she went off script from what we'd agreed about the weekend.

I edge away from the leer in Bruce's face. 'We need to worry about getting to safety first.'

He drags me close for one more kiss and that's when I realise. The menthol smell. It's coming from my husband. I turn my face into his neck, inhale. 'New aftershave?'

His smile shows teeth. 'Nicolaï Pour Homme. Including notes of mint and tobacco. Thought our guests would like it.' He has the look of a puppy wanting praise.

'You mean that it would mess with their heads because of Jonny?'

'Exactly.'

I press a kiss to his neck, unwilling to admit the ghost of Jonny Rake haunted me too.

Even at the end, Elsie would talk about Jonny as a tortured genius, despite being his biggest victim. Selfish, self-centred, superstar Jonny Rake. He was one of those people who drew trouble to him. If Bugsy hadn't killed him, bungling his attempt on Edward – impressive sleuthing from Monet, I have to admit – he would have found a way to die young by his own indulgences or pissing someone else off.

Once I realised I wasn't the only one on the island with a plan, I made some adjustments to my own. Because you have to be able to think on the fly if you want to succeed. If you don't want to become a target yourself.

Like dealing with that snivelling coward Edward in the butcher shed.

I can't say I didn't enjoy watching the accountant beg. It was a guess that he knew more than he was letting on about where Lara is, but not needing much of a leap. I don't know details about his marriage, but like all of them, it had to be one wrong comment away from all-out warfare.

His recreational efforts with Bugsy must have given him some courage.

'Can she rest now?' Bruce asks, breaking my chain of thought.

He's talking about my sister and the cause that has driven me for so long, but I know what he's really asking is, *can you?*

Elsie was a dreamer, and she left a light touch on the world for the most part. She didn't light up a room with wild energy, nor did she take control of every conversation, but for those of us who really saw her, well, we saw something... we saw someone who lived more deeply than the rest of us.

I found her on her windowsill. It wasn't a seat so much as a wooden ledge just wide enough for a narrow slip of a girl to sit, sheltered by the gauze of her curtain, and write herself onto a page.

Turned out it was also wide enough for her to curl up after she took whatever it was that allowed her not to hurt any longer.

Mum and Dad followed soon after. Not in quite the same way, more that the energy that kept them looking after themselves evaporated with their older child.

I've been alone ever since.

Other than Bruce, who turned out to be useful. His expertise setting the fires to detonate across the island means that little boat that's even now out of sight will have its work cut out to save anyone.

He's given up his family home and his good name, and changed the course of his life for me.

And he'll want repayment.

He reaches out an arm towards me, beckons for me to come back into his embrace. He doesn't seem to care about the blood stains on my dress. Maybe the opposite. I think he's been staring at the way the red is smeared between the buttons at my cleavage.

Nice.

I paste a smile on my face and give in to his insistent stare. I let his meaty hands touch my skin. Let him cover my mouth with his. Let him think I want him as much as he so clearly wants me. I can't disappear with a man like Bruce at my side, but I knew that and I've planned for it. My solution has to wait until we make land.

There will be time for the last piece of the puzzle to fall into place.

Adam – Sunday

The sight of Monet in an old dinghy, battling oars through the clear waters of Hawk Bay, blurs before my eyes. I let the tears fall, unashamed.

'How the fuck did she do that?'

'She's pretty amazing,' Ivy murmurs.

With Dylan going to meet the boat, I move closer to where Ivy's propped up in the golf cart we used to get her down the trail. She's been drifting in and out of consciousness since we found her in the suite along with Monet's note, but for now her gorgeous eyes are open and they're filled with tears just like mine.

For a blissful moment she's just a woman, and there's the buzz of attraction and the knee-trembling knowledge that maybe I'm not alone feeling a connection so far beyond the ordinary it yanks the air from my lungs. But then, as always, I blink and she's Ivy St Fleur.

Jonny's Ivy.

And the shame of what I've done is a black sludge that drowns any flickering spark. It turns the pure into the guilt that's dogged me nearly half my life. Guilt for the most beautiful of mistakes, but one I'd make again because I simply couldn't do anything else. It's that knowledge that hurts most. Knowing how we left things. I might as well have fucking killed him myself.

Any moment, Monet will reach the sand and Dylan will come back and I'll lose Ivy again. Already, her gaze has flicked beyond me to the water.

'What did you mean before?' I ask. 'About Monet's name and Jonny and it being too late.' It's sheer desperation. Begging her to explain exactly how idiotic I am. But I'm past not being willing to do anything to keep her talking to me.

I don't think she's going to answer.

But then her eyes close as if in a beatific moment of prayer. When she opens them, they're filled with so much pain I'm reaching to comfort her before I can stop myself. 'Jonny Rake didn't care at all about art, but you did.'

There's a lump in my throat.

'You mean that she's...' I can't say it because I can't – in this moment, with smoke and ash and Monet maybe about to save us all – bear to be wrong. I had the thought, briefly, when I found out she was pregnant, because no matter that the world thought she and Jonny were together – that he told me they were – I didn't believe she'd sleep with us both at the same time.

Ivy's lips tremble. 'She's yours.'

I lean my head so close to her that she can't do anything but meet my gaze. And for once there's something more important than the instinctive urge to kiss her. 'She's my daughter?'

'Yes.'

'Does she know?'

A nod. 'Told her.' A gasp of air. 'Just before she...'

I touch my finger to her lips. 'We can talk about this later.' But she's changed my whole world. I have a reason to be better. I will be better.

And I'll get us off this stupid island.

With the dinghy pulled in, Dylan approaches us, and when I look at Ivy again she seems to have shrunk in the blankets she insisted on despite the heat. There's no way she'll be able to walk to the boat. Dylan's got this easily with his bulging muscles and sheer size, but I know I can't step aside again.

I face Dylan, know that I'm asking a lot and, hell, appreciate that I might need his help anyway, but I ask, with a nod to Ivy. 'Can I?'

His gaze swings between us and then to the small boat even now rocking on the sand. 'I'm here if you need.'

She's both heavier and lighter in my arms than I would have guessed. I lift her awkwardly, but when she's against my chest it's like it's where she was always meant to be.

Her eyes flutter open and she presses against me. 'Do you get the feeling it was inevitable we'd end up here?' she whispers.

I study her face, her beautiful face, grasping at the opportunity to let myself look when I've had her only in my head for so long. 'You mean stranded on an island and hoping not to get burnt alive?'

A half-smile quirks her lips. 'Destroying each other.'

'Don't write us off yet.'

I stagger across the sand, hurrying and careful all at once, and constantly aware of Dylan ready to take over. Pride means I don't want him to, but I've learned something these last few days about what it means to have a relationship with someone, so I nod my assent when he's there for the last part as I step into the shallow water. He helps take her weight, helping lift her as carefully as possible over the side of the boat to settle on one of the benches.

I clamber in after her, trying not to wince at how mine and then Dylan's weight lowers the small dinghy in the water.

Monet's frowning as she kisses her mother's forehead. 'She's okay?'

'She just said how amazing you are,' I tell her. 'We'll get away from here and get her help, thanks to you.'

Colour appears in Monet's cheeks. 'I think it's going to be a team effort.'

I've been a loner for so long, but when I look at my daughter I kind of like the sound of working together. Ivy said she knows, but I don't waste time attempting some gushing reunion. Hopefully, there will be time once we're safely back on the mainland.

I realise I'm staring and she's staring, and on impulse I lean across and give her a quick hug. And I feel like a right idiot but then, then she hugs me back, and I'm grinning so wide my face hurts.

Dylan clears his throat. 'Want me to take a turn at the oars and get us away from the ash?'

'Thanks,' Monet says. She edges out of the way, then points down at a small metal box I hadn't noticed. 'That probably has a flare or something, but it's locked.'

Remembering the note on the back of the poem, I grab the key I shoved in my pocket. 'What do you reckon?'

She grins. 'See, teamwork.'

She takes the key from me and unlocks the box to reveal flares, a life jacket and a waterproof torch. Then, at the very bottom, a Nautilus two-way marine radio. She turns the switch at the top until it clicks. She presses the button on the side and says, 'Mayday, mayday. We're in a boat trying to escape a fire on Sparrow Hawk Island. Can anyone hear me? Over.'

There's a long second and then it crackles. 'MAYDAY Nautilus, Nautilus, Nautilus. This is Sea Rescue Adelaide, Sea Rescue Adelaide, Sea Rescue Adelaide. Received Mayday. Our rescue craft Sea Rescue 1 has just launched. They are proceeding to your distress location at 30 knots. Approximate time to your location is 50 minutes OVER.'

Ivy stirs, drawing my attention from Monet's conversation with the Sea Rescue Squadron. Her eyes open again.

'Help is coming,' I tell her, relieved it's the truth.

She grasps for my hand, squeezes it.

I mean to ask her why she did it, not sending the letters Monet wrote to me. Why she ignored and rebuffed the pitiful attempts I made to reach out to them. I might be new to this family thing, but I managed not to give *that* detail away to Monet when she asked.

But as Ivy's chest rises and falls, I just don't say the words.

Not because it doesn't matter. *It matters.* She took something from me, and that knowledge just about rips my heart from my chest, but it wasn't something I tried hard enough to keep, and blaming her won't help.

She must have had her reasons, and I want to find out and work through whatever they are. I want to do better.

On a sudden surge of pure instinct, I feel that if I don't tell her now I may never get the chance.

I lean in close to her.

'I loved you,' I say. And then – because if you can't be honest when you've just escaped a massive blaze and still might drift out to sea never to be seen again, you'll never be – I keep going. 'I still love you. Thank you for looking after our girl all this time, for guiding her into the incredible young woman she is today.'

'I heard that,' Monet says from the front of the boat, flashing a grin over her shoulder.

'I'm not ashamed to admit I think you're a walking marvel,' I reply. Then I lower my voice so only Ivy can hear me. 'Keeping that promise all this time to stay out of your life, and therefore hers, nearly killed me.'

Her hand reaches up, and her fingertips brush the side of my face. 'Me too. I was angry then, so afraid for myself and my baby. I didn't want to ruin Jonny's legacy when you never fought for me.'

'I thought you didn't want me to fight.'

'I didn't know what I wanted. I had betrayed Jonny, and he was dead. I couldn't see a way that having you in my life would be possible.' She lowers her gaze. 'I didn't think I deserved to be happy.'

I lift her chin so she meets my gaze. 'We can start now. Be together.' Even as I say it, I know I'm asking a lot. For so long, I've been looking for what I lost when Jonny died. I was so sure it was the music, but it was what the people in this boat offer... family. 'Not necessarily romantically,' I add quickly. 'But as family.'

She grabs my face and drags it to hers so she speaks against my lips. '*Oui.*'

It's the goddamn best kiss of my life.

SINGLE BODY FOUND AS
THE CEDRICS BAND REUNION
MYSTERY DEEPENS

PORT ESTE – The body of Bruce Harper, the black-sheep sole heir to the Harper fortune, was found in the early hours of this morning after a long search by police and rescue personnel.

Mr Harper had been missing for three days. He was last seen by members of The Cedrics Band on Sparrow Hawk Island. They believed he, with his wife, Florence Harper, had gone to get help given the fire danger the guests were facing.

There has been widespread social-media coverage of the missing couple with fans of the band pleading for the public to come forward with any information.

Thanks to a tip-off from neighbour William Tucker, who was lucky to flee ahead of the blaze, police searched a secluded property some distance away belonging to the Harper family and found Mr Harper in a boat believed to be the vessel used to escape the terrible tragedy on Sparrow Hawk Island, where the keyboardist from The Cedrics Band is believed to have perished in the fire.

It is believed Mr Harper was alone, but police have so far refused to comment on the likely whereabouts of his wife. Given his death, which appears to be suicide, and links to manslaughter and murder charges stemming from incidents in his past, grave fears are held for Mrs Harper's safety.

Anyone with any information is urged to contact police.

Lara – One year later

The interviewer leans towards me, her interest echoed by the attentive faces of the studio audience. 'I appreciate that you've been over this a million times, but can you share with the viewers how you managed to battle against all the odds to be sitting here with us today?'

This question I know exactly how to answer.

'It's because of the fans,' I reply. 'Ordinary people, complete strangers, in fact, who followed my little anonymous blog and saw what happened that morning as my livestream for them was interrupted, my device fell to the ground and the camera captured the horror of what would unfold.' I let my voice catch a little. 'These people shared and talked, and filled in the blanks about where I was and that my life was in danger. As I crawled beneath the stage, dragging my useless shattered leg behind me,' – I pause and brush the limb in question, which still requires a cane for me to walk – 'they were so determined to work out what was happening that they crashed the website. Then dozens of them worked together to first contact and then to both convince authorities that there was a chance I was alive and direct them to exactly where I was.' I stare into the camera and let my eyes fill with tears. 'I owe all of them my life and I will be forever grateful.'

The interviewer shakes her head, admiration radiating from

her. 'Tell me, Lara, in that explosion, in the shocking moment captured for all the world to see, as your device recorded you being thrown from the stage and the satisfied face of your beloved husband watching on, did you think you'd survive?'

The memories slam into me and I don't need to fake the flinch back into my chair. Fighting with Edward about sleeping with Jonny first, and then in the early hours finding the note I'd been so sure was from Bugsy that promised me a chance at fame.

I'd feared having to use my body to sweeten the deal, but never imagined it was a set-up by Edward. Never thought he'd do such a thing then throw off the rest of the band, who actually tried to search for me. Sometimes, I ask myself how I could have missed him bringing the components to make an explosive, but then I can almost hear him in my head.

I've always been a lot smarter than you.

Knowing it will only help in creating sympathy, I pull myself together and wait a beat, feeling the interest and anticipation in the room rise to almost breaking point. Then I blink so that a tear slides over the rough skin of my left cheek, and I lift my hand to the deep ragged scars that run from my other cheekbone to disappear into the low neckline of my carefully chosen dress.

Every gaze in the room follows my fingertips, along with what I know will be millions of viewers at home.

I let my lip tremble as though the whole thing is nearly overwhelming. 'I've always known deep inside that I have the strength of a survivor. My family always believed I'd make something of myself, and I carried that knowledge with me through those horrific, long hours.'

On cue, Mum manages a loud, prideful sniff from the front row of the audience.

The part of me that wants to be fair appreciates that she was at my side, holding my hand, through all the surgeries and rehab I needed to pull through after my ordeal, but I can't be sure she wasn't already thinking about the aftermath and how she might benefit.

I guess I can't really blame her. After all, I had to get the thirst for the spotlight from somewhere.

No one is better than me.

I let the murmurs die down and then contort my features into the twisted smile that most shows off the ravages in my face. The smile that has graced more news sites and magazine covers than I could have imagined lying there alone and in agony on that terrible day, having crawled into the bushes under the stage, whispering for help into my phone, convulsing with the pain and fear of Edward – Edward! – coming back to finish what he started as more explosions went off and the smoke from fires swept over the stage area. The same smile that will be on the front of the memoir that is out tomorrow in thirty-six countries and has already been optioned for film.

'I knew I had to live so I could fulfil my destiny of helping others who suffer trauma at the hands of those they love.'

The woman takes my lead and rattles off the website for my foundation and waxes lyrical about my good works. Good works that have made me rich and famous.

Then she leans in again. 'And how is your relationship with the band these days? I saw they all attended your husband's memorial.'

If not for how it would have looked to the world, I would have thrown a party over Edward's remains rather than give him the dignity of a service, but there were the boys and my image to consider.

'We're close,' I tell her, knowing no one from the band will want the bad press that would come with them denying my exaggeration. 'Given Ivy's prognosis, I understand why they've been reclusive this last year, but I was speaking to Monet the other day and she said that her mother is doing as well as can be expected. From what I gather, both Adam and Dylan have been there to support Jonny's daughter through Ivy's battle.'

'Did she say anything about a possible romance between her uncle and her mother?'

I hesitate and lower my voice, then give them all what they're asking for. 'I don't want to break any confidences, but I will say Adam Rake seems to be a brand-new man, and his upcoming album isn't the only special thing in his life. He's certainly been very caring of Ivy.'

I let my voice drift off, saying a whole lot without saying very much at all. It's something I've gotten rather good at since being in the public eye. Ivy has never said if she remembers where we met before. Passing each other in that hotel hallway, her sneaking from Adam's room, and me from Jonny's. But none of that matters now. We discuss my book and the speaking tour I have coming up and then the interview is nearly over.

'One last question,' she says. 'If you could go back in time, would you have stepped onto the boat that carried you over to the band's reunion?'

I pause again, although I don't really need to. I look straight into the camera. 'I believe we need to look to the future and make the best of it that we can.'

The truth is, this is all I've ever wanted. And I always get what I want.

Acknowledgements

I'D LIKE to acknowledge the Kaurna people and the Kaurna Country on which *The Last Encore* was written.

Although my name goes on the cover it takes a team to get a story that starts with an idea all the way into the hands of readers, and it's so very much appreciated, so thanks to anyone not explicitly mentioned below.

Thank you so much to my editor, Peyton Stableford, who worked with such good humour and enthusiasm to bring this story into the best possible shape. Many thanks, also, to the rest of the wonderful team at Head of Zeus Publishing. Thanks to Jenni Davis for the copyedits and Simon Michele for the cover design. Thank you to the wonderful Australian Bloomsbury team who provide so much brilliant support. I'm lucky to have so many great people on my team.

Hattie Grünewald, you've helped me so much through every book and I cannot thank you enough. Thanks too, to all the team at The Blair Partnership for everything you do.

My dad was involved with the local Sea Rescue squadron, so I was not at all surprised when they so readily helped answer my questions around emergency calls at sea. Very much appreciated.

Another fictional band, 'Super 5,' helped inspire the beginnings of The Cedrics Band. Thanks to creator Armin and the band: Dave, Derek, Rich, Strop and Tim. So much gratitude, too, for all the live music I've been lucky enough to experience over the years. From school shows to stadium tours, watching music being performed is always something special.

Thanks to Fiction Distilling for the gin-making tour and answering my questions, as well as for your support to the SA bookish community.

One of my favourite pieces of writing advice I always share is to find your writing community. Writer friends understand and help with the day-to-day of getting the words down and taking the story from an idea to the page. The crime and thriller community in Australia is so great for both people and books, and my TBR pile reflects this. The SA crew is smashing it, and it's so great to watch you all shine!

Thanks to the Monday Murder club, Cat, Louise, Con and Liam, and particularly to Bev Goldfarb who read an early draft! Thanks to Emily Madden, Lisa Ireland and Amanda Knight for Writers Camp. And to Amanda for the cheering and Voxes and support – it means so much. And to Rachael Johns without whom I am not sure I would always turn up at the keyboard. Your friendship and feedback are both brilliant.

Non-writer friends who ask about the book and then buy it and read it and support it are pure gold. All my family friends, school friends, and friends-through-kids – thank you. Thanks to Caroline and Rowan, Alison, Amy and Julie in particular.

Harriet (the very best dog) and Karma (is a cat) keep me smiling every day no matter how the book is going.

Family is everything so many thanks to Dick, Shirley and Lyn, and remembering Dad and Wendy. My big sisters and their families are always so supportive, thanks so much.

Again, you answered questions when I needed so thank you Mitch and Chloe. Thanks to Fi and Kirst with all my heart for everything. Still miss you, Mum, and couldn't have done this without you believing in me.

My most heartfelt thanks to all the wonderful readers, booksellers, bloggers, Instagrammers, TikTokkers, podcasters and reviewers who supported the release of all my books so far. Without you I couldn't have kept doing this and you've literally made my dream come true. Thank you.

And to my family. Amelie, James and Claire – thanks for all the love and support and voting on important bookish decisions like island names. All my thanks, and even more love, to Dave who reads everything I write, listens to everything I need to say to work stuff out, and is always there for me when I need him.

About the Author

REBECCA HEATH studied science at university, worked in hospitality and teaching, but she always carved out time to write. She lives in Adelaide, Australia, halfway between the city and the sea with her husband, three children and a much-loved border collie. She is the author of *The Summer Party, The Dinner Party* and *The Wedding Party*. This is her fourth adult novel.